CATCHING HELL

D. B. SIEDERS

CITY OWL
PRESS

CATCHING HELL
Jinx McGee, Book 1

CITY OWL PRESS
www.cityowlpress.com

Cover Design by MiblArt. All stock photos licensed appropriately.

Edited by Tee Tate

For information on subsidiary rights, please contact the publisher at info@cityowlpress.com.

Print Edition ISBN: 978-1-64898-101-2

Digital Edition ISBN: 978-1-64898-100-5

Printed in the United States of America

To all my favorite authors,
Thank you for the inspiration

CHAPTER ONE

Life goal number 666: Be the kind of woman that when your feet hit the floor each morning, the devil says, "Oh, crap. She's up!" — T-shirt worn by Jinx McGee, demon hunter.

I saw my first demon when I was five. I was looking in a mirror.

I'd been brushing my teeth when I glanced at my reflection and noticed I wasn't the only one there. A presence lurked behind my eyes. It wasn't nice. It was angry, and it wanted out. I don't know if the demon living inside me had always been there, but that was the first time I saw her. My scream almost burst my own eardrums—and my older sister's since she'd been standing beside me. She didn't see the demon. Neither did my mom. They both thought I was imagining things.

They were wrong.

Still, when life gave you lemons, you were supposed to make lemonade. Life gave me a demon, so I became a demon hunter. I never learned how to make demonade, let alone market it.

Since becoming a demon hunter, I'd seen six hundred and sixty-four demons...not that I was counting. Demon number six hundred and sixty-five targeted the man I was currently surveilling on my latest stakeout. The man and his demon stalker were my latest demon-hunting assignment in downtown Nashville, and shit was about to go down.

Like the fact that said demon stalker was currently speeding through the air on a collision course with a wagon full of drunk tourists who, being strictly human, couldn't see it.

"Look out," I yelled. Damn it, where was my partner? She'd texted to tell me she was stuck in traffic, but I could've really used some backup. While unseen, the freaking demon could do real, visible damage.

Crap, I couldn't wait for Lacey. I'd have to break protocol and go after the demon and its mark on my own.

The demon, who was a streak of black only I could see, whizzed past the man it was targeting and through one of those pedal taverns clogging up Broadway and Second Avenue. The damned demon knocked the penis headband right off one of the intoxicated bachelorettes. Bummer. I enjoyed phallic party favors almost as much as I enjoyed drunken revelry. It would've been fun to pick it up and crash the party. I could shove one of those drunk gals off her stool and take her spot, pretending to be a sixth cousin twice removed who no one really knew, but she endeared herself to the group anyway.

Jane McGee the jolly bridesmaid had a nice ring to it. It was what a gal my age should be doing.

Too bad I was working.

I was Jane "Jinx" McGee, demon hunter, and would be until I figured out how to get rid of the demon currently possessing me. Long-term relationships, marriage, white picket fences, and a whole lot of normal weren't possible for me at the moment. I'd have to settle for keeping drunken bridesmaids and the rest of humanity safe from unauthorized demon shenanigans.

"Oh! Sadie lost her wiener."

The shout came from another one of the rolling bar's occupants, who nearly fell out of her seat laughing, blissfully unaware she'd been dive-bombed by a demon. Damn it, tempters moved fast. I hoped this one was corporeal. They weren't necessarily easy pickings, but easier to catch than the immaterial variety. Corporeals were still fast as all get-out, even with a body, but at least they couldn't transform into ether and vanish into vents or gutters.

I needed to slow the demon down, but first I had to follow it to the more private location it had chosen to claim the human it was after.

One of the gals on the pedal tavern handed me a shot glass as they passed, and I downed the contents in a single gulp while they hooted and hollered, giving me high fives and shouting, "You go, girl." The bachelorettes had good taste in tequila, at least. Ah, to be an ordinary human, blessedly unaware of creatures that go bump in the night. With a nod of thanks, I returned the glass and set off at a light jog to catch up with the demon's target.

The oblivious human hadn't noticed the demon tracking him, of course. Poor sap. He just had the inexplicable compulsion to go wherever the demon had chosen. Demons had all kinds of nasty mind tricks they used to manipulate their prey. If they went around openly on the attack, people would soon become too afraid to leave their houses and hunting would be harder.

Demons were ambush predators.

I'd been watching the demon's target, a middle-aged father of two, for over a week. He'd been demon marked, and when one of our patrollers spotted the demon's mark—invisible to humans but a clear signal to other demons the bearer was already taken—she'd called us in. I'd been waiting for the demon, intent on siphoning his soul—or stealing his life-force for those who didn't believe in souls and such—to lure him to a secluded location so it could claim its next meal.

The poor guy looked more like Santa Claus than demon chow with his jolly round face, salt-and-pepper beard, and generous belly. The red Hawaiian shirt really tied the look together, but thankfully he wore khaki pants instead of red crushed velvet.

That would have been completely over the top.

I wondered what this guy had done to get a bull's-eye on his back. The case file was scant on details but flagged as urgent.

No matter. I'd find out soon enough based on the flavor of tempter demon he'd attracted. He ducked into a dark alley—how original—as his demonic stalker finally stopped zipping around and stepped out of the shadows. With my enhanced senses, I observed the demon stalker assume a form that halted the man dead in his tracks and turned him into a quivering mass of lust and longing.

Ah, a succubus had tagged him. My demon stirred within me, excited by the prospect of hunting.

She's hungry. So am I.

I shuddered as my demon's thoughts echoed in my mind along with her ravenous excitement. Fortunately for me and the rest of the planet, my demon was under my control and on a tight leash. She'd only taken over fully once when I was young, but once had been enough.

Nothing would ever be as bad as that, and the memory sent a shiver down my spine.

I couldn't afford that little trip down memory lane. I had work to do. And I needed my personal demon, who I called Hannah, to do it. When I summoned Hannah, she gave me the strength and demon magic to subdue and capture rogue demons. The fact that she was much more powerful than the tempter demons we hunted—and currently an unknown entity in the demon hierarchy—made us a winning team if a tad unstable. The obsidian mirror Hannah was bound to was supposed to prevent her from taking over and going off on any unauthorized side quests or killing sprees.

That made the two of us unsuited for normal careers like banking or public relations. Since it took a demon to find one, however, being demon possessed made me eminently qualified for my current job.

I reached the alley and took a closer look at its occupants. The corporeal shape-shifting succubus's appearance surprised me. Instead of going all hot, sexy, and ho-bag, she went for plain and unassuming. Her baggy skirt, oversize sweater, and mousy brown ponytail screamed librarian. Maybe her mark had a book fetish?

Nah.

I unsheathed my enchanted knife, crept down the alley, and prepared to kick some demon ass.

CHAPTER TWO

"Oh, God." Santa's low, husky voice echoed through the alley. Stumbling footsteps followed, muffled as the man went deeper into the side street, closer to the succubus. I couldn't see him as clearly but spotted his shadow.

It quivered like an honest-to-God bowl full of jelly.

Gross. Then again, if he finished...prematurely, it would give me more time to nab the demon before he recovered enough to give it another go. My knife flashed with streaks of dazzling purple light and then glowed a brilliant red. I nearly dropped the damned thing.

"Oops." I scrambled and ducked behind a stack of boxes to avoid being spotted. Amateur move. Shaking the knife and slapping it against my thigh didn't do anything other than leave a bruise. My blade was still switching from blazing red to flaming purple, and purple wasn't a demon color. Demon hunter training 101: red was for demons, blue for celestials, green for ghouls, yellow for mythical or elemental creatures, and white for vampires. The brighter the glow, the stronger the creature.

I totally remembered that from my training.

Members of the seven tempter demon classes didn't produce purple, and they didn't get such a powerful reaction from my weapon/demon detector. I'd only ever gotten a screaming neon glow around my powerful demon boss and his associates. Bizarre. Cue the *X-Files* music.

Red and blue mixed to make purple, at least in the mundane world. Did that mean there was a celestial in the vicinity? They only ever visited "special" people to bestow help, blessings, or some nonsense like that. Demon-hunting operations didn't encounter them as far as I was aware. None had ever come my way.

Didn't matter. And I needed to stop dicking around.

I fired off a text to HQ so I'd have additional backup on standby in case Lacey didn't show up in time. There were about six texts from my partner, probably telling me to wait for her instead of going off on my own and doing something monumentally stupid. Again. But really, I didn't get in over my head often.

Okay, who was I kidding? I got in over my head all the time.

I might have had some very minor issues with impulse control.

The smart choice would be to wait for Lacey. Then again, if Hannah was right and the succubus was super hungry, she might feast on the man's soul before my partner arrived.

The succubus lured the man in with her mojo as he continued his slow march toward her, sobbing and moaning. "Is it really you?"

If I didn't do something, he'd be dead, and his kids would be left without a father.

I'd lost my father at a young age, before I even knew him. Mom said he'd bailed, leaving her with two girls to raise on her own. By all rights, I should hate him and want nothing to do with him. But like all gals with daddy issues from absentee fathers, there was a hole in my soul with his name on it.

And somewhere in the depths of my soul, I missed him terribly, even after all these years.

Nothing I could do about my dad, but this man's kids weren't going to lose their dad tonight. Not if I could help it.

I'd just have to wing it.

Peeking to make sure the coast was clear, I slithered down the alley with my back against the grimy brick wall. Night-vision goggles would have been nice. My big bad boss—BBB or Triple B for short, though I never called him that to his face—totally needed to spring for some state-of-the-art equipment. Fortunately, my eyes adjusted quicker than the average mortal's—a side effect of demon possession I could control without Hannah—and I spotted the man, Jack Murkowski, now chatting with the succubus-in-librarian's-clothing. Desperation wafted off his aura in sickening waves, along with something else I couldn't identify. He stank like gloom, doom, and bad news with a hint of brimstone, but that was what happened after repeated exposure to inhabitants of the hell realm.

Cliché for sure, but some stereotypes were true. While the alternate dimension we called hell wasn't all lakes of fire and eternal suffering, it apparently had an abundance of sulfur. They should bring some Febreeze there, or maybe deodorant.

The scent bothered me, and not just in the literal sense. It also alerted the senses and instincts I'd developed by tracking and capturing all manner of demons. Succubi didn't smell like brimstone. They smelled like whatever scent most attracted their victim. Given the form the succubus assumed, Murkowski most likely favored musty old books with a hint of rose water. Something was off.

Everything about this assignment was off—the lack of detail in the case file, something wonky with my knife's supernatural threat detection system, and a succubus seemingly going off script.

Anxiety warred with adrenaline as I prepared for attack, but adrenaline won.

The succubus had the patience of a seasoned hunter. I'd give her that. She didn't go in for the soul-sucking kiss or shag right away. Instead, she toyed with her ponytail and lowered her gaze to the dirty ground. The act didn't exactly fit the location, not to mention the honky-tonk music and hoots from downtown tourists moseying along in Music City. The succubus reached out and placed a small hand on his shoulder, demonic gaze aglow with anticipation and hunger her victim couldn't see.

But I could.

Time to strike.

Steeling my resolve, I reached into my shirt and pulled out the locket that held my obsidian mirror, the instrument that allowed me to control my inner demon. I kept it on a silver chain, close to my heart. Well, more like between my boobs, because I guarded my girls with my life.

I popped open the locket and gazed into the polished obsidian's shiny black core as reality and time slipped away. My brown eyes glowed with a thousand sparks of light as my features twisted and my face split into an evil grin. "Okay, Hannah," I whispered. "Let's do this."

The demon merged fully with my consciousness and took over my body, though I held the proverbial leash. I closed the locket and tucked the black mirror safely between my girls. Then my demon-controlled body crawled up the wall and into the shadows, masking our movements and scent so the succubus wouldn't detect us before we struck.

I'm hungry. May I eat her?

Hannah always wanted to eat our targets. Sometimes the boss let her. I hated it when that happened. It gave me heartburn for weeks.

"No." I had control of my mouth—and my rational mind. Hannah seemed inclined to press the issue, so I put my foot down. Metaphorically. Stomping my feet for real would be silly. "You don't need to eat her, and you know it."

She didn't have to drain the full life-force out of the lesser demons we hunted. Unlike tempters, Hannah mostly sustained herself through her own magic as well as the energy that fueled me. I think she ate other demons for funsies or as treats, which was more twisted in my humble opinion. All she had to do was ingest part of the essence of another demon to weaken it for capture. The boss decided what happened from there. Hannah and I were strictly a capture-and-retrieval operation.

Like bounty hunters, only supernatural.

And way cooler. We totally rocked the camo pants, black Doc Martens embroidered with roses and with custom rhinestones I'd bedazzled myself, and tank top. Very paramilitary chic, but with bling.

Murkowski moaned and took another step toward the succubus. Time to stop her before she drained him dry.

I dropped to the ground beside the man and the succubus and then leapt onto the demon's back, pressing the enchanted knife to her throat with one hand while I clung to her ponytail with the other. Thankfully, the knife glowed red this time. Demon, check—demon-killing blade, check—demon hunter making her move, double check.

"Mr. Murkowski." My warped demon voice echoed through the alley as a husky rasp. "You need to leave."

The man's gaze went wide. And if I wasn't mistaken, it was filled with more than a little annoyance. Why wasn't he scared? Was it because I was a woman? That was just so sexist and wrong.

Maybe it was my height, or lack thereof. I clocked in at five feet three with boots. Whatever. I wasn't short. I was concentrated awesome.

At least he didn't seem turned on. Had to take the positives when and where I could.

"Thank you, Mara." Mr. Murkowski's voice also echoed through the alley. "You may go now."

Wait, did he say "Mara?"

No, it couldn't be.

"Mara?" Focusing my attention on the succubus rather than her victim, I cursed myself for not recognizing her sooner.

I'd tracked this particular succubus before. Mara was harmless. Okay, not really. She was a succubus who consumed human life-forces during carnal passion. But she only targeted the bad ones. That was our bargain.

"We had a deal, Mara." I tightened my grip on her ponytail while digging the knife into the flesh of her throat. The demon steel could kill her if it sliced through her jugular. If I hit something less vital, it would hurt like hell—literally—and would slow her down long enough for my demon to trap her.

She didn't fight. In fact, her body slumped and shrank. That was new. No demon had ever used sympathy as a ploy, which was a good thing. I was a sucker for the downtrodden, the lost, the sad sacks and sadder cases.

Pathetic, I know, but we all had our weaknesses.

Hannah didn't share my empathy, so I channeled my demon's power and let her cruelty infuse me before I caved. "We gave you a list of fair game humans to snack on and a map to the state penitentiary. And the state capitol. You get a small sip of their life-forces, but no killing, remember?"

If she'd already burned through the local fare, we could probably book her a flight to D.C. It would take her more than a few decades to make her way through that many politicians.

"I know." Her voice was squeaky yet infused with that breathy, Marilyn Monroe quality that drove men and some women out of their minds, not to mention their pants. "I'm sorry, Jinx. He made me do it so he could get to you."

Get to me? Someone had set me up? What for? I was a great demon hunter and totally fun at parties, but I wasn't exactly high on the food chain.

"Who made you do this and why?"

I yanked a little harder than necessary on Mara's hair to show her I meant business. I didn't want to hurt her, but she didn't need to know that. This case was already all kinds of weird. Throw in a setup, and I had a sneaking suspicion things were about to go south. I needed answers. Fast.

I glanced at Murkowski, remembering he'd called Mara by her name and had said something about her going. That didn't make sense, unless—

"I did," Murkowski said. "You're a hard woman to find, Ms. McGee."

I examined him more closely while scrambling to figure out who—or what—he was, not to mention how he knew me.

"Not really," I said. "I have a website. It lists my email address and mobile number, and I'm on social media and demonbusters.com." Of course, finding any of that information required access to the demon web within the dark web. Anyone who'd heard of me in the first place ought to be able to swing it.

Murkowski grinned, his Santa-like features shadowed with malevolence as his aura grew darker. Holy guacamole. This guy wasn't Mara's dinner.

He was a demon-possessed human, which was way worse.

Well, that explained why my knife had been blazing a brighter shade of red than a run-of-the-mill succubus could produce. Whatever type of demon was lurking inside Murkowski was powerful. He might even be in the same fighting class as Hannah, or more powerful. I'd find out soon enough because we *would* fight. I couldn't let a demon of his level run loose on earth.

But I didn't want to hurt his human host.

The demon inside Murkowski didn't care about his host, and I had no idea if I could save the man from the demon.

But I had to try. Time to improvise. Things were about to get messy.

CHAPTER THREE

My knife flared, glowing like a neon sign in Vegas, even brighter than before. Whatever type of immaterial demon had taken up residence in Murkowski had been hiding its power. Not anymore. He was more powerful than any demon I'd encountered, other than my own. And the boss.

I was in such deep shit. So was Murkowski, the unwilling human host.

"Thanks for cluing me in, Hannah," I muttered.

She didn't answer. In fact, if I had to guess what she was thinking or feeling, I'd have gone with curiosity. Great. At least her presence imbued me with demon strength and power. I hoped it would be enough to get us out of this sticky situation.

Murkowski's eyes glowed as the demon inside him glared at me.

"You have my attention, Bad Santa," I said, shrugging as best I could with my body wrapped around a frightened succubus. "What do you want?"

He laughed, with his cheeks like roses and nose as red as a cherry.

This meat sack does have its advantages. So ordinary and unassuming, even for a human, he's come in very handy. You didn't recognize me at first."

He was right, and I could have kicked myself. No worries. If I survived, the boss would do that for me later. First rule of demon hunting, aside from covering your ass? Suspect everyone. Then again, the boss had put me on Murkowski's tail, so either he hadn't known the man was demon possessed, or *he'd* set me up.

My combat instincts kicked into high gear, and Hannah grew impatient. She wanted to fight so badly I could taste it, and her hunger infused my mind, body, and soul with battle lust. Good. We had to protect the human.

The powerful demon wouldn't give up his host willingly, and he'd have no qualms about tearing Murkowski's body and soul apart if he needed to make a quick escape.

"You're good," I conceded. "You'd be trapped already if you weren't."

He laughed as his gaze went black save for the glowing red motes of power floating within them. No longer bothering to hide behind the facade of humanity, he said, "Thank you. I almost wish I could say the same about you. Alas, for who and what you are, I must say I'm disappointed. Luring you here was far too easy."

Who and what I was? Whatever. Contain and capture first, interrogate later.

I snorted. "You didn't lure me. I was sent. I've been tracking you for weeks. It's kind of my thing, you know, being a demon hunter and all."

Where the hell was Lacey? I needed my partner. Sure, she was a trainee, but she and her demon were great fighters and wicked fast. No help for it, though. Time for plan B. Stall and hope she'd show up soon. The cramp in my leg from perching on to Mara had become almost too much to bear. My mortal body did have its limits, even with my demon.

"Are you going to tell me what you want?"

"So many things," he said, his hooded gaze traveling over me, leering. Gross.

I'd need a shower and a brain scrub after this, and I doubted I'd ever be able to sit on a male stripper dressed as Santa's knee—again—without a few shots of tequila.

Wait a minute...

He wasn't really lusting over me so much as Mara. No matter her form, a succubus radiated intense sexual magnetism, and no human or demon was immune. That was what made them one of the most dangerously underestimated tempter demon classes. If I hung around Mara long enough while she was throwing off that kind of energy, I'd want to hit it, too.

And I wouldn't even need tequila.

The demon inhabiting Murkowski shook his head and tried to focus his glassy-eyed demonic gaze on me, but it kept returning to the succubus, who'd grown hotter in both the physical and metaphorical sense.

Oh yeah, Mara was hitting us with some major mojo. If I didn't get away from her soon, the heat pooling between my legs might become a fatal distraction. It wasn't her fault. She had strong survival instincts, too, and using sex as a weapon was her thing.

It was also a thing I could use that to my advantage.

I loosened my grip on her ponytail and slowly moved my hand to her shoulder, giving it a light squeeze. She flinched before lifting the shoulder, leaning into my touch, and going along with the act.

Or maybe she was sore. Having a demon hunter hanging off her back couldn't be comfortable.

I responded to Murkowski's demon, my voice low and husky, "Me too." I was acting. Sort of. Mara's turbo-charged pheromones were hard to resist.

"What?" Murkowski's demon muttered. His pupils dilated as his jaw grew slack, drunk on the sensual energy surrounding the succubus. A thick bulge appeared at his crotch, pushing against the fly of his khakis. Ugh, I'd be scarred for life.

I'd have to get over it.

"I want things too." I pretended to fall under the succubus's spell— mostly. Licking my lips, I gave him a wink and added, "Naughty things."

Location notwithstanding, the dank alley had decent acoustics.

Sultry guitar chords and a yearning baritone floated in the air from some nearby club. Mara had no doubt added her succubus glamour to the ballad, using it to her advantage in the act of seduction.

Was she seducing Murkowski's demon, or was she after me? I was playing a dangerous game, but it was my only chance.

I bent and kissed Mara's long, graceful neck. She tilted her head to give me better access, moaning as I trailed my tongue down the column of her throat. I enjoyed it more than I had the right to, but it had been a while since I'd gotten any action. And she was hot. I nuzzled her neck, moving back up to place a light nip on her earlobe while risking a glance at Murkowski to gauge the demon's reaction.

Bad Santa growled. Oh, yeah, he was into it, and based on the state of things below the belt, he was getting more into it by the second. The demon possessing Murkowski fed on his human desire.

I tucked my head against Mara's neck, letting my hair fall in front of my face, and whispered, "We're going to give him a show. When I lean in to kiss you, be ready to strike."

"Yeeeeesss," she hissed. Reaching her hand back to grasp my nape, she pulled me closer. My nipples grew hard, and I squirmed a little.

It might be more difficult to keep my wits than I thought.

But it was working. The demon inside Murkowski was mesmerized.

Hannah must have sensed my urgency, or maybe it was the frenzy of sexual energy. Either way, hunger surged through her and into me as she wrestled for control.

Cut it out, Hannah! We're working here, I screamed at her in my mind, hoping to get her back on track.

I pulled my knife away from Mara's throat and dropped to the ground to stand in front of her, close enough to feel her white-hot, sensual energy coursing over my body. It sent blood racing between my legs and left me gasping. My demon purred. Guess she was on board with this plan.

Or maybe she was just horny. Hannah only got action when I did, and I hadn't been all that active lately. I'd have to work on that for both our sakes.

Mara's gaze drew me in, and I had to struggle to resist, to stay focused. We might be on friendly-ish terms, but she was a tempter demon. All demons were slaves to their appetites, especially tempters—embodiments of the seven deadly sins. It was possible to redirect those appetites, but not to tame them. She'd suck out *my* life-force if I wasn't careful. And if Hannah didn't stop her.

Hannah growled. Great. If Hannah stopped behaving and went berserk, we'd probably all get eaten. Mara smiled, baring her teeth in feral triumph as she pulled me close, pressing our bodies together.

It felt so good. Soft, warm, and inviting in that way unique to women. She was taller than me. At five one, without the boots, practically everyone was taller than me, but the height difference enhanced the sense of warmth and security. Safety. That was one of my greatest desires.

I resisted, my instincts for survival fighting against the lure of the succubus. She pulled back and shimmered, a sign she was changing form.

I gasped as Mara's librarian glamour melted away and she assumed the shape of a hard, decidedly masculine body cloaked in shadow, made for sin. The long lines of that body were at once foreign and achingly familiar. When I'd last seen and touched that body ten years ago, it had been hard and muscular, but still held the last traces of boyhood—eager, yet as inexperienced as my eighteen-year-old body had been.

That encounter had been all too brief, but it burned in my memory and...other places to this very day.

In my fantasies, the body and the soul encompassed by it had grown and matured into that of a man, strong, powerful, and with a desire to match my own. There was nothing awkward in those fantasies, no shy fumblings in the dark. In my dreams, I got dinner and a show.

Go big or go home.

I looked into the face of the succubus, but Mara was gone, replaced by my fantasy come to life. It was Dominic, my long-lost childhood demon best friend who'd turned into so much more than that for one brief, beautiful moment. The man—demon—who disappeared just when I'd needed him most. He'd vanished after our first kiss. Well, more like first make out session, but it technically counted as a single kiss since we hadn't come up for air.

I'd been looking for him ever since.

This wasn't D. He was gone. Had to be. No matter how hard the boss and I had tried, we'd never been able to summon him, so we concluded he was dead.

My heart was still mourning his loss.

"Jane." His whispered voice was smooth and smoky as single malt whisky, and just as intoxicating.

D never called me Jinx, always Jane, and it set my heart racing. I didn't meet his gaze, but I didn't need to. Instead, I ran trembling fingers over his face, exploring its contours through touch. How could I forget the strong jaw, those impossibly high cheekbones, and that mouth?

I'd shared the deep bond of trust with D. That bond shattered when he disappeared, and I'd lost more than an object of lust that night. I'd lost my best friend, my confidant, and my heart.

Never again.

I tried to pull away, but strong hands gripped my waist, pulled me closer, and lifted me until I was forced to wrap my legs around his hips. He was all hard lines and lean muscle, and I couldn't stop my traitorous body from pressing against his, gasping as delicious friction set my most sensitive nerve endings on fire.

"That's right," D whispered.

No, not D. Mara. I had to remember that. I had to resist the lure of the succubus. But my heart longed for D as much as my body did. He trailed his hands down my back to cup my ass, pulling me against his body as he groaned and grew harder.

"This isn't real. It's not D. It's not real." I hoped chanting this mantra would keep me from falling into Mara's spell.

The succubus's glamour and power couldn't be denied, and it ignited every cell in my body. That was tough to resist. But her most insidious weapon, her true power, was the near-perfect embodiment of my heart's desire.

Longing was far more dangerous than lust.

"Where have you been?" I asked before I could stop myself. The succubus was good, very good, but I couldn't allow myself to fall deeper under her spell. Nor could I afford to rip open the wound D had left deep in my heart. I was acting, damn it.

"I never left." He lifted my chin.

I met his gaze—no, Mara's gaze—trying to resist temptation. Those sweet words whispered in D's dark, husky voice pierced my heart. But this was not D. These were not his words. This was not the reunion I'd dreamed about. D was dead and forever out of my reach.

The succubus leaned down, lips parted, ready to deliver her deadly kiss. Shagging was preferable, but a kiss would suffice if a succubus only had time for a quickie. The kiss of a succubus was supposed to be orgasmic, so I guessed that still counted as the moment of release that would drain my essence. And after she'd taken all that made me who I was, the empty shell of my body would expire. Hell of an awful way to go.

I bit my lip hard, the pain snapping me out of my stupor, and pushed against the succubus with all my demon-fueled might.

With one last look at the facade of my best friend and almost lover, I yelled, "Now!"

CHAPTER FOUR

Thankfully, Mara snapped out of her hunger-fueled lust just as I drop-kicked Murkowski to the ground. I grabbed my knife and straddled him, landing on my knees in some foul-smelling liquid that would ruin yet another pair of camo pants. Then I jerked his head back with my free hand and held the blade against his neck. Damn, I hope I didn't injure Murkowski too badly, but I had to subdue the demon controlling him.

We barely escaped the attention of two lost tourists. The pair sported new cowboy hats and wore T-shirts emblazoned with "Welcome to Nashvegas." They turned away at the last minute, trading the dark and foreboding alley for neon and noise along the main drag.

Nothing to see here, folks. Move along.

Murkowski reached up, growling as he tried to wrap his thick hands around my throat. Mara took him by the wrists and held tight, channeling her inhuman strength as she crouched low and bent to place her mouth over his.

"Wait." I shoved her hard and earned a snarl for my trouble. I'd never seen a succubus in the throes of such hunger. She was scary.

Still hot as all get-out, but scary.

I bent down, my nose barely an inch from Murkowski's. "Tell me who sent you."

I couldn't allow Mara to consume Murkowski's soul, nor could I let her drain the demon within Murkowski, at least not until I interrogated him. Murkowski would die, and even powerful demons took a long time to recover from a succubus attack. Getting him out of Murkowski's corpse would also be difficult and messy. Better if Hannah extracted the demon and held on to him.

Murkowski grinned. "That was quite a show, demon hunter. Clever. No wonder the general wants you," he said, voice hoarse and wheezy.

Oops. I might have broken a few of Murkowski's ribs. God, what if I'd punctured his lung?

Wait, a general wanted me?

That was weird. I mean, I did love military guys. I'd worked my way through more than a few privates, lance corporals, the odd airman, and even a petty officer or two—I was a true patriot, after all. But a general seemed a bit out of my league.

And based on the messenger, the general had to be from the hell realm. A demon general wanted me. That couldn't be good.

The demon lunged, breaking Mara's hold and probably Murkowski's arms in the process. It didn't stop the demon from wrapping Murkowski's meaty fingers around my throat to choke off the air my human side needed. I lifted the knife, trying to figure out how to disable the demon while doing as little damage as possible to the host. I slashed his chest through the Hawaiian shirt, and he howled in agony, loosening his grip just enough to for me jerk out of his hold.

He grinned again, his expression triumphant. "The armies of darkness are at the ready. All they need is you."

Time seemed to slow around us. He opened his mouth and inhaled. My body went rigid. I was paralyzed.

And not just me. Hannah was paralyzed too.

Murkowski's demon tugged at my demon, trying to rip her from my body and consciousness.

Besides Hannah herself and my boss, I'd never met a demon who could do that—summon a possessed human's inner demon or tear it away from body and soul. It was what made us such a great team for demon hunting. I had no idea what kind of demon Hannah was, only that she was formidable, dangerous, and impossible to defeat.

Until now.

Adrenaline spiked and fear gripped me as I struggled to hold on to Hannah. Part of me had always wanted to separate from her. Honestly, what human wanted to share a body, mind, and soul with a demon? I hadn't asked for her and all the trouble that came along with demonic possession.

All I'd ever wanted was normal.

But separating from Hannah was dangerous, possibly fatal. The boss had been searching for the means to free me from Hannah since I joined his demon-hunting operation. That was our bargain—he would help me find and summon D and find a way to rid me of my demon. In exchange, I would work for him as a hunter, tracking and capturing rogue tempter demons who roamed the earth.

If Murkowski's demon took Hannah, she might die. I would most definitely die.

Murkowski's bearded face split into a triumphant grin. "Don't worry, pet. We won't leave you behind."

I assumed he was talking to me and not Hannah. Apparently, he thought I would survive his extraction of Hannah. While I was naturally curious about the hell realm, I wasn't up for a spur-of-the-moment visit, especially without the strength and extra abilities my demon gave me.

My head ached and my limbs weighed heavy with fatigue as Hannah slipped away from me inch by inch. Did she want to leave? Had she realized this demon was her ticket to freedom?

"Please," I pleaded with Hannah, begging her. I would've fallen to my knees if I wasn't already on them. "We have to save Mr. Murkowski and Mara. Please don't leave me."

Mara hadn't fled, which meant she was too weakened, too scared, or possibly too hungry to take the opportunity to hightail it out of the alley. If she did, Murkowski's demon might go after her once he finished with me. Demons didn't like loose ends, and the lesser demons and humans they used as pawns in their power plays normally didn't outlive their usefulness in those games. I couldn't protect her if she ran, not without Hannah.

I couldn't protect myself without Hannah.

"You can't have my demon," I said through gritted teeth.

"Demon?" Murkowski's face split into a sinister grin that looked all kinds of wrong on a Santa-looking man. "Oh, dear, you have no idea what you're carrying within you, do you?"

Without warning, something broke inside me. It bubbled up from deep within the core of my being and strengthened my resolve. Curling through me in tendrils of a newly ignited fire, it latched on to Hannah like a grappling hook. I couldn't pull her away from Murkowski's demon with the leash tied to my black mirror, but this new power matched him in terms of force, a veritable well of strange, untapped potential.

Hannah's essence stretched between us in a metaphysical tug of war as the knife in my hand shot out bursts of purple sparks.

I had no idea what this new force was or how it matched the strength of a powerful demon, nor did I care. I lurched forward and pressed the blade of my knife against Murkowski's neck, marveling as it flashed from red to blue and back again.

"Hannah, fight back. We've got this. Come on."

Something happened. A sense of awe, wonder, and understanding coursed through me. It had to be coming from Hannah. My own consciousness was too worried about survival to be awed by anything. What had she realized? Why was she calm?

And what did that have to do with the strange surge of power that had allowed me to maintain a grip on my demon?

Hannah finally responded, wrenching free of Murkowski's demon, and slamming back into me. The force of it lifted my body into the air and banged me against the alley wall.

She'd snapped back like a rubber band. And bonus, she'd ripped the demon right out of Mr. Murkowski. It appeared as an amorphous cloud of black smoke and howled with a mixture of fury and pain.

Relief coursed through me, as did the horrid aftertaste. *Yuck.* Hannah had taken a big bite out of this one to weaken it, and I'd yet to find an after-demon dinner mint that could wash that nastiness out of my mouth.

I managed to land on my feet—barely. The immaterial demon morphed into the shape of an oversize gargoyle, complete with phantom teeth, and bit me. I sliced it with my knife, and its piercing shriek nearly burst my eardrums.

"Damn it, Hannah, swallow him!"

Waiting for Hannah to do her freakin' job, I kept stabbing at the immaterial demon, who'd now taken the form of an ugly, horrifying giant spider that spat mini-spiders out of its maw and covered me with eight-legged terrors that also bit. Resisting the urge to scream bloody murder and flee the alley, I gritted my teeth and put my years of training to use by holding my knife out and spinning with demon-fueled speed, hacking at the connections between the spider's body and the tiny spiders crawling all over me.

I used the last connection to pull what was left of the demon's misty form to me. Apparently, the demon had only been playing with me before, since he released some magic that sent electrical shocks through my body. I screamed in agony but held on. The bastard had claimed he wanted me and Hannah. Presumably, he wasn't trying to kill us—but that might change if he got desperate enough about escaping.

"Hannah! Please," I called to my demon out loud.

She flung my body into the air, dislodging the demon from my grip in the process. Instead of landing gracefully on my feet, she let me fall into what I could only assume was the city's most disgusting cesspool of a dumpster.

And I'd thought the alley smelled bad. Ugh.

I struggled to stand up, stumbling on the unstable heap of revolting waste. Hannah didn't help me. I yelled at her in my head, *Hellooooo! It's your job to keep me alive and catch the demons, remember?*

I found my footing and peered out of the dumpster, scanning the area for the immaterial demon. It had floated away from Murkowski's body and now hovered near the entrance to the alley. I tried to climb out of the dumpster so I could apprehend it, but something held me back.

Hannah. She was working against me. What the hell?

Hovering in place, the shimmering patch of darkness that was the demon opened its maw and grinned, eyes glowing. When he spoke, his voice was high and piercing, like the shriek of a banshee.

"Remember."

The demon flickered briefly and then vanished, leaving a whiff of brimstone in its wake.

CHAPTER FIVE

Damn. Damn. Damn. The demon got away. Hannah had *let* it get away.

I hated it when they got away. Double the paperwork, not to mention the strong possibility it would latch on to another host and come back for round two of Let's Stalk Jinx McGee. Hannah had to know that. She'd nearly been captured by the demon in Murkowski, but she'd stopped me from going after it.

She'd friggin' let him go.

And she'd dropped me into a dumpster. Not cool. I gagged as I tried to wrap my mind around this clusterfuck of a case.

Had she failed to capture the demon due to distraction or injury? She'd gone strangely quiet. Not at all like her. Instead of insulting me or screaming like an angry lioness after an unsuccessful hunt, she'd faded into the depths of my consciousness. Normally, I had to summon her back with my black mirror. Why had she let Murkowski's demon go? And what exactly did the demon want us to remember?

Add that to the tally of inexplicable screw-ups associated with this case. Then there was the weird power surge that helped me keep my demon, and my misbehaving demon going AWOL somewhere in my subconscious.

Mara groaned, pulling my attention to the other, more urgent task at hand. Holy guacamole, she *was* still hungry, and what was left of Mr. Murkowski lay on the ground, injured, unconscious, and ripe for the picking. I hoisted my aching body out of the dumpster. After pausing to pick bits of gooey noodles out of my hair, along with what I hoped was a napkin and not part of a stinky diaper, I limped over to get between the predatory demon and her prey. Good thing I hadn't eaten before going on the hunt. The dry heaves were bad enough.

Upchucking on poor Mr. Murkowski would add insult to injury.

Mara was trying to control herself—she really wasn't a bad demon. Most tempter demons weren't bad, or all bad. They were just different. Religion and myth focused on the worst of them, scratching the surface instead of digging deeper for the big picture. Whether they'd been created by demon lords or evolved to feed on the essences of their fellow demons and humans, they couldn't help their natures.

"Mara." I filled my voice with a warning I couldn't back up without Hannah. Nice of her to leave me in a jam. "Get it together. This one's not for you."

"I know," she whined, scooting away from the juicy, defenseless human despite her obvious longing. Her pupils had dilated until her eyes appeared black, and she'd transformed back into her normal sex kitten form. Buxom, curvaceous, long-legged, and dripping sensuality.

Too bad. I'd enjoyed making out with the librarian almost as much as making out with the form of D, but I'd have to deal with that later. Compartmentalization and prioritizing were crucial life skills I was working hard to master.

Mara groaned and doubled over, somehow making agony look sexier than the entire cast of one of those top model reality television shows—or so I'd heard, since I didn't watch that sort of thing—and filling me with alarm. I had to feed her, but I didn't exactly have any vetted candidates on hand. She was only allowed to drain her fellow demons or nibble on approved souls from humans. Humans approved by the boss, not by me. I'd have let her devour half my exes had Triple B not nixed the idea. He was such a stickler.

"Hold on, Mara. Let's stabilize Bad Santa and call 9-1-1. After that, I'll find you the best meal this side of the earth realm, okay?" I only hoped I could deliver.

I ran my hands over Mr. Murkowski's limbs and torso to check for injuries. The good news? No broken bones. His cuts, scrapes, and bruises were superficial. Shouldn't take him too long to recover from those. That dislocated shoulder might sting a bit more, but I'd make certain he had state-of-the-art orthopedic care my commission from this botched job could buy.

The bad news? His breathing was shallow, and he looked like the kind of guy who was about two steak dinners away from a heart attack. I wasn't a doctor, but I played one in the field and figured it was time to get some professional help involved.

I dug my phone out of my pants pocket and called for an ambulance. Fortunately, my tech demons made it impossible to trace me via mobile. I could stay on the line long enough to give the dispatcher a general idea of Mr. Murkowski's injuries and potential cardiac arrest on the horizon without any follow-up from law enforcement. After hanging up, I dragged a very agitated succubus behind the dumpster to hide with me while we waited for a pickup.

No way was I going to ruin my own ride. I smelled like a sewer. Time to call for my delinquent backup. Again. I swear HQ left me hanging on purpose.

A chipper voice shot out of the phone, down my spine, and directly to my ass, making it twitch in irritation. "Demon Hunters, Incorporated. You find 'em, we bind 'em. How may I serve you?"

"I don't have time for this, Lacey. I need a ride." I propped the phone between my shoulder and ear and gave Mara a shove. The succubus had started eyeing me like a slab of prime rib. "Where've you been? You were supposed to be here ages ago."

"Hi, Jinx!" My partner, trainee, and sometimes best frenemy ignored my question. I hated it when she did that.

"Do we have to do this every time I call you? It's getting old, and I need a pickup pronto." I didn't have time for her Gen Z nonsense. This was an emergency.

Infusing her voice with all the snark she could muster, she asked, "Is that what you've been into tonight? Hijinks? Get it?"

I groaned. "Yeah, I got it the first time. And the million and one times after that. You need some new material."

Lacey Green was another member of the very exclusive demon-possessed-since-childhood club. We were a rarity since most humans didn't survive demonic possession very long. She'd named her demon Simon. Funny name for a mammon, otherwise known as a greed demon, but she rolled her eyes whenever I suggested she change the greed demon's name to Gordon Gekko. She also noted I was older than dirt and the reference proved it.

While incorporeal and reliant on possession, Simon wasn't as powerful—or volatile—as Hannah, and Lacey didn't need to summon him with a black mirror. Her little immaterial tempter spent most of its time in her mobile phone, surfing the Internet. Her data storage fees were probably astronomical, but it made her and Simon hella good trackers. That demon could find anyone, anywhere, anytime.

He could also find the best bars, dance clubs, and parking. Handy demon, that one, especially for his twenty-three-year-old mistress. Like her own personal Yelp.

"You need to be nice to me if you want pickup service," Lacey said. The singsong in her voice made my ass twitch harder. "What happened to *your* car?"

"Nothing happened to my car. Jeez, forget where you park one time and people never let you live it down." I peeled something green and gooey off my left boot. I could replace the pants and shirt, but these were my favorite pair of boots. Hopefully someone at HQ could magic the dumpster crud off them. "I'm just a little messy. Fought with a dumpster and lost."

Lacey laughed. "You do get yourself into the most interesting situations. Did you catch the demon? While you've been rolling around in trash, I've bagged three. Nasty little gremlins."

Seriously? That's what she'd been doing? "Let me get this straight. You were supposedly stuck in traffic, but somewhere along the way, you decided catching vermin was more important than joining me for our stakeout and coming when I called you?"

"I had to," she said indignantly. "They were chasing drunk tourists down Printer's Alley. I think they may have some form of hell realm rabies."

Fair point. A chorus of low growls rumbled in the background as if to confirm Lacey's diagnosis. Then again, she'd probably poked at them with a stick. She laughed when I said as much.

"They need to be put down. I should really off-load them before they start foaming at the mouth. At least, I think they have mouths. Hard to tell one end from the other, really. Did I mention I caught three?"

I rolled my eyes. Lacey's competitive nature surpassed even her penchant for the five-finger discount. The boss had recruited her much as he'd recruited me, minus the death threats. The threat of prison sealed the deal for her since Lacey had a thing for shoplifting. More of a compulsion, which was why her greed demon had latched on to her in the first place.

"Yeah, yeah, three points for you. As far as interesting situations, you don't know the half of it," I said. "You won't believe the night I've had. I tracked a succubus who I thought had targeted my mark, but it was a setup that put me in the cross hairs of another demon. I had to make out with the succubus to distract the other sneaky demon, who the boss didn't mention, by the way. Then Hannah yanked the sneaky demon out of the host before it could kill the poor guy."

I left out the part where the sneaky demon had escaped. The last thing I needed was Lacey rubbing my failed capture attempt in my face. It would add insult to whatever injury the boss had in store for me when he found out.

I pulled my knife out of its sheath and waved it in front of Mara to keep her at bay. It glowed with a pale-red light appropriate for the power level of a succubus. Thank goodness, or maybe badness, for small favors. I had no idea what was up with the blue and purple I'd seen earlier, but for now, it seemed to be functioning properly.

I didn't want to jab it into Mara, but if she kept staring at my lips, I might have to give her a little slice to incapacitate her.

"You made out with a succubus?" Lacey asked, awe evident in her voice, along with a hint of jealousy.

Mara started stroking my hair while whispering sweet nothings in my other ear. Damn, she must be desperate to get so close to me in my smelly state. I pushed her away and smacked her hand lightly with the flat of the blade, making her whimper.

Glad she didn't have the strength left to morph into my ex again.

"Um, yeah." I put more distance between myself and Mara while keeping an ear and eye out for the approaching ambulance. "She's still with me, and she's really hungry. If we don't get out of here soon, she might eat the paramedics when they get here to pick up the human host."

Lacey snorted. "Not my problem. You really need to get a car locator app."

"I did not lose my car." I knew exactly where it was. I'd left it parked on Commerce Street. Or was it at the state capitol? Farmer's Market? Maybe I did need an app.

"Why would I let you in my car after you've been dumpster diving?" Lacey was clearly not on board with the urgent extraction operation of Jinx McGee and her not-so-trusty succubus sidekick.

"I wasn't dumpster diving," I said, huffing while I tugged a greasy lock of hair out of my face. "Hannah dropped me in there. I think she's mad at me."

"Of course she is. You're good at making demons mad. And people. Animals too. I bet puppies don't even like you."

If she only knew. Presumably, Hannah went off to brood after dumping me in the trash. I had no idea why she was pissed. She'd let the demon go, not me. This mission fail was on her.

And why hadn't she escaped when she'd had the chance?

"Hello? Earth to Jinx? You're a little off tonight." I heard a thwack and envisioned Lacey smacking her head with feigned disbelief. "Wait, what am I thinking? You're always off. Off-kilter, off your rocker, and don't even get me started on how you sing off-key whenever we're on stakeouts."

I grumbled, Lacey's insults distracting me from my own brooding. "Whatever. I'm a big hit at parties. Anyway, aside from being in imminent danger of consumption by a raging succubus, I've got a major incident report to file at HQ. The boss sent me after the wrong mark."

Lacey sucked in a deep breath. I'd shocked her, apparently, by casting doubt on the boss. She was in awe of the guy. Ah, to be young. Also, she clearly hadn't been listening to me earlier when I said the boss didn't tell me about the sneaky demon.

"The boss doesn't make mistakes, and technically he sent *us* on this assignment."

"And you didn't show. Since you ditched me, you're welcome to the paperwork." Score one for Jinx.

I cut her off before she could launch into a tirade. "And in any other situation, I'd agree with you about the boss. But Murkowski was already demon possessed. The succubus was a decoy. The demon in Murkowski was looking for me specifically. He almost yanked Hannah out of me."

"Why would he do that?" she asked.

"Dunno," I said, the distant sirens growing closer making my stomach twist. "Something about joining an army of darkness."

"If I had a quarter for every time I heard that one." Lacey giggled. Her sense of humor almost made up for her shenanigans.

"I know, right? Oh, and apparently, I'm important. Important enough to be a 'who' and a 'what.'" I wished the sneaky demon had given me a little more information about that.

Hey, Hannah, got anything on that?

My personal demon didn't deign to respond.

"Yeah, you're something," Lacey said. Going by her tone, I probably didn't want to know her theories on what I was.

"Oh, and Murkowski's demon said that I didn't know what I carried within me. I assume he meant Hannah, but what did he mean by that?"

"Maybe he knows what kind of demon Hannah is," Lacey said. "No one this side of the hell realm has been able to identify your demon. Ask him when you interrogate him."

Yeah. I'd have to have the demon in my possession before I could ask him, but I wasn't telling Lacey that.

"So about that ride..." I had to convince Lacey to get her ass—and more importantly, her car—to our location before the paramedics arrived and before Mara took a bite out of my soul, and possibly my person. Time was wasting.

Lacey heaved a deep sigh—the one that conveyed a level of bored disdain that was a trademark of her generation. I didn't have any dirt on her, which meant blackmail was out, and I didn't have anything she wanted.

Something flashed in my periphery at dizzying speed. I stood up—too fast, apparently, since my knees cracked loud enough to startle Mara—and put myself in the path of whatever the threat was, my knife at the ready.

It blazed red. Another demon.

Out of the shadows, a tall figure in a dark hoodie emerged holding a jar filled with mist, swirling like a miniature tornado. I couldn't see the hooded man's face, but I recognized the jar as demon realm in origin, and what was inside as an immaterial demon. It was Murkowski's demon, the one Hannah had let get away, only to be recaptured by a demon hunter I didn't recognize.

A deep voice laced with humor spoke. "Looking for this?"

I was about to ask who the hell he was when headlights flooded the alley with blinding white light. I turned, squinting to save my night vision while trying to figure out if the vehicle's driver was friend or foe.

After my eyes adjusted, I realized it was Lacey's car. My chariot had arrived at last, but in keeping with her MO, Lacey had the worst timing.

When I turned back, the jar holding Murkowski's demon was resting on the dirty asphalt, but the stranger who'd been holding it was gone. Attached to it was a note. Elegant script flowed across what looked like parchment paper.

Meet you at headquarters.

CHAPTER SIX

I squirmed in the back seat of Lacey's car, knowing we were being followed by the unknown demon hunter who'd bagged Murkowski's demon. Whoever he was, I owed him, since I wouldn't have to tell the boss we'd lost the demon. But I didn't like it. Demon hunters were territorial, and we rarely trusted hunters outside our personal teams. And since he'd left the demon for me rather than claiming it for himself, he'd want something from me in return.

Something told me I wouldn't like it.

I tapped the glass, which made the demon within swirl faster and emit a scream that hurt my ears.

"Stop it!" Lacey said, wincing and gripping the steering wheel tighter. "I already have a headache from your stink. That scream is making my ears bleed."

Right. I had more pressing matters, like what was up with my incommunicado personal demon. Hannah still wouldn't answer me when I called for her. I could've used the black mirror to force her out, but maybe this situation called for diplomacy. I'd have to give her some time to get over being mad and then hope she'd tell me why. Or get over it.

She'd come out again when she was hungry.

Unless...had Murkowski's attack injured her? Maybe she was traumatized.

I'd have to deal with Hannah later. Right now, I had to confront the boss about this FUBAR mission and take care of Mara. The succubus had enjoyed a three-course rabid gremlin meal, and I'd promised Lacey a cheeseburger kiddie meal after I cleaned up.

In the meantime, I needed some intel. I shifted in the seat Lacey had insisted on covering in a thick plastic tarp—I didn't blame her, since it would be a crime to mar the perfection of her Mustang's leather interior —and dialed my favorite roommate, Boice, aka the hell realm's number one tech demon.

Of course, if you asked his brother, Roice, he'd tell you *he* was the number one tech demon and my favorite roomie. Guys were so competitive. The twins were pains in my ass but worth every penny the boss paid them when it came to intel gathering, research, financial planning, and all-around best buddying.

In exchange for these invaluable services, I gave them a pass on rent and let them cook for me while I enthralled them with fascinating tales of my exploits as a demon hunter on the mean streets of Nashville. They were demon hunters, too, but I did more fieldwork and was therefore way cooler. They were better at paperwork, research, and making mischief and mayhem online. Our arrangement worked beautifully.

I also pretended not to know about all the time they spent on Porn-Web. We all needed hobbies.

"What do you need?" The surly male voice on the line managed to infuse both seriousness and boredom into the question. Boice was all business. He needed to get out more.

"A million dollars and a trip to Tahiti would be nice," I offered, picking more bits of nastiness off my tank top. "But I'll settle for a favor. I need you to find out which hospital Jack Murkowski's been admitted to and make sure his medical costs are covered."

"Murkowski. Got it. What if he's insured?"

"Transfer enough to cover his deductible and missed work."

The sound of lithe fingers clicking across the keyboard let me know my roomie was on it. The deep sigh let me know he disapproved.

"You're a big softy," Boice said.

"My money, my business." I calculated how much this little mishap was likely to set me back. At this rate, I'd never be able to retire from the demon-hunting mafia to live it up in the style to which I would like to become accustomed.

I totally needed a sugar daddy.

He grunted. "If you keep this up, you'll have no money left to eat, let alone retire."

"Whatever," I scoffed. "Just remember, the longer I work as a demon hunter, the longer you and your bro get to live rent free."

"True," he said. "Anything else?" The steady stream of keyboard clicks continued. That demon could type. I hoped he was typing up my field reports instead of writing fanfic. Boice had a thing for slash.

"Actually, there is." Given the nature of the encounter, I was far from done with this case. I needed to find out how a powerful, immaterial demon infiltrated both the earth realm and its host undetected. Getting more information on the host would help. "See what you else can dig up on Murkowski—his business dealings, vices, associates, you know, the usual. The file I got from the boss left out a lot of details. Aside from the bio, it just said the guy was marked by a demon, but that was apparently a ruse planned by the sneaky demon who was possessing him."

Boice uttered a startled grunt, as if he'd been punched in the gut. Uh-oh. This might be worse than I thought. When he recovered enough to speak again, he asked, "What kind of demon?"

I looked at my jar full of demon, wishing I had more to go on. I'd been trying to engage Hannah since we got in the car, but no luck. If she had some extra intel on the demon, she wasn't sharing.

"Immaterial. Not a tempter, at least not one that I've ever tangoed with in the field. He's powerful too." I shuddered at the memory. "Powerful enough to almost nab Hannah before he got away."

"Definitely an unauthorized demon. No summoner would let one that powerful pass through the portals. You said he tried to take Hannah?" Boice asked between clicks. "And you let him go?"

"I didn't let him go, Hannah did. Lucky for me, another demon hunter handed him to me in a magical mason jar. I didn't know the boss hired a newbie, and I had no idea a demon could take my demon out of me against our wills."

"No new hires. Maybe someone from another jurisdiction?" Boice kept typing, bless him. Such a good little minion. "As far as Hannah, it's tricky to forcibly evict a demon of Hannah's strength and caliber, but not unheard of if you have the right tools, enough power, and know the proper incantations," he replied coolly. "But your demon is unique. She's tethered to you and doesn't seem to follow the normal rules of possession. And since she's been attached to you for so long, summoning her out of your body would probably kill you."

I could almost hear his unspoken like-I've-told-you-a-million-times.

I shook off that happy thought and focused on the more immediate issue. "That's just it. He didn't *summon* Hannah. He pulled her out of me physically, or metaphysically. Not sure. But it was like he was on the verge of ripping her out of me—literally."

The clicking stopped, and there was a long pause. I hated uncomfortable silences. Fortunately, he spoke before I could get too squirmy. "What else?"

I leaned a little to the right as I gathered my thoughts, reaching down to remove a gelatinous mass that had detached itself from my tank top and was now stuck to the plastic covering my seat. I used the wet wipes Lacey had given me to get its remnants off my fingers.

"He used a succubus to lure me into the alley. Pretended to be an ordinary human about to lose his soul to her. He didn't seem to think taking Hannah would kill me. Come to think of it, he said I'd be going along for the ride to the hell realm. Even asked for me by name."

My mind raced with the implications. I knew most eviction attempts for long-term demonic possessions didn't end well for the host, which was one reason why the boss had never tried to summon Hannah. But what if there was a way to get Hannah out of me safely? Had the boss been holding out?

"Why would an unauthorized demon want you?"

I didn't care for Boice's tone or incredulity. "Aside from the fact that I'm awesome, he said a general in charge of an army of darkness wanted me. Does the hell realm have a draft?"

More silence. Not good. A draft seemed so official. Sure, I could fight, but I was more soldier of fortune than loyal warrior ready to give her all for a cause. Unless the cause involved world peace and free donuts, but only if they were fresh and glazed with chocolate. The donuts, not world peace.

Then again, chocolate glaze could very well be the key to world peace.

Boice's irritation brought me back to attention.

"Some hell realm militias are filled with conscripts, and their recruiting methods are a bit more...forceful than those used in the earth dimension in this era," he said carefully. "Your realm has a particularly nasty history of forced military service. Don't even get me started on the celestial realm's military system."

Good grief, demons could be so touchy about their reputation, mostly because the bad apples from their realm had been immortalized in myths, legends, and holy texts on earth, striking fear into the hearts of humans since the beginning of recorded history. I'd have to remember to be more culturally sensitive around Boice.

Nah. Needling him was so much more fun.

"Well, I'm definitely not militia material. I'm not joining any armies in the hell realm, the celestial realm, or anywhere else."

"You're a highly skilled demon tracker with lethal powers," he said.

"So?" I countered. "What if I don't like the uniform?"

"You wear camo pants, and your black mirror hangs around your neck like a dog tag," he added helpfully and resumed his furious typing.

"But they won't let me wear neon camo," I said, getting back to the important issue. "And my rhinestone and rose Doc Martens aren't regulation in any dimension. I won't go anywhere without them. They're my secret weapons."

He sighed, loudly. I was totally winning the argument. He was obviously frustrated with my mastery of the art of debate. "Do you actually wear neon camo? That blends in exactly nowhere."

I scoffed, going in for the kill. "Says you. I'm a stealthy ninja in Vegas."

We'd reached headquarters by then. The imposing glass-and-steel monstrosities towering over downtown cast a long shadow on our more modest brick-and-mortar center of operations. Low profile was our motto. I'd voted for "Don't Let Your Demons Get You Down," but management had not approved. They hadn't approved Taco and Tequila Tuesday, either. Clearly, the bureaucracy was stifling my creative genius along with office morale.

"Right. Moving on. An unauthorized, powerful demon managed to sneak past portal security, possess a human, subdue a succubus, and wants to rip out your demon and recruit you to fight in a rebellion." Boice was good at summaries. "Anything else?"

"This other hunter. He's following us back to HQ."

"Aren't you just the belle of the ball? I'll check the roster for demon-hunting assignments from all regional jurisdictions, but you didn't give me much of a description. Roice can search recent reports for anything out of the ordinary with demon crossings when he gets back from grabbing takeout. Maybe we can track down which portal your demon used."

"Can you get something for Mara too? She'll need to crash with us for a while." I carefully extracted my foul person from Lacey's car. Wasting no time, she popped the trunk and replaced the plastic seat cover with an impressive assortment of Christmas tree–shaped air fresheners.

I mouthed "sorry" before turning my attention back to the phone. "Let me know as soon as you find anything interesting."

"A succubus as a roommate? Talk about making me an offer I can't refuse. Have fun with the boss," he said before ending the call, the little bastard. He loved it when someone else got in trouble.

Maybe that was why he and his brother kept living with me.

"Time to sort this mess out," I muttered, blowing a greasy lock of hair out of my face and nodding at Mara. The look of post meal contentment drained from her face along with the blood. She was terrified of facing the boss, with good reason.

"I'm sorry." Mara took a step back, her gaze darting wildly. "He knows my name—my real name—he summoned me to do his bidding. I had no choice."

Crap on a cracker. That was how the bastard demon had done it. To know a tempter demon's true name was to have power over it. The more powerful the summoner, the more compelling the summons. My colleagues and I knew the lower-ranking demons and tempters we tracked only by their street names or classification, so we had to rely on negotiation, diplomacy, bribery, brute force, and skill in hand-to-hand, or rather demon-to-demon, combat to rein them in or subdue them.

Mara's voice brought me out of my philosophical musings. Damn it, I had such a hard time staying on task. "I can't go back to the hell realm. I'm sorry, Jinx, I just can't. He'll kill me."

Mara had fled the hell realm to escape a nasty demon who'd put a hit out on her. She held refugee status, but it could and would be revoked if she broke the rules.

The succubus took a step back and seemed on the verge of bolting. She'd go into hiding if I couldn't talk her down. Then I'd have no way to protect her from the boss or from the demon who'd used her to get to me.

"Mara, you can't run. I'll have to chase you and trap you, and I really don't want to do that." I placed my palms up, one empty and one holding the demon-filled jar, and took a slow, careful step in her direction. "It wasn't your fault. I'll make sure the boss knows that. I'll take care of you. He'll be more interested in this," I said, nodding toward the jar.

"You can't protect me from your boss or from the demon who summoned me," she said, pleading, gaze darting from my face to the angry trapped demon. "You don't even know what he is. You won't keep him trapped for long."

I took her arm, gently but firmly, and gave it what I hoped was a reassuring squeeze. "I won't let you take the fall for this. I promise."

I braced for her skepticism and another round of protests, probably an attempted escape, but she surprised me, gazing into my eyes as if I'd hypnotized her. It couldn't be Hannah. I didn't feel her.

But I felt that strange sensation again. The bubbly thing that had held on to Hannah in the alley had returned, only this time it was calmer, like a gentle hand instead of a red-hot grappling hook. Mara must have sensed it too. Her stiff shoulders relaxed, and the wild-eyed look of panic fled from her gaze.

Even weirder, I could taste her terror and anxiety, like I'd drawn it out of her. Lucky for me, demon emotions tasted a whole lot better than demon essence.

"Okay," Mara said, nodding while Lacey stood dumbfounded. Lacey had pushed herself off her car and was fiddling with her curly red locks as she stared in slack-jawed awe. Apparently, I had impressed her too.

Whatever. I had questions that needed answers and a demon to deliver. I dragged Mara a few feet before she stopped, jerking me back as she stood frozen with a similar expression of disbelief and wonder plastered across her face, just like Lacey.

Then I realized they weren't staring at me. They were staring at the vision in front of the door to HQ, his broad shoulders nearly obscuring the entrance to our lair. Tall, dark, and stunning, shadows wafted around him as if caressing his form, accenting his curves and edges from the chiseled features of his impossibly handsome face to the lean muscles of his body. The demon hunter who'd recaptured Murkowski's demon. I recognized the hoodie, though the hood no longer covered his head and face, and that wasn't all.

He was magnificent, he was a god, and he was exactly as he'd appeared when Mara took his form.

Only he was the real deal. And he was supposed to be dead.

Mara tugged on my hand and let out a little gasp. "Wow, he's perfect. I thought you'd dreamed him up. I had no idea he was real."

"Oh, he's real, all right." Shock and disbelief gave way to all-consuming rage. Ten years of searching before coming to the heartbreaking conclusion that he was dead, forever beyond my reach, and he shows up now? Where had he been? Why hadn't he come back when I summoned him?

Why was he back now?

My eyes stung and my chest went tight. No, I would not cry. Damn it, I would not cry in front of him. I wouldn't let myself drown in years of grief. I couldn't. Anger was better.

He smiled. The bastard demon who'd disappeared all those years ago without a word stood before me and had the audacity to lift his full, sensual lips into a smile—nay, *smirk*—as if he could win me over with a grin and a wink.

I jerked out of Mara's grip and marched over to him. He watched me with interest. Drinking my body in with his sultry gaze, his eyes flashed red with the light of some faraway corner of the hell realm made of fire and sin and forbidden pleasures. His gaze grew wary, however, as I came closer. He squared his shoulders and adjusted his stance as if braced for impact.

He wasn't dumb.

I slowed, taking a moment to savor the sight and scent of my long-lost demon, and sighed. He was even more beautiful than I remembered. He looked away briefly, as if chagrined, but not before a rush of pain flashed in his otherworldly gaze.

No. That vulnerable, wounded, sexy-as-hell act wasn't going to get him off the hook. He owed me answers.

I would not run to him. I would not wrap my arms around him and sob. I would not hold on to him and never let go. My poor, wounded heart wouldn't survive when he disappeared again.

I smiled and ran my fingers over his chest, reveling in the sensation of his hard muscles as they tightened in response to my touch. He parted his lips as his gaze filled with hunger.

"It's good to see you, Jane." His voice was low and husky.

"Welcome back, Dominic," I said, before planting a gentle kiss on his sensual lips.

Then, I reared back and punched him square in the jaw.

CHAPTER SEVEN

He rubbed his jaw and looked more amused than annoyed, the prick. Come on, that had to have hurt. My knuckles ached so bad I thought I might have fractured them. I prepared my aching fist for round two, but he grabbed my arm and pulled me close as he loomed over me.

"I probably deserved that," he said, gaze growing serious. "I owe you an explanation. I don't expect you'll forgive me right away, but—"

I tugged out of his hold and took a step back, planting my sore hand on my hip while trying not to wince or drop the jar holding Murkowski's demon. I seriously needed some ice for aching fist of fury. "Right away? How about never? I thought you were dead."

I squared my shoulders and gave him my best glare. "You're lucky I didn't stab you with my knife. And don't bother with the explanation unless it involves alien abduction."

The corners of his lips twitched as he fought back a smile.

"Alien abduction with anal probes," I added. "I hope they went good and deep too. Without lube."

Lips still twitching, he coughed and cleared his throat before speaking. "I'm sorry to disappoint you, but aliens had nothing to do with my disappearance."

"Whatever. It's not like I care." I didn't mean a word of it. Of course I cared. My heart was racing, and my stomach had filled with butterflies. I was dying to know what had happened, where he'd been, why he'd walked out on me.

But I would rather die than admit it. I wouldn't tell him how much I'd missed him. How I still dreamed of him at night. How I sometimes peeked in the corner of my closet, hoping against hope the grown-up version of my childhood demon companion would miraculously appear, take me in his arms, and never let me go.

He grinned again and took a step forward as if daring me to back away. I refused to give him the satisfaction, but I really hated it when people did that, especially demons over six feet tall. I already had to look up at him. This close, I was bound to get a crick in my neck from throwing it back far enough to meet his gaze.

Thankfully, he did me the courtesy of leaning down, his gaze locked on my mouth before it rose to meet mine. God, those eyes. I'd almost forgotten. The first time I'd seen him, I'd been frightened by his red eyes. But when I'd looked closer, I realized they weren't red at all. His irises were a vivid shade of green with sparkling red light swirling and twinkling within them, as if he glowed from somewhere deep inside.

I shook my head and channeled my scorned woman fury, glaring at him.

"But you do," he said, his smile widening in triumph.

"I do many things." I cocked my head to the side. "You'll have to be more specific."

"Care," he said, low and sensual.

"Do not." It sounded lame even to me. I looked away so he wouldn't see exactly how much I did care.

He leaned in closer, moving slowly lest I unleash my fist of fury on his vulnerable jaw or perfectly straight nose. His hot breath caressed my ear as he whispered, "I saw what you did with the succubus—what you wanted to do with me. I wish it had been with me. I missed you so much..."

I was about to snort in derision, but he sounded sincere, his voice filled with such longing. Was it? Did he long for me the way I still longed for him?

It didn't matter. He'd hurt me. I could admit that to myself, even if I'd never in a million years let him know. I couldn't trust him. He was right about one thing. I did care enough to want answers.

But not enough to beg for them. I had my pride—the only thing I had where he was concerned. And if he wanted me to listen, he was going to have to work for it.

"Liar." I resisted the urge to rub my cheek against his as I whispered, "And the only thing I want to do with you is watch you burn in hell."

He pulled back, still smiling, but this time it didn't reach his eyes. "If that's what you truly want, you're ten years too late."

What was *that* supposed to mean?

Then it dawned on me. "You were summoned to hell? You've been there all this time?" Why hadn't he answered my summons? If he'd survived this long in the hell realm, he must be as cunning, devious, powerful, and strong as he was deliciously attractive. Surely he could've come back or at least contact me had he wanted to.

I shook my head and stopped focusing on his masculine beauty and magnetism. I'd thought he was dead, but he'd been alive all this time. And he'd stayed away. He hadn't cared about me as much as I'd cared about him. That had to be it. It was the only explanation that made sense.

Damned if I let him know how much that hurt. "Why are you back now? And why did you catch Murkowski's demon for me? You didn't bother telling me back in the alley. Of course, you didn't bother to identify yourself either. You always had terrible manners."

"You were doing remarkably well on your own, and I wasn't sure you'd welcome the help, or the distraction, especially if you knew it was me."

Okay, he had a point, but still. "Fine, but what about—"

He held up a hand and cut me off. "The demon? I trailed him as far as midtown before I caught him in an ambush. I know his type. Messenger demon. Emissary of a high-ranking demon lord who has no business entering the earth realm. I'll interrogate him and find out what he's up to."

A messenger demon working under orders from a demon lord?

Demon lords were barred from traveling to earth and interfering in earth's business. It was the reason demon travel was highly regulated. Nothing more powerful than tempters, who were weak and vulnerable in the hell realm, were permitted on earth under the same refugee status that allowed Mara to stay.

Sounded like someone was breaking the rules to come after me and my demon. And I was going to find out why, not D.

"No, I'll take him to the boss, and we'll interrogate him. It's my job. My case. You stay out of it." I poked him in the chest with my index finger, which now resembled a good-sized sausage link. I needed to take something for the swelling.

Amusement returned to his gaze as he crinkled his nose. "As much as I'd love to continue this conversation, I have a meeting to attend. You do, too, but I'd suggest you shower first. You smell fouler than the pit of Hades. We'll talk later."

My cheeks flamed as outrage and humiliation flooded my being. He turned and walked toward the entrance of headquarters. My headquarters. What business did he have—

Realization dawned. He had a meeting. The tall, dark, and dastardly demon was off to a meeting with my boss, *the* boss.

I marched over to him and placed my hand on the doorknob, blocking his access. He could've easily pushed me aside, but he simply paused and stared down at me, one brow arched.

"You aren't...working here, are you?" I asked, dreading the answer.

He grinned again, the fiend, before answering. "Not officially. I'm here as a consultant."

My jaw dropped. "A consultant? On what? We've never used consultants before. And who called you?" Presumably someone at HQ had been able to contact him, which meant the boss had been holding out on me. I was starting to think the boss had been a big fat liar on all fronts.

D grew serious once more, brows furrowed and jaw ticking. "You've never faced such a powerful demon before. And you aren't the only one. Your boss, the Arbiter, is concerned. We haven't had such a high-ranking demon breach a portal in over a decade, and that one was the first in centuries. I've been tracking him through the hell realm and came here just after he did through...unofficial channels."

I froze, mind racing as I took it all in. Dominic was here. He knew more about the demon in Mr. Murkowski than my boss had bothered to share with me. I hated to admit it, but that would make him useful as a consultant.

Wait, he'd called my boss the Arbiter?

"The boss is called the Arbiter? Like a title?" I asked, incredulous. "How do you know him?"

He shrugged. "I don't know what he calls himself on earth, but Arbiter is his title in the hell realm." Then he furrowed his brow and studied me, like he was trying to figure me out, or maybe wondering how much he should or shouldn't tell me.

Or maybe he was wondering why I looked and smelled like a landfill.

"We've been working here for years, and he never told us he had a title," a slightly breathless female voice spoke, giving me a start.

I turned to find Lacey and Mara behind me, eavesdropping on my conversation with The Betrayer, a title I'd just invented for Dominic. I'd have to print some business cards for him. I'd incorporate some miniature pitchforks and poop emojis.

D cast a wary glance at Lacey and Mara before turning his attention back to me. "I've never met The Arbiter in the...flesh, but he and I share similar interests." He emphasized the last word while staring hard at me.

"Okay," I said, backing away from the door. "Don't let me keep you. The boss hates people who show up late."

He smiled. "Thanks for the tip. We'll talk later."

My mind raced. Finding D and getting free of my demon was why I agreed to work for the boss's demon-hunting organization. It wasn't just because I was highly qualified, being demon possessed and all. I'd wanted D back. We hadn't been able to find or summon D, and the boss had told me—not unkindly—that D was probably dead. I believed him. I'd given up hope.

Oh, I was about to have it out with the boss. Big time.

I backed off. D opened the door and strolled in with Lacey and Mara practically tripping over themselves to follow. I couldn't blame them. D had a great ass, especially framed in tight black denim. He moved with the fluid grace of an athlete—I'd kill to have that kind of stride, so confident, as if he owned the place. D could definitely do swagger.

"Stay out of my business and off my case," I yelled.

The show ended too soon once D disappeared behind the elevator doors. He'd be heading to the lowest level of the building. The boss occupied an expansive underground office that was a combination reverse penthouse and dungeon. At least I assumed he kept his dungeon down there.

"So?" Lacey said, arching a winged brow and leveling her green-eyed gaze on me. "Care to spill?"

"What?" I feigned ignorance.

"Don't be coy. Who on earth is that fine creature who fell from the heavens and into our office?"

I snorted. "He didn't fall from heaven. He slithered out of the pits of the hell realm like the demon he is. No offense, Mara," I added.

"None taken." Her breathy succubus voice had grown breathier. "He is a demon. More powerful than a tempter, and a bad boy. But he's *so* pretty."

Lacey laughed. "Well, I wouldn't mind having him slither over to my apartment later. Unless, of course, he's spoken for." She turned her inquisitive gaze on me again.

If she was expecting me to claw her eyes out or descend into a fit of jealous rage, she was about to be disappointed. I gestured to the elevator with a casual flick of my wrist, regretting the movement as soon as I made it. I winced again when I bothered to look at my injured hand. It had swollen to nearly twice its normal size.

"Be my guest. Just be warned, he'll ghost you. You may think you've captured and tamed the beast, but when you least expect it, he'll disappear on you."

Lacey smirked. "Duly noted." She looked at my hand and said, "You might want to wrap that up, but I have to say, I'm impressed. It was a nice punch."

"Thank you. I've been saving that for ten years. Now if you'll excuse me, I need hot water, a few gallons of soap, and a serious convo with my inner demon before talking to the boss. Mara, you stick with Lacey."

Mara looked dubious, but Lacey shrugged. "Wanna grab some real food? Bet you haven't been on an actual dinner date in ages," she said, wagging her eyebrows at the succubus.

"Thank you." Mara sounded genuinely surprised. "I would love to share a meal with you after your generous gift of the gremlins. But doesn't that normally come before the date?"

Lacey laughed. "Hey, I'm all for bucking convention. See you in a bit, Jinx."

I waved good-bye, pleased they'd hit it off, and headed to the team locker room for my date with Kohler, god of the shower.

Once I was clean and reasonably presentable, I hopped on the elevator and descended thirteen stories below ground level for my meeting with the so-called Arbiter with Murkowski's demon-in-a-jar. Arbiter of what, I couldn't say. I'd have to ask D, assuming he decided to stick around.

He'd apparently been in the hell realm for a decade, according to his story. That would be useful. I could possibly bring myself to extend him a tiny bit of professional courtesy until he left me to get on with my work and my life since he could tell me more about messenger demons and demon lords.

Damn it, why hadn't he answered my summons? Why was he back now?

The more I thought about it, the more I was convinced that the boss had known D was back and he hadn't told me. I'd bet every last dollar in my dwindling bank account that the boss had known where D had been all along, which meant he hadn't kept his side of our bargain.

Then again, demons were treacherous, sneaky creatures who caught unsuspecting humans in loopholes by bending the rules and conniving.

The doors opened to an elegant, if shadowy, reception area. The walls were covered in dark carved panels that cast shadows over the black marble flooring in the low light. Mr. Barbatos, the boss's secretary, looked up from beneath long lashes and nodded in greeting from behind his antique mahogany desk. It was as elegant as the demon himself. Mr. Barbatos didn't use a computer, mobile phone, or any other modern gadget, though he did maintain an old-fashioned rotary dial phone on one corner of his freakishly neat desk. The phone served as a link between our squad of demon hunters and the boss, as well as an intercom system. I wasn't sure how it worked, though, since it didn't seem to be plugged in.

"You're late." Mr. Barbatos's deep, velvety voice jolted me out of my musings and brought me back to attention.

"Sorry," I said. "I had a little run-in with a dumpster."

He grinned, his pale skin glowing from within as he leaned back in his fancy-schmancy office chair. "I heard."

His expression grew serious, then, and the sparks of demon light swirled in his obsidian irises as he rose from his chair. He buttoned his tailored suit jacket, ever the gentleman, and glided around the desk, leaning in a little too close for comfort. With jet-black hair, chiseled features, and immaculate dress, Mr. Barbatos was swoon-worthy, but all he inspired in me was apprehension. Kind of like a modern-day Samurai warrior—beautiful, powerful, and deadly.

That was probably why he'd chosen this form while working on earth. The guy was a high-ranking demon, one I suspected held rank and power on par with the boss. How the two of them wound up stuck on earth doing what amounted to menial demon cleanup duty was beyond me. I'd never asked. None of us had. We valued the sanctity of our lives and souls too much to pry.

"One day you little demon hunters will learn to control your personal entities, but until then, I'll never lack for entertainment," he said.

Ouch. That stung. But since he seemed to be in a good mood, I channeled my bravery to ask him a few questions. If I couldn't get the
lowdown on my ex from my ex, I figured Barbatos would know.

"So," I began, striving for casual as I adjusted the ice pack on my
wrist. "D's back. Did you know? The boss must have. Funny, he forgot to
tell me."

He arched a brow, feigning ignorance.

"The consultant?" I pressed, giving up any pretense of casual interest. Barbatos wasn't buying it anyway. "The new demon who dropped by
when I got back to HQ?"

"Ah." Mr. Barbatos leaned against the desk and strummed his long
fingers hypnotically over the antique wood surface. "That would be
Dominic. Of course that's not his real name. He's not ranked highly
enough to avoid control by a summons—yet. Dominic is one of many
aliases he maintains."

Duh. Of course he couldn't avoid control by summons. That was why
the boss and I spent years working to summon him and assumed he was
dead when we couldn't. Without his true name, we'd resorted to complex
summoning rituals and work-arounds that involved personal effects, a
lock of his hair, and blood. My blood. And the whole time the boss knew
who D was and had been faking me out.

"Why is he here now, after all these years?" That was the most important question at the moment. It wasn't for me, surely. He would have
come back sooner if it was. A small pang stabbed at my heart, but I
pushed it away. He was apparently here for a case—my case. But was it to
help, to take it over, or maybe to offer protection?

That thought made me bristle. I didn't need his protection. The team
and I were highly trained professional demon hunters.

Barbatos grinned like the Cheshire cat. "Why don't you ask him yourself? He's waiting for you along with the Arbiter."

"Again with the Arbiter," I blurted. "How come I don't know these
names and titles and the new guy, this *Dominic*, does?"

Barbatos sighed, his gaze condescending with a hint of challenge.
"You and your ragtag band of hunters didn't need that information

before. It was—what's the human expression? Ah, yes, above your pay grade."

The smug bastard irked me, but I knew better than to rise to the challenge, especially without Hannah to back me up. Instead, I glowered at him. "Why now?"

"Because, pet," he said, leaning down and putting his face mere inches from mine. People and demons kept doing that to me today. What was up with that? "Shit's about to get real."

CHAPTER EIGHT

Mr. Barbatos led me into the boss's lair. If I hadn't already been on edge from the whole shit's-about-to-get-real thing, that would've done it. He never accompanied any of us lowly demon hunters for the mandatory postgame wrap-up. It was beneath him.

I got the feeling it was beneath the boss, too, but he was a control freak.

My boss and his snarkily delicious colleague had been in charge of policing demon activity in the earth realm for centuries. Before that, demons moved as freely to and from their realm as angels—also known as celestials—and wreaked havoc on humanity. Versions of those encounters survived in religious texts and folklore throughout the world, but those stories varied widely in accuracy. Sometimes, demons were helpful. Seriously, the Black Plagues of the Middle Ages could've been extinction-level events were it not for the boss.

He was a freakin' legend.

Some might call him a hero, but not me. I doubted he cared very much about a few hundred thousand human souls, give or take. No, he probably wrangled his fellow demons so he could drain their energy for himself, or collect trophies, or prove that he was the biggest badass in this realm and all others.

Male posturing was apparently universal.

And since he'd apparently been lying to me, I wasn't inclined to think charitable thoughts about the old demon.

The air left my lungs once we crossed the threshold of the door, and as always, I got the sense that I'd entered a portal into another realm. The sleek black desk and ultra-modern accessories appeared standard issue and ordinary for the average egomaniacal human CEO—it was funny, considering how old-school Barbatos was by contrast. Everything in the boss's office screamed Euro-style cool, from the smooth metal shelves filled with ancient tomes from earth and who knew how many other realms to the rows of flat-screens lining the tiled walls to the multiple computer screens and keyboards neatly aligned on his desk.

I almost giggled at the thought of Mr. Barbatos and the boss being paired as some sort of hell realm odd couple. I wondered if they had their own reality show. Wow, what if we were unwitting stars of a hell realm version of *The Apprentice*? Or *The Dysfunctional Demon Office*?

"Jane Aurelia McGee." The boss's icy voice sent goose bumps erupting over my arms and shoulders. What was it about hearing one's full name? Maybe he'd been talking to my mother.

I spun around, searching the dark, cavernous recesses of the office for the Big Kahuna. He seemed to materialize out of thin air using tricks of light and one of a series of hidden doors to his lair—sneaky corporeal demon—and sauntered toward his desk. The large screens lining the walls came to life as he passed them. The displays were...eclectic. Everything from digital stock tickers to documentaries to images of the never-ending wars and conflicts that raged all over my planet leapt off the screen in high-definition detail. He often had them on when we had a post-case wrap-up, but I'd always been too wrapped up in my case notes to comment.

"Do you watch all of these at the same time?" Then, remembering my manners, I added, "Sir?" I wanted to launch into a tirade about how he'd broken our bargain, but I'd be in a better position to renegotiate terms if I stayed calm, kept my wits, and used the element of surprise.

I was surprised when he answered. "Of course. I make it a point to stay informed about anything that affects our little business here in the earth realm."

Of course he did.

Getting right down to said business, he gestured to the black leather chairs in front of his desk, inviting Mr. Barbatos and me to sit. It always made me squirm. I liked leather, but not being swallowed whole by it in the principal's office. And my feet didn't reach the ground. It was so undignified. The boss enjoyed reminding me that he was in charge, and this was one of his more annoying power games.

I gave Mr. Barbatos the side eye, but he only grinned, the smug demon. He knew what was going on.

I wasn't sure if I wanted to know.

The boss stood behind his desk, looming over me in another power play. He wore a perfectly tailored suit like his executive assistant, only in dark gray rather than the light gray Barbatos favored. It worked for him, with his tan skin and salt-and-pepper hair.

I arched a brow and set the jar full of angry demon on the boss's desk. For once, I kept my mouth shut and waited for the boss to explain. I could play power games, too.

The boss leveled his gaze on me. "Your demon captured an entity you weren't expecting?"

Humor deserted me as my ire rose, but I resisted the urge to yell. Snark was more my style. "Technically, *Dominic* caught him. Funny thing, the case file mentioned that Mr. Murkowski likes hamburgers, Hawaiian shirts, and spending summers in Destin with the family, but it didn't include anything about a preexisting demonic possession," I said a little too brightly. "Then again, it failed to mention his Bad Santa fetish, too. Hate it when that happens."

Barbatos smirked, not because he liked me or thought I was particularly funny, but because he thrived on conflict. It was a demon thing. The boss, however, narrowed his gaze and said, "I see. You and your demon failed to capture the demon possessing Murkowski."

"No, Hannah managed to capture the demon and almost got ripped out of me in the process, but then it escaped." I decided it wouldn't be wise to mention that Hannah had let the demon go. "The whole situation could've been avoided if I'd known what I was dealing with. I don't like being blindsided, and I don't like lies."

"Fieldwork is often unpredictable. It also comes with occupational hazards. Did you forget that, or have you become complacent? You've always been too brash. Seems Dominic arrived right on time."

I should have kept my temper in check, but I had my limits. I stood, fists clenched at my side and body vibrating with barely contained rage. "We had a bargain. You told me failure to summon him meant he was dead. You lied—"

Quick as a snake, his face was in front of me, close enough that my eyes crossed. It took every ounce of training and fortitude I had not to flinch. The fact that I was in the right gave me strength.

"I didn't lie. I never lie. If we were in the hell realm, I'd be within my rights to slay you where you stand."

My heart pounded and fear sweat leaked from my pores, but I held my ground. We weren't in the hell realm. He couldn't kill me. It was against the rules. Of course, as far as I knew, he made the rules and could unmake them. But he owed me an explanation.

He backed away, straightened his jacket, and said, "Dominic's appearance came as an unexpected surprise for me. My intention was to inform you at this meeting, but against my orders, he chose to make his presence known to you first."

I kept my face neutral, but my jaw almost fell to the ground. D had surprised the boss? Nothing demon-related ever caught the boss off guard. Coupled with the weirdness of the Murkowski case, this couldn't be good. I nodded, and in response to his arched brow, I took my seat again.

"Summon your demon. I need to know what happened when this one"—he looked at the jar on the table with disdain—"tried to take her."

"Yeah, about that..." Hannah was still incommunicado. I wasn't sure if a summons was a good idea. Then again, if the boss wanted her, she might be more inclined to listen.

"Never mind." I tugged on the chain at my neck. Reaching into my shirt seemed inappropriate in the office setting. I stared into the center of the obsidian and watched as my reflection morphed into a scowl that really brought out the red demon sparks in my eyes.

"Greetings, Arbiter." Hannah surprised me by speaking first. She hijacked my voice, and she shouldn't have been able to do that. Then again, I was grateful that she showed up at all.

The boss's gaze widened for a fraction of a second, but he quickly schooled his features to calm. Meanwhile, Barbatos leaned forward to get a better view, his eyes alight with giddy anticipation. All he needed was popcorn and 3-D glasses.

"You remember me." The boss spoke carefully, with a hint of warning in his deep, cold voice.

"I remember everything." Hannah's calm disturbed me more than the boss's anger.

Remembered him? Remembered everything? That didn't make any sense. They talked all the time. The three of us had been through countless debriefings and postgame wrap-ups, not to mention all the times she tried to help us summon D.

Then again, Hannah had called him the Arbiter when she appeared this time. She'd never used his title before.

The escaped demon messenger had said, "Remember," before he vanished. Perhaps that message had been meant for Hannah. My gut sank as I wondered what she'd remembered. We'd never figured out exactly what kind of demon Hannah was, where she'd come from, or why she'd wound up possessing me. She couldn't remember anything about her past, and the boss figured she'd lost her memories after some sort of altercation with another demon. She'd been smuggled out of the hell realm and had taken up residence in me shortly thereafter.

The boss never said it, but I knew why she'd chosen me as a host. There was something in me that was wrong, malevolent. Had to be.

Demons were attracted to bad humans, drawn by the darkness within them. I'd always been the bad kid. It was why my dad left us, why my mom always disapproved of me.

If Hannah was remembering her past, maybe she could tell me what was in me that was evil enough to get a demon's attention.

The boss cocked his head to the side and studied Hannah, and me, with interest. It was weird. I wasn't the focus of the boss's scrutiny. Hannah was. Only this time Hannah seemed calmer, more in control of herself, than she normally did. I tugged on the black mirror and her leash a little more tightly. We seemed...closer, for lack of a better word. True, anger still coursed through her consciousness in dark waves, but she and I meshed without the push and pull of our normal dynamic.

Did that demon do something to you when you took a bite out of him?

For once, I didn't voice the thought aloud, but Hannah caught it and, surprisingly, answered me.

Yes. He gave me clarity. Fear not, my other. I will keep us safe.

My other?

I turned my attention back to the boss. When he spoke, his deep voice warped, and his essence vibrated with more malevolence than I'd ever seen in him.

"If you remember everything, then you'll remember my policy. Tell me everything you know about this demon."

The corners of my mouth tugged into a smile I suspected was equally cruel—Hannah's doing. I preferred smirks, personally, infused with mild to moderate disdain and a dash of sarcasm. I almost dug out the black mirror again so I could see. I'm sure she made us look badass.

"I let the demon go," Hannah said. "And I wouldn't have given him to you if I'd kept him. Mephisto sought to capture me and my host. I wanted to know why, so I questioned him. He...enlightened me. And then I released him."

Barbatos chuckled. "I haven't seen Mephisto in ages."

"He hasn't had a message to deliver in ages," Hannah replied.

Mephisto. I'd read about him once during the countless hours of study and online training that came along with the demon-hunting gig.

How much of it was history versus myth was anyone's guess. Dubious sources of information aside, while Mephisto wasn't quite a hotshot in the hell realm hierarchy, the messenger himself ranked higher than any demon I'd yet encountered during my hunts. As far as I knew, he'd been holed up in the hell realm for centuries since the banishment of demon lords from earth. In addition to capturing tempter demons, demon hunters and portal guards were meant to keep demons like Mephisto from traveling to earth and wreaking havoc like they had prior to portal closures and travel restrictions.

"What message?" It was me who asked that time. I hated meetings. All posturing and cryptic back-and-forth without substance. Waste of time. I was a woman of action. "And what's going on with Hannah?"

The second question was directed at the boss, but I'd be perfectly fine if Hannah answered.

At first, I thought the boss would ignore my questions, but he nodded, surprising me. "If this message is what I believe it is, perhaps it's time to rally the troops from our side. Have you shared the message with your host?"

Yay! Looked like I'd be getting info.

"Not yet." Hannah took over the voice function again. "Rumors of war are eternal in our realm. And theirs. There have been no other signs. Unless, of course, you've experienced unauthorized opening of your portals, recruitment of summoners to the cause, or unrest among outsiders inhabiting the earth, there's nothing to substantiate your theory."

Well, that sucked. My hopes for finally being in the loop were dashed. And since neither the boss nor Hannah had seen fit to clue me in on whatever clarity Hannah had gained from Mephisto—not to mention her sudden "recognition" of the boss—I was less in the know than ever.

Thanks, Hannah.

And what was this "ours" and "theirs" business? There was only one demon realm as far as I was aware. Then again, maybe that was yet another piece of information that was above my pay grade.

Barbatos, Mr. Helpy Helperton, chimed in, renewing my hope of getting some real information. "If there are no open portals, how do you suppose Mephisto made it onto this plane?"

The boss moved from behind his desk and began pacing. The wall monitors flashed with seemingly random images. A wooden doorway to some rundown building, a sewer cover, a large tree with a split at the base of its trunk, the small opening covered with a tangle of gnarled roots. I was confused at first but caught on quickly.

These were all portals.

I had no idea this many existed around the city. Demon hunters generally weren't allowed near the portals since our energies and the demons we carried could accidentally send us on a one-way trip to the hell realm. The boss employed others to guard the portals—summoners—deciding who went in and out and when they were permitted to travel between realms. But like most other non-demon-tracking operations, the rest was shrouded in secrecy.

I was getting really fed up with secrecy.

Apparently, so was the boss. Either that, or he didn't like sass from Hannah and Barbatos. Implying that he had anything less than absolute control of demonic activity on his home turf tended to make the boss a tad testy.

The boss walked back to his desk and placed his hands firmly on the smooth wood surface. Then he graced us with yet another malevolent smile. "I believe it's time we questioned Mephisto."

Hannah's next words floored me and everyone else in the room. "No. Mephisto will go free and deliver my reply to our mutual acquaintance."

The glass container holding Mephisto cracked. I stared in horror as the swirling demon inside expanded and then ducked when the glass shattered and the incorporeal demon shot out and started flying around the room, presumably looking for an exit.

CHAPTER NINE

What. The. Actual. Fuck?

Hannah released the demon again? Not normal and not right. We captured demons. We protected the earth from them. We didn't just set them free to eat people, especially unauthorized demons as powerful as Mephisto.

The boss recovered quickly. He snarled, and for a split second I caught a glimpse of the demon hiding behind the facade of a businessman. "Summon him back. Now."

"No," Hannah said. Personally, I would have considered complying, but this had apparently turned into a demon-style pissing contest.

Barbatos rose and began creating sigils from demon magic, waving his hands as glowing symbols appeared. A trap. He shot the trap at the demon zipping around the room, but Mephisto evaded it and disappeared into a vent. "The lower levels are secure," Barbatos said. "I'll catch him."

The boss nodded and then turned his angry gaze to me. "If you refuse to cooperate, Intercessor, I'll simply have to question Mephisto's accomplice."

Intercessor? Was that Hannah's title? That wasn't her real name, but surely it had something to do with her past, her nature.

Hannah was powerful. I'd only had a glimpse of her true power once, and it had been enough. She was scary. And it seemed she'd known the boss sometime in the past, possibly when they'd both been in the hell realm, which meant the boss had probably known who and what she was all along.

He'd known, and he'd never told me. Something about that past association was connected with Mephisto, hell realm wars, and a demon lord who wanted Hannah—and me—as his newest recruits.

But how?

A loud noise from behind us made me turn in my chair. All thoughts philosophical, snarky, and otherwise fled my mind. A platform rose from the floor. It had a glowing, magical pentagram swirling above it, sigils twinkling in the corners. No candles. True demons used magic for summoning, though they still needed names. It wasn't the hypnotic power of the pentagram that had my heart racing, though, or even the impressive figure of D—Dominic—as he stood outside the circle, controlling the spell.

It was Mara. She stood in the pentagram's center, helpless gaze darting around the room. Hands bound in front of her and feet in enchanted chains, her form shifted in rapid succession in a desperate attempt to appeal to any entity in the room with the power to set her free. I wondered if the damsel in Medieval getup was meant for the boss or D. Then there was a sleek African queen, and an alluring seventeenth-century lady in powdered wig with a bodice that left little to the imagination. The prim schoolmarm with the tight bun surprised me, but I'd learned not to judge.

Then, turning to me, she assumed the form of D.

I would have been mortified if outrage hadn't already seized my heart. I rose to my feet—me, the tiny human, not Hannah the Intercessor —and faced the boss in outright challenge. Hannah had gone silent. Again. Looked like I'd have no backup.

"Let her go," my feral voice sounded through clenched teeth. "She didn't help Mephisto willingly. He forced her through means of summoning."

"Just as I intend to obtain answers from this temptress by means of summoning. She's already on probation. If she cooperates, I'll send her back to the hell realm rather than casting her in solitary confinement in one of your little human penitentiaries in this plane."

No, he couldn't.

"You unbelievable bastard. She'll starve." Shocked and appalled, I imagined the limp and emaciated body of the succubus wasting away in some sterile cell, devoid of sustenance or even the comfort of companionship.

The boss scowled at me. "Ah, yes, Jane McGee, the bleeding heart. I'm surprised you've lasted this long as a demon hunter."

"And I'm surprised you let an unauthorized demon lord slip through the cracks so he could make threats in your domain," I countered.

What was I doing? I'd never crossed the boss openly before. Sure, I talked smack when he wasn't listening, but apparently, I'd located my ovaries and decided enough was enough.

And it was. I'd given my word to Mara that she'd be safe. I promised I wouldn't let her take the fall for this. I had to protect her. I wasn't sure how I could do that without Hannah's cooperation, but at least she didn't seem inclined to stop me.

Pain gripped me as an invisible hand closed around my throat and squeezed. The pressure wasn't enough to choke me. It just reminded me of who—and what—I was up against. The lines of the pentagram's glowing sigils blurred, as did the images flashing on the boss's television screens as my vision faltered. My heart pounded in my chest as adrenaline combined with moxie I hadn't realized I'd possessed.

It wasn't Hannah. This was all me.

"The truth will set you...free," I whispered through my aching throat. D had moved, slowly inching toward us as if ready to step in. "But first it will piss you off." If ever there was a time for Gloria Steinem, it was this sausage fest.

At least my vision had cleared enough to see the boss's face in the middle of the spots dancing in my vision. The spots really brought out the red demon menace in his eyes. Mine probably just looked bulgy and bloodshot. Not my best look. I totally needed a makeover if I survived.

I had bigger fish to fry now. I scrambled to formulate a plan, a bit of brilliance I could use to put my money where my big fat mouth was.

"You're an insolent whelp of a mortal. I could snap your neck and take the Intercessor from you in a heartbeat. Think carefully before you speak again." The boss's calm voice contrasted the iron grip his demon mojo had around my neck.

"Thought...you said..." I spoke between gasps, "separating from Hannah would...kill...us both."

I'd caught him in another lie. We might both survive, like Mephisto implied. Maybe I wouldn't, but it was possible that Hannah would kill him. I'd call his bluff.

"If...you let...me...breathe...we can have...a civilized conversation." I almost wished I hadn't wasted precious breath on back talk. My mouth would be the death of me someday.

But I didn't plan on checking out quite yet.

That strange sensation I'd experienced earlier in the alley bubbled up within me again, going from slow, rolling boil to violent maelstrom in the making. It was more powerful than any demon strength Hannah had ever loaned me.

I hoped the new power could save me from the boss like it had saved me and Hannah from Mephisto, but I wasn't sure it would be enough. I could really use some demon mojo right about now.

"How...about a little...help here?" I asked Hannah. She answered inside my head.

I cannot give the Arbiter what he seeks. Too much is at stake. You must find a way to save the tempter.

Wonderful.

If I couldn't use Hannah's demon strength, I'd have to hope that the strange energy creating a storm within me would help. I jumped into the maelstrom and let it swallow me as power coursed through my conscious-ness, fueling my resolve and strengthening my body. It wasn't Hannah's demon power, but it would do. Throw survival and protective instincts into the mix, and I'd be a force to be reckoned with.

At least for a few minutes—I didn't know how long I could keep it up. I placed my hands over my throat and seized the intangible force that held me in its grip. Casting off the enchantment, I barely managed to stay upright. At least I could see clearly again. The television screens flickered, and the sigils surrounding Mara seemed to dim a bit. Weird.

I caught sight of Barbatos out of the corner of my eye. He'd returned empty-handed. Not good. But I'd apparently floored the boss and made Barbatos's jaw drop to the ground. D, on the other hand, looked pissed. He probably hated not being able to rescue the damsel in distress.

Too bad.

"Here's what's going to happen," I said, my voice still hoarse. "You're going to release Mara into my custody so she can help me find out how Mephisto got to this realm. I want access to everything you have on Murkowski, and I want access to every portal Mephisto could've used to travel from the hell realm. The rest of the team can question local summoners and demon associates to gather intel."

Wow. That sounded good. Professional, even. Score. I should've located my ovaries years ago.

Barbatos threw his head back and laughed. I wasn't sure if that was a good thing or if I'd just signed my own death warrant, but at least I'd impressed someone in the room. And I'd apparently landed a high-stakes demon-tracking case. I should really ask for a raise.

"Add finding Mephisto to your list, pet. He's gone," Barbatos said. He was *so* helpful.

The boss's tan skin had gone from red to a very interesting shade of purple.

Yeah. Best save any discussions about my salary for later.

"And why in the name of Lucifer's Legions would I do that?" the boss asked.

He held his stance, but I had his attention. The maelstrom of power swirling within me held, too, for now. I doubted it would last much longer. I needed to bargain with the boss. If I made it worth his while, perhaps I'd walk away with my life, Mara, and my demon.

"You're going to do it because I'm going to solve this case for you and make sure no more demon lord messengers—or demon lords—go sneaking through unsecured portals or by means of rogue summoners. I've got a bigger stake in this than you. A rebellion leader in the hell realm is after me, too, not just Hannah. I'm highly motivated to save my ass from a one-way trip to your hometown."

His face returned to its normal hue as he considered my proposal. He walked back to his desk and sat on his leather throne. Mara had stopped whimpering and appeared to hold her breath while waiting to see if her head was off the proverbial chopping block. D stared at me with a whole lot of "What the fuck?" written over his face.

Barbatos was the only creature in the room enjoying the show.

"And if you fail?" The boss's gaze lit with demon sparks.

We were bargaining for real now. He'd expect a substantial sacrifice on my part if I didn't manage to pull off what I'd promised. And he'd basically confirmed that Mephisto was indeed set on capturing and delivering me and Hannah to the hell realm general. If I failed in my mission, I'd be in the hell realm's boot camp before being shipped off to certain death. How much worse could the boss's idea of a punishment be?

I shouldn't have asked.

He grinned. Uh-oh. Second rule of demon hunting? Never make a deal with a demon. They were masters of the loophole, always stacked the odds in their favor, and were experts at winning something from their victims no matter the outcome.

I should've learned my lesson by now, especially since the boss hadn't produced D like he'd promised—thus failing to keep his end of our first bargain—for years. And he hadn't separated me from my demon, which he apparently was capable of doing.

I'd keep that one in my back pocket for leverage.

Drawing a deep breath, I channeled my inner lawyer. "If I fail, that will stack the odds in the rebellion leader's favor. That's not a win for either of us."

"It's not a win for anyone aside from Belial. But I'm not bargaining with him. What do you expect to happen when he captures you? Do you think I'll bargain for your release?"

The boss was good. My maelstrom of confidence waned. I needed to wrap this up. Still, I'd learned something important. I now knew the rebellion leader's name—I'd have to get my roomies on research duty for this demon while I investigated Murkowski so I could hopefully track where and how Mephisto the messenger traveled to earth and snagged himself a body.

I'd also have to locate Mephisto's new host. Immaterial demons needed a human host to remain anchored to earth, or so I'd been taught. But I dealt with tempters. Maybe higher-ranking demons weren't bound by the same rules.

The boss's arched brow brought me out of my musings. He was waiting for my answer.

"No." I snorted. "I'm not worth that much to you. The way I see it, you have nothing to lose."

He appeared to consider my argument. "And what do I have to gain?"

Oh, for the love of lollipops... "Peace on your turf? No more illegal crossings through whatever portal Mephisto used? Your reputation? Seriously, a demon messenger slipped through the cracks on your watch. That's got to be embarrassing."

The lights flickered, and Mara gasped as the sigils around her pentagram glowed. Not good. Had I pushed him too far? I was terrible at bargaining. I couldn't even haggle my way to a decent price for my car. Roice had to do it for me.

"You owe me, and you know it," I said, low and menacing. "You didn't summon D. Told me he was dead. He's not. You were supposed to bring him back to me in exchange for demon- hunting services. That was our bargain. You failed. You also didn't release me from possession by Hannah. Mephisto almost managed it, so I know it's possible. You. Owe. Me."

The boss casually strolled from behind his desk and walked over to me, looming. I hated it when anyone used the height advantage. Had none of these demons heard of the Napoleon complex?

Leaning down until we were nose to nose, he spoke. "You will solve this case, secure the portal, and root out the traitor in the summoning community, and you will do it in a week's time. Should you fail, I will consume the souls of your mother and sister before I devour their flesh. I will cast Mara into mortal prison until she goes mad with hunger. Then, and only then, will I pull you from the hell realm and teach you the true meaning of eternal damnation. That is my bargain, you insignificant bag of meat. Now get out of my sight."

Panic seized my body and mind. My soul was one thing. Loved ones were quite another. He'd threatened me plenty of times in the past, but never my mother and sister. "No, you can't take my family, I—"

He reached down and wrapped his hands around my throat again, only this time with his own slender and surprisingly strong fingers.

"I can and I will. Don't ever forget your place, Jane McGee. Dominic!" He turned his gaze to D as he barked out his name. The pentagram disappeared, along with Mara's chains. D was in front of us before I could blink and grabbed the boss by his arm.

Then D growled. He actually growled. "Let her go."

The boss looked back and forth between us and smiled before dropping me on the ground. Being short had its advantages, though, since I drew on Hannah's strength to do one of those cool leg flips that brought me back to a standing position. D tried to stand in front of me, and I almost let him assume the macho protector stance. But I couldn't in good conscience endanger the life of one more entity. It was bad enough that I'd put my family's life in jeopardy, and Mara's.

I couldn't risk D, either, no matter our history.

The boss had outmaneuvered me. I realized too late what he'd done. I was a loose end, proof that he'd broken his word and, I suspected, proof that he'd been keeping secrets—like Hannah's identity—from his fellow demon bosses. This business with Belial and a brewing hell realm rebellion would put him under unwanted scrutiny. If I solved the case and sent Mephisto packing, the boss's colleagues wouldn't find out. If I failed, he'd kill me, my family, and then deal with Hannah himself—weakened from extraction from my body—and tie up loose ends.

In his haste, however, the boss hadn't secured my agreement. And he'd broken our first bargain. That gave me more power in this negotiation. I still had some leverage and, given the stakes, plenty of motivation.

"Give me full access to all resources, *all* information you have on Belial," I said. "I want his dossier, his history, and his agenda, everything I need to work out what this rebel demon lord is up to and how to stop him. And I want command of the entire team. Give me that, and I'll release you from our first bargain."

"Jane, don't do it," D said, and I heard something in his voice I hadn't since we were kids—desperation.

The boss smiled in triumph. He reached into his breast pocket to pull out a small knife. It glowed with a bright-purple light. Again with the purple. I'd never seen any metal from the hell realm glow purple, aside from the sparks back in the alley. And holy crap, just how powerful was the boss? Grabbing my wrist, he scored it with the sharp blade and then cut his own. Ew. And it hurt like the blazes.

I had to swallow hard before speaking. "Can't I just sign a contract? That is so unsanitary."

Plus, he'd scored my sore wrist, the one I'd injured by punching D. It still hurt like a bitch.

The boss clasped my bloody wrist to his, and an electric jolt of power shot through me. I gasped as some sort of unnatural wind swirled around us and miniature lightning bolts illuminated the room. Wow. Demons had a flair for the dramatic.

"It's done," the boss said. "The pact is sealed. You have five days to complete your task."

"Whoa, whoa, whoa," I said, refusing to let him separate our linked wrists. "A week is seven days."

"Not in the hell realm," he said, doing his best to yank out of my grasp.

D put his hand over our joined wrists, helping me keep a grip on the demon. "We're not in the hell realm. You must abide by the rules of this

plane. And she's right. You didn't keep your end of the original bargain."
The look he gave the boss was hot enough to burn lava.

"No thanks to you," the boss said, glaring at D.

"Six days, counting today," he said.

As soon as he let go of me, a book materialized in my hand, and the
lock to the chain that kept it closed vanished. He looked at it with what
could only be described as tenderness.

I gasped, recognizing the treasure I held. Yeah, I'd have some leverage
as well as much-needed information.

Glowing sigils decorated its cover in the primary demon language.
Roughly translated, the title was *Compiled Grimoires of the Wicked and
Wise*. No human, mundane, demon hunter, or summoner was allowed to
read it, probably because it held the secrets of summoning powerful
demons along with demon lore and history. Real history. I'd need that
kind of information to solve this case. It was also the only book our team
scholar Trinity hadn't read, since she'd managed to get copies of the other
forbidden texts from her personal demon.

I'd set her to work translating and researching ASAP. If nothing else,
I'd be contributing to her continuing education.

Plus, I could hold the book for ransom if the boss went after my
family. I'd have to get them some extra protection and put my emergency
plan into action. No way would I let the boss touch them on my account.

The boss took one last, longing look at the book before turning his icy
gaze on me. I caught a flash of what looked suspiciously like sorrow
before he spun on his heel, stalked toward his desk, and said, "Now get
out of my sight."

CHAPTER TEN

He didn't have to tell me twice. I grabbed Mara and scrambled to the door, not waiting for Barbatos to escort me out and not waiting for D to tell me what I horrible mistake I'd made. I staggered out of the elevator, holding on to Mara for support until we made it out of the building and into the night. The slight chill helped chase away the dizziness and excess adrenaline and thankfully allowed me to walk unassisted. My wrist and throat hurt like the devil, but I still had a bit of the confidence from that strange power surging inside me. I wanted to ask Hannah about it, but she'd gone back into hiding. It was probably for the best. I needed to get home and tend to my injuries before dealing with my demon and my new assignment.

We got as far as the parking lot when I remembered that I did not, in fact, have my car.

An engine roared to life behind us, and I spun in time to spot a gorgeous black sports car of some sort—I was bad with the whole make and model thing—pull up beside us. It shimmered in the glow of a nearby streetlamp, but the edges seemed to melt into the darkness, as if camouflaged.

I was instantly in love.

The driver rolled down the window, and a deep voice said, "Get in."

Seemed like D was determined to get back in my good graces with all this chivalry. Who was I to refuse such a noble gesture? I hadn't forgiven him. I just really needed a ride.

I nodded to Mara, who stood beside me in a dazed and frightened stupor. Poor thing. I'd have to let her rest and get settled before questioning her.

Then again, as the magnitude of my mission sank in, along with the consequences of failure, I couldn't afford to delay too long. I'd have to get the twins on research and interrogate Murkowski ASAP.

After we hopped in D's car, Mara in the back while I opted for shotgun, and buckled up, I sent a group text to Lacey, my roomies, and our colleagues, Alexi Volkov and Trinity Jones, telling them to check the various portals around the city for the rest of the night. It took me three tries. Those virtual keyboards were tiny, and I had to type with my bad hand. After fixing more than a few autocorrect snafus, I managed to get the messages out.

Lacey texted back right away to remind me I was not "the boss of her." Alexi, bless him, was much more cooperative and promised to put his sniffer to work on the portals from midtown to east Nashville. He had a gift for it, or rather, his wolf demon did. After I asked Barbatos to tell Lacey I was, in fact, the boss of her for the next five and a quarter days, she agreed to cover from midtown to west of the city to see if the portals in that area were secure.

Trinity agreed to help but said it would cost me. Figured. Then again, she was the supergenius of the group. Her demon had come to her voluntarily, and they worked together in harmony. When she wasn't busting criminal demons for the boss, she put her considerable skills to use doling out vigilante justice for the "greater good."

Hey, we all had our thing.

When I told her about the grimoire and said I'd grant her unlimited access in exchange for assistance and her legal expertise, she all but squealed with delight. Trinity had a knack for demon languages and laws and could find any loophole in a demon realm contract. Given my current situation, those skills were priceless.

That left the summoners. And the question of what the hell this demon lord Belial wanted with me. And how to handle my family.

I was so screwed.

My chest tightened, and stars danced in my vision. Sweaty palms and shaking hands rounded out the symptoms, as did the knives of pain stabbing through my aching wrist and bad hand. Did I have a fever? Had BBB infected me with some horrid hell dimension virus through our blood vow? It would certainly solve my problem. All demon pacts were rendered null and void upon the death of one or both agreeing parties.

"Breathe."

D's voice jolted me out of my panic attack. Seemed I'd been on the verge of hyperventilation rather than succumbing to a mysterious hell flu. Damn. So much for the easy way out. I took D's advice and took several deep, cleansing breaths.

After a moment, I said, "You can drop us off at my car. I think I'm off Commerce Street." I hoped so. It would be super embarrassing if I hadn't left my ride there.

D shook his head. "You're in no shape to drive. I'll take you home. We'll get your car tomorrow."

Wait, what was this "we" nonsense?

He appeared as tense as I felt. His jaw ticked, and one of the veins at his temple pulsed with every beat of his heart. Surely he wasn't worried about me. I was nothing to him. Just an old acquaintance, the girl he'd left behind. Since he wasn't dead, his failure to come back to me had to have been a conscious choice. Wasn't the first man to leave me. That would be dear old Dad. D had probably picked up some charming habits during his time in the hell realm, like ruthlessness, calculation, and a hunger for power. That was probably why he was here "consulting" on my case.

Or maybe he saw me as a pathetic damsel in distress he felt compelled to save.

That was worse.

"Don't worry about it," I said. "I'll grab my car tomorrow when I go check on Mr. Murkowski, interview him, and pay a visit to Nashville's summoners."

He slammed on the brakes so hard, the forward momentum sent me flying as far as the seat belt would allow before snapping me back into the seat. With a series of jerky shifts that could permanently damage his transmission, he reversed and parked on the shoulder of the deserted street.

"What the hell, D?" I yelled. Somehow Mara had managed to sleep through D's attempt at recreating *The Fast and The Furious*, as well as my outburst.

He grabbed me by the shoulders, pulling me as close as my seat belt would allow. Anger rolled off him in thick, almost palpable waves, and I had the strong suspicion that he was fighting not to shake me. God, I was sick of being manhandled and bullied by demons. I pushed against his solid chest and yelled again.

"Let me go, asshole! What is wrong with you?"

He gripped me tighter. "What's wrong with *me*? You take on a demon lord and a hungry succubus on your own, you challenge your demon boss—who could destroy you, in case you hadn't noticed—and you make a deal with the demon boss that put yourself and your family in danger? What the hell is wrong with *you*?"

I yanked one shoulder out of his grip and slapped him across the face, sore wrist be damned. He growled, grabbed both of my wrists, and pinned my arms at my side, using his size and strength to his advantage, the bastard.

"Hit me again, and I'll turn you over my knee and spank you," he said, his face red with fury.

"Insult me one more time while manhandling me, and I'll rip off your balls and put them in a mason jar on my mantel." Pain shot through my wrist and shoulders, but it was nothing compared to the rush of anger and indignation. I could stand a lot, but my former BFF's judgment might tip me over the edge.

I struggled against his hold as he visibly worked to get his temper under control. Oh, no, I wasn't having it. We were long overdue for this knock-down, drag-out, and given the total crap day I'd had, it was the perfect time, perfect place, and he was the perfect punching bag.

But since I couldn't hit him yet—my wrist hurt like a bitch—I settled for a tongue-lashing. "First of all, how dare you come waltzing back in after all these years with the audacity to judge me? I thought you were dead! Not a word, not a note, or even an email in all these years, and you just show up? Yes, I took on a demon and a succubus, and you know what? I beat them. Just me and my demon. It's my fucking job, and after ten years, I am *very* good at my fucking job."

He opened his mouth to speak, but I cut him off.

"As far as the deal, I didn't have a choice. It was deal or let Mara take the fall, and I promised her I'd keep her safe."

I fought back angry tears that threatened to spill from my cheeks. No way would I cry in front of him. Swallowing past the lump in my throat, I managed to speak with more composure. "I did what I had to, and I'll do whatever it takes to solve this case. I won't lose my...my family, and..."

Him. I was about to say, him.

Had he come between me and the boss...well, demon pissing contests tended to end badly, often with a great deal of blood and severed limbs. D had clearly grown up to become a powerful young demon, but he was young, and the boss outranked him.

D's gaze went wide and then softened. I stiffened. Had he figured it out? Did he know I was protecting him, too?

He let go of my arms and raised a finger to catch a solitary tear before it fell down my cheek. I couldn't deal. Angry D, snarky D, sexy D? Oh, yeah, I could hold my own.

Tender D? No way. I would not let him break my heart again.

He must've sensed the wave of panic that seized me, since he backed off and leaned his head against the seat, running a hand over his face. I settled on massaging my throbbing wrist and shaking like a leaf. I curled into the seat and pulled my knees up, resting my forehead on them. It also let me hide my face from him. I hated this. All of it.

"Here," he said.

I didn't look up but felt a cold glass cylinder being shoved into my palm. A vial of some sort, its markings resembled the ones on the vessel he'd used to capture Mephisto.

"What's this?" I rolled the vial around in my good hand, surprised at the warm feel of the glass.

"Medicine," his gruff voice answered. "Swallow half now and half before bed. Won't do anything about that wicked temper or foul mouth of yours, but it'll heal your wrist and anything else that's injured. Kills pain, too."

I uncorked the vial, pausing to admire the intricate swirls and patterns in the glass. Demon made, of course. Most things that came from the hell realm were old-fashioned by modern earth realm standards, but even the most basic and utilitarian of objects bore the hallmarks of master craftsmanship. I only hoped the hell realm apothecary's skills matched that of the glassblower.

I sniffed the contents, surprised when a pleasant aroma wafted out instead of something nasty. It smelled a little like mint and some floral base I couldn't identify. I swallowed half the contents and recorked the vial, leaning against the comfortable leather seat and closing my eyes. After a few minutes, the throbbing in my wrist eased, and a pleasant, warm sensation bloomed within me, spreading from my center through my torso and limbs.

I opened my eyes and gazed in wonder at my hands, flexing my fingers and rolling my wrists. The right one was still stiff and a bit achy but improved with less swelling. The windows had fogged, casting the car's dark, luxurious interior in shadow and seclusion. Had someone passed by on the street outside, they'd probably think a hot and heavy make out session was unfolding inside.

I turned in the seat to stare at my ex. D was still angry, but his rage had cooled from a rolling boil to a slow simmer. He wouldn't look at me, but I took a moment to stare at him, running my gaze over his tense, feral, otherworldly form. Damn, he was fine. Memories of longing I'd felt when the succubus took his form made me warm in all kinds of inappropriate places. I could devour those lips. I could run my tongue along the column of his neck and trail it down his delectable body, and I grew hungry just from running my gaze over him.

"Jane, I'm doing my best here, but if you keep looking at me like that, I may not be able to hold back."

I swiped the tears away from my lashes and cheeks, thankful he didn't watch me do it. "Looking at you like what?"

Wait, how was he watching me without looking at me? With demon mojo?

"Looking at me like you want to rip my clothes off and ride me to the hell realm." He shifted in his seat, turning to face me while he curled his lips into a half smirk. "Or are you still planning to collect my balls as a trophy?"

I laughed, glad for a respite from the tension—sexual and otherwise—between us. "Maybe. The jury's still out. Besides, it isn't you," I lied. "I'm still under the influence of the succubus. Now, if you're done yelling at me for being stupid, I'd like to get Mara home and start working on this case." Sure, I had a million questions for him, but none of those answers would matter if I died at the hands of the boss or a demon lord.

He cocked his head and examined me. "I wasn't yelling at you for being stupid. You're not."

Well, that was a surprise. Did he just give me a compliment? I looked away and started fiddling with the hem of my T-shirt. "You don't think I'm stupid?"

Yeah, I was fishing. Pathetic, but it would be nice to get a little emotional pick-me-up.

D sighed. "I think you're reckless, and I think you need to learn to when to shut up around your demon boss, but no, you're not stupid. You're one of the bravest souls I've ever encountered."

A large crack formed in the armor I kept around my heart. Instead of brushing off what might have been the best compliment I'd ever received, or yelling at him again, I did something completely out of character.

I remained silent.

Thankfully, so did D. He revved the muscle car's engine and drove to my place in silence. I wasn't sure how he knew where my place was, but I suspected stalking. Or he could've gotten my address from Barbatos.

Nah. He'd totally been stalking me.

I gently roused Mara from her slumber when we arrived at my building. It was a little awkward with my still gimpy wrist. Hopefully the second dose of hell realm medicine would put me back at one hundred percent by morning. Hannah sure wasn't doing her job on the healing front. D exited the vehicle, too, and stood beside it, not waiting for an invitation to come in. We weren't there yet. But he'd been kind to me in spite of my outrage and the less-than-warm welcome I'd offered him—which he richly deserved, but still...

"Thank you, Dominic," I said, liking the way his name rolled off my tongue. I even smiled at him. See, I could be gracious.

"You're welcome, Jane," he replied. "Now that we're playing nice, tell me what I can do to help with your investigation, besides get your car." He leaned against the car's sleek black frame, arms crossed. Shadows danced over the hills and valleys of his lean muscled body, doing terrible things to my insides.

I bit back a snarky reply. Asking for help wasn't my strong suit, but he'd made it easy by offering. I needed all the help I could get. Plus...

I put my hands on my hips and sized him up as he quirked a brow, clearly wondering what I planned on doing next. I liked to keep people guessing. "You know, since you're officially part of our demon-hunting team, being a consultant and all, and since the deal with the boss included access to all resources, that kind of makes me your boss now, right?"

He smirked. "Yeah, I suppose it does. Plan on making me scrub toilets?"

"Tempting," I said. It was, too, since Boice had reminded me of my bathroom cleaning duties. But I had something else in mind, something better suited to D's skills and temperament. "But I have something else in mind for you if you're up for it."

"I'm up for anything." He said it in a way that made heat creep up my cheeks and down to a few other places. Then he frowned. "You trust me?"

"Not as far as I can throw you," I said, which wasn't quite true. "You owe me some answers." I wanted those answers, but at the moment, I was more concerned about survival.

"I'll explain everything to you, I swear," he said. Then, he pulled out his demon knife from its sheath on his hip, and without taking his gaze off me, he held up his arm and scored his wrist. He held up the knife, its crimson glow brightening as drops of his blood sizzled on its sharp edge.

Oh no, no way. I wasn't making another demon bargain tonight.

"Relax," he said. He took a deep breath and locked his gaze on the glowing knife. "I swear by my blood to guard your back, to fight at your side, and to protect you from your enemies, Jane McGee. If I betray you or this sacred vow, I forfeit my life and my soul."

Magic washed over me in dark tendrils. D vibrated with its power as the knife lit up with a series of sigils that sealed the pact. I stood, stunned. He'd sworn allegiance to me with his blood. Demons didn't make pacts lightly, and they were binding. Sure, there were loopholes and provisos, but D hadn't left any ambiguity in his promise.

Shaking off the effects of the magic, he sheathed his knife and looked at me, brow arched. "Now that we've established my intentions, what can I do to help with this case?"

I cleared my throat, not quite sure what to say. "Thank you" wouldn't be right, and I didn't think he'd appreciate "are you out of your freakin' mind?" I settled on giving him a task that would help me while giving me time to process ten years' worth of emotions unleashed by his sudden and unexpected return.

"I'm assigning you to investigate all the known summoners in the city. I don't care how you interrogate them or for how long, find which ones helped Mephisto gain access to earth. I'd also like to know if he went back to the hell realm by the same portal or if he might still be on earth. Oh, and find out if they let any other unauthorized demons through."

He nodded, his grin turning positively wicked. "Good call. I happen to be an expert at interrogation. Text me the list, and I'll get on it."

Wow, that was...easy. I'd half expected him to argue for a more important assignment or to react with stoicism, but he seemed excited at the
prospect. It was weird. It was also kind of hot. Heat crept into my cheeks.
Was I blushing? Ugh. I was far too old to be blushing. I didn't look and
rarely acted my age, but blushing like a silly schoolgirl?

Ridiculous.

"Okay, good," I said, faltering a bit. He'd thrown me off, the bastard.
"I'll get busy on Murkowski and then figure out what to do with my
family. How about we meet up tomorrow night? You can come here if
you want. We can talk about the case."

I was silky smooth. He'd come over under the guise of working on the
case—which we would be—and I would blindside him with a little interrogation of my own. He owed me more than a few answers.

"Midnight," he said. "I'll have answers one way or another."

The way he said another sent shivers down my spine, but that
was why I'd put him on the summoners. The midlevel ones would
be easy to screen. With any luck, Roice would have that done by
now. It would take Lacey and Alexi a little longer to hit all the
portals, so I'd have to settle for hitting the books, or rather, the
book. I hoped it would give me the lowdown on Belial and his
rebellion.

I'd have to get Trinity in on the book research, too. She'd been itching
to get her hands on this one for ages. I might not even have to bribe her
with donuts this time.

And I was totally going to bend the corners of the pages just to spite
my asshole boss.

I fished out my car keys and tossed them to D. "I assume you know
what I drive."

"Yes."

"Can I also assume you know where I parked?" Because I didn't
remember.

He laughed. "I'm sure I can work it out. Get some sleep. You're going
to need it."

Not likely, but I appreciated the sentiment. He'd just fired up the engine when I yelled, "Wait, I don't have your number." I kind of needed it to text him my demon summoner hit list.

My phone pinged, and I dug it out of my pocket to read the text message.

Dominic's number.

That was it? Guess he wasn't into small talk or sexting. I gave him a thumbs-up and dragged Mara inside the building and into the elevator. Thank goodness I didn't run into any of my neighbors or management. Didn't really matter. I was the building weirdo, and they generally steered clear of me. When we exited at the ginormous penthouse suite I shared with my demon roomies—paid for by the boss—I arranged a date for Mara with my shower and checked in with said demon roomies.

My two favorite pains in the ass, one for each cheek, were settled at their desks. Identical twins who assumed the appearance of tall, lanky teens with dirty blond hair and the usual fascination with smartphones, their forms betrayed their true natures and their true ages. They were the twin demons of technology. At least, that's what they told me. More powerful and higher ranking than the average tempter demon, they were relatively young, as was mortal technology in the grand scheme of the hell realm time scale—appearing on the scene sometime after the end of the Civil War and rising to power during the Industrial Revolution. I wasn't sure whether the damning article from an evangelical website that they'd produced as evidence was legit, but they were freakishly good with electronics, computers, and mechanical devices, so I decided to just go with it.

They'd insisted on mirror-imaging their workstations to creep me out, or possibly confuse me. It worked. I could only tell them apart by their T-shirts and by getting a peek at their computer screens. Boice spent his time writing fanfiction and surfing the stock market, while Roice enjoyed online RPGs and stirring the political pot with fake news and scandals.

Mostly harmless. He also made killer memes.

Boice deigned to look up from one of his screens first to greet me. "Hey, Jinx. Heard you caused quite the shit storm at HQ."

His brother looked up then, identical faces staring at me with interest and something suspiciously like admiration. Roice grinned. "Wish I'd been there to see it. You're like one of those yappy little chihuahuas who barks at everybody because you're so tiny."

I snorted. "You mean the ones who make pit bulls turn tail and run? Yup, that's me. Did you get that list of scumbag summoners for me?"

"Did I get the list? Pshaw, that was easy. Already texted you the deets. Give me a real challenge next time." He rolled his chair over to another part of his workstation and started clicking away on a keyboard in front of a screen filled with images of contraband materials and Bitcoin values.

"Surfing the dark web again?" I shuddered at the thought of the transactions made on whatever site Roice had found. Drugs didn't bother me much, but weapons and human trafficking did. The ordinary humans running these rackets were even worse. The twins took out said human trash in their spare time.

"Yeah." Roice grinned at the computer screen. "No demons tonight, but I've got a ring of kiddie porn distributors lined up. Hungry, bro?" While the twins found and banished the occasional mammon, aka greed tempter demon, behind contraband trade, the souls of human traffickers and their clientele were fair game for the demon brothers, satisfying their considerable appetites. I was cool with it. Good riddance to the dregs of humanity.

"Save some for Mara, okay?" I figured the succubus could use her talents to help flush out their prey. She'd need more than a few gremlins to tide her over. "And find out everything you can on a demon lord named Belial and any hell realm rebellions he may or may not have led— and any he's planning to lead."

"Why not ask his demon messenger? Hannah's got him, right?"

"No." I said it extra loud so my demon could hear it from wherever in my consciousness she was hiding. "That would be too easy. D caught him and brought him to HQ, but then he got away. Apparently, he traded information to Hannah for his freedom and she let him go. Anyway, Mephisto's in the wind, or maybe in the sewer. Not sure how he travels. Hannah said she was sending a message back to his boss, this Belial demon lord."

Roice whistled long and low. "There's a rabbit hole I never thought we'd go down." Turning back to his screen, he said, "If that's the case, odds are Mephisto hightailed it back to the hell realm to deliver Hannah's reply in person, or he may have sent the message back through other channels so he could stick around, grab another host, and have another shot at taking you and Hannah with him. I'm on it."

"And before you ask, no, Hannah hasn't told me anything. Mephisto told her something. I think he helped her get some of her memories back, but she's not sharing any of them with me. I don't know why unless she's mad at me for making that bargain with the boss."

Roice laughed, twirling in his chair. I got a glimpse of tonight's T-shirt, a lovely mocha number emblazoned with "Shh... Nobody cares" on the chest. I'd have to steal it when he wasn't looking. "Who isn't mad at you?"

He made a fair point. I turned to Boice. "Murkowski?"

He nodded. "I took care of the medical bills. You're lucky he's insured. Otherwise, you'd be in the red this month. Again." Pushing a stray lock of dirty blond hair off his forehead, he gave me a frown that seemed suspiciously like concern. "Seriously, let me invest for you. I'll make you a billionaire in less than a year."

Oh, man, that was tempting. But that was what demons did. "I never pegged you for the patron demon of greed, but I might have to reclassify you. I am not a cheater. No insider trading. Period."

Boice's shoulders sagged, obscuring the message on his red T-shirt. It read, "If you need anything from me, reconsider." Oh, the irony. My demon boy really did have his heart in the right place, just not his methods. Still, I was seriously rethinking my ethics. At the rate I was going on my own, I'd never be able to retire.

"Suit yourself," Boice said. Perking up, he asked, "Where's our guest?"

Naturally, Roice perked up, too. "I haven't seen a succubus in ages. Is she hungry?" He wagged his brows, and I rolled my eyes.

"Give her a break tonight, fellas. The boss almost sent her back to the hell dimension through a reverse summoning portal."

Their gazes darkened, and they both muttered "asshole" under their breaths.

"I stopped him," I said, earning more admiring glances—or maybe they were just ogling my boobs. "But I kind of, sort of forged a blood pact with the boss to find out how Mephisto made it onto the earth dimension. I have to root out the summoner or summoners who helped him and close the portal so we can stop Belial from kidnapping me and Hannah for his demon rebellion. If I don't do it in six days, counting today, my family and I will face a fate worse than death."

"We heard," Roice said.

Then both of their gazes went wide, and they turned to one another and said, in unison, "I call dibs on her half of the suite."

Ah, demons. Loyal to the bone.

CHAPTER ELEVEN

I managed to catch a few Z's before getting up at the butt crack of dawn—something I rarely did—and heading out to interview Mr. Murkowski. I left notes on the twins' computers reminding them that my soul, and thus their squatters' rights, were in jeopardy, and that Mara was off-limits. They had work to do, not fellow demons. Like most males, they thought they could handle Mara if they worked together—gross—and it would be totally worth the recovery time to get with a succubus.

And I was pretty sure she'd devour them for their sparkling personalities alone.

I also left Mara a legal pad and a note asking her to write down everything she knew about Mephisto's mission and Belial. Then I sent a text to Lacey, setting up a rendezvous at the portal through which Mephisto might have entered. I texted Trinity and told her about the book, which I'd left with my roomies, and her research assignment. The twins' cell phones rang about two seconds later, forcing them out of bed with a slew of groans and curses.

Trinity had been drooling over that book for years and was no doubt gunning to get started. I loved that woman, and not because she was the perfect alarm clock for my lazy demon roomies.

That was just a bonus.

Finally, I scheduled an evening staff meeting at my place using food and an open bar as incentive.

I was totally charging that to the boss's account. It might be one of my last meals.

I pushed worry about the loss of my soul and my family's safety aside —I'd had contingency plans for them since I started the demon-hunting gig—to focus on investigating. Feeling uncharacteristically professional, I parked my freshly washed and waxed car, courtesy of D, and waltzed into one of the many midtown hospitals and asked to see Murkowski. Boice had gotten me on the list of authorized visitors. I loved having hackers at my service. Gathering my bag of goodies, I knocked softly on his door.

"Come in." Murkowski's hoarse voice was barely audible through the door. No wonder. He'd been intubated. Because I was a masochist, I'd read his chart and mentally flogged myself over the man's injuries.

At least the tube was out now.

The room was bright and seemed cheerful for a hospital suite. Balloons and flowers crowded the counter and floor space around Murkowski's bed, well wishes from friends, family, and colleagues. The man formerly known in my mind as Bad Santa appeared less than jolly, but his eyes sparkled, and his beard had been neatly trimmed. He sported the standard-issue hospital gown, of course.

Too bad. I kind of missed the Hawaiian shirt.

"Good morning." I plastered on my best winning smile as I walked in, dodging balloons, vases, and medical equipment. "How are you feeling today?"

He chuckled. "I've had better days. You a nurse?" The question was infused with humor. I'd skipped the camo and tank top, but jeans and a formfitting V-neck T-shirt weren't exactly nurse attire.

"Nope, I'm an investigator." I straightened, doing my best to look more authoritative. "I'd like to ask you a few questions about your attack in the alley last night if you're feeling up to it."

He grimaced as he adjusted the bed, bringing him to a sitting position. He had an IV drip running through his right arm and was also tethered to a blood pressure monitor. The flimsy hospital gown did little to bolster his jolly Santa appearance.

Nor did the bruises.

"I told the police all I remember," he said, averting his gaze. Didn't take a demon lie detector to spot that big fat whopper. Then again, who'd believe him?

I pulled up a rolling doctor's chair, plopped down beside him, and took out my very official-looking pad and pen. "I get it, and I'm not with the police. I'm part of a special investigation unit that investigates unusual cases. You can speak freely." I leaned in closer. "This is strictly confidential. My only concern is catching the entity who did this to you and making sure it doesn't hurt anyone else."

His body jerked, and he sat up straighter. Ouch. That had to hurt. I put my hand on his shoulder and eased him back. "Take it easy, Mr. Murkowski. You've got a concussion. No sudden moves."

He leaned back but still eyed me through a narrowed gaze. I got that a lot. People were so mistrustful. Then again, I had several advantages in delicate situations like this, not the least of which was a nice pair of boobs. I adjusted Santa's blankets while my girls hopefully put him at ease.

My height, or lack thereof, worked, too. Gave folks the idea I was younger than I was, cute, and totally harmless.

Murkowski squared his shoulders and sat up again, though not as quickly. He cocked his head to the side and examined me—my face, not my boobs. Weird. Finally, he said, "I don't remember everything, but I do know you were there."

"Yes," I said.

"You did some pretty freaky stuff, too."

"I did indeed. So did you, as I recall." I wagged my eyebrows at him, and a blush spread across his cheeks. I caught a flash of deep sorrow in his gaze. Poor guy.

I sat back down on the rolling chair and put on my best I'm-in-charge-here face. "What else do you remember? Do you know how you got to the alley?"

He laughed, or tried to. It started as a laugh and ended in a dry, rasping cough. "You're the first person who's given it to me straight in the past twenty-four hours. What were you doing in the alley?"

I grinned. Bad Santa was no fool. "I asked you first."

To sweeten the deal, I pulled out one of the items from my goody bag. I draped the thick, fuzzy blanket over Murkowski's feet. Hannah infused it with a bit of warmth. At least she was communicating with me again, even though she hadn't deigned to give me any answers. And at least she was helping.

"If you want to keep me as a host," I said in my head, "you'd better get with the program and help me solve this case so we can save my ass."

Do not fear. I am with you, and all will be revealed in time.

She didn't seem concerned. In fact, I sensed smugness and calculation before she retreated into the depths of consciousness.

Cryptic much? Maybe I could get that little nugget of nonsense stitched on a pillow.

Murkowski groaned as he wiggled his toes underneath the toasty blankie. I almost had him. Digging into my bag, I pulled out a smaller paper sack from which the mouthwatering scents of deep-fried goodness wafted. I'd read his updated file, generously provided by my roomies. It confirmed the guy loved burgers and fries. Honestly, who didn't?

I'd also followed him to his favorite restaurant about fifteen times over the past few weeks. I knew the specifics about his favorite food vice. Demon power aside, surveillance was my specialty.

Murkowski perked up when the smell of deliciousness hit him. "Is that for me?" he asked, a hopeful look painted over his formerly jolly, white-bearded face.

"Maybe." I reached into the sack to snag a fry and took a bite, making a show of chewing and savoring the crispy-on-the-outside, soft-on-the-inside magical potato creation. "Feel like talking?"

He scowled. "That's not nice. I'm in the hospital on account of you.

Least you could do is feed me. Then I might consider dropping the lawsuit."

It was my turn to laugh. I popped another fry. After swallowing it down with a moan of ecstasy, I said, "Nice try, Bad Santa, but you might want to rethink your strategy." I fished out a file from my bag and plopped it on his lap.

He snatched it up and started thumbing through the pages. His heart monitor ticked up a notch as he read. I unplugged it and sent a quick text to Roice asking him to work his magic with the computer system that linked monitoring equipment to the nurse's station. Didn't want any interruptions to throw us out of the moment.

"Hey, are you trying to kill me?" His brows shot up in alarm as he reached for the call button at the side of his bed.

"I wouldn't do that. Not unless you want the contents of that file to get back to your family. Or the cops."

"That's blackmail." His gaze darted around the room. He was probably looking for something he could use to bash my skull in. I got that a lot, too.

"No. It's a reminder of what got you into this mess in the first place. Did you know you were demon possessed?"

His gaze went wide as confusion, disbelief, and realization raced through his mind—at least that was what I read. Could've been gas, but I waited patiently for reality to set in. He wouldn't be ready to talk until then. In the meantime, there were plenty more fries.

"What do you want?" he asked at last. "Besides my fries."

"Well, Santa, I'd like to know when and how a powerful messenger demon targeted you." I took pity on him and gave him a fry.

He snatched it and gobbled it down with an appreciative grunt. "Not why?"

I snorted. "I know why, and so do you. You got in over your head with gambling debts. Made a deal with the devil, right?"

He scowled but didn't respond. It was all in the file—the updated file Boice had left under my door last night, which included bank records, travel patterns derived from his cell phone, ATM, and credit card transactions, and what was available by way of mundane surveillance. Putting it all together, we figured out that Murkowski was broke. He liked betting on pro sports and was very, very bad at it, which probably explained the broke part. But like most gambling addicts, desperation and the adrenaline rush had him placing the mother of all bets in the hopes he could dig himself out of an already sizable hole.

It hadn't worked.

He owed one local loan shark over a hundred grand and had no way to pay for it without selling the house he shared with his two high school–aged children. He'd tried to secure a loan against the value of the home, but the bankers had smelled the risk and said no. With no retirement funds available, since he'd already burned through them, he'd turned back to gambling.

At least he hadn't touched the college funds for the kids, but probably because he couldn't legally get his hands on them.

Then, all of a sudden, he'd stopped the desperate quest for cash—at least as far as the electronic paper trail indicated. Boice thought he'd managed to lay hands on enough cash to pay the debt. Didn't take a genius to figure out what happened. The man had become easy prey for a tempter demon, or so it appeared on the surface.

After last night's fiasco, however, we deduced Mephisto had come to Murkowski under the guise of a mammon, aka the most common species of immaterial greed demon, like Lacey's demon. Being immaterial, Mephisto likely employed a corporeal henchman to broker the deal, someone other than Mara. I needed to know more about the henchman.

"Look," I began, going for a gentler approach. "I figure you came up with the money somehow, and since you didn't win the lottery—we checked—you haven't donated a kidney on the black market—your chart would've shown that—and you don't have a Genie—because they're rare and come with some pretty hefty price tags to go along with those 'wishes,' I'm guessing you found another loan shark who made you a deal that was too good to be true."

He sighed, dragging a hand down his face and along his beard. "Yeah, well, I thought the lady was nuts. I didn't realize the demon thing was real until it was too late."

I gave Murkowski a sympathetic nod, offering him the rest of the fries. I held on to the burger, though. He wouldn't get that until I got the info. He took the fries and gobbled them down like they were the first meal he'd had in weeks. It had been less than twenty-four hours, but hospital food sucked. As a man who obviously appreciated a decent meal, I'd nailed the bribe.

"No one ever thinks the demon thing is real until it's too late." I gave him a rueful smile. "Demons are tricky. Tell me what happened."

After licking the salt from his fingers, he cocked his head, seemingly lost in thought. "You're right. I'd gotten in way over my head. I knew it was wrong, but I had a lot of bills. That's what got me started. My wife had cancer. Damned insurance didn't cover half of it. We were already in the red. Wiped out all our savings and retirement."

I nodded. The file had mentioned that, too, which is why I'd brought the blanket and a few other items in my goody bag. Bad choices aside, the guy had been through hell. Yeah, I was a total softy.

"Right. Then you took up gambling, and it didn't work out." I scribbled on my notepad. It helped with the professional look, and my doodles weren't half bad. I should have been an artist. "How did the demon come into the picture?"

He shifted uncomfortably in his bed. "Gal turns up after I lost my last bet—no, wait, it was a few weeks after I lost the bet and had been scrambling to keep my bookie's goons from paying a home visit to me or my children." Murkowski's face turned red, though I couldn't tell if it was from shame or anger.

I nodded, encouraging him to continue while digging out the burger.

"That smells awful good." He eyed the wrapped bit of all-American goodness with longing.

"You'll get it when you tell me what I need to know." I held it just out of reach. "Be quick, or I'll eat it in front of you."

I was a softy, but not that soft. After all, I did work with demons.

He sighed. "Like I said, this gal shows up with a suitcase full of cash and tells me it's mine if I'd let her demon take over my body. I told her that while I was flattered, I didn't go for jailbait. I mean, she could've been over eighteen, but I'm not into girls young enough to be my daughter. She just laughed and said she had a demon in need of a host body and wanted to borrow mine for a few days. Said the demon was looking for someone and needed cover."

Given the form Mara had assumed in the alley, I doubted he was lying. I stopped doodling and took down his description of the girl. Not Mara, based on her preferred shapes, and I believed her when she told me she'd only met Murkowski the night before. I'd run the description he gave me against known female summoners and demon associates, though Mephisto could've used or blackmailed another shape-shifting demon like Mara as his broker. It was a lead, though. I'd take it.

"You just took the cash?"

"Well, yeah," he said, defensive. "I thought the girl was nuts. Crazy money is still money. After I shook her hand, I went straight to my bookie, settled up, and got out of there before I got tempted again. I waited for the girl to show up—thought she'd want to do some weird stuff and that I could play along for a while and then tell her to get lost. But she didn't, so I figured I was home free."

Yeah, classic demon entrapment. I had to admit, it was a little disappointing. I'd expected more finesse from a high-ranking messenger demon, something with more flair. Or more creative. This was about as lame as passing a note in study hall.

Still, the tactic had clearly worked. As soon as Murkowski accepted the cash, he'd sealed the pact. It only took a yes and a single, miniscule drop of blood. Mephisto's courier could have gotten that from a tiny needle planted on the cash case's handle, or with the handshake. Murkowski would've been none the wiser.

"When did the demon take over?" I asked.

"A few days later. I woke up with a splitting headache and a weird feeling in the pit of my stomach. When I went to shave, I saw a shadow in the mirror, and my eyes went all freaky—black with red sparks. I don't remember too much after that, just bits and pieces. It was like, well, like after I came out of surgery here. I woke up a few times and caught a face here, a conversation there, but nothing made sense."

I shuddered, remembering my first glimpse of Hannah in the mirror. Shaking off the distraction, I turned my attention back to Murkowski. "Classic demonic possession. Do you remember meeting Mara?"

"Mara?"

"The demon from the alley, the one who looked like a librarian? She's a succubus. Mephisto, the demon who possessed you, forced her to target you so he could attract a demon hunter." I didn't mention that the demon wanted me specifically. He didn't need to know that.

A pained expression crossed his face, full of sorrow and agony. I had to look away.

"Yeah, I remember." His voice was broken when he spoke. I risked a glance at him, caught him wiping tears from the corners of his eyes. I gave him the burger then. I hated to see anyone cry, especially a guy who looked like Santa.

"She was the spitting image of Margaret—my wife, at least the way she was before the cancer got bad. We lost her not long ago."

I hated Mephisto already. Now, I loathed the bastard. How incredibly cruel, using the man's grief against him. It was inhuman. It was so very demon.

I gave him a moment to regain his composure and enjoy the first bite of his burger. As much as I despised Mephisto's methods and lack of flair, they'd worked exceedingly well. He'd been able to lure me, and apparently the boss, into his trap and almost managed to send Hannah and me on a one-way trip to the hell realm. Before that, though, he'd needed a portal and a summoner. Glad my team was working that angle. We needed to find the summoner and secure the portal.

"I'm sorry." I took his hand and gave it a squeeze. "We caught the demon who possessed you, and he's going to pay for what he did. I promise." At least I hoped he would. Considering Hannah just let him go, he could be long gone back to the hell realm by now.

Murkowski chewed his burger and nodded. After swallowing hard, I offered him the soda I'd also stashed in my bag. He smiled and accepted it, taking three large gulps before setting the can down and letting out an appreciative belch.

"Excuse me," he said, sheepish.

"Not at all." I chuckled. "Is there anything else you can tell me about what happened to you? Did the demon take you to any strange locations? Do you remember anything about his associates?"

"Not much." Murkowski frowned. "But I thought you said you caught the guy—demon—whatever he is."

Bad Santa was sharp. I supposed I could give him a little more information as incentive. "Here's the thing, Mr. Murkowski—"

"Call me Jack," he said. "You pulled a demon out of me. I figure we don't have to be so formal."

I laughed again, liking the guy even more. "You can call me Jinx." I fished out a business card. He took it, quirking a brow at the logo—my sigil—and the strange symbols under my name. It was demon for "Eat at Moe's," but humans wouldn't know that.

"Here's the thing, Jack. The demon who possessed you was a messenger, and he was also sent on a retrieval mission for another, more powerful demon. I need to find out how he got here and who helped him. Anything you can remember could help me do that."

He leaned back and patted his belly. Closing his eyes, he said, "After he took over, he took me someplace strange, a park, I think. I don't go to many parks. I remember talking to someone. I heard a voice, but it wasn't clear. Maybe a woman's voice? And there was something that growled, like a dog, only...bigger. Anyway, the whole thing seemed weird, going to a park at night. That's what serial killers or perverts do, right?"

Or demons looking for a portal and a summoner.

I pulled out my phone and loaded some pictures of the locations Lacey had scouted in west Nashville. There were a few large parks out there and at least two portals that fit the description. I showed them to Murkowski. He said it could've been one of them. The guy didn't remember much else except an odd-looking tree.

It was something. I took more notes about the voice and the growls and sent them off to my roomies, along with instructions to be on the lookout for demons or human associates who fit the description of the girl who'd brokered the deal between Mephisto and Murkowski. I had Murkowski make a rough sketch of the cash-for-possession courier and the tree, and then decided to let him get back to the business of recuperating. After plugging his heart monitor back in and texting my roomie a message to restore the hospital computer system to normal operations, I thanked him for his time and warned him to stay out of trouble.

Hannah chose that moment to get with the program, yanking me to my feet and turning my body toward the door in a very awkward and less-than-grateful manner. Why was she suddenly in such a hurry to get out of there and go hunting? It was weird.

"Cut. It. Out," I whispered through gritted teeth. Wrestling control of my body, I turned back and stepped closer to the bed to deliver a final message to Bad Santa.

"No more gambling, mister." I issued the stern warning with hands on hips, barely resisting the urge to shake my finger at him. "You need to take care of yourself and your kids, okay?"

He chuckled. "Like I haven't heard that one before." Then he grew serious and said, "So this demon thing is real? I was possessed?"

"Yup," I said. "Afraid so. You shouldn't have any lasting side effects, but I suggest you don't pick up any more bad habits, unless you want another target on your back for tempter demons."

He nodded, but then he frowned. "But demons? I mean, seeing is believing, but..."

I tugged on my black mirror and asked Hannah for a small demonstration. To my surprise, she came through. Murkowski's gaze flew wide as he stared at my eyes. No doubt he found the sparks of red swirling in my irises familiar and unsettling.

I probably should have done that before plugging the heart monitor back in.

In moments, a nurse popped in to check Murkowski out in spite of his protests. Eyeing me with suspicion—I got that a lot, too—she said I needed to get out and let the man rest. She crinkled her nose and gave me another scowl. Damn it, nurses had the best sniffers when it came to contraband food. Murkowski reassured her we were almost done and promised he'd lay off the junk food.

Liar. I didn't blame him, though. Junk food was one of life's more appealing guilty pleasures, as long as it didn't come with a gluttony demon. Once a beelzebub got its hooks into its victim, other compatible vice demons tended to tag along. Succubi and incubi worked with the bubs—augmenting lust for excess food and drink with, well, lust. Sloth often followed, and the belph demons of laziness were such a pain in the ass to evict.

I hoped none of Mara's bub and belph buddies showed up on my doorstep looking for a place to hide or hang out. I wasn't running a demon hotel, and the demons of gluttony and sloth were messy.

When we had the room to ourselves again, he said, "You've got one, too? You're possessed?"

"Not exactly." I struggled for a way to explain my unique relationship with Hannah. "My...companion helps me with cases and is a pretty cool roommate." I hoped Hannah heard that part. "It's part of the demon-tracking gig. Takes a demon to track a demon. If you think of anything else, even if it seems trivial, call me, okay?"

"That what you really look like?" His gaze had grown wide and filled with suspicion. No wonder, given his experience with demons and deception.

"Yup, this is all me." I swept a hand down my compact body. "My demon pal is immaterial, like the one who possessed you. Only corporeal demons can shape-shift, like Mara and maybe like the girl who gave you cash in exchange for possession."

He grinned, this time checking out my boobs. "Your demon keeps you in pretty good shape."

I laughed. "It's not all fun and games. I train hard, and I've got good genes, except when it comes to height." I also healed fast and didn't suffer the aches and pains other humans complained about. I suspected it had something to do with Hannah's prolonged occupation of my body, one of the few perks that came with demonic possession.

"Will more demons be coming for me?" Murkowski asked, growing serious. Poor guy was probably terrified.

I smiled. "Not likely. It isn't like being possessed once puts a bull's-eye on your back."

He relaxed visibly and fixed me with a quizzical expression, gaze narrowed as if I were an interesting puzzle he was trying to piece together. No idea why. I wasn't that complicated. Then again, maybe he wondered if the demon in me might jump out and try to take his soul. No, that couldn't be it. He didn't appear afraid. Just curious.

He leaned back and put his hands behind his head. "You know, someone picked up the hospital tab for me. Covered everything my insurance doesn't, plus the balance for my wife's cancer treatments. You wouldn't know anything about that, would you?"

I put on my best poker face and shrugged. "Not a clue."

He smiled. If I didn't know better, I'd swear he didn't believe me. No way. I had the best poker face. "Sure you're not an angel? Assuming they exist, too."

My chest went tight, and I fought a grimace. I'd spent most of my childhood wondering if I could find an angel to rescue me. That was what angels were supposed to do. I tried to be good, hoping a guardian angel would notice me, see I was doing my best despite the demon inside me, but none ever came.

Guess I wasn't good enough.

I coughed and looked down at my feet. "Oh, I'm no angel, believe me. But if they're out there, I'll bet they'll be keeping an eye on you and your girls. You folks deserve a break."

I felt a hand on mine. Murkowski didn't hold on long enough to make it weird. He just gave my hand a light squeeze. "I think you're wrong."

I was about to scoff, but his chuckle caught me off guard. I looked up to find Bad Santa grinning like a fiend, his gaze full of mischief. "Okay, maybe a fallen angel. You did bring me a heart attack special," he said patting his belly.

Bless his heart. I grinned in spite of myself and made a mental note to have Boice and Roice keep an eye on the guy so he'd stay out of trouble.

To be sure, I slapped him on the leg gave him a gentle reminder of my own. "Just remember what I said about bad habits and tempters, okay?"

He nodded. Then after a quick glance down at my business card, he gave me a funny look. "Jinx, huh?" The corners of his mouth curled into a smirk. "I hope you're luckier than your name."

I smiled back. "Like I haven't heard that one before."

My phone chimed, and I tugged it out of my tight pants. There was a text from Lacey. Weird dog reported in Percy Warner park, possibly a hellhound. We were scheduled to meet up at the park anyway. I'd never seen a hellhound. Maybe it had something to do with this case since it had apparently been spotted by the mundanes.

Time to go check it out, along with the portal and summoner in charge of the area, and possibly play dogcatcher.

Good times.

CHAPTER TWELVE

I met up with Lacey at Percy Warner Park. The stone-and-wrought-iron gate lining the grand entrance near Belle Meade fit the genteel, old-money South feel of the area. Ah, nature—the air was filled with pollen, gnats, and the aroma of enough mulch to choke a demon tracker.

Yeah, I was a city gal. Pretty sure I was allergic to grass and natural sunlight. I spotted Lacey sitting on one of the stone steps and hauled ass to join her.

"What's for lunch?" she asked. She sported shades and the telltale scent of SPF 100 sunscreen. Wise move for any ginger.

I pulled out some gourmet sandwiches and a couple of bottles of iced tea, earning a nod of approval. While we ate, I told her what I'd learned from Murkowski and showed her his sketches of the girl and the weird tree. She didn't know the girl, but she recognized the tree, and a jolt of adrenaline shot through my veins along with hope. It matched the tree I'd seen on the boss's screen.

"It's one of the portals," she said, confirming the lead.

"The one you texted about?"

"You got it." She grinned, apparently happy to be on the hunt. "The guard in charge reported some unusual activity a week and a half ago.

Nothing came of it at the time, but your buddy Roice might have a hit on the security cam."

"Score. What about demon traces? Tempters, or something else more powerful? And what's up with the hellhound?"

My partner stood up and dusted grass and debris off her butt. "We'll probably find Rover the demon dog when we find the portal. As far as demons, I'd say it's something more powerful, but you should probably have Hannah get a read on it. Speaking of reads," she said, putting her hands on her hips and giving me a hard look. "Did you really get the boss's favorite book?"

"Sure did," I said brightly. "Straight out of the forbidden section. Pretty sure it's hiding demon porn. Want to make doodles in the margins?"

She snorted. "You are so immature. I thought you'd be a tad more serious given the stakes. Why did Hannah let the messenger demon go instead of coughing him up and making him spill his evil plans?"

"No idea. She's playing the whole cryptic mentor card." I grimaced. I hated that card. "And apparently I need to 'work this one out' on my own to unlock my 'true potential' so 'all will be revealed' in time."

"Lay off the air quotes. It's not helping with the maturity thing. If Hannah's not going to help, we should get cracking. Ready to take a look?"

"Hell, yeah." I bounced up and down. Hey, if I was immature, I might as well live up to my reputation. Go big or go home. "And is that a yes to project doodle?"

I stopped after three bounces, though. Cowgirl boots and bouncing without a sports bra did not mix.

She caved and offered me a smirk. "Sure, I'll help with project doodle, but only if I get to read the book first."

That surprised me. I had no idea Lacey was interested in demon lore, at least not beyond classifications, descriptions of powers, associated sins, and tracking and capture methods. Trinity was the scholar in our little outfit.

My disbelief must have showed—I really needed to check my poker face—since Lacey gave me a scowl. Freckles aside, that woman had elevated the looks-that-could-kill thing to an art form. Maybe that whole myth about redheads stealing souls had an ounce of truth.

"Sorry," I said. "I just didn't realize you were, you know, interested. What I've read so far has been pretty dry."

She jerked back, and her scowl deepened. "Seriously? Of course I'm interested. Aren't you? Don't you want to know why?"

"Why what?"

She shook her head at my apparent thickheadedness. Jeez. I wasn't a mind reader, for Pete's sake. "Why us." Lacey said it nice and slow, as if that would somehow clarify this cryptic statement. "Haven't you ever wondered why demons chose us?"

"Of course I have." I'd done nothing but wonder for the past eighteen years. When it came to the standard demon drawn to sin scenario, however, Lacey's case seemed a little more...cut-and-dried, given her penchant for shoplifting.

My face must have given Lacey some idea of what I was thinking, since her gaze went wide and then she looked away. Crap. I needed a better poker face.

"The world's filled with shoplifters. I guarantee every mall within a twenty-mile radius is full of them, not to mention car thieves, hedge fund managers, and three-quarters of the hacks on Wall Street," she said. A hint of pain bled through her mask of indignation.

I should've realized. I wasn't the only member of our demon-hunting operation haunted by guilt and shame. I wasn't the only one asking, "Why me?" I wasn't the only one wondering what made me so bad I had drawn a demon.

I needed to be a better friend.

"I'm sorry," I said, and meant it. "You didn't deserve it, no matter how many graphic T-shirts you lifted. You're a good person, Lacey. You just lost your way for a while. That's all."

"You think so?"

I put my hand on her shoulder and squeezed. "Yes, I do. I don't know why our demons came to us, but maybe it was so we could do some good in the world. After we solve this case, we'll see if we can find answers in the grimoire. Deal?"

She gave me a lopsided grin and nodded. "Deal."

We hiked about a gazillion miles before leaving the trail. I totally forgot to bring my machete, so every branch, vine, and twig repositioned by Lacey the leader came flying back to hit me in the face. And somehow, I managed to hit every spider web along the way despite bringing up the rear. I'd have to make a note of that on Lacey's employee evaluation.

We stopped in a clearing, and I sensed the demon magic before I spotted the ugliest tree I'd ever seen in the middle of the small patch of clear forest. Its branches split and twisted at random angles that made it seem more crooked than a politician. Pockmarked with lumps along its trunk and full of hollows, the tree was as imposing as it was hideous.

And it matched Murkowski's drawing to a T.

"Which hole is the portal?" I asked. There were so many. Maybe this was some kind of hell realm hub.

Lacey pointed to hollow at the juncture of a pair of branches. Then she nodded to the ground and the unnaturally regular pattern of leaves and debris that formed a circle around the tree. "Don't cross the boundary."

"I know that," I grumbled. I wouldn't have been able to even if I forgot. Ordinary humans could walk right up to the tree, blissfully unaware of how close they were to an interdimensional gateway. Since I harbored a demon, the magic would deny me access to the portal without permission from an authorized summoner, setting off all kinds of triggers, traps, and defenses to prevent tampering.

And speaking of summoners...

A man dressed in camo, the kind that actually blended, appeared from behind a nearby patch of shrubs. He'd painted his face in a haphazard pattern of greens, grays, and black with the odd brown smudge here and there, though that could have been dirt. Leaves clung to his hair, which he'd gathered into a ponytail behind his head. I appreciated the lack of a man bun almost as much as I appreciated the tall, lean frame and startlingly blue eyes.

Oh, yeah, I'd get a little dirty with him given half a chance.

"Hi there." I waved and smiled. "We'd like to ask you a few questions about the portal."

The guy whipped out a gun, leveled it on me, and pulled the trigger.

CHAPTER THIRTEEN

Lacey summoned her demon and sent him flying at Mr. Shoot-Em-Up before I could blink. Hannah, having located her sense of self-preservation, came as soon as I tugged on the black mirror, and we leapt into action. Literally. We jumped into a nearby tree, ripped off a heavy branch, and threw it at camo man while he was distracted by Lacey's immaterial demon's aerial assault just outside the boundary. He couldn't shoot it, but he had a demon blade and knew how to use it.

The summoner was protecting his portal, but this was overkill. Shoot first? Seriously?

The tree branch hit his back between the shoulder blades and sent him to the ground. Simon buzzed above him, pulsing with anger and possibly hunger.

The summoner did one of those cool as hell backbend jumps to his feet, which had to hurt since I'd nailed him in the back. Glaring at Simon and Lacey, who was spinning her knife in rapid circles to create a shield against material and demonic attacks, he turned his attention to the trees. I chucked another branch at him, this one decorated with a scrap of whitish fabric that might or might not have come from my undies.

"We come in peace!" I yelled, motioning for Simon and Lacey to fall back. When he lowered his knife, I jumped down—this time Hannah cushioned my knees, and I didn't get an owie—and approached, hands up and smiling at the psychopath on the other side of the boundary.

He scowled and spoke in a low, gravelly voice. "Ticket."

"Oh, no." I patted my pockets and looked sheepish. "I seem to have left it at home. Anyone else show up recently without a ticket?"

"From the other side," Lacey added. Wasn't she helpful...

"No one comes or goes without a ticket." His deep voice dripped with disdain. It wasn't attractive. I dropped him from a ten to a high eight on my hotness scale.

"That's so weird." I smiled sweetly and batted my eyelashes. "Because a messenger demon named Mephisto came to the earth realm recently, and he forgot his ticket, too. You haven't seen anything strange around here lately, have you?"

"We're from Demon Hunting HQ, by the way," Lacey said.

I'd forgotten to identify myself. But honestly, the scuffle had been too much fun.

His frown deepened, as did the furrow in his brows. Maybe he was thinking. Or maybe he was a natural frowner. Hard to tell. I fished out my phone and held up a picture of Mr. Murkowski, waving it at the stern outdoorsman to get his attention.

He took a step closer and studied the photograph.

"This is the human he possessed," I said. "The guy doesn't remember much, but he said Mephisto dragged him somewhere in the woods. We think Mephisto dragged him here."

The guard shrugged. "If he already had the demon inside him, he wouldn't be able to cross the threshold."

"But he might have been with someone—maybe a woman—and she could've crossed the threshold if she wasn't possessed. Maybe they were checking to make sure they could get back through the portal after securing their prisoner."

"Prisoner?" he said, gruff voice alight with interest. Yeah, he seemed the type to be interested in prisoners. I wonder if he had handcuffs.

What a delicious thought.

Lacey nudged me after a moment. I'd been staring. In my defense, the guy had started pacing, which gave me a nice side view of his ass.

"Yeah, um, anyway..." Where was I? Oh, right. I was investigating. Definitely not ogling. "We have reason to believe Mephisto traveled to the earth realm to kidnap someone for a hell realm demon lord. We need to know if there's a chance he used this portal."

His gaze turned hard, and I held up my palms. "Not that you would've let him. You seem...dedicated. But is there a chance another summoner commandeered this portal while you were out? On break or out camo and war paint shopping?"

He didn't respond, so I kept going. I hated uncomfortable silences. "Oh, and Murkowski mentioned something that growled. Do you have a dog, wolf, coyote, or maybe Cerberus hanging out around here?"

"The mundanes have reported strange animal sightings, too. Any hellhounds running around?" Lacey asked.

His gaze drifted off, apparently lost in thought again. Or maybe he was stoned. Then he turned and started hooting and chirping and making other odd animal noises that made me take a step back. Lacey did, too.

Yup, our cray-cray senses were tingling.

All summoners were a little off—it was a job requirement. No sane person would hang around a demon portal, let alone police it. But even by summoner standards, making weird animal noises in the middle of the friggin' woods during an interview was off the rails.

"What's he doing?" Lacey whispered from the side of her mouth.

"No idea," I said. "But dat ass."

We fist-bumped, and then I cleared my throat, hoping to get his attention. Before I could speak, a swarm of woodland creatures invaded the clearing in a blur of fur, feathers, fangs, and scales. They gathered around Dr. Doolittle, who went from surly nutjob to oh-my-God-adorable in a nanosecond. He cooed to the birds on his shoulder and scratched fox and coyote ears before wrapping some kind of snake around his neck like a boa.

Wow, if I hadn't had Hannah, I would've jumped right in there to cuddle all of them, rabies risk be damned.

Lacey could have if she'd put down her phone, aka demon carrying case, but she'd taken another step back. Maybe she was allergic to woodland creatures. That had to suck.

The summoner turned back to us, this time with a big grin that showcased the cutest dimples. A red-tailed hawk landed on his shoulder—the biggest one I'd ever seen—and the summoner nuzzled it with his nose. "My friends tell me there were some people here around ten days ago. I reported it to our boss around that time. You have anything from the man? Something they could scent?"

Oops. I hadn't counted on that. Then again, I'd let Murkowski handle the file. I fished it out of my bag, placed it on the ground, and nudged it toward the boundary of the clearing. One of the foxes leapt over the boundary and sniffed it. I crouched down and watched in fascination, falling in love with the scruffy little redhead.

"Can I pet her?" My fingers itched to stroke her soft fur, and the fox seemed just as eager for a rubdown.

The summoner did some sort of chirp growl thing that I assumed was fox talk. Sounded more like squirrel to me, but animal linguistics wasn't my thing. The fox approached my outstretched hand slowly, sniffed, and then pressed her forehead into my palm to my utter delight. After a wonderful scratching session, the fox circled Lacey and then went back to the file, sniffing and pacing around in apparent excitement.

"Ricky recognizes the scent." The summoner beamed, smiling at the little fox with obvious pride.

I squealed in delight, showering the creature with more scratches and praise. "Who's a good fox? Who's the best fox in the whole world? That's right, Ricky's the best."

She accepted my praise with a few enthusiastic yips and a love bite or two, careful not to break the skin, before leaping back into the circle with her buddies.

"Has she detected any other scents? Other humans?" Lacey asked.

After another back-and-forth in fox talk, the summoner shook his head. "Nothing other than yours," he said, nodding at my partner.

She sighed. "I was here last night. That's how I knew the portal had been used recently. I'm surprised you didn't."

The summoner scowled and stepped forward, his muscles tense. "I suspected it had, and I reported it. Demon tracking is your job, not mine."

The cute little woodland critters turned their unblinking gazes on us, and the trees and shrubs seemed to close in. Was it creepy in here, or was it just them? Even the gnarly tree quivered with something like menace, and I caught a flash of tooth and claw from some of the creatures within the protective sphere surrounding the portal.

Lacey tried to take another step back, but I grabbed her arm and yanked until she stood beside me. No way I would let her bail on me. "Okay, okay. We're working on it. Did your buddy get any other scents?"

Thankfully, the tension eased and quickly returned to fairy-tale cuteness. The summoner chatted with Ricky and the other creatures for a bit and then turned back to us. "They're going to sweep the area for more human scents, but perhaps your host's companion concealed it. It's not outside the scope of tempter demon magic."

"Yeah, but why not cover Murkowski's, too?" I asked. A small finch landed on my shoulder, tickling me with its tiny little bird feet. Yup. I was officially in love with the bird, too.

The summoner frowned. "A good question. Has the Arbiter reviewed video and demon surveillance?"

"Arbiter?" Lacey cocked her head to the side.

"One of the boss's titles," I said. "I just found out last night. Hannah's apparently 'The Intercessor.' Fill you in later."

Lacey shook her head and rolled her eyes. "They never tell us anything."

"Don't I know it." Turning back to the summoner—I should really get his name, possibly his number—I answered his question. "He's reviewing the video now, I think. Not sure about the demon surveillance."

The summoner put a couple of fingers in his mouth and whistled. One of the other hollows in the ugly tree glowed as a creature emerged, its golden fur sleek and glowing in the sunlight. Roughly the size of a lion, the beast looked more like an oversize greyhound with a thicker coat and—

"You have a dog with wings?" Lacey said, gasping in awe.

"I want one." I marveled at its graceful lines and gorgeous eyes filled with otherworldly cunning. I'd seen a few animals from the hell realm, mostly vermin on the order of the gremlins Lacey had captured the night before, but never anything as elegant and powerful. This beautiful creature must've been what Murkowski heard. Anything that big could produce a growl of epic proportions.

It also explained the "hellhound" sightings.

The summoner chuckled. "Archimedes is a cadejo. He's an excellent tracker, and he helps me guard the portal."

"Where was he the night Mephisto showed up last?" Lacey asked.

I hated to play bad cop, bad cop, but Lacey had a point. "Or the night Mephisto came from the hell realm in the first place, assuming he came through this portal."

The summoner dropped his gaze as if sad or possibly ashamed. "Archimedes was ill. I thought perhaps he'd eaten something that disagreed with him—sometimes species differences give visitors from the hell realm indigestion—but now I think perhaps it was deliberate."

My blood boiled at the thought. "Poison? What makes you think so?"

He shrugged. "He didn't recover within a day after the symptoms hit. Most of the time it only takes a half a day. I was worried. I gave him a potion from the hell realm. One of the regulars who uses this portal brings me supplies for him. It still took three days, but he pulled through."

"Bastard," I muttered. Animal cruelty was inexcusable as far as I was concerned.

"I agree," he said, giving the amazing creature a scratch behind his ears. "I'll send Archimedes out to scent the area for traces of demon linked to human. If we find anything, I'll send word."

"Awesome. Can I have a cadejo?" I asked.

"No." The summoner frowned. Again. He was much prettier when he smiled. "They're not pets, not in the same sense as earth realm pets."

"But he hangs out with you. You give him meds. Do you feed him?"

"Yes," he said, lips twitching.

Ah-ha. I was totally going to win this. "Do you walk him?"

He fought a grin, blue eyes alight with amusement. "We patrol together, but that's strictly professional."

Damn it. That was a point for Dr. Doolittle, but I wasn't finished yet. "Do you give him baths and scoop his poop?"

He finally gave in and grinned again. It made him look almost sane. Maybe he wasn't crazy. Maybe he was simply feral. A wild beast among wild beasts, at home in his element. But surely he had a home somewhere. I'd have to find out so I could send him a thank-you note.

I was nice like that and would never dream of breaking in and stealing his cadejo.

"Don't even think about it," he said, grin still in place. Archimedes sauntered over and licked his hand. Doolittle was such a liar. This hell realm pup was totally his pet.

Crestfallen but not completely defeated, I gave it one more try. "Fine, but if one ever comes up for adoption at the hell realm shelter, keep me in mind." I pulled out a business card and handed it to him. He looked at it and then examined me with wide eyes.

"You should get going, Jinx McGee. You have a case to solve and less than five days to do it."

My jaw dropped. Seriously? Did everybody know I made a deal with the boss?

Lacey patted my shoulder. "Your roomies put it all over the message boards. You're famous in our circles."

I pouted. "I thought I was already famous for table dancing at the annual Yule party." I'd wowed the whole gang with my mad skills and had the video to prove it, too. Perhaps I needed a repeat performance at tonight's staff meeting.

"Okay, well, thanks for your cooperation, Mr...."

"I'm Cooper." He grinned again. The man's grin was almost as enticing as his ass.

"First or last name?" I teased, pulling out my pad and pen to record the facts. I was on a case, after all.

"Just Cooper. If you need anything, send your sigil on the wind."

"Can't I just text?" I asked, hopeful.

He put his hands out and gestured to the area. "Sorry. No signal out here. Send your sigil, and I'll get a message to you."

"Via cadejo?" A girl could hope.

Lacey picked up my file, grabbed me by the arm, and started dragging me away from the clearing, much to Cooper's amusement. I cast a last longing glance at Archimedes and his companion. He grinned wider and waved.

"Good luck, Jinx McGee. I hope you don't die."

That makes two of us, buddy.

After sending Lacey off to check on video footage from the Warner Park portal, I sent a text to Boice and Roice promising a slow and painful death to the brother who'd spread the word about my unfortunate situation. They'd even started an online betting pool. The odds of my death were about ten to one. So much for the vote of confidence.

They sent a message back asking if I wanted in on the betting pool. How thoughtful. I declined on the grounds that it represented a conflict of interest, which seemed to confuse them. Demons...

I asked them to get an update from Trinity on the boss's book—how much she'd translated and if she'd found anything useful. Then I sent a message to Alexi asking him to bring some vodka to the meeting. At a loss for what else to do, I stopped at a local coffee shop for a pick-me-up—after I located my car—and sent a text to D.

Did you know there's a betting pool on my death?

I took a sip of the most delicious chai latte I'd ever tasted, savoring it as if it were my last. Of course, it could be, but I decided to focus on the positives. We'd identified the portal, and we had a lead on the messenger demon's broker. Great progress for the first day.

Speaking of...

Did you find the summoner? We know which portal he used.

He texted back immediately.

Yes. I've been questioning him since this morning.

Well, well, well. Looked like I picked the right muscle for the old interrogation job. D might've been an unreliable friend/almost boyfriend, but he was turning out to be a pretty good errand boy and hired thug. Now if he could only get me a cadejo. I texted back.

Don't keep me in suspense.

He didn't send me a message right away. Apparently, he liked suspense, the bastard. I took another sip of the warm and delicious beverage while checking my email. The damages for Murkowski's medical care weren't as bad as I thought. I'd be able to eat out at least twice a week until payday. My roomies would have to bail me out for the other days. Or cook for me.

I typed another message.

Hello? It's only my life and soul we're talking about, and my family. But by all means, take your time.

He sent a photo. I wasn't sure I recognized the summoner, but that could've been the bruising. And the split lip. I knew D was capable of brute force. He'd taken care of more than a few bullies in our youth—not to mention would-be attackers who thought they'd take advantage of a young, beautiful boy out roaming the streets after dark—but as a demon in his full powers, he also had more creative tools at his disposal. Judging from the look on the summoner's face, D had also included more metaphysical means of persuasion.

It wasn't pretty, but few things about illegal demon activity were. I only hoped D hadn't scrambled the guy's marbles before getting the info we needed.

He confirmed the message was from Belial and that he was supposed to send you and Hannah back through the portal with Mephisto. Claims Mephisto didn't show for their scheduled rendezvous. He hasn't seen the demon since.

Wow, D had the summoner singing like a canary and turning on his demon master? The summoner had probably signed his own death warrant, assuming D didn't kill him first. I swallowed hard, wondering how to broach the subject of the summoner's immediate future—assuming he had one.

He'll live. He's lucky I found him before Mephisto did. Demons hate loose ends.

I breathed an audible sigh of relief. D knew me a little too well, knew I'd been worried about how far he would take things. Of course, I had good reason. But he was older now, more in control of his strength and powers, more confident. It had taken brass balls to stand up to the boss on my behalf.

It took brass balls to stick around after the welcome I'd given him.

I fired off another text.

Okay. See what you can find out about his accomplices, especially a female summoner or demon who might have helped broker the deal with Murkowski. You can tell me all about it at the staff meeting tonight.

I sat staring at the phone, giddy with anticipation as I waited for the response he was typing. Pathetic.

I was such a fool.

He replied shortly after my heart took off at a sprint.

I don't interrogate human females. You and your colleagues will have to handle that. We're still on for midnight, right?

That was an odd code of chivalry for a demon. Most demons had no qualms about attacking women or females of their own species, a fact the boss had brutally reinforced last night with Mara and with me. I couldn't decide whether it was pro- or antifeminist. Instead, I focused on the warm fuzzies that filled my soul at the prospect of my midnight rendezvous with Dominic. I had to stay cool, though. Just because I was on top of the world, the roller coaster that got me there would inevitably come crashing down at breakneck speed.

Yup. Definitely needed to play it cool. Keep things professional. Make him squirm as much as I was. I sent another text.

Fine, but you still have to attend the staff meeting. Staff meetings are mandatory.

Oh, yeah, buddy. I was the boss of him, and he'd better show up at this important gathering of demon hunters for strategic planning over tequila shots and tacos. I was an awesome manager. I'd just have to remind Roice to order tacos.

I had the tequila covered.

Still no reply. I clearly needed to turn up the heat, crack the whip, and make sure he knew exactly with whom he was dealing.

I should probably tell you that failure to attend mandatory staff meetings could result in severe punishment and loss of taco and tequila privileges.

I waited, chewing on my nails and contemplating all the ways I could punish D severely. I'd need one of those leather corsets and a riding crop. Possibly spurs. I'd just started surfing online sex shops when a text alert sounded, setting my little heart all aflutter.

You can punish me all you like, but can you handle all I like?

Holy hotness, Batman. I practically jumped up from my seat and did a happy dance. Scratch that—I did jump out of my seat to do a happy dance, earning more than a few raised eyebrows and strange looks. I'd have to take it down a notch. Before I grabbed my bag and got ready to leave, I fired off another text to D. Two little words full of promise and hope.

Game. On.

CHAPTER FOURTEEN

The heavenly scents of tacos and queso wafted from my penthouse, which was probably why Alexi arrived first. I totally understood. Tacos rocked. Plus he was a big guy with an appetite to match.

He knocked and stood at a polite distance from the door, head down, feet shuffling, waiting for me to ask him to in.

"Are we going to do this every time?" I asked, stepping aside so he could walk right in without a gold-embossed invitation.

A shadow of a smile crossed his face. How anyone that big and burly could be so timid was beyond me, but then again, the Russian import had issues. Worse, they were daddy issues. He'd inherited his demon from his Russian mob boss father, and it manifested as a wolf, which pretty much explained the whole werewolf myth. It gave him enhanced senses, speed, and strength, which he used to subdue demons.

And sniff out tacos.

The man was built like a linebacker but had the golden hair and chiseled features of a male model. Too bad he'd missed his chance to play college or pro. He was good and could have earned a scholarship, but a jealous teammate had goaded him on the field out of spite. Alexi had accidentally injured the guy during a high school state championship game, and it had completely crushed his spirit. Worse, his teammates were too scared to play or practice with him after the incident. It sucked big time.

"Jinx, you know my rule. I do not enter where I am not welcome," he said in his deep, accented voice, and I struggled not to giggle. Or melt. I had a thing for accents.

"I thought that only worked for vampires." I loved teasing the big marshmallow of a man. With a low bow, I said, "Enter freely and of your own will."

He chuckled and ducked as he came through the door, case of vodka in hand—his own creation, distilled to perfection and infused with an eclectic variety of sweet and savory flavors. I called dibs on the caramel batch and set him to bartending duty. Lacey came in next and sat down beside Mara. Those two had really hit it off. My roomies took their sweet ass time getting offline, but since they'd come through with the food, I forgave them. The boys lined our conference/goody table with baskets of chips interspersed with tiny bowls of fresh salsa and delectable queso. We'd snack on those before visiting the taco bar and hitting the booze.

Trinity arrived next, curls bouncing as she walked in like a boss in jeans and a T-shirt that read, "Black Girl Magic." In her case, it was literally true. She held the boss's book, *Compiled Grimoires of the Wicked and Wise*, in one hand and a plastic container filled with fresh guacamole in the other. It was official. She was my favorite teammate. She sat down, adjusted her glasses, and called the meeting to order. "Are we ready to get started?"

"Not yet." I hated to do it. She was better at calling meetings to order, and running meetings, and scheduling meetings—she really should be our manager. She was way better than me, except on the entertainment front. "We're waiting on the newest member of Demon Trackers R Us to arrive."

Mara and Lacey sighed in unison. Alexi's brows shot up, and Trinity pushed her glasses up her nose and steepled her fingers beneath her chin. "We have a new team member?" Her voice went a bit higher. She hated surprises.

Roice smirked. "You haven't heard? Jinx has less than five days and counting to find out who let a messenger demon lord through an unsecured portal and stop a demon lord from coming to earth from the hell realm. She needs all the help she can get."

Roice wore an army-green T-shirt that read, "I'm not always rude and sarcastic. Sometimes I'm asleep." I'd have to steal that one, too.

"I know that." Trinity gave him the side eye and heaved an impatient sigh. "What I don't know is why we have a new team member and who that team member is."

Boice flashed a smirk that matched his brother's—nothing like getting it in stereo—and said, "He's a consultant brought in from HQ. We've never tracked a demon lord, so they figured we needed backup. Or cleanup if we screw up. Oh, and he's also Jinx's ex."

That little shit. Of course he'd blab everything he knew. Tonight's T-shirt read, "In my defense, I was left unsupervised." How apropos.

"He's not my ex," I said, exasperated. "That would imply we dated. It didn't get that far." My demon bristled, too. What bug had crawled up her butt all of a sudden? I tried to subdue her with a few whispered incantations into my black mirror, but she still suffused my being with that strange mixture of anger, longing, and fear that had my head spinning and made my limbs twitch.

That was so embarrassing.

I reached for a shot glass and filled it with high-quality tequila purchased on my demon boss's tab, hoping the twin demons of technology and gossip would let it go. If my neck was on the line, I was for damned sure enjoying booze. I also hoped it would subdue my demon, or at the very least render my limbs less susceptible to Hannah's agitation.

Of course, my roomies didn't let it go. Roice shook his head and offered me a wide-eyed gaze of mock surprise. "Didn't he live in your closet when you were kids?"

Lacey choked on a mouthful of chips, eyes watering as she recovered. "That hot guy lived in your closet? I thought you said he wasn't taken."

I downed my shot, sucked on a delightfully sour slice of lime, and immediately poured another. "He did once live in my closet—long story

—and he's not taken. Not by me anyway." It killed me to say it. Thank God for tequila. Flirting by text aside, I had no claim on D.

Did I want a claim? I missed the friendship. Losing my best friend had left a gaping hole in my heart that I had never fully filled. And sure, I wanted his hot bod. Who wouldn't? But to be honest, I wanted much more than his body. I'd come to that uncomfortable realization during that tender little moment in his car last night. It brought back a lot of memories and stirred emotions I'd buried years ago. But I had too many abandonment issues, some of them thanks to him. I still couldn't trust him.

And lack of trust was a deal breaker for any kind of serious relationship, working or otherwise.

I did *not* want to have this conversation now. It would ruin my image as a crack-the-whip, hard-ass manager.

Mara walked over to me, eyeing me with a mixture of curiosity and not a little sympathy. Of course she understood my dilemma. No way she could've assumed the form of D without seeing into my mind and heart, knowing deep down I wanted and needed him. She took the tequila bottle out of my hand and settled it back on the bar, but not before I took another shot of liquid courage.

"We're not here to talk about Jinx's past relationships." Mara's sultry voice and gorgeous form cast a spell on the room. Her true form, or what I assumed was her true form, was beautiful, but in a strange, generic way like a Barbie doll but with reasonable proportions. It probably made it easier to assume the shape to fit her target's desires. "We're here to help her stop the demon lord Belial from starting a hell realm war."

She led me to the head of the table, her hand silky smooth in mine, and sat me down in the executive chair before filling a plate full of my favorite munchie combinations, with just the right ratio of chip to salsa, sour cream, and guacamole. Looked like she'd learned more about me than just my taste in men after our make out session.

"Wow, Mara." Heat crept over my face, and I squirmed. I wasn't used to being cared for. It was weird and more than a little uncomfortable. No worries. The alcohol would take care of that soon enough. "Thanks, but you don't have to serve me."

She laughed, the sound like an ancient, sensual melody. "It's the least I can do. You saved my life."

Roice and Boice had the decency to stop teasing me and sit down. Not that I minded anymore. With three shots of tequila and a near-empty stomach, I'd soon be feeling no pain. I'd just created the perfect bite of nachos when I realized everyone was staring at me.

"Wha?" I said, my mouth full.

Trinity rolled her eyes. "You're supposed to be holding a meeting."

"Oh, right." I wiped my hands on my napkin, dropping it twice before succeeding. "The meeting is now in session."

Lacey raised her hand. Seriously? How could she have a question when I'd just called the meeting to order? I thought about ignoring her, but Roice raised his hand, too. Naturally, his brother joined in. Trinity and Alexi were the only employees getting a gold star for behavior after this little gathering.

"Yes, Agent Green?" I used my official voice, as befitted my title as temporary boss lady.

"What about Dominic?"

"What about him?" I asked irritably. "He's late. He can catch up when he gets here."

A deep, accented voice chimed in. "Technically, you've started the meeting early. He has five more minutes."

Oh, right. I'd forgotten. Damned tequila. Okay, I would so not be giving Alexi a gold star now.

I sighed and rolled my eyes, making the room spin along with my head. Maybe that third shot had been a bad idea. I pulled out my mobile phone. Yup. Alexi was right. D had four and a half more minutes to show up. With a shrug, I stuffed another bite of tortilla chip paradise into my mouth, motioning for everyone else to dig in.

"Would anyone like some vodka?" Alexi asked, hopeful. The only thing the man took any obvious pride in was his homemade hooch. It was a very healthy step toward self-confidence.

Mara flashed him a brilliant smile. "I would love some."

Alexi blushed, clearly awestruck by the succubus. She was a knockout, of course. But it was more than simply lust or longing. Alexi's smile held genuine gratitude. He'd appreciated the courtesy. Poor guy didn't get much appreciation, or he hadn't until he'd joined our demon-hunting gang.

I'd have to think on the complexities of human-demon relations later. When I was sober. And when a demon lord wasn't out to get me.

A knock sounded at the door about a minute after the meeting had been set to begin, bringing me out of my daydream and back to the staff meeting I was supposed to be running. I needed to get a grip. Lives were at stake—namely mine, not to mention my family's. Lacey and Mara practically fell over themselves in a fight to answer the door, but I beat them to it. Barely. I was having a little trouble walking. I opened the door and looked up into the face of the demon boy I'd once saved and who'd saved me in turn, before he left.

D had grown into quite the man, but I caught a glimpse of the frightened, lost boy he'd once been. Maybe it was the tequila, or maybe it was the realization that most of my memories of him had been good. In point of fact, they were the best memories I had.

"Where have you been?" I asked in a small voice. That was the alcohol talking. Not my wounded heart.

He smiled and then leveled an intense gaze on me as if reading my thoughts. I'd never been so acutely aware of my heartbeat, the quickness of my breath, or my weakened knees. I didn't get weak in the knees. I wasn't that kind of girl.

Except, apparently, with D.

He took my hand and gave me a look of such sincerity, laced with agony and yearning I didn't understand or quite believe, that I had to look away. He put two fingers under my chin and forced me to meet his gaze.

"I'm sorry I'm late." I didn't think he was just talking about the meeting.

He clearly wanted to say more, but my butthead roommates had to go and spoil the moment by yelling, "About time," and "Don't company rules apply to consultants?"

After making a mental note to have Trinity change the Wi-Fi password without telling them, I turned and said, "Everyone, this is Dominic, our consultant. Dominic, this is everyone. You've met Mara and Lacey Green. The big guy over there is Alexi Volkov. He's one hell of a demon tracker and a pretty decent bartender."

Alexi blushed, and I felt bad for about a nanosecond. Then I remembered that one of my missions in life was to get Alexi to see what a great human being he was. I'd probably have to beat him over the head before he believed it, but I wasn't above desperate measures.

I pointed to Trinity and said, "That's Trinity Jones. She's the brains behind the operation—knows demon languages, customs, and demon law." Trinity smiled. She knew herself and her worth, and I was glad of it, but I also made a point of giving credit where credit was due.

Rolling my eyes and gesturing to the twin asshats with whom I lived, I said, "And these clowns are Roice and Boice. They're the techies."

Dominic eyed them curiously. "You're both pure demons."

Roice nodded, giving him a once-over. "Takes one to know one."

Dominic smirked. "I've heard of you guys. Did you really cause the Great Northeast blackout of '65?"

Boice smiled. "Yup. And the NYC blackout of '77—"

"And the Northeast 2003," Roice added.

"Yes, yes, and proud we all are of your ninja level pranks." I cut them off before they really got on a roll. They were a little too proud of their work. "Now that we're all here, I'm calling this meeting to order."

Settling back at the head of the conference table, I kept an eye on D while running down what I'd gotten from Murkowski, as well as what Lacey and I had learned from Cooper the summoner. Judging from the size of the plate he filled, D's appetite was still healthy. He gave Alexi two thumbs-up after sampling the vodka and took his seat next to Mara.

My fists clenched, and something thick seemed to lodge itself in my throat. They sat too close, and Mara's hand was too close to D's leg when she leaned forward.

Clearing my throat, I said, "We know which portal Mephisto used, we know at least one summoner who helped thanks to Dominic, and we know there's at least one other entity who helped, and she's likely a human woman since she was able to cross the threshold to Cooper's portal and disable his guard dog. There may be two, or more. What do we have on Belial?" I asked.

The twins turned their gazes to Trinity. They'd all been working on research, but naturally made her their spokeswoman. Smart move. She was the only tracker in the group who'd acquired the assistance of a demon voluntarily. After summoning Fidria the Unknowable during an advanced ritual—she'd done her homework and nailed the rites and incantations—she'd negotiated with the powerful demon keeper of knowledge to teach her all about the hell realm. He'd been so impressed by her scholarly drive and tenacity that he'd sent her a personal demon to assist in her studies.

That immaterial demon had become her personal spirit guide and made her the envy of every demon tracker, summoner, and hell realm visitor to the earth realm.

Yeah, she was that good. I just wondered about the price she'd had to pay for such a valuable resource. Demons didn't work for free.

Clearing her throat, Trinity began what would no doubt be a lengthy dissertation on the demon lord.

That woman loved to lecture.

"Belial, also known as Belhor or Beliar among other names, is known as the Wicked One in Hebrew texts and is often confused with Satan. He's not, actually." She looked around the table, probably to make sure we were engaged and paying attention. She was such a good speaker. I should really take notes.

Then again, it was much easier stealing notes from my roomies.

"He's neither the absolute nor a primal emanation, but he is a powerful lord in the hell realm."

That was reassuring. Primal emanations were supposedly capable of unleashing hell on earth with the demonic magic. On a scale of biblical plagues to natural disasters on steroids, these demons made tempters look like garden gnomes. They'd been banished from the earth realm long ago after a truce between the hell realm and celestial realm and were most definitely not allowed to travel to earth through portals, or so we'd been told by the boss and Barbatos.

The absolute, big baddy Lucifer himself was a myth as far as any of us demon-hunters knew. Good thing, since demon lords were more than bad enough.

I nodded and Trinity continued. "He's painted by Milton and The Bible as the evil demon of lies, but character assassinations aside, he did lead a war against the Sons of Light—angels, or more accurately, residents of the celestial realm—by the Sons of Darkness."

Boice snorted, no doubt testy about the reputation of his fellow demons. "Can we skip the bullshit and get to the part that matters?"

Trinity gave him a stare that reminded me a little too much of my third-grade teacher, who was, in fact, demon possessed. "Don't get your panties in a wad, B. Background first."

Roice grumbled, "Fucking angels wrote the history books as propaganda. And they accuse us of lying."

I sighed, hating to do it, but... "I'm going to have to agree with Boice, just this once. Can we get to the part about why he wants to steal Hannah and recruit me for his latest round of hell realm war games?"

Trinity gave me a similar look, but then, after a few eye rolls, she shuffled her stack of notes and got to the good part. A flash of red shone in her gaze before she spoke. Her personal demon assistant was in on the research too. "After a long and illustrious career as a hell realm general, he got into politics. Nothing unusual there, but he apparently ran afoul of Duke Astaroth, another powerful hell realm leader, which led to his first failed hell realm rebellion a few millennia ago."

Wow. I totally needed to incorporate words like *afoul* into my vocabulary. It sounded impressive.

D surprised me by speaking up. "What got him in trouble with Astaroth?" His voice was low and guttural, almost a growl.

A great question, but the way D asked it gave me pause. Why was he so interested in the history of this demon lord? I made a mental note to follow up on that observation later.

Trinity beamed at him, giving her hair a little flip. Yeah, she wasn't immune to D's charms, either, though I suspected she was more impressed with his question. She loved being the professor.

"Aside from being a rival for power in the hell realm, Astaroth is said to have taken issue with Belial's skill with magic. Much more powerful than the kind used by ordinary citizens of the hell realm or tempters who still inhabit earth. Rumor had it he was dabbling in the kind of magic known only to primal emanations. Naturally, rival demon lords wanted to stop him—or steal his magic for their own use. It seemed to be your garden-variety demon pissing contest on the surface, but I dug a little deeper and found something more interesting."

I liked interesting, especially when "interesting" could help me save my family, not to mention my own neck.

Trinity paused as everyone sat on the edges of their seats in rapt anticipation. Except for Roice. I swear that demon boy had the attention span of a gnat. I threw a wadded-up tortilla wrapper at him to get his attention. Did I know how to hold a meeting or what?

"Hey." He rubbed his head and scowled at me. I'd nailed him right between the eyes.

"Two points for Jinx." I prepared another tortilla wrapper ball in case I had to go for round two. "Next time I'll hit you with a Molotov cocktail. We're talking about my life here."

Lacey snorted. "Your staff meetings are much more fun than the usual."

"Open bar, babe," I said, taking a little bow as best I could while seated. I nearly fell out of my chair.

"Perhaps you should switch to water," Alexi suggested.

"No way." I poured another shot from the bottle I'd secretly stashed under the table. "I need this for medicinal purposes. It's helping with the whole anxiety over my impending doom thing."

"Anyway," Trinity said, loudly. "As I was saying, I found something interesting after reviewing the grimoire and a few other sources my demon brought from the hell realm. It seems Belial was less rebel and more reformer, depending on whose side you're on. He wanted to improve relations with the earth realm and celestial realm, set the record straight on demon culture and history, that sort of thing."

"Amen to that," Boice muttered.

"But wait. There's more." Trinity held up an index finger. "There are others who claim that the reformation angle was a ruse to gain more power and renew war with the celestial realm. Once he amassed enough demon magic and power, he planned to attack. Other accounts suggest he was dabbling in celestial magic. It would have given him advantage in negotiations or battle."

That *was* interesting, but still didn't explain his interest in me.

"Which account is accurate? And what does any of it have to do with me?"

Trinity smiled. I would be getting a gold star, too. "It may not be one or the other. He could want both. As far as where you come in, I have a couple of theories, but nothing solid."

I spread my hands wide and spun in my chair. Spinning was a mistake. After I stopped seeing double, I said, "I'm all ears, girlfriend."

She scowled, clicking her nails on the table and waiting. For what, I had no idea. I was paying attention.

"Don't ever call me girlfriend again."

Oops. I'd meant it as a term of endearment, affection even. "My apologies," I said. "I'd be most interested in hearing any theories you have to offer, my esteemed colleague."

D seemed to be interested as well. He leaned forward in his seat, hands on the table and fierce gaze fixed on Trinity. Boice remained interested, too, and no wonder. I wouldn't be surprised if he left us to join Belial's rebellion. Anything in the name of fighting negative demon species stereotypes.

I wasn't unsympathetic. I just had bigger fish to fry.

Trinity said, "Your personal demon has a long-standing relationship with you. She's been in the earth realm for long enough to have plenty of experience with modern humans—something Belial might find of value if he wants to open formal relations with humanity and recruit allies against the celestial realm. That's one possibility."

I didn't buy it. Plenty of tempters had been around earth for much longer. They'd be easier to recruit or manipulate. They'd also be easier to reach and control than Hannah.

"Another possibility is your demon's power," Trinity said. "We don't know what she is, but we know some of what she can do. Any general would find those skills valuable. She might be an untapped well of demon magic. It fits with what Mephisto said about you not knowing what you had within you. Maybe Hannah is some sort of weapon or power source."

"So he wants Hannah and not me." It made sense. Mephisto had tried to separate us, to pull Hannah away from me. And in spite of my intrinsic coolness and great ass, I didn't have any superpowers that might attract the attention of a demon lord. A few combat skills? Sure. Demon-level combat skills without Hannah? Not so much.

Except for that strange power that had bubbled up from somewhere inside me back in the alley and in the boss's office, but I didn't even know what it was, let alone how to control it.

Trinity studied me. "Don't underestimate yourself," she said. "We don't know everything about you, either. Most humans couldn't host such a powerful demon for so long and live to tell the tale. It's practically unheard of. Most long-term possessions end with the demon consuming the human host's soul, or with the demon wasting away if it refuses to feed, which is rare. There's clearly something about you and your relationship with Hannah that's helped you survive, thrive even, while hosting a demon."

And there it was. The elephant in the room, the one I didn't like to talk about. Hannah had come to me as a child. I always assumed I'd been born bad. I'd survived, thrived even, making me a great host. Did that confirm it, my worst fear?

I was evil. Something about me was wrong, twisted, and wicked enough to deserve a demon as horrible and powerful as Hannah.

I didn't voice the thought aloud, mostly because I didn't want to set Boice off on a tirade against demon speciesism. I knew they weren't all bad, just like I'd always figured angels, aka celestial realm citizens, weren't all good. Of course, I'd never actually met a celestial. They didn't deign to associate with demon hunters. But still, tempter demons always targeted humans who suffered from some major character flaw. Lacey's demon had targeted her on account of a compulsion to shoplift, and Murkowski had a gambling problem. Mara inspired and fed on lust, like others of her kind.

While Boice and Roice had no hosts, their mischief and mayhem came from stirring the pot of human greed, anger, and envy, while other demons had a taste for pride, despair, and sloth. The seven deadly sins were real, and it helped tempters gain access to vulnerable hosts and targets.

What about powerful demons and their hosts?

And what was my sin?

To deflect, I giggled and asked, "Does this mean I'm the chosen one?" That would be so cool. "I don't have a scar or anything, but I could use a badass wand to defeat an evil wizard."

Lacey groaned along with my roomies while Alexi looked confused. D didn't react, but he'd been gone for a while. I'd give him a pass on pop culture references.

"You're too old to be the chosen one. How about you go on a side quest for sobriety first?" Boice said, high-fiving his twin.

Whatever. I wasn't drunk. I could hold my liquor like nobody's business.

And I was young at heart, damn it. Why was it always some teenager who got to save the world? Why not an almost-thirty career woman who worked for clandestine supernatural police forces?

"What about Alexi?" I said, pleased with my flash of brilliance in the midst of intoxication. "He's been inhabited by his demon a long time." I turned to face my colleague. "How old are you?"

He ducked his head. "I'm thirty, but I have only carried the demon since I was fifteen. The wolf is...different. He has more compatibility with people than other demons. Those who are afflicted can live as long as normal humans, if not as happily."

My heart broke a little more for Alexi. After losing control of his wolf demon back in high school, he'd become a hermit. When the boss found and recruited him, he was withdrawn and depressed, convinced no one was safe around him. At least the boss had given him the tools and skills to better control the wolf.

He'd done nothing to deserve his fate. His horrible Russian mafia thug father had cursed him with the wolf demon. If I lived through this, I swore I'd find a way to help the guy. He deserved a shot at happiness.

"I'll see what else I can dig up on Belial with your roomies," Trinity said, ignoring both my excellent suggestion and the twins' snark. That lady was all business. "The boss's grimoire is missing several pages, and my demon guide hasn't worked out how to fill in the gaps."

"What?" I did fall out of my chair then, but a rush of adrenaline and anger had me on my feet and ready to rumble. "That sneaky bastard. He tricked me." Of course he had. Freakin' demon.

For once, Boice didn't automatically rush to the defense of his fellow demon, and the rest of the team seemed to share my outrage. Still, I could've kicked myself. I should've checked the book before leaving HQ. I should've been more specific about terms and conditions while negotiating with the boss. I should've seen this one coming.

I flopped into my chair and put my head in my hands. Trinity's voice snapped me back to attention. "It's a setback. Shake it off. We'll find a work-around."

I jerked my head up, a move I regretted as soon as my gorge rose. When had the room started spinning? It took a minute, but once Trinity's face came back into focus, I met her gaze. She smiled and said, "And you're forgetting one thing."

"What's that?" I had a sneaking suspicion she wasn't going to confirm my status as the chosen one, but I held out hope.

"What you did to break free of the boss's hold, when you were trying to save Mara. Hannah didn't help you with that, did she?"

"No, she didn't." I'd known the power I'd manifested was not something from Hannah or the demon realm, but I'd been a little too preoccupied with the case to consider the implications. It could come in handy if and when I could call it to my service, since it had already helped me to stand up to BBB, had allowed me to keep Hannah from being ripped out of me, and had kept Mara from bolting. "That was pretty badass, right?"

"I've never seen or felt anything like it." Mara spoke, her sexy voice filled with awe and wonder. "It was some sort of magic and powerful. Have you done anything like that before?"

"Not really." But then I remembered something. One night just before the boss found me and we'd struck the bargain that gave me control of Hannah, work as a demon hunter, and get help looking for D, I had lost control of Hannah.

It was the night I'd lost D.

In a rush of panic, I'd been gripped by a sudden surge of power that had scared me almost as much as Hannah's rage. It helped me regain control and bury her so deep into my subconscious, it had taken the boss to coax her back out. When he pulled her back to the surface, she had no memory of what she'd done, or maybe what we'd done. Since I'd never managed anything like that again, I hadn't given it much thought.

"Wait," I said, deciding to share with the class. "Once, when I was younger and lost control of Hannah, I got the same feeling and...power surge, for lack of a better description. It put me back in the driver's seat then, and I kind of, sort of think it helped me keep her from being nabbed by Mephisto last night. What does it mean? Do you think it has something to do with Belial's interest in me?"

"It might. I don't know yet, but I'll find out." Trinity had that hungry look in her eyes. She loved nothing more than a fact-finding mission, a reason to expand her vast knowledge of demons and their ways.

"I'll keep working the summoner angle and reviewing video and magical surveillance from the portal," Lacey said. "If we can figure out who's working with the summoner and with Mephisto, maybe we can find out who else is in on this. I'm sure this demon lord has a backup plan to get you and your demon into the hell realm."

I gulped, suddenly nauseated, and not just from the shots. "Good call. Thanks."

Turning to Alexi, I said, "Would you mind keeping an eye on my family? If things go south, I'll need to move them to a safe location. I'll give you the details later."

Alexi smiled, glowing as if lit from within. "I am honored that you trust me with your family's protection. I will do all in my power to keep them safe."

"As will I," D said. Of course he would. He'd grown fond of my mom and sister while hiding out in my childhood home, protecting all of us from the nastier supernatural forces most humans didn't know about. Looked as if he'd appointed himself our protector once more.

I gave both gorgeous guys on my team a bright smile and then remembered my conversation with D from earlier. "Hey, what happened with that summoner you interrogated?"

D flashed a wicked grin. "I locked him up in a warded safe house and told him I'd be back for round two of Q and A tonight. A couple of associates are guarding him. I've sent Lacey what I've got so far. I couldn't get him to share the identity of the woman who approached Murkowski. Yet. But he will."

The way he said "yet" made me shiver. It was easy to forget what he was sometimes. I wasn't sure if that was a good thing or a bad thing. I was glad he was on my side.

"We can check out his known associates and ties to the demon realm," Lacey said. "Text me the address, and I'll ask Simon to try to get more information out of him."

D fired off a text to Lacey, and Lacey fiddled with her phone while we reviewed other open cases and demon hunter business. Research, she said. She wasn't fooling anyone. Online shopping, most likely, or one of those time-suck game apps. Gen Z was not sly.

"Well, I'd say that's great progress." I was just about to adjourn the formal meeting in favor of dinner when Trinity spoke again.

"You're forgetting something else. Your demon. She let Mephisto go, and if she's part of what Belial wants, we need to know why she let him go and what he told her."

No kidding. I hadn't forgotten. Hannah was just refusing to cooperate.

"Yeah, about that," I said, taking another shot. "Hannah and I aren't exactly on speaking terms right now. And she wouldn't give up anything about Mephisto to the boss. Not sure she'll do it for me."

Trinity gave me a glare that could bring a dragon demon to its knees.

"What? I've been trying, I swear." Geez, first I was the chosen one, then I wasn't because of ageism, then I might have had some awesome extra mojo that has nothing to do with my demon, and apparently, I was the hell realm's most wanted military recruit? It was enough to make my head spin. Damn it, I needed more brain space or a clone to figure this stuff out. "I begged her to spill the deets about Mephisto, but she won't do it. She says it's not safe for me to know yet, or that I'll figure it out in time —something like that. It's all very confusing. I think I need some diagrams."

Trinity leaned back and gave me a look that seemed a tad judgmental. "Well, you'd better get on speaking terms fast. You've got four more days to solve this case. I'd suggest you get started."

D, who'd been glancing at his phone, jumped up fast enough to knock over his chair and said, "Son of a bitch!"

"What?" I asked, head spinning. I wasn't sure how much more I could take.

"The guards I set to keep an eye on the summoner just texted. Summoner's gone. Bastard got out of the safe house.

Double fuck.

CHAPTER FIFTEEN

We'd driven around until the wee hours of the morning, every pothole, sharp turn, and sudden acceleration ricocheting through my inebriated brain until my skull pounded with the mother of all headaches. I wasn't sure how D was tracking Keith Pendergrass, aka shady summoner serving the scum of the demon realm underbelly, who'd managed to get away. All I knew was his attempts at reenacting *The Fast and The Furious 18* hadn't gotten us anywhere so far.

"Pull over," I said as inspiration struck.

"Are you going to throw up?" D was probably more concerned about his leather interior than the state of my stomach, but he complied.

I opened the door and tried to step out, but a tight band across my chest stopped me.

Damned seat belt.

I extracted myself and stumbled onto the sidewalk, begging Hannah to give me a little more coordination than I could manage on my own. I normally held my liquor better than this, but that was Hannah's doing. She wasn't deigning to help me tonight. There was little in the way of traffic in midtown at the hour, and the streetlights illuminated one of the city's green spots in the middle of the urban sprawl. My destination sat in the middle of the large park, and I focused on putting one foot in front of the other to get there.

A hand landed on my shoulder and spun me around.

"Hey, stop manhandling me." I pushed at D's chest in an effort to get away. "Don't make me pull my knife on you."

"I don't know where you think you're going, but you aren't going alone. Stay here and wait until I park the car."

He waited for me to nod before heading back to the muscle car and getting in. Once he'd turned into the park's entrance, I sprinted across the grass and over a few demons disguised as homeless humans as I headed for the large building ahead. Its thick columns and stone roof, a throwback to a long-ago time and faraway land but somehow fit the eclectic Nashville cityscape. The near-perfect replica of the Parthenon was also a hotbed of paranormal activity of the demon variety.

There was a demon bar hidden beneath it. If I was a summoner on the run, I might look for a place to hide among the patrons of this shady establishment, particularly if Mephisto or Belial had allies in the local community. Or maybe some of the locals could give me some intel.

While I considered waiting for D, I figured it couldn't hurt to go in and see if any of my contacts had some information. Climbing the steps, I scanned the columns for a glowing sigil marking the entrance to the bar. After two tries, I finally got my hands in the right position and muttered the incantation that opened the hidden door. With a deep breath, I stepped inside and fell.

Once I landed in the underground chamber, I pulled myself up, dusted off my ass, and made my way down the musty tunnel. A few demons loitered in the nooks and crannies, their glowing eyes watching my every move. Hunters weren't popular here for obvious reasons, but as long as they didn't make a move against me, I'd be happy to leave well enough alone.

But I kept my hand on the hilt of my knife just in case.

I followed the glow of neon that illuminated a sign reading "The

Hellbound." The entrance to the bar was a stone boulder guarded by a burly, winged demon roughly the size of a linebacker.

He took one look at me and said, "No."

I sized him up and crossed my arms, sighing internally. Why was it always a pissing contest with these clowns? "Mishkinis, I'm not in the mood for your bullshit tonight. Let me in."

"No."

Leshy demons made excellent guards, and this particular import from Eastern Europe took his job seriously. Last time I'd seen him, he'd been working as a bouncer in the human world. Like Mara, he could shape-shift and blend. Maybe he was moonlighting at The Hellbound, but I suspected he'd lost his job after use of excessive force. Impulse control wasn't his strong suit.

"Dude, I'm not after any of your buddies. I'm looking for a loose cannon summoner who's been letting unauthorized big baddies through his portal. Know anything about that?"

He snorted, but the slight flicker in his glamour told me I was on the right track. I needed to get in that bar, but I didn't want to get Mishkinis in trouble. I liked the guy. Plus, I owed his wife a favor. She'd helped me catch a bog beast demon off the Natchez Trace and let me keep the bounty.

Without warning, I lunged forward and slapped the flat of my blade against the leshy's arm. He howled and threw a punch, but only caught air as I ducked and slid underneath him. I got in a few good slices as I went, weakening the demon, but it wasn't enough. He spun and flung himself on me, his weight crushing and immobilizing.

If that wasn't enough, the stench of the creature was almost enough to make me lose my tacos.

Mustering my training, I went limp and pretended to be unconscious. After an agonizing few moments, Mishkinis slowly lifted his bulk off me. Using scent and sound, I formed an image in my mind of the demon, the location of his buff arms, and the vulnerable spot at his throat. This would take finesse since I didn't want to kill him. When he exhaled, I struck, slicing a thin line from his chin to his collarbone that made him fall backward. Struggling against aching ribs, I straddled the demon and slammed the hilt of my knife against his thick skull, knocking him unconscious.

"Sorry," I panted. "Nothing personal."

Standing on shaking legs, I did my best to wipe off the dust and grime covering my clothes and slipped into the bar.

Aside from a collection of horned, scaly, and tailed demons, the bar resembled a standard earth establishment. I slid into a booth near the door and did a scan of the room. A vamp or two stood out in the crowd, but they weren't my jurisdiction. At a nearby pool table, a winged man with bright blond hair, a hooked nose, and a wicked smile flirted with a petite woman who, despite her unassuming appearance, radiated power. She struck the cue ball and sank three solids, earning a high five and smoldering kiss from the winged man. Elemental Fae. Generally not a problem. An incubus sat at the granite-topped bar nursing what looked like a champagne cocktail. When he caught my eye, his glamour shifted, and he turned into D's doppelgänger.

I giggled but shook my head no. Not looking for a date tonight. Some of the bar's other supernatural patrons could hook up with an incubus and walk away relatively unscathed, but I had too much human in my lineage to risk it.

The laughter in my throat died when the real D appeared out of nowhere and slid into the booth across from me, expression murderous.

"You should smile," I said brightly. I pointed at the incubus. "See, he's really pretty when he smiles."

"Is this a joke to you?" Mr. Grumpy's jaw was clenched so tight he'd probably crack his back molars. Hopefully consulting came with a good dental plan.

"No, obviously not. I had to wrestle a leshy to get in. I'm trying to find the summoner." I'd been super helpful on the drive over, too, asking D where he'd last seen the summoner and if he'd checked his pockets. Then I might or might not have asked if I could check his pockets for him.

Sadly, he hadn't let me.

I didn't think he'd let me anytime soon. "Damn it, Jane. I told you to wait. We're supposed to be working together."

"We are," I said distractedly. I'd spotted what looked like a human in the middle of a cluster of imps. "Any sign of this Pendergrass guy?"

"Yeah, he's here, and I'm going after him. You stay put."

He stood, glaring at me in warning. I supposed I deserved it, but it still pissed me off. I'd been taking care of myself for a long time and didn't need an unreliable demon babysitter.

The bar went quiet. Uh-oh. We'd been made, or rather, D had been made. A pure-blooded, powerful demon of the nontempter variety tended to attract attention.

The incubus, who must have thought better of glamouring himself to seduce D, grabbed his drink and disappeared into the shadows. The imps parted and left the hapless human exposed to D's scrutiny. The bartender, a tall, handsome-from-the-waist-up satyr, stepped between D and the human, his cloven hooves echoing through the eerily quiet bar.

"We don't want trouble here." The satyr lowered his head, horns gleaming in the low light and breath coming in snorts. For a guy who didn't want trouble, he seemed ready to charge like a raging bull.

"Then you shouldn't be sheltering wanted criminals," D said, fists clenched and stance wide.

"Warrant?" the satyr said.

D growled. "There's been an APB out on him for hours. It's been broadcast. Try to keep up."

I was going to choke on the testosterone cloud.

And Pendergrass was slinking away. I spotted him stepping behind the bar, and while the demon versus satyr stare down commenced, the little sneak pushed through the door to the kitchen. Right. My turn. I ran across the bar and jumped over the granite top...sort of. I might not have stuck the landing, but I was still a wee bit intoxicated.

Pushing through the swinging door, I entered the kitchen, startling a couple of ghouls cooking some kind of mystery meat best left a mystery. "Which way did he go?"

The ghouls pointed to the freezer, which was weird. Why would

Pendergrass go in the freezer? Trap doors and hidden exits could be anywhere. I dashed through the kitchen and threw open the freezer door. Pendergrass was pushing against the back wall, presumably the hidden door, and it cracked open. I pulled out my knife and leapt on his back, planning to immobilize him by holding the knife to his throat.

He wasn't a demon, but in my experience, anything with a pulse stopped with a knife to the throat.

"Let me go, woman," he said.

I laughed. "Not a chance in hell. I've got a few questions for you."

He yanked the door and slammed me against the wall beside it, clocking my noggin, but I held on, jabbing the knife into the tender flesh of his neck. He stilled once more as I twisted the knife. Just a little. Just hard enough to let him know I meant business.

"You've been a naughty boy, Keith. Word on the street is you let a big, bad, nasty demon through your portal. I want to know where Mephisto is, if you let a demon lord named Belial onto this plane, and any other unauthorized activities you've been up to."

He stiffened. Good. He should be afraid. Dealing with dangerous demon lords and smuggling schemes was tricky, and he was just as likely to be torn apart by the demon he summoned as he was by the boss when I dragged his ass back to HQ.

"You Jane McGee?" he asked, muscles twitching.

I twisted my knife a little. "I'm asking the questions here. Did you summon Mephisto?"

He grunted and struggled harder against my hold.

"I'll take that as a yes. Makes my job a lot easier."

Pendergrass twisted, and something closed around my wrist, burning my skin with white-hot agony. I held on, stabbing at any part of his body I could hit. I scored a few hits, but not enough. He flung me off and then dragged me by my wrist as he pushed at the hidden door. Hannah stirred within me, but I couldn't reach my black mirror to summon her.

I tried to call on whatever power allowed me to defeat Mephisto when we first met, as well as bargain with the boss, but it didn't come. Figured. I'd have to do this the old-fashioned way. Gritting my teeth so I wouldn't howl in pain, I threw my body back and used my weight to jerk Pendergrass away from the wall.

As Pendergrass stumbled, I saw what was holding me—some kind of glowing handcuff-like contraption powered by sigils. The other cuff was attached to the summoner's wrist. Where had the bastard gotten that kind of demon magic? The only magic summoners were supposed to have was the kind that for creating portals. It tended to run in families, and back before regulation, summoners used it to bring demons over to do their bidding. For a price.

These days, no souls had to be exchanged, and the only thing a demon had to promise was to behave while on earth and register with the network of demon-monitoring agencies scattered across the globe. This was higher-level magic, likely provided by Mephisto or the demon lord he served.

It didn't matter. I had to keep the bastard from dragging me out of the bar and to a secondary location. I wasn't a damsel in distress. I was a demon hunter.

I slashed my knife at the cuff, but it didn't make so much as a scratch. Switching tactics, I twisted and moved behind Keith, putting my full weight into pulling on the magical cuffs. A sick pop and gasp of pain told me I'd pulled the bastard's arm out of his socket.

"Let go, or I'll pull your arm off."

Keith muttered another incantation I didn't understand. The cuff disappeared, but not before it sliced my wrist. I collapsed to the ground, bereft, as if someone had ripped my soul right out of my body.

He couldn't do that, could he?

Keith made a grab for me, but something burst through the freezer door like a whirlwind and slammed into him. It was D. He and the summoner tumbled into the darkness beyond the hidden door. I stayed put, exhausted and probably going into shock, which made no sense. I'd had worse fights. The only thing I could do was place my knife against the black mirror around my neck and give Hannah a taste of the summoner's blood. She could track him. Eventually.

But she didn't respond. I couldn't believe it. Of all the times to leave me high and dry.

That was my last thought before I closed my eyes. Then, the world went dark.

CHAPTER SIXTEEN

Things were obviously a bit fuzzy after I recovered from passing out. We'd made it back home, and D had tended to my wounds before tucking me into bed. He'd given me another demon potion that probably had some sort of sedative in it to help me sleep.

It worked, but a little too well. I woke up around two in the afternoon feeling well and truly hung over. Crap. I'd wasted half a day. I only had three days left to figure out how Mephisto got here, secure the portal and summoners who helped, and avoid being dragged to the hell realm for mandatory military service.

Three days until the boss came to claim my soul before going after my family. Alexi had been keeping tabs on them and had some of his demon informants trailing them as well. If I didn't make decent progress today, I'd have to have Alexi grab them, haul them to my safe house, and guard them until I found a get-out-of-a-soul-bargain-free card. Those things were hard to come by.

I rolled over and ducked back under the covers. I needed to get moving, but between my throbbing head and lead-weighted limbs, it just didn't seem to be an option. How pathetic was that? I'd fought through a lifetime of demonic possession, bad luck, the loss of my best friend and would-be boyfriend, and the hell of combat training for demon-tracking fieldwork, only to be taken down by an evil little bastard named Jose Cuervo.

Come to think of it, maybe I could make it through hell realm militia basic training. But I didn't want to. Once had been more than enough.

But with all that truly excellent motivation, I couldn't seem to lift my head from the pillow. What was wrong with me? The feeling reminded me of surgery, or what I'd heard about it. Thanks to Hannah, I rarely got sick. Injured? Oh yeah, but I couldn't remember the last time I had a cold, let alone a hangover. Hannah always healed my injuries, and I assumed she kept my body, the body she shared with me, healthy. But the fatigue and malaise plaguing me was what I imagined coming out of anesthesia in a thick fog of dread was like, missing a part of myself that had been removed.

The delectable scents of coffee and bacon distracted me.

The glorious aromas traveled from my nose to some deep-seated part of my brain that contained my center, the core of my being, my purpose. If portals were the gateway to the hell realm, bacon was the gateway to heaven—or at least to getting my ass out of bed and into action.

I rose with extreme caution and shuffled toward the aroma of my salvation, practically drooling in anticipation. Or maybe that was just the horrendous taste in my mouth. It was a toss-up. Mara must've made breakfast. It certainly wasn't the twins. If anything, they'd probably taken pictures of my incapacitated ass in compromising positions and posted them all over social media. It was kind of their thing.

When I made it to the kitchen, the sight that greeted me left me breathless and made my heart melt in a puddle of sticky goo.

D stood in the kitchen—my kitchen—his long, lean torso draped over my counter as he sipped a cup of coffee and read a book. He was reading a book, in my kitchen, and it was so ordinary yet completely amazing and—

"Holy guacamole, where's your shirt?"

D looked up and flashed me a wicked grin. Oh my God, between sleep mussed hair, a way past five-o'clock shadow, and sinfully charming smile, I must have died and gone to bad girl heaven.

Wait, was that a contradiction?

"Sorry." He said it, but he didn't mean it. "Didn't mean to scandalize you. Should I go get decent?"

He took a slow sip of coffee as I stood and stared in awe, mesmerized by how he savored his morning cup of joe as it slipped past his lips, and he swallowed it down the column of his throat. He licked his lips and winked before standing up to his full height, giving me an eyeful of broad chest that tapered down to mouthwatering abs and a trim waist, an enticing trail of dark hair drawing my gaze and daring it to slip down to drink in the bulge below the waistline of pajama bottoms.

He looked like a dream. I, no doubt, looked like a hot mess. And I still felt weird and not quite myself. Had I killed essential brain cells by keeping company with my dear friend tequila? Maybe it had been wrestling with a summoner who used demon magic to whammy my ass. I searched for Hannah's presence in my subconscious, but all I got back was silence. I decided to let her be for now since she seemed content to either be incommunicado or as cryptic as a prophecy from Nostradamus when she bothered to talk to me.

Dropping my gaze, I pushed a lock of tangled hair behind my ear. "No, you're fine. I should probably go freshen up. Still mad at me for jumping the gun and going after Pendergrass without you?"

How humiliating. I normally had no shame, but where D was concerned, I'd apparently hit the mother lode.

I didn't dare look up, not even when he moved to stand in front of me, giving me a great view of his bare feet. I was surprised, though I shouldn't have been. No gnarly toenails for this guy. He was too perfect.

"Jane, look at me." His voice was soft, kind, unlike last night when he'd dragged me out of my apartment to go on the hunt. Fierce and gentle by turns, just as he had been when we were growing up.

But could I trust him? Could I trust myself around him? Not likely. He already had me dripping with lust. No big deal there. I'd appreciated men and the amazing things they could do for a woman's body since

Mikey McFarrin had given me the first big O I'd ever received from someone other than myself. That boy had magic hands. I had no doubt D would rock my world in bed, in the shower, on my sofa, against a wall...

I really needed to get a grip.

It wasn't fear of the physical that had me ready to bolt. I'd hit that in a heartbeat. No, the problem was D and I had a history. There was too much between us for anything to be simply physical, and I didn't relish the thought of having my heart trampled beneath his beautiful feet.

"Jane." He whispered my name again, coaxing me to meet his gaze. He ran a finger down my temple and along my jaw, his touch leaving a trail of fire in its wake. I had no choice but to look at him. He was so close I could feel the heat of his body wafting over me along with his scent. He'd been in the shower and smelled of something warm, spicy, and sensual. I wanted to lick his damp skin, to savor him like smooth whiskey.

"I'm not mad, not anymore. Wish you'd work with me and let me watch your back, but I get it. You've got trust issues. So do I. But one thing hasn't changed. You are the most beautiful thing I've ever seen. Always have been, always will be. You're the only thing that's kept me alive the last ten years."

Wow, talk about silver-tongued devils. That was possibly the most heart-melting praise I'd ever received. I wanted to believe him, but that was laying it on pretty thick.

"Where've you been for the past ten years?" I straightened, jutting out my chin and channeling my inner wronged woman. "Someplace without phones? Mail? Passenger pigeon service?"

He sighed and looked away. I'd have called it guilt, but it seemed more like pain.

Or shame.

No, he was that lonely, frightened demon boy in my closet again, hungry and lost and looking for a home. So much for wronged woman outrage and bravado.

"D." It was my turn to reach out to him. I cupped his stubbled jaw with a shaking palm. He leaned into my touch, placing his large, warm hand over mine and making me dizzy with his closeness. "What happened to you? Something bad?"

He stiffened when I asked the second question, and his gaze met mine again, hard and distant. "I was summoned to the hell realm and bound by a demon lord," he said. "Couldn't get away until I came into my full power. I couldn't answer when you tried to summon me all those times over the years. I really wanted to."

The boss had been way off about D then, assuming his lack of response meant he was dead. Instead, a more powerful demon had summoned him. I'd assumed my boss was powerful enough to break any other demon's hold, but it appeared I was mistaken.

Unless the boss was lying at that, too.

Speaking of powerful, D clearly was. He'd been more powerful than a tempter demon when we'd been younger, too. I had no idea what his rank was in the demon realm. But even demon lords were vulnerable when young. I'd worried that D might have been injured, lost, or that he'd simply vanished. Then my wounded heart and teen brain assumed I'd done something to frighten him off or repulse him.

Then I'd figured he was dead.

"Who summoned you?" I asked, anger rising. I was a highly trained demon tracker and investigator. I could find the bastard. D would want to get his own revenge, but that didn't mean I couldn't help.

Better to be angry with the jerk who'd taken D away from me than be mad at myself for how I'd treated him since his return.

He pulled away, taking a step back as his gaze darted warily around the room, like a wounded animal caught in a trap. I didn't think he'd answer me, but when he regained his composure, he said, "I was summoned by my father."

His father? Wow, talk about awkward family reunions. His absentee father had summoned him to hell, a father who didn't let him come back to earth. My absentee father walked out on us, but at least he didn't haul me away and keep me prisoner.

Judging from D's reaction, it hadn't been warm or welcoming. I had about a million questions, but all I could think to say was, "That had to suck."

Damn me and my big, fat, stupid mouth. "What I meant was, I'm very sorry that happened to you. Want to talk about it?"

"Not especially." He ran a hand through his thick mass of dark hair. The move gave me a chance to ogle his mouthwatering bicep, but I chastised my inner ho-bag, telling her to pipe down. For now. If she was a good ho-bag, I promised I'd let her come out and play later.

"Oh, come on." I followed him as he walked back into the kitchen so I could prod him for more information. He poured me a cup of coffee, God bless him. "You can't just say you were summoned by your dad, who kept you trapped in the hell realm, and leave it at that. Why are men so weird about talking?"

His scowl softened, and he offered me a sideways smirk. "Why are women so keen on talking?"

"That's easy." I stole a piece of bacon off his serving plate. Was there any food more perfect than bacon? "Superior emotional intelligence."

He grabbed a plate and started filling it with bacon, waffles, and fresh strawberries. I reached for the cabinet before remembering I needed a step stool. Boice kept the dishes on the highest shelf just to be an ass. Freakin' tall people. D surprised me by handing me the plate he'd been filling, turning me around, and parking me on one of the barstools flanking our kitchen island.

"Eat," he said and turned to fill his own plate.

I did, savoring a bite of crispy waffle topped with strawberries and whipped cream. But I wasn't about to drop the conversation. "Changing the subject?"

He walked back over to the kitchen island and sat down across from me. "You're not eating," he said, looking at my plate and pointing.

"I had a bite." I took another, irritated by his refusal to share. I chewed and swallowed politely before I continued my interrogation.

"Are you going to talk to me?"

"Are you going to eat?"

Jeez, what were we, five? Going toe-to-toe with D used to be my favorite pastime. The guy was as snarky as I was, and he wielded pop culture references with the same mastery as a samurai wielded his sword, or at least he used to. It would probably take him a little while to get current now that he was back on earth. But much like me, he was a master of deflection. I'd have to bring my A game if I was to win a serious conversation with Mr. Tall, Dark, and Tight-lipped.

I grinned as a wicked plan unfolded in my devious brain. "What if I let you feed me?" I eyed his plate. Chockablock full of food porn in the form of a savory waffle topped with delectable white sauce, fresh fruit, and a mountain of whipped cream, it had me salivating almost as much as its creator. "Will you talk to me then?"

His gaze went molten. I watched as he cut a corner of waffle, making sure to capture just the right proportion of the delectable flavors. Leaning forward, he held his fork in front of my mouth and said in a low, husky voice, "Open."

I wanted to open more than my mouth, but I needed to stay focused. I couldn't let him distract me with sex appeal. I wanted to know what happened that night, why he'd been taken, and what he'd been doing—or forced to do—since.

I needed to know if I could've done something to stop it, to find him.

I played along, opening my mouth and enveloping the culinary delight D offered. The flavors exploded over my tongue, and I had to fight the urge to moan. But then a thought occurred to me. If I was caught in a maelstrom of arousal, of bone-deep longing for the man who could disarm me with a glance, he was caught up in the storm right along with me. His breaths quickened, and his green eyes filled with sparks of demon light as he eyed me like a meal he'd dearly love to devour.

Oh yeah, he wanted me as much as I wanted him. I was going to win this.

I savored the bite, swallowing slowly and licking my lips, hoping to drive him as crazy as I'd been ever since he showed up at HQ. It worked. He placed the fork back on his plate with a forced gentleness, leaned back on his barstool, and crooked a long index finger at me.

"Come here."

I was powerless to deny him. I still wanted to talk, and talk we would, but who was I to refuse such a summons? If I sweetened the deal with a kiss, I'd have him singing like a canary in no time.

I hopped off my stool and closed the distance between us on shaking legs, my skin too tight under his hungry gaze. I stopped, stood beside him, and placed my hands on my hips, challenging him to ask for what he wanted. Our heights were matched when he sat, for once putting me on eye level with him. I liked it. I'd like it even more if I could hover over him, his body locked beneath mine as I rode him to ecstasy while he writhed and groaned and cursed with pleasure.

As if reading my mind, he reached out and lifted me onto his lap, giving me a thrill as I landed on the evidence of his interest.

I hissed. He was so hard, his arousal straining against my center in the most enticing way. I dug my fingers in his hair and pulled him to me for a kiss. Our lips met and I held him tighter, tried to deepen the surprisingly gentle kiss that amounted to little more than a brush of lips, light, teasing. I wanted more. Much more.

I couldn't force him to do my bidding, but I was a master at the fine art of persuasion. I slid my arms down his shoulders and wiggled, bringing my body closer to his. I rolled my hips, shivering as friction stoked the flames of my desire. He groaned, grabbed me by the hips, and pulled me tight against his hard length as he buried his face in my neck.

"Fuck, Jane, what are you doing to me?" His whispered curse filled me with raw lust, and I wasn't alone. His muscles twitched with the visible effort it took to hold back. I didn't want him to hold back, not this, not anything.

"Same thing you're doing to me." My voice was almost as breathy as a succubus. I pressed against him, writhing and squirming as pleasure coursed through me. I'd sell my soul for the ability to make clothing magically disappear. I wanted to be skin to skin, to feel every inch of him as he glided into my body.

I'd lost this game as soon as I climbed on top of him, but by now I didn't care. Animal instinct trampled on my resolve, my self-control, and rational thought.

Without warning, he stilled my movements with his strong hands on my hips. I growled. He flashed a wicked grin before leaning in to kiss me on my nose, my forehead, both cheeks, and my chin. Warm lips danced over my sensitive skin, teasing me when all I wanted was to finish what we'd started.

"No," he whispered. "I waited so long. Let me savor this. I want you to savor this. The slower we go, the better it will be."

I didn't want slow, normally didn't do slow, but for D, I'd do just about anything. Wait, he'd stopped moving, stopped those too-soft kisses. His eyes, fathomless and dark except for red sparks that marked him as a demon, stared into mine. What was he waiting for?

"I want to try something," he said, voice low and husky. "It's...a bit of demon magic I think you'll like."

"Try it," I said, desire and frustration sharpening my voice. "Try anything, just don't stop."

He said a few words in one of the demon languages. It wasn't my area of expertise, but I recognized the demon words for "many" and "fingers." Before I could think too much about it, waves of sensation pulsed through my body and filled every nerve ending with delicious pleasure. D held my hips still, but somehow, he'd magicked invisible fingertips and bid them to run over my skin from the sensitive nape of my neck to my nipples, hard and straining against my thin T-shirt, as I gasped, wanting more.

But he took his time, teasing me, chasing those phantom caresses with his tongue, bringing me to the brink of completion before pulling back, only to begin the game again.

"You like it?" he asked, almost shyly.

"Yes," I hissed. I needed more. Wanted more. I hovered over the precipice and begged him to bring me over the edge.

The strange, bubbly sensation I'd been experiencing suddenly burst from within me. D cried out in surprise and, I hoped, pleasure as I pulled his strong hands away from my hips so I could move against him and find the sweet friction I craved.

God, this was so good. Incredible. With time and his exquisite, undivided attention, I was on the verge of a climax before the main event. D could do that for me. I was close. All I needed were his hands, his mouth, a little more pressure and time.

And the strange, new, wonderful power coursing through me.

"Jane." He whispered my name in wonder and awe. "What is this? Magic?"

"I don't know," I said between gasps. "But I like it."

"Keep going," he commanded, his gaze glittering as he leaned back a fraction to watch, to revel in what we were making together. Then he pulled my mouth to his and kissed me, really kissed me, his tongue hot and greedy as it mingled with mine. He raised his hands to my breasts, running his thumbs over the hardened peaks. I didn't think anything could feel better than the magical sensations he created, but I soon found there ain't nothing like the real thing.

I paused to yank my shirt off while D held me steady, his gaze running over my bare breasts. Feminine pride surged as he surveyed the terrain, but it was quickly replaced by raw need when he took one peak into his hot mouth, running his tongue over my nipple and sending a jolt of electric pleasure through my body. He grabbed my ass and pulled me to him, setting a rhythm that had me inching toward the edge of climax.

Delicious friction and pressure, his hands, his tongue, his scent, everything that was him coalesced into this moment. Damn, we'd both burned for it for over a decade, and this was just the beginning. It was the spark, the beginnings of a blaze that would surely consume us both.

"Jane." His voice caressed me between hot kisses, snaking his hand between my legs to massage my clit. Oh my God, it was too much, too good to last. "Come for me. Come for me now."

His voice, husky and full of passion, was my undoing. I came in an explosion of crashing waves and shimmering stars. D held me through it, whispering sweet words into my ear as I trembled in his arms. At least, I thought they were sweet words. He was speaking one of the demon languages again. I really needed to brush up.

D seemed content to hold and caress me, but we were far from done.

God, if he could do that as an appetizer, I couldn't wait to find out how he'd serve the main course. But sadly, I would have to wait. Earth-shattering orgasms aside, I was still a woman on a mission. Until he told me all the details on his summons and its aftermath, we would not be getting to the main event. I wanted to know him, truly know him, and reconnect before the big shebang.

But I wasn't cruel.

I slipped off his lap, and before he had the chance to stop me, I pulled down his pajama pants enough to release him from their confines, marveling at his length, at what I'd done to him, what I was going to do to him.

"Jane." I didn't know if the plea in his voice was for me to slow down or to put an end to his agony by flooding him with the delicious pleasure of release. I went with the latter.

I took him in my mouth, intoxicated by his responses—a sharp hiss of breath followed by a deep groan and muttered curses. He put his hands on my head, tried to pull me back, but I reached up and took his hands in mine, stilling them, inviting him to sit back and enjoy. I took my time, bringing him to the brink and then pulling back, making him work for it, driving him out of his mind.

"Fucking hell, Jane." I risked a glance up and was treated to the sight of my beautiful demon coming unglued. Jaw clenched, head thrown back, corded muscles as taut and rock-hard as his cock in my mouth. "I'm going to come."

A smile threatened to undo my good work, but I fought it. Of course he was going to come. I wanted him to come. That was the idea.

I gripped the base of his cock and increased the pace of my strokes, running my tongue under his sensitive head as he bucked and trembled beneath me. After another moment, he exploded with a deep, guttural groan that made my heart sing. I held on until it ran its course and then sat back on my heels and surveyed my work with no small amount of female smugness.

Yeah, we were good together. We'd be even better when we got to the main event.

"Damn, that was amazing. Wasn't my plan, but it was fucking incredible," he said, breaths still uneven.

"What do you mean?" I couldn't think of anything better than what had just happened.

He grinned. It warmed the cockles of my heart to see the man in my kitchen so satisfied. At least I think it did. I wasn't exactly sure what cockles were. I'd have to look that up.

"That was supposed to be just for you."

I grinned, too. "While I appreciate your enlightened views on giving, this particular activity is always better when a friend comes along for the ride." Then, suddenly shy, I dropped my gaze and said, "I loved watching you."

He leaned forward, took my chin in his hand, raising my head to meet his gaze. "I loved watching you more." Demons were so competitive. "And I'd love to explore the magic you unleashed."

"Me, too." It had saved my demon back in the alley, saved my ass when I made the deal with my boss, and now, it seemed that this power could unleash earth-shattering orgasms. Bonus. "It must be some kind of demon mojo. Maybe from Hannah."

D shook his head. "Not demon magic. It's the wrong...flavor."

"I can't imagine what else it could be. After all, we still don't know what kind of demon Hannah is, so maybe her magic is as unique as she is."

"Maybe. We can explore that, too." His face split into a wicked grin full of promise and sin. He was temptation itself, but I would resist. For now.

I grabbed my shirt off the floor and pulled it over my head. He gave me a quizzical look but followed my lead and pulled his pajama bottoms back up. I missed the view, but it was time to put my diabolical plan into action. I sat down on the floor across from him, cross-legged, and leaned forward, placing elbows on knees and chin in my palm.

"Okay, now that we've gotten that out of the way, talk," I said. Short, sweet, to the point. He was under my spell. He'd have no choice but to obey.

He watched me, brow arched, and jaw set in a stubborn line. D was a worthy opponent. I'd give him that. But he was no match for Demon Hunter Extraordinaire, Jinx McGee.

"I never actually agreed to talk."

"Oh, no, mister, I followed the terms of the agreement. I allowed you to feed me." I wagged my eyebrows as I eyed the juncture between his thighs. "Quid pro quo. Talk."

He chuckled. "While your meal could be classified as cannibalism, you're not quite as intimidating as Dr. Lecter."

Oh, he was such a bad boy. I'd have to give him a spanking. Later, after I'd secured his cooperation. "I'm serious." I waved a hand down the length of my body, proudly displaying my wares with the flair of a game show hostess. "If you want more of this, you're going to have to pay the piper."

His brows furrowed, and he appeared thoughtful. "You've already made one bad deal with a demon. Sure you want to make another?"

He tried to look menacing and succeeded a little too well. But I was the woman in charge here and would not be deterred or distracted. "It's not a deal. I'm not trading sexual favors, and neither are you. No man-whoring here. It's simply a condition of moving our relationship to the next level. Honesty is key in all relationships, and so is communication."

"Where did you get that crazy notion?" The corners of his lips curled as he fought a grin.

"From the Internet. Duh." I gave him my best stern look, the one that let demons, humans, and everyone in between know I meant business. "Now talk."

He cocked his head and grinned, a wide, feral smile that had me on edge. He was scheming. Thinking of a way to get out of chatting about his sordid past, assuming it was sordid.

At last, he spoke. "You get three questions. I'll answer them as honestly as I'm able."

I practically squealed in delight, bringing out an adorable chuckle from my demon boy. God, I'd missed his laugh. He didn't laugh often, even when we were kids. I hadn't either back then. Laughter was hard to come by in the naughty corner. Still, once out of school and gain-fully employed in a profession that suited my unique condition, I'd embraced my wicked sense of humor with a bear hug and refused to let go.

I decided then and there that making D laugh would be my new personal life goal. It ranked right up there with a million dollars, a trip to Tahiti, world peace, and unlimited tequila and tacos.

"I can ask anything at all, and you'll answer?"

"Is that your first official question?"

"No, jackass." I shot eye bullets at him with my steely gaze. They were mostly blanks.

"Yes." He flashed me a smirk before schooling his features to resting stern face, which was a step above resting bitch face. "And I'll answer as long as I'm able. Some information is classified."

I stood in front of him, giddy in my triumph. He reached out to snatch me, no doubt attempting to distract me from my mission by pulling me back on his lap. Tempting as that was, I would not be denied this rare and wonderful opportunity to delve into the psyche of this fasci-nating male specimen.

"You're way too excited about this."

"Can you blame me? Anyway, enough stalling. Tell me why your father summoned you."

He averted his gaze and heaved a deep sigh. I waited. After a long moment, I worried he'd shut me down by telling me that the answer to my question was "classified." He surprised me by speaking. "He summoned me because he'd been looking for me. Orphan, remember?"

I remembered all too well. Part of me wanted to throw my arms around him and keep him safe and warm forever, but this was a sensitive subject. He didn't like pity, never had. Nor did he like to talk about or remember his life before he found me. I just nodded, hoping he'd continue.

"Yeah," he muttered, running a hand through his hair and scrubbing his face. "He couldn't find me until I grew old enough to track by my demon magic. Once that hit, anyone who knew my real name could summon me. Dear old Dad knew it, of course, and he summoned me the night I...left you."

He pinned me with his gaze. For once, it was open, earnest. "I didn't want to leave you. I've spent the past ten years working on a way to get back to the earth realm and back to you."

Heart. Melt.

"I'm so sorry." I meant it, too. And knowing he'd been forced to leave me went a long way to soothing the old wounds I'd carried with me for the past ten years. "I had no idea. I was worried, anxious, and so..."

"Angry?" He curled his lips into a smile.

I laughed, sheepish. It wasn't like I could deny it. "Yeah, well, that too. You were dead as far as I knew. Before that, I didn't know what to think, except sometimes I, you know, wondered if you, you know, had second thoughts about us. Our relationship did take an interesting turn that night."

He stood up and pulled me into his arms, instantly putting me on high alert. I didn't want him to coddle me—well, I did, but I didn't want to need the coddling. I'd spent many years building my armor against the world. D was one of the few people who could shatter it like glass. Double standard, but I was much more at ease being the comforter rather than the comfortee.

"Speaking of fathers, you ever find your dad?"

The question should have shut me down, rebuilding the armor around my heart. Instead, my voice was steady and my heart mostly free of the old deep ache when I answered. "Nah. Boss used all his resources, and I did a lot of investigating on my own. Nada. He's either dead or living so far off the grid that he might as well be."

"I'm sorry," he whispered. Then he held me tighter. I fought to keep my tears at bay. Total losing battle.

I squirmed, trying to wriggle out of his hold. When that failed, I tried to start a tickle fight, but he managed to catch my wrists, holding me firm against his hard body. Putting his mouth close to my ear, his hot breath stoked the flames of arousal anew. "Don't you dare. Never, ever doubt what I feel for you, what I've always felt for you."

He was talking about that night. The night he disappeared was also the night we stopped being best pals and took it to the next level, succumbing to attraction and longing that had built over years. At least, I had succumbed. I hadn't realized he'd been burning for me just as long.

"N-No." My voice was little more than a squeak. He was doing terrible things to my self-control. He pulled me tighter against him, letting me feel him again, hard and ready. "M-Maybe. But it's nice to hear."

He ran his tongue along the sensitive shell of my ear. It sent the most delightful waves of warmth coursing through my body that pooled low in my belly. I'd never get enough of him. Even after the amazing, earth-shattering orgasm he'd just given me, I was hot and hungry and ready for more.

And so was he. I was the luckiest demon-possessed girl in the earth realm.

"Good." He blew gently on my ear, sending delicious shivers down my neck. "Can we get your two other questions out of the way? I can't wait to touch, tease, and taste every inch of you."

Tempting. He was tempting beyond belief. The only thing that saved me from giving in was the knock that sounded at my door.

CHAPTER SEVENTEEN

"Jane, are you home?"

My sister's dulcet tones could wake the dead, something that normally grated on my last nerve, but for once I was grateful.

"Coming," I yelled. "Give me a sec."

I felt D's smile against my skin as he spoke. "Sadly, you aren't coming. Do you want me to go?"

I didn't, and why should he? I was a grown-ass woman in my own grown-ass woman's apartment with a grown-ass man doing what consenting adults did. Besides, scandalizing my big sister was my third favorite thing to do.

I pulled away from D with great reluctance. "No. Stay. But put a shirt on. Otherwise poor Megan might never be able to look at another man again."

He grinned. "Be nice to her. I'll be right back."

"You clearly don't remember what a pain in the ass she is." Speaking of asses, I admired the shape of his as he walked away. I really needed to get a view of his bare derrière during our next Q and A session.

I smoothed down my hair as best I could before walking to the door so I could harass my favorite sister. "What's the password?"

"Really? We're going to do this again?" Oh, goody. She was already exasperated, and I hadn't even brought out my best material. Messing with Megan was so much fun.

Waiting a beat, I pulled out my stern, drill sergeant voice. "You're not even close. Password or no entry."

I leaned my back against the door and waited. After about ten seconds and a very loud sigh, she uttered the magic words. "Jinx, Jinx, the nimble minx, she'll kick your ass before you blink."

I collapsed in a fit of giggles. That never, *ever* got old.

"Can I come in now?"

I opened the door and marveled at the sight of my sister. How did anyone look that put together in the morning? Oh, right, it was well past noon. She probably thought I'd been on a bender, which, oddly enough, I had been. We had the same dark hair and round face, but she was pale, especially next to me. I had what appeared to be a natural permanent tan. It was a source of endless jealousy, made worse since I worked nights and didn't have to work for it.

Then again, she stood a good eight inches taller than me. That made us even in the jealousy department. Oh, and she had gorgeous blue eyes, a winning personality—if a bit on the sanctimonious side—and a bless-edly ordinary life. She had the perfect husband by society's standards, a chance for children, and she looked like a runway model. She had all the things I couldn't thanks to my demon. Guess we weren't so even after all.

"You look terrible." She walked in like she owned the place, though she'd only been to my apartment a half-dozen times. I didn't entertain family members or nondemon friends all that often.

"Thanks," I said. "Coffee?"

"Sure." She set her bag down on my counter and eyed the two plates filled with breakfast treats with undisguised curiosity. Let her be curious. I'd just had a mind-blowing orgasm delivered with a side of breakfast. She'd meet D soon enough.

Crap, I hope she didn't recognize him.

Surely not. She'd only caught a few glimpses of him when we were kids. Once D got better at hiding, there had been no need to worry as much. Sure, he spent nights in my closet, but he'd soon started roaming during the day and some nights, too, once he got comfortable. He was such an explorer.

He'd only ever scared me once when he came back bloodied and bruised from a run-in with someone bad. I'd treated his wounds, but he wouldn't tell me who or what he'd fought. Only that he'd won. I'd faked being sick and convinced my mom I'd be okay staying home from school on my own.

Aside from D's injuries, it had been one of the best days of my life.

We'd had full run of the house, and I'd been able to sit with him on the couch and watch the big TV. I'd even made him the most ginormous roast beef sandwich in the history of the earth realm—seven layers of bread, cheese, and tender, juicy deli roast beef. And though I'm sure it had given him horrible indigestion later, he'd eaten every bite. After that, I'd cradled his head in my lap and stroked his hair until he fell asleep.

"I need to talk to you about something." Megan's tone dragged me out of my reverie.

That didn't sound good. I handed her a cup of joe and braced for whatever lecture or judgment was to come.

"Sure, what's up?" My voice was too chipper, but she'd set me on edge.

"Are you alone?" Her gaze surreptitiously roamed over the expanse of my huge combination kitchen, conference room, and living area.

I leaned against the counter and sipped my own cup of joe, savoring the flavor and rush of caffeine before answering. "My roommates are robbing banks right now, possibly planning a cyberattack on the entire U.S. banking system, so they're out. I think I have the rest of my demons safely tucked away."

Megan rolled her eyes and walked away, plopping down in one of the chairs in the wide expanse of living area. These were the nicer chairs that I assumed Boice and Roice kept for show, or possibly as an attempt to contrast with my own eclectic and fabulous furnishings. I liked the way my brilliant patterns shone out of the dark corner into which they kept tucking my stuff. They were jealous. I could tell.

After taking in the view for a moment, because having a penthouse came with perks, Megan turned to me, back straight and gaze narrowed, full of suspicion. "Jane, what exactly do you do for a living?"

And...here we go again.

I flopped down on the boring couch across from sister dearest and mock groaned. "We've been through this like a million times. I'm a consultant."

Megan arched a skeptical brow. "So you keep telling me, but what exactly do you consult on?"

I balked. "I don't know. No one knows. That's the beauty of consulting. It's a vague job that still sounds fancy and pays a crap ton of money. All the cool kids are consultants."

She shifted gears, moving to the after-school special, concerned big sister tactic. "Jinx, it's okay if you don't have a conventional job. As long as you're making a living—legally—that's all that matters. You are making legal money, right?"

Oh, this was too much fun. "You got me." I raised my arms in surrender. "I didn't want to have to tell you, but I'm an international woman of mystery."

"Jane—"

"No, it's totally cool. I get to dress up, go to nice restaurants and hotels, and spy on the ambassadors from Uzbekistan, Kazakhstan, and a few of those other -stan countries. I've got at least two hot guys lined up in every city I work. Very James Bond, or would that be Jane Bond?"

She shook her head and frowned, turning her gaze away from me. "Fine. Keep your secrets. It's not my business anyway. I'm only your sister."

I hated it when she went for the jugular. She apparently thought I harbored some inferiority complex based on the fact that she'd attended a Southern Ivy League university while I'd attended community and online colleges—sporadically—earning an associate's degree in criminal justice. Whatever. It had totally worked with my demon-hunting duties and schedule, and I also had street cred in the human world. Win-win.

"Right, I should give all the sordid details of my employment to my sister, the kept woman who has one of those cushy rich people jobs."

Okay, maybe I did have a bit of a complex.

I couldn't help it. I was the bad sister. Not only that, I was also the bad *little* sister. I was duty bound to be a pain in the ass.

Her husband, Brad, was some kind of hotshot investment banker who could support Megan and at least ten other sister-wives if he'd been into that sort of thing. So instead of working for a paycheck, Megan devoted her time and energy to all sorts of charities. Still a Goody-Two-shoes. She probably ran a home for orphan kittens on the side.

And she'd never even given me one.

Megan sighed, failing to take the bait. "You're right. I don't have to work a nine-to-five. I know how fortunate I am, and I give back as much as I'm able," she said, not giving me the satisfaction of a snarky comeback or starting a fight. "And speaking of giving back, I stopped by to return this."

She held out a slip of paper that looked suspiciously like a check. What the hell? I hadn't loaned her money since high school. Wait, maybe I'd forgotten about one of the few times I'd spotted her for gas money. It would be just like her to remember and give back the money with interest.

Or maybe she thought I was hard up.

"Whoa." I waved my hand and backed away from the check as if it were a small explosive device. "I was kidding about the spy thing. I'm a superhero."

"Really." The corners of her mouth twitched as she fought to stay serious. Or maybe she was just covering her shock and awe at my revelation.

"Oh, yeah. The yoga pants and sweater are part of the disguise for my alter ego. By day, I'm Jane McGee, 'consultant,'" I said, making air quotes and winking. "By night, I'm Jinx the Jaunty Purveyor of Justice. Vigilante style, of course, because, really, is there any other kind?"

"Jaunty Purveyor of Justice?"

"Hey, Batman was already taken. I had to come up with an original superhero name." I struggled to climb out of the thick plush cushions of the fancy sofa and moved over to my own sofa, my beauty, she who embraced my backside like my favorite pair of jeans. Much better than my roomies' furniture, and not so close to Sis.

Megan followed me to my dark, cozy corner of the room and sat primly on one of my mismatched chairs. I'd tacked several swatches to one of the armrests, torn between new neon tartan creations and glow-in-the-dark skulls.

"Well, that certainly is...original." I wasn't sure if she was referring to my superhero name or the swatches, but I'd take it either way. Then she shook her head and leveled me with one of her determined looks.

Uh-oh.

She held up the check. "This isn't charity for you. It's what you donated to one of my charities last week, and it's too much. I'm giving it back."

Damn, she really knew how to suck the wind right out of my sails. I almost sank back into my sofa, and I had to fight not to fidget with the nubs covering the well-worn fabric. No, I wouldn't let her get to me. I wasn't little Janie anymore. I was a seasoned warrior, a professional. No way would I let Megan get the upper hand.

I gave a dismissive wave and snorted. "What? Me give to charity? No way. I'm the bad sister, remember?"

How had she found out? I'd asked Boice to make an anonymous donation to Megan's local cancer patient advocacy chapter, emphasis on *anonymous*. I'd have to have words with the little snitch later.

"You aren't bad." Megan's voice was gentle, soothing, but I was immune to emotional sneak attacks. Megan, however, was a worthy opponent, remaining firm and unconvinced by my command performance, damn it.

"And it's not that I don't appreciate this, but you should be spending your money on you."

"I do." I gestured to the splendor around us, from tricked-out kitchen to our high-end electronics and amazing panoramic view. "Just look at this superswanky apartment."

"I thought you said the boss of your *consulting* firm paid for this as a home office." The way she said the word "consultant" was laced with more than a little skepticism. Why did no one take me seriously? No matter. I knew how to throw her off.

"Yeah, but I paid for all the décor." I patted my faded sofa. "This is vintage, a rare find. Can't get this kind of quality just anywhere, you know. Not to mention this awesome upholstery."

I then placed my bare feet on the coffee table, kicking away some old Chinese takeout boxes to make room. "And I'll also have you know this table is made of very special wood from a rare species of baobab tree. They only grow in Madagascar. Cost me a fortune on the black market."

"Jane, I'm serious," Megan said, and she was. She really was worried about me. No idea why. I was living the dream.

"So am I," I said, pointing to the check. "I'm not admitting to anything, mind you, but if I allegedly made a substantial donation to an organization that may or may not be championed by my sister, I would not have cut into my savings or my takeout budget."

"Fine." She sighed, stuffing the check into her pocket. "There is something else I wanted to ask you about."

I sat up ramrod straight and bowed my head in faux contrition. "Yes, I stole your Malibu Barbie and buried her in the backyard. Whew." I threw my head back and spread my arms over the sofa's expanse. "Glad I got that off my chest."

"Why is a large blond man who looks like the Terminator following me and Mom?"

Double damn it. I'd told Alexi to be sly, but the poor guy just stood out in a crowd. A big, blond god of a man, good-looking, and with that accent? Yeah. Still, I thought it would take a little longer for Megan and Mom to catch on.

I crossed my eyes and shook my head at her. It was my flabbergasted I-have-no-idea-what-you're-talking-about look. Or maybe it was my crazy look. Whatever worked. "I have no idea what you're talking about, and frankly I'm surprised. It's not like you to be paranoid."

She furrowed her brows. Oh, yeah, I sowed seeds of doubt like a pro, throwing her off my scent. It was for her own good. No need to worry her or Mom. Yet.

Still, I'd have to text Alexi and encourage him to be more discreet, and I'd have to do it in a way that wouldn't hurt his feelings. He was a giant marshmallow on the inside.

Megan was about to open her mouth again when a vision emerged from my room. A vision wearing tight jeans, a tighter T-shirt, and with a freshly shaved jaw that would have made him appear clean-cut were it not for the damp locks that framed his impossibly handsome face and brushed his shoulders. I let Megan ogle him for a bit, mostly because I wanted to ogle him, too. He was just too delicious.

"Good morning," he said with a wink, walking over and planting a soft kiss on my lips. He surprised me by turning and extending a hand to my sister. "You must be Megan."

My awestruck sister accepted his hand and shook it, clearly on autopilot. After shaking her head, she said, "Pleased to meet you, Mr...."

"Bellatore," he said. "Dominic Bellatore."

He walked back to the kitchen and began cleaning up after breakfast. Holy guacamole. He was cleaning? That settled it. I was keeping him. And Bellatore? That wasn't his real name any more than Dominic was, but it had that sexy Italian ring to it. Dominic the Warrior. The tall, dark *Italian* Warrior. It fit him like the jeans that molded to the enticing contours of his ass.

I beamed at Megan, who eyed me with a mixture of awe, confusion, and more than a little envy. The last part faded fast. She and Brad were soul mates, and she loved him more than life itself. The awe and confusion stuck around.

I let her stare for a minute before taking pity on her. "He's a colleague and friend. We're working on a consult together." I glanced at the antique grandfather clock in my corner. "Speaking of, we need to get to work. Our deadline is in three days."

"Of course," Megan said, slowly coming out of her stupor. "I won't keep you. But you are coming over for Sunday dinner, right?"

Oh dear. I'd forgotten about Sunday dinner. After much wrangling,

I'd finally caved and accepted Mom's summons for a family meal with just the four of us—Mom, me, Megan, and Brad. At least Mom and I had the swinging single gal part in common. Well, at least until now, assuming D was planning to stick around this time.

Which gave me a fabulous idea.

"Hey, D, want to come to a family dinner with me on Sunday?"

He froze and turned around, nailing me with his startling green-eyed gaze. I could see the demon sparks swirling in his irises and wondered if I'd crossed a line. He was interested in the physical, and I suspected he might want to rekindle the emotional relationship, too, but meeting the family in the official capacity might be too much too soon. Or maybe he wasn't keen on reliving his days as the hungry, frightened orphan demon who once shared our home. I was about to make another joke to diffuse the situation and hide the wave of disappointment and pain threatening to crash into me upon his rejection.

Then he smiled. "Does this mean we're dating?"

I smiled back, my heart leaping with joy. "You'd have to take me on an actual date for that to be true."

He nodded. "As soon as we're done *consulting*," he said, his voice laced with amusement. "I'll take you wherever you'd like. I'll even pay."

"Oh," I said, giddy with anticipation. If I were a dog, my tail would be wagging at light speed. "I'd love to go to Tahiti."

I'd love to go anywhere with D, or nowhere at all. He'd shown me a glimpse of paradise right here in my apartment. I'd be perfectly happy for a repeat performance. Low-key was my middle name.

Stifling a chuckle, his eyes twinkled with what I thought might be affection. "I'll see what I can do."

"So you'll be my dinner date at the old family get-together?" I tried to sound casual and failed miserably. For some reason, I really wanted him to come with me. That was where I'd met him, after all. Where it had all started.

Where we had started.

And while he knew my family as well as I did—what with years of living with them in secret—they didn't know him. It was a shame, really.

He'd done a lot for us. If I was a walking disaster around anything electronic, D was a born mechanic. He'd fixed my mom's car in secret on many a night when she'd been fretting over how to pay for the necessary repairs. He'd done the same with our furnace the following winter, and he'd somehow managed to make our food stores last longer than usual. Megan used to joke that we had a friendly elf who made certain we never ran out of her favorite sugary marshmallow cereal, or bread, or peanut butter, or anything else we needed until Mom's paycheck cleared.

It wasn't just because he shared our food. He hated sugary marshmallow cereal. He'd done it for her.

The memory tightened and warmed my chest all at once, and I held my breath, holding on to ridiculous hope that he'd come with me.

"Consider it a date," he said, then turned around and got busy loading the dishwasher.

I walked Megan to the door, gushing in hushed tones about how fabulous D was. Megan smiled. "It's good to see you happy, Jane."

"I'm always happy," I said. "Unless I'm stuck in line at a drive-through. Then I get cranky."

"Joke all you want, but I mean it. Keep him around. Seriously, if I wasn't happily married, I'd hit that with a Mack truck."

"I know, right?" I said, giggling.

She surprised me, pulling me into a warm embrace. We weren't normally touchy-feely. I'd always kept my family at arm's length. Between my demonic possession and the secrecy that came along with it —including D—I'd made keeping to myself standard operating procedure. And as recent events proved, I was a danger to my family. My line of work had put them in harm's way. I couldn't have that.

"I know about the money you put in Mom's account, too," she whispered in my ear.

I stiffened. Damn it. I was busted. I needed better money launderers.

Pulling back, she said, "See you Sunday."

After seeing my sister off, I returned to the kitchen, my coffee cup, and my friend with benefits. "What's on the agenda today?" I asked.

I assumed we'd pick up the search for Keith the missing summoner. I'd be much more helpful sober. Of course, I'd tried to touch base with Hannah, but she still wasn't answering. She was apparently still off somewhere deep in my subconscious since I couldn't feel her presence. I didn't have the luxury of dealing with her recent mood swings. Guess it was good, old-fashioned detective work today with the assistance of a corporeal demon.

D nodded. "I asked your roomies to monitor police reports, hospitals, news, and cameras all over the city. Between the two of us, we dinged him up pretty good. If the summoner turns up, we'll spot him."

That made sense, though it was a little disappointing. Still, conventional detective work got the job done in the earth realm more often than not. Speaking of...

"Who was helping him?" I asked, remembering our text chat from yesterday after I left Warner Park. D mentioned he knew who had helped Keith bring Mephisto from the hell realm. Maybe that guy, or gal —I really shouldn't make such sexist assumptions—could help us locate Keith.

D's gaze turned hard. "The same man who helped my father summon me back to hell."

Wow. Talk about a bombshell. No wonder D's interrogation of Keith had been so brutal. Then again, if D were out for revenge, was it clouding his judgment? Could he work for me on my case while settling old scores?

"Who is he, the summoner who sent you to your father? And where is he?" I asked.

"I don't know his name, only his methods. I have very little to go on, but Keith used the same methods to summon Mephisto. The sigil patterns were practically identical aside from the name. I've also got a few associates on the hunt. If anyone can track them, they can."

"Demons?" I asked.

He nodded, averting his gaze briefly before he said, "They specialize in sensing and parsing magic. If Keith is in league with Belial, he's most likely using some powerful demon magic to stay under the radar. It has a different...flavor, for lack of a better word, than tempter magic. He can't escape to the hell realm through legal portals, and my colleagues and I believe we've located and secured all unauthorized portals, which means he's likely gone into hiding. They'll be able to sniff out any concealment magic."

That fit the profile we'd built of the demon lord. Belial was known for magic and could wield much more sophisticated sorcery than the glamour, persuasion, or possession techniques used by tempter demons. "That's impressive. How'd you manage that?" I asked, genuinely curious.

And a little suspicious.

I knew D was powerful, but I'd been thinking about how he'd been operating. He'd followed me to the alley where I'd had the run in with Mephisto and Mara, and I hadn't detected him, wonky knife notwithstanding. I was usually quite good at detecting demons in the area, even powerful demons. Hannah had apparently missed him, too.

And the boss had missed Mephisto altogether.

D had also appeared at HQ after following us. True, he could've used his car, but the niggling in the back of my mind made me suspect he had other ways of tracking and traveling. Plus, how would he know about unauthorized portals, let alone how to find rogue summoners who could hide using magic, if he didn't know more than a little magic himself? If Pendergrass could get his hands on high demon magic, why not an actual demon?

"D? How much demon magic do you have?"

His gaze turned hard. "Is that question number two?"

That was right. I had two questions left in our little game. While I wanted to know more about his father, his time in the hell realm, and all his delicious secrets, this line of questioning seemed more important. More immediate.

"Yes," I said, "it is. Are you going to answer?"

"That's classified," he said, crossing his arms over his broad chest.

I scowled and then grinned as a thought occurred to me. "I'll take that as a lot," I said. "And you still owe me two answers since you didn't actually answer that question."

"Damn it, Jane, the less you know about this right now, the better. Safer. I'd say trust me, but..." He trailed off.

Smart man. We'd woven a few strands of trust between us, but they were thin, fragile, in danger of snapping at any moment should either of us tug a little too hard.

"Fine," I said, turning on my heel and heading off to my room. "Go do your supersecret thing. Alone."

"What'll you be doing?" he yelled.

I held up my middle finger and said, "That's classified."

CHAPTER EIGHTEEN

After showering and leaving my empty apartment, which D had apparently vacated in a huff of testosterone-fueled indignation, I met up with Lacey. We'd received a hit from an Internet chatroom Boice had been monitoring. KashvilleKeith47, our summoner's oh-so-clever and original handle, had logged on from an IP addressed located somewhere in east Nashville.

He'd been scared, warning the online rogue summoner community—which was a thing, and its membership had quadrupled over the last six months—about demon hunters and a crazy demon hitman sent to take him out. I could only assume he was talking about D. No surprise, there. What really got our attention, however, was the warning Keith issued.

End times at hand. Be ready to open the gates to the glorious rebellion.

These guys talked a lot of smack for unemployed thirtysomethings living in their mamas' basements.

"Are you sure this is the right place?" Lacey asked. She was always questioning my directions. Of course, the empty-looking warehouse did seem a bit questionable. Situated in a pocket of urban decay, the large, bland building with pockmarked concrete and boarded-up windows could've been hiding anything from a meth lab to a zombie horde. But where else would a sneaky little underground summoner on the run hide? We'd already checked his mom's basement.

"According to my good friends Siri and Boice, yes," I said, testily. "But you could always double-check with your demon. And while you're at it, why don't you ask him to sneak in the building and make sure the coast is clear? Better yet, have him let us in. Unless there's a serial killer in there."

She rolled her eyes, not deigning to look up from her phone. She appeared to be furiously texting. That was weird. She normally just talked to her demon. Or maybe she was playing Candy Jam or some other online game. Kids these days. Always on their phones.

She finally stopped texting and pinched the bridge of her nose. "What the hell did you put in those drinks last night? I haven't blacked out since that party in Jimmy Livermore's lake house."

"Tough night?" I asked, sympathetically.

My hangover had disappeared thanks to a combination of breakfast, a gallon of water, the heavy petting session with D, and the hangover remedy Mara whipped up for me. Taking sympathy on my partner for the day, I fished what was left of the potion out of my bag and handed it to her.

She eyed the vial warily, wincing as she pulled down her sunglasses. "What is it?"

"I think it's the demon version of hair of the dog. Mara made it."

That seemed good enough for her. She took off the cap and downed it in a single gulp. "Hey, that's not bad."

"Great. Now can we play Simon says open the friggin' warehouse door?"

She scowled. "Simon doesn't like that, and he doesn't like you, either."

Sticks and stones. All I cared about was getting in. Sure, we could pick the lock, but it was easier to have a demon fly in and open the door for us. Lacey talked to the demon inside her phone. He materialized as a wisp of black smoke and slipped through the cracks of the warehouse door. Lacey kept an eye on the phone, presumably monitoring Simon's activity.

"So he really doesn't like me?" I asked.

"Not even a little," she said and then frowned. "Something's wrong."

She took off toward the door, which flew open thanks to Simon, and ran inside before I could blink. Damned long-legged people. I stumbled after her, nearly tripping on bits of crumbled sidewalk and uneven, unkempt lawn. If I fell and jacked up my knee, I'd be sure to make Lacey my personal assistant while I convalesced. On the other side of the rusty door, I scanned the dark interior for Lacey, following the echoes of her footfalls. By the time I caught up, she was disappearing around the corner. I ran after her and then stopped dead in my tracks. The stench hit me before I got a look at the gruesome sight.

And the flies. Holy guacamole, how did they all get there?

"My God," I said. "There are flies, and then there's this pitch-black, Satan-like swarm of flies."

"I know." Lacey's voice was muffled and shook, much like my knees. "And the stench. I had no idea dead bodies smelled this vile."

We were both unnerved. I'd seen dead bodies before, up close and personal, but this was different. Most demon-possessed humans were still alive when we tracked them. They stank faintly of sulfur, and if the demon in possession was an amateur, they walked with a strange gait. Some of them survived their demonic possessions or demon deals, but they were shells of the people they'd once been. alive. Others died from demon-draining, but the boss had special cleanup crews for that. We normally made ourselves scarce when we found a dead body after calling HQ, but the sight, scent, and sick feeling was memorable.

I'd seen blood, too, and smelled it. I'd seen maimed, injured, and close-to-the-brink-of-death human bodies, but nothing like this.

The flies cleared, perhaps in response to Simon's presence, giving us a better look at the horrific sight. A thin white male in his thirties lay face up in a pool of blood, unseeing gaze locked on the ceiling, his face contorted in a rictus of terror. I almost didn't recognize him, but it had to be Pendergrass.

I walked cautiously to where Lacey stood, pulling my shirt up to cover my nose. Lacey had done the same. Simon hovered over the body, presumably doing some sort of demonic detective work. Gritting her teeth and squaring her shoulders, Lacey started snapping pictures with her phone while I fired off a series of texts to my roomies, the rest of the team, and the boss.

Work now, unhealthy coping mechanisms later.

We should call the police, but not before gathering evidence for our own investigation. There was a remote possibility Keith had run afoul—hey, I finally had a reason to use my new favorite word—of some garden-variety human bad guys and wound up dead in a pool of what might have been his own blood.

But garden-variety human bad guys didn't normally use blood to paint a pentagram and authentic demon sigils around a dead body.

"I'll get shots of the sigils," I said to Lacey, who'd finished photographing the area around him. "You get what close-ups you can of Keith the unfortunate summoner."

"You sure it's him?" Lacey asked, though there could be little doubt. "And why do I have to take close-ups of the dead guy? I'll never get the smell out of my memory as it is."

I rolled my eyes. I recognized him. But she was apparently unwilling to take my word for it. I showed her the picture Boice had sent me. This was our guy. Lacey nodded, making a grimace of distaste.

"Perk of being temporarily in charge, babe," I said. "I've got eternal damnation hanging over my head. You take Mr. Stinky. What's Simon got?"

She looked down at her phone. "He smells traces of demon, but that could just be residual scent. The guy was a summoner. He spent a lot of time with demons. Wait," she said, holding up a finger.

Simon dove into the body, his incorporeal form undulating in and out of the guy's open mouth, nose, ears, and pores in sickening waves. Gross from my perspective, but demons like Simon had no aversion to death and decay. He was likely examining the body for signs of trauma and a clear cause of death.

"Well?" I asked, my gut filling with dread. "Don't keep me in suspense."

"No open wounds, no broken bones or obvious internal injuries. Just exsanguination."

"You mean something drained all the blood out of his body without opening any veins or arteries?" I asked, flummoxed. The demons we normally encountered could inflict a lot of damage to a human body from the inside or the outside, but the patterns followed the rules of the earth realm—blunt force trauma, stab wounds, bites, cuts, scrapes, and all manner of other injuries. This didn't fit the MO for any other known supernatural entities, either.

This kind of carnage was a new one for me.

"Is it the summoner's blood?" I asked.

Lacey sighed. "We won't know without a DNA test, but I'm *not* going to collect any blood or tissue," she said with vehemence. "Simon can do it."

"Right." I was still feeling...off, for lack of a better word, but my brain fog had cleared. As much as I balked at the idea and wanted to deny the possibility to myself and anyone else who might bring it up, I had to consider every possible suspect, including my long-lost demon friend who'd shown up right when the shit hit the fan with this case.

"Can Simon sort out different types of demon magic? Not just the kind we see with tempters, but something more powerful?"

Tempters like Mara could use glamour to lure their victims into a passionate frenzy, and Simon had used his powers of persuasion to tempt Lacey into upping her shoplifting game. Anger demons, maces, had mind-control powers and could amplify rage in their human victims, much as levi demons could boost envy, ego demons could magnify pride, belphs could inspire sloth, and bubs gluttony. These and other ordinary citizens of the hell realm who came to earth used their own brand of rudimentary basic magic to trick mortals, playing on their natural inclinations toward pride, covetousness, lust, anger, gluttony, envy, and sloth to sow discord and get a meal in the bargain.

But magic that could kill a man, draining his blood by means that didn't involve the usual exit routes, was something I'd never seen before. Sure, ancient texts and myths told tales of demon-inflicted horrors, but those had always seemed like exaggerations of, well, mythic proportions. The summoner's gruesome murder was on par with the magic and power that had nearly ripped my demon out of my body.

The kind of magic and power a hell realm general of myth and legend might possess. Or a mysterious demon from my past.

"Never mind," Lacey said, making a face of disgust. "Simon has the, um, samples. And I'll ask about the magic thing."

"Ugh, I don't want to know about his samples." I gagged, biting back bile. We needed to get out of there and shower.

I checked my phone. The rest of the team had texted back right away with similar questions about how and why our summoner died. All except for D. That was weird. Keith had been his find. He'd interrogated the guy—the photographic evidence he'd shown me certainly seemed to corroborate his story.

But the body looked pale. That was a no-brainer, considering he died from extreme blood loss, but did that include blood stuck in bruises?

"Any bruises or other injuries?" I asked.

Lacey shook her head. "No. Weird, huh? I thought your boyfriend worked him over."

"So did I." Why would a demonic entity first heal and then murder a rogue summoner? It didn't make any sense.

"Do you think D killed him?" Lacey asked. The look on my face made her take a step back and lift her palms. "I'm thinking out loud here, but what if he, you know, accidentally killed him during the interrogation and covered his tracks?"

"But I saw Pendergrass last night. D and I chased the guy down, and he got away."

Lacey shrugged. "Maybe he went back out after you passed out. He could have killed Pendergrass then."

"Why would he do that?" Rhetorical question. I knew, of course. Demons didn't like to let go of what they considered theirs, including humans they targeted. D was a demon through and through. Then again, if Keith was the only person who could lead him to the summoner who'd helped his father abduct him ten years ago, D would want to keep him alive.

Unless Keith had already answered his questions. If D knew who the other summoner was, he could be tying up loose ends before taking the guy out. But why lie about it? It wasn't as if his agenda conflicted with mine.

"I don't know," Lacey said, cocking her head to the side and squinting. Apparently, she was racking her brain too. She'd likely reached the same conclusions but had thought better of voicing them. "It's just weird you get attacked by a messenger demon right before your ex shows up out of the blue, gets assigned to the case, and then his first suspect ends up dead."

I started pacing. I hoped I wasn't getting any "samples" on my boots. Probably a bad idea since I could also be leaving all kinds of forensic evidence behind at a crime scene, like footprints. But the twins would fix that. They'd erase any evidence of our presence from the lab reports by hacking into the Metro and TBI crime lab computers.

Handy little demons.

Lacey could be on to something, but clearly my judgment was clouded by a very personal relationship with my ex.

"But why?" I said again, frustrated and a little heartbroken. I didn't want to think D would ever turn on me—according to his story, he hadn't abandoned me all those years ago. He'd been taken. But I still didn't know how he'd escaped.

Maybe he hadn't.

Lacey's words echoed my thoughts. "What if this was a setup? Maybe the boss or someone else is trying to throw you off so you don't solve the case. I mean, if you don't, he gets your soul and the souls of your family, right?"

"Right, unless Belial gets it first. Do you think D might be working for the boss?"

Or worse. Belial.

I kicked a few stray bits of glass shards as I paced the grimy floor. I didn't want to think about this, didn't want to face the possibility. How much did I know D—beyond childhood memories and the pleasures of the flesh? We'd been apart for a long time. I wasn't the same frightened girl he'd grown up with, and he was clearly no longer the shy, lost demon boy. Our reconnection had gone a long way to restoring the bond we'd once shared, weaving frayed threads of trust and longing between us, but was my demon man friend, foe, or a bit of both?

Lacey watched me struggle, not without sympathy, and shrugged. "Maybe, maybe not. I just think you should watch your back. Oh, and you were right. Keith's body has traces of demon magic all over it. Simon's never seen anything like it in this realm before."

Lacey summoned Simon back to her. He flew out of the body and into her phone, his shape like that of a huge raven disappearing into the device in a series of sparks and weird green light.

"I had no idea you cared," I said, touched.

Before she rounded the corner on her way back to the car, she said, "I don't. Oh, and until you know what's going on with D, you should probably keep it in your pants."

Busted

CHAPTER NINETEEN

Just when I thought my day couldn't get any weirder, Trinity called and invited me over to her place so she and her demon could share what she'd learned from the boss's grimoire. Don't get me wrong—I was thrilled she'd made progress on the missing page front, but she never let any of us come to her place, let alone with her demon there, presumably out in the open.

I'd never met the demon. None of us had ever seen her demon.

She never summoned it in front of me or the team and seemed awfully protective of the immaterial entity, who was apparently neither tempter nor lord. According to Trinity, it was something of a mage in the hell realm. More magic than a tempter, but she was evasive about how much more. I was curious but didn't push. We needed her on the team, and I didn't want to piss her off enough to leave us.

The boss wouldn't let her or any of the rest of us leave, but I'd always been a little worried that she was embarrassed of us.

Okay, I worried she might be embarrassed of me. I tried, I really did, but I could only manage to fake being a functioning adult for thirty-minute stretches. Maybe an hour in a pinch. I couldn't help it. It was who I was as a person.

Bottom line—an immediate invitation could only mean one of two things: really, really bad news or a super awesome breakthrough.

I wasn't sure I could take more bad news, so I convinced myself it must be something super awesome. Yup, definitely a subscriber to the power of positive thinking. It was a survival skill.

Trinity lived in one of the newer upscale high-rises in downtown Nashville, the ones that came with an Olympic-sized indoor pool, twenty-four-hour concierge service, and celebrity neighbors. I wasn't jealous or anything. I had a killer view, and the twins sort of acted as concierges. At least they brought takeout and took out the trash...sometimes.

It took some wrangling, three forms of identification, and a more than a little cleavage to convince the security guard to let me in. After dashing into the elevator, in case the guard changed his mind, I breathed a sigh of relief and tried to summon Hannah—again. No luck. Too bad sweet talk and cleavage didn't work on her.

I rang the bell and waited with bated breath. Naturally, I was dying of curiosity. I'd expected a freakishly tidy, sparse, and decidedly scholarly vibe from Trinity's lair. When the door opened, however, I was greeted by dark woods complemented by rich earth tones, though I'd guessed right when it came to the scholarly angle—she had an impressive collection of books filling floor-to-ceiling shelves.

I was so caught up in awe that I didn't notice who'd answered the door, not until a deep voice laced with amusement caught my attention. "Welcome, Jane McGee. It is an honor to finally meet you."

I spun around and came face-to-face with a striking man with dark hair, a silky, black beard, and sparkling red eyes. Gleaming white teeth showed between a pair of sensual lips, and his cheeks dimpled as he smiled. He wore a tunic like the one I'd seen on D when he first showed up in my closet. Obviously, this guy was a demon, but he seemed familiar.

"Who are you, and what have you done with Trinity?" I pulled my knife from its sheath and assumed a fighting stance. No sign of Hannah, damn her, but I could bluff with the best of them.

The demon's smile widened, and he held up his hands, palms up. "I am Marquess Samagina of the hell realm, currently in the service of Mistress Jones."

My jaw dropped, but fortunately, my knife did not. "*You're* Trinity's demon? But you're corporeal," I stammered. He had to be lying. The demon standing in front of me was solid, and there was no sign he was possessing a human body. It was his body. But I'd seen the red gleam of the demon in Trinity's gaze too many times to count. Her demon was immaterial.

"He's not lying, Jinx."

Instinct kept my knife trained on the demon, but my gaze darted to Trinity. I'd never seen our resident scholar look sheepish, but her slumped shoulders and averted gaze alarmed me more than the bombshell she'd dropped on me. As far as I knew, and as far as any of the demon hunters in our circle had been told, demons were either immaterial or corporeal, not both.

"Well, this should make our next refresher course on demon species more interesting." So much for maintaining maturity, but I really couldn't think of anything else to say.

"You can't tell anyone." Trinity's gaze met mine, hard and determined. "The boss thinks Sam is an immaterial, midlevel demon of scholarship, not a—"

"Powerful demon lord capable of going from corporeal and incorporeal? Yeah, I'm sure the boss wouldn't appreciate that."

The demon coughed, clearing his throat before speaking. "Not a lord, I'm afraid. The distinction is no doubt inconsequential to you from an earth realm perspective, but my rank and legions are not as impressive as that of a lord or duke in the hell realm."

Okay. That settled it. With a lecture like that, this guy *had* to be Trinity's demon. And judging by the sidelong glances and tension in the room, I guessed there was more to their relationship than "Mistress" and "Marquess." I couldn't blame her. Tall, dark, gorgeous, *and* smart? She'd be crazy not to hit that.

Plus, she'd called him "Sam." It was kind of cute. Color me impressed.

Trinity shot me a look of pure murder, which I ignored as the corners of my lips curled into my trademark smirk. I'd *totally* be ribbing her about this later. But we had bigger fish to fry at the moment. I sheathed my knife, which had gone all wonky again, wavering between a brilliant crimson and bright purple, and looked back and forth between my teammates.

"Okay, now that we've gotten introductions out of the way, maybe you and *Sam* here can tell me what you've got on the boss's book." I walked over to one of the gazillion bookcases, grabbed the gilded volume, and planted my ass on one of the comfy chairs surrounding Trinity's coffee table. I flipped through the pages, being deliberately rough with ancient fabric, at least until my colleague snatched it out of my hands.

Before I could protest, Trinity opened to a section from which several pages had been ripped and placed it on the table in front of me. The pages were still missing. I was tempted to start creasing the corners of the remaining pages when Trinity started chanting. Sam the demon scholar joined in, conjuring a pentagram around the book on the table's surface. It reminded me of the boss's pentagrams, with lights and floating sigils that cast the room in an eerie glow.

Not to mention my knife. I yanked it out of its hilt before it could burn me. More powerful demon magic. How much of this shit was hiding right under our noses?

Without breaking his rhythm, Sam said, "Place your knife on the book."

"Not sure that's a good idea," I said. "I think it's malfunctioning."

"We need it. Trinity's knife didn't work, nor did any of my weapons. Yours might. It's reacting to the book and its magic."

He was right. I placed my knife on the book, which made more of those weird purple sparks fly. The book levitated, hovering above the pentagram, and pages appeared out of thin air. Well, not exactly pages—more like holographic images that resembled pages. Ghost pages. Could a book be haunted?

Trinity stood up and grabbed a quill and a piece of parchment from one corner of the coffee table. Where had that come from? I shook my head in a desperate attempt to wrap my mind around what was happening. I'd barely recovered from the shock of dead summoner and dual-natured demon species. I wasn't sure I could handle what appeared to be a display of higher demon magic, which was supposed to be safely contained in the hell realm.

"There," Trinity said, furiously scribbling on the parchment. She was good. I could barely translate one in three words on the ghost pages, but she had no trouble reading and transcribing the words into English.

Interpreting them would be another matter entirely.

In the days of the great ancient war, Belial was defeated, and his allies exterminated or banished. Should the banished one, the one who has long slumbered, awaken, this Fallen of the Host of Seven is she who has the power to open the gates to the Realm of Darkness.

To defeat her, a Warrior forged in turmoil must rise and battle the Harbingers of Doom, which are Seven Sins and Seven Virtues.

The Warrior will lead seven into battle; imbued with the Power of Three Realms, they will stand against two.

Arbiter and Intercessor, in Harmony or Discord, will decide the course as they should have long ago.

With the Warrior, or against the Warrior, to stand or fall with the Steadfast or the True.

"Well, then," I said after the third read. "That clears it all up."

"I'm very pleased to be of service." Sam offered me a beatific smile.

Trinity patted him gently on the shoulder. "That was sarcasm, hon. We've talked about that before." She smiled apologetically. "He doesn't get out much, and I'm truly sorry about that, too." The last part was addressed to Sam.

"Oh, yes, of course." The demon's shoulders slumped in defeat, and I almost felt sorry for him. "My apologies. Naturally, the meaning is shrouded in metaphor and poetic language—"

"Right, I get it. I've read Nostradamus."

Trinity arched a brow at me.

"Fine, I watched a few documentaries on Nostradamus. Cryptic prophecies, ancient histories, blah, blah, blah. But some of it makes sense." I started pacing, ticking off items on my fingers. "One, the boss is the Arbiter and Hannah's the Intercessor, and they're definitely not in harmony. Two, according to our intel, there's a war brewing in the hell realm, presumably between Belial and...someone. Maybe that Astaroth guy?"

Trinity shook her head and held up a finger. "Belial led a rebellion against Astaroth, and we've been chasing the magic angle, but this passage deals with the realm of darkness, and three realms, presumably the hell realm, the earth realm, and—"

"The celestial realm," Sam added helpfully. "Lord Belial did lead a hell realm army of demons against the celestials."

"Right," I said. "Which just leaves us with a warrior plus seven versus seven sins and seven virtues. Seven allies? What is it with the number seven?" I turned my attention to Sam. "I thought demons were into sixes. Is this a celestial thing, you know, since angels on high are all about the number seven?"

He shrugged. "Perhaps, though the translation of what appears to be an archaic demon battle plan and prediction isn't necessarily reliable. You might as well ask why prophecies take such license with spelling and punctuation."

"Look at you," Trinity said. "You made a joke." She gave him a high five, which made the poor guy blush and shuffle his feet. Oh, they were adorkable.

As cute as it was, we needed to stay focused. I couldn't solve the riddle of the warrior and sevens, but I did know I needed to get in touch with my demon ASAP. Maybe she could shed some light on this, or at least tell me what her beef with the boss was—or would be in the future. At the very least, she could help me stop whoever wanted to open the gates to the realm of darkness. That hit a little too close to Keith Pender-grass's final message to his fellow summoners.

End times at hand. Be ready to open the gates to the glorious rebellion.

Yeah, that couldn't be a coincidence.

"What now?" Trinity asked.

"Our priority is still securing the portals. Opening any hell realm gates is a no-no, since that seems to be step one in the prophecy of doom, not to mention that was the deal I made with the boss in the first place."

Trinity pushed her glasses on her nose, squared her shoulders, and nodded. "Secure your soul first, worry about the rest later. What can I do?"

Best. Colleague. Ever.

"Keep working the magic mojo to find and translate the other missing pages. See if you can dig up more about the warrior, team, and these harbingers of war. And don't worry, your secret's safe with me." I turned to the demon and gave him a wry smile. "Sam, glad to have you on the team, especially if you can give me an advantage over the boss."

He took my hand, bowed low over it, and kissed it. Oh, wow, that was hot. Old-fashioned and a little awkward, but totally hot. I winked at Trinity and wagged my eyebrows while mouthing "keeper."

She grinned back. "We can do that. What are you going to do?"

I grabbed my knife and put it back in its sheath, resisting the urge to scratch the book's cover. I was so petty.

Instead, I headed for the door and yelled over my shoulder, "For starters, I think I need to get my knife fixed. I also need to talk to Hannah. She's been sulking and avoiding me long enough. I'm going to get in touch with my inner demon."

CHAPTER TWENTY

By the time I made it back to my apartment, news of the ritualistic slaughter of a local Nashville man was all over television, radio, and the Internet. The story had even gone national. Jeez, nothing like gruesome and gory to ignite morbid curiosity and spread it like wildfire. My roomies were digging up anything they could find on the guy. He had a mile-long rap sheet in our circles for illegal summoning of course, but somehow, he'd managed to beat every charge levied against him.

Kind of like he'd beaten every charge filed against him for drug trafficking and other unsavory activities. His demons likely offered protection in exchange for illegal passage onto this realm. Either that, or he'd simply been smart enough to cover his tracks or slip through the cracks of the overworked criminal justice system.

Or maybe D's summoner was covering for him.

As for the charges related to demon summoning, the boss apparently had some ethics where humans were concerned—not me, obviously, but he hadn't punished the man in spite of overwhelming circumstantial evidence. Maybe this was his excuse. Maybe he'd sent D or someone else to get rid of this thorn in his side and make it look like the result of his meddling with demon lords.

I was down two days and had more questions than answers. I needed to get Hannah on board with the save Jinx's ass program. I was her host. She couldn't ignore me forever, especially if she wanted me to keep being her host. Good grief, she seemed oblivious to our dire situation. I could've used her expertise on who or what killed Keith Pendergrass. She hadn't even responded to my summons at the warehouse. I'd tugged on her psychic leash and rubbed my black mirror until my fingers were raw but with no result.

Then there was the minor issue of the grimoire's prediction about wars and balance and some beef she had with the boss. She could clue me in about that.

And I still felt weird. Had ever since I'd stumbled out of bed, but the feeling had amplified as time passed. Almost like I'd lost a limb, or I'd lost my best friend.

It was probably just a residual hangover.

I made a cup of coffee and tried to focus. I needed all the help I could get in order summon to Hannah with Mara's assistance. She'd never ignored me when I summoned her before this case. We figured a proper summoning circle with sigils and the use of her official title would work where scrying failed. I had a lot of questions for the Intercessor. True, she never gave straight answers. She'd never even given me a straight answer when I asked why she'd chosen to possess me. She simply stated all would be revealed in time.

At first, I'd assumed it was because I was born to be bad. But having a powerful demon like Hannah at least allowed me to work for the boss and with my team to control the flow of hell realm visitors on earth and monitor their activities. It had let me to do some good in the world. But now I wondered if there wasn't more to it than that, especially after Hannah's cryptic conversation with the boss the other night. It was like she'd been speaking to an old friend, or possibly an old enemy.

She'd called him Arbiter, and he'd called her Intercessor for the first time.

Hannah had been different, like she was aware on a whole new level.

Should the banished one, the one who has long slumbered, awaken, this

Fallen of the Host of Seven is she who has the power to open the gates to the Realm of Darkness.

Crap on a cracker. Was that about Hannah, meaning she had the power to open the gates, the portals? Was her refusal to cooperate part of her diabolical plan to start a war? But why? Hannah helped me capture demons and protect humans and the earth realm from them. That seemed like the exact opposite of a demon who wanted to start a war. And she'd promised to keep me safe.

She'd called me her other. What did that even mean?

As Trinity pointed out, most normal humans wouldn't survive long-term demonic possession like I had. What was up with that? I knew I was weird, but this was a seriously next-level FUBAR situation. Full-time occupation by a powerful demon sapped the host's life-force. Alexi was the exception, since animalistic demons did less damage to their hosts and tended to work in harmony with the humans who got saddled with them.

But I certainly wasn't special as far as demon trackers. The rest of the team had me matched in terms of weirdness. Nope, I was just one of the gang. Except I was in charge of the gang, at least temporarily, and I actually didn't hate management yet.

Maybe I had some executive leadership skills and that made me special.

Nah.

Boice and Roice joined Mara and me in one corner of our expansive living area as we prepared to initiate a summons. Mara seemed more relaxed and at ease. I was glad. She'd been terrified when the boss had threatened her. I didn't blame the succubus. The boss had scared me, too. In spite of everything, I was glad I'd channeled whatever mojo allowed me to keep her out of harm's way, and not just because of her succubus charm and glamour.

She hadn't mentioned anything about leaving. Instead, she appeared to be enthusiastic about helping. I had to admit, she made a nice addition to the team. If I lived through this current case, I'd see about hiring her so she could be a bona fide, paid member of our operation.

My roomies were bespelled enough for all of us. I had a sneaking suspicion they cared less about my fate and more about spending time with a member of the hell realm's most beautiful and magnetic species. Fair enough.

"So," I said, sitting on the edge of the pentagram Mara had constructed on one of our area rugs. "How do you want to start?"

I fought the urge to giggle. She'd constructed the pentagram out of uncooked spaghetti noodles and had floating tea candles placed at the tip of each star point. The sigils sparkled around the noodles. We had glitter? I had no idea the twins were crafty. It was cute, so cute I wondered if it would actually work. Then again, Mara didn't exactly have a lot to work with in our apartment.

"Like the pentagram?" Boice asked, smirking. "We helped."

I gave him a saccharine smile while surreptitiously flipping him off. "What an incredibly sweet gesture."

"Only the best for you, boss," Roice said, snorting.

That was the final straw. I was raising their rent.

"Oh, before I forget," I said, pulling out my knife. It glowed red in the presence of the twins and Mara, but it still flickered with a bit of purple. "I need you guys to look at my demon-hunting knife. It's doing weird things."

A heavy sigh preceded my roomie's snarky reply. "You want me and my *demon* brother to help you with your *demon*-killing knife? Seriously?"

Well, when he put it that way... "Point taken, but it's flashing weird colors, not just red. We're taking blue and purple. Any ideas?"

"No. Blue is for celestials. Never heard of demon steel glowing purple," Roice said with a shrug. "And before you ask, I've never heard of a hybrid demon and celestial. Our kinds don't mix."

"No celestials here," I said, waving my hands around. "Unless you've got one stashed in the storage closet."

"Maybe purple's for aliens," Boice said helpfully. When I glared, he sighed and shook his head. "I'll research it."

"How do you normally summon Hannah?" Mara asked, getting us back on track.

"With my black mirror," I replied, fishing it out from between the girls. It felt strange in my fingers, cold and devoid of any tangible power. Normally I could sense the demon energy coursing through it under my fingertips, a pulsing power that grew stronger as I prepared to unleash Hannah. Now I felt...nothing. Come to think of it, I hadn't felt anything since being dragged back from my all-night drunken summoner chasing the night before.

Come on, Hannah. Give me a break, will you?

Would she cooperate, or was she determined to hold out on me until we both got sucked into the hell realm?

"Wait, that's weird," I said, examining my black mirror more closely. The obsidian gleamed in the glow of candlelight. But the black core in that normally reflected the demon sparks floating in my irises was now marred by a white streak. The streak bulged in the center and tapered at either end.

Roice leaned closer to examine it. "What the hell is that? I told you to stop drawing vaginas on all your stuff."

I shoved him away. "I didn't do this. What does this mean?"

Mara scooted over to look, her gorgeous gaze widening in alarm.

A wave of panic and dread threatened to engulf me. "What?" I asked, my voice an octave higher than usual. "What's wrong?"

Mara shook her head and said, "Try calling her."

I closed my eyes and worked to get my breathing under control. I didn't know how many more surprises I could take. My heart raced, and a cold sweat broke out on my forehead. After a moment, I focused my energy and reached deep within, seeking, calling, and pleading as I fought against the unthinkable.

"Hannah." My voice came out as a harsh whisper. "Can you hear me? Please come out."

Nothing. The feeling of unease that had followed me all day, that sense of emptiness, it all made sense now. My eyes stung, and I couldn't speak past the lump in my throat. Warm arms enveloped me—Mara's, I thought, though I sensed Boice and Roice come closer, drawn by my uncharacteristic display of grief and sorrow.

"No," I said. "No, this can't be happening."

"What the hell, Jinx?" a voice said—Boice's.

"She's gone." The void of anguish threatened to swallow me whole. "Hannah's gone."

CHAPTER TWENTY-ONE

I only thought I'd felt like crap yesterday morning. Boy, was I wrong.

Compared to this morning, yesterday was a dream. If only I could go back and have my future self tell my past self that I was a fool. I should've seized the day and done something fun, something exciting, something useful—some combination of *Back to the Future* and *Ferris Bueller's Day Off*. With only one day to go until I lost my soul, with the added bonus of a prophecy of doom hanging over my head, we'd lost the rogue summoner, all our leads, and my personal demon.

This was the most sucktastic Sunday ever.

Seriously, stuff like this was only supposed to happen on Mondays.

I thought about hitting the tequila again, but that would be counterproductive. It would also reflect poorly on my image as a budding midlevel manager. D had shown up sometime during the night. He'd climbed into bed with me and held me close, like he'd done when we were kids. No demands, no frisky business, he was just...there for me. When I needed him.

I had a sneaking suspicion he was hanging out in my closet again. He needed more space. He was a big boy now.

Maybe I could leave him my apartment in my will. He could have full run of the place.

Shaking off that unpleasant thought, I rolled over and wrapped my body around his, reveling in the sensation while I could. In spite of my fears and doubts about him, his presence soothed. It anchored me and gave me strength to face the obstacles ahead. But I had questions for him. Given the nature of those questions, I might unravel the fragile strands of trust I'd woven between us.

But I still needed to ask.

"What's on your mind?" he said, his voice deeper with the remnants of sleep.

"How did you know I had something on my mind?" I snuggled closer, holding him tighter.

He chuckled. "I know you. You only hold me tight enough to cut off my circulation when you're worried."

It was my turn to laugh. "Yeah, what could I possibly be worried about?" I asked, rolling over and putting my index finger to my chin, miming deep contemplation.

He rolled over, too, and landed on top of me. I was about to get excited, but instead of pinning me with his body weight in an effort to ravish me senseless, he pinned me down so he could dig his fingers into my ribs, tickling me until I dissolved in a fit of giggles that had tears streaming down my face.

"Say uncle." He granted me a brief reprieve to catch my breath and voice my surrender. Like I would give him the satisfaction.

I started to hyperventilate, my breaths coming in short bursts that deprived my body and brain of much-needed oxygen. He loosened his hold on me by a fraction, and I used it to my advantage. I snaked a hand down between our bodies and caught his impressive manly bits, causing him to gasp in surprise, scowl, and then grin in the space of a split second.

"Sucker." I smirked as he let go of me. "You fell for the oldest trick in the book."

He smiled down at me, his gaze playful and brimming with sensual interest. "You're the one touching my junk. Who's the sucker now?"

Oh my God, he was right. He did know me well, along with my inner brazen hussy. I thought about suspending my Q and A session in favor of a hot and heavy tumble on the bed session, but he stilled my hand, much to my disappointment.

"What's on your mind?" His firm tone brooked no argument.

I let go, and he rolled off me to sit up on my comfy mattress. I sat up, too, dread replacing the all-too-brief sensation of carefree playfulness. D and I never seemed to catch a break.

I sat up and started fidgeting with the hem of my tank top. "I need to ask you some questions, but I'm afraid you'll be mad at me when I do."

He sighed and ran a hand through his dark hair before scrubbing his face. "I didn't kill him," he said.

Wow, that was easier than I'd expected. "Wait, how did you know what I was going to ask?"

He gave me a sad smile. "How could you not ask? I would've been angry if you hadn't. You can't hold back in this investigation, Jane. The stakes are too high. Question anyone and everyone, including me."

A wave of relief and gratitude filled me. He was being reasonable, so earnest. And he was answering questions. In fact, he was more than open, more than willing—he seemed eager, like a man in desperate need of confession and absolution. Maybe I should work in a few more questions while he was in the mood.

"How much demon magic do you have?" I asked. Before he could cut me off, I said, "Not the regular magic tempters use, but the powerful, high demon magic that can destroy a body from the inside out. I need to know what kind of entity killed Keith Pendergrass. He was exsanguinated without a mark on his body."

I gulped before I voiced my next thought, the pain of last night washing over me anew. I gripped the covers, wrapping my grandma's quilt protectively around my legs and wishing I could use something similar to bandage my aching heart. "And I need to know what kind of entity could've taken Hannah. That would take some powerful demon magic, too."

Assuming she'd been taken. I didn't want to face the fact that she might have left voluntarily. I had a habit of making people leave. First my dad, then D—even though he'd explained that one and was here now, the insecurity lingered—and now Hannah. When I needed her most, she'd vanished.

He'd gotten up off the bed and now stood over me. Two fingers lifted my chin. "I don't think she was taken." His words confirmed my worst fear. I must've flinched, since he gripped my chin tighter, forcing me to hold his gaze rather than turn away. "And I don't think she abandoned you out of spite or fear or anger. I think she's trying to help you. I think she wants to protect you."

I sat up as disbelief morphed into a tiny sliver of hope. Could it be? How?

"Wait," I said, holding up a finger as a thought occurred to me. "How could she just leave? She's never done it before, and my black mirror holds her to me and allows me to contain her and summon her when I need her help. And anyway, separation is supposed to be lethal for both of us."

D quirked a brow and gave me a look that seemed suspiciously like do-you-seriously-believe-that. "Do you really think a demon as powerful as Hannah could be held by that little trinket around your neck? Especially since she's somehow figured out her identity as the Intercessor?"

He had a point. I'd told him a bit about the text Sam and Trinity translated—the part about the Arbiter and the Intercessor holding the keys to the outcome of some future war of apocalyptic proportions—but what was I supposed to think?

I threw my hands up in exasperation. "The boss told me it would, and until now, it has. What else could get her to work with me to track demons?"

He held up his palms in apparent surrender. "The Arbiter found you when you were young and vulnerable, just like the rest of your crew. He told you what he wanted you to believe and what you wanted to hear. I don't blame you," he said before his gaze turned hard. "But you're not a young, vulnerable girl anymore. You're a seasoned tracker. You need to think for yourself, trust your gut and instincts instead of trusting your so-called boss."

So-called boss? The guy paid me. That made him more than a so-called boss. But maybe D was right. Maybe he really was more like a mob boss than a legit businessman, especially if he'd known more about Hannah and her true identity than he was saying.

Duh, of course he was. But I'd always figured him for an honest boss. A scary, surly, garden-variety asshole of a boss, but an honest one.

"Do you think the boss set me up with Murkowski? You think he had something to do with Hannah's awakening and is trying to use it to his advantage?" I asked. "He's a demon. Would he benefit from a hell realm war?"

D started pacing. "I don't know. I don't think he's in league with Belial. That's not the way the rebel demon lord operates. He negotiates, persuades, works to make his recruits come willingly because they believe the rebellion is just and righteous. The Arbiter would see right through that kind of scheme—he's a master of those tactics himself."

I studied D as he talked. He moved with the unconscious grace of a warrior, a soldier. He stood straight and paced with even steps, muscles rolling with practiced ease as he walked. Though seemingly lost in concentration, I would bet every last dollar in my dwindling bank account that he was keeping an eye on every corner of my room, every nook and cranny, just as he'd done while on the hunt for the rogue summoner.

Wow, what if he was the warrior—as in The Warrior—the one who could defeat battling armies of demons and angels? I'd add that to my list of questions to ask after I got an answer about his magic. The two had to be related. The Warrior would have to have a boatload of magic to take on two realms.

"Back to my question." I struggled to concentrate on the task at hand rather than how much I enjoyed ogling the fine male specimen in front of me. "Aside from your demon associates who specialize in detecting advanced magic—where were they last night, by the way?—and your uncanny ability to secure rogue summoners in hiding and observe yours truly, a seasoned demon tracker, in an alley without my noticing, do *you* know high demon magic? Do you practice it?"

He stopped pacing and gave me his pissed-off demon look. "I told you. That's classified."

"So much for questioning anyone and everyone, including you," I said, giving him *my* best pissed-off demon hunter look. "If you're going to help me, cut the shit and help me."

"Fine," he said, growling. "I know high demon magic. I'm a decent practitioner. That's how I escaped from him."

Before I could blink, he was gone. I jumped off the bed, heart racing, as I scanned the room. He'd vanished. Just as suddenly, he reappeared in front of me. His body remained tense, but a hint of a grin curled the corners of his lips. Clearly, he'd been trying to impress me.

He'd succeeded.

I wondered what else he could do, other than materialize across a room and conceal himself from demon trackers. Could he travel through the space-time continuum? That would be cool. Or maybe he could read minds or tell when people or other demons were lying. That'd be handy. I bet he knew some good card tricks, too.

If I lived through this, I'd have to take him to Vegas. We'd make a fortune.

"Where'd you learn it?" I asked.

"You're down to your last question," he said, turning away, but not before I caught a glimpse of the hard line of his jaw. If he clenched it any tighter, he'd crack his back molars. "Sure you want to squander it on that?"

"Maybe," I said. "If it'll help me solve this case and live long enough to pick up where we left off, then yes. If it helps me crack through your shell and get close to you again, then that would be a definite yes."

He braced his hands against the thick panes of my large bedroom window, leaning as if fighting some battle within himself. I wanted to go to him, to wrap my arms around him and either hold him or shake him until he came to his senses and told me the truth.

I wanted to know everything. Where he'd been, what he'd been through, why and how he'd come back.

Because Lacey was right. He'd shown up when the whole mess started. I didn't believe in coincidences. He might not have something to do with the demon lord and the demon boss both ironically out for me and my soul, but he knew more than he was telling me. I'd have to put a stop to that.

Especially if he was the warrior who could save all three realms.

"My father taught me," D said, his voice a harsh whisper. "He taught me a lot of other things, too. Terrible things. Things that would make your skin crawl and your blood boil. You think you're bad? Baby, you've got nothing on me."

That wasn't good. It took a lot to make my skin crawl and blood boil. I'd seen things. Bad things. But apparently D had seen and done worse.

"Who exactly is your father? And what about your mother?" I asked. Technically, I'd burned through my allotted three questions, but he couldn't just leave it there. I wanted to go to him even more now, to hold him and tell him he wasn't bad. Whatever he'd done, he'd surely been forced to do by his father. The hell realm was different, and the demons who lived there operated under their own set of rules that would make ordinary humans balk. Was that it? He'd grown up in the earth realm. His moral compass had been forged here.

A fine tremor ran down his back. I rushed over and put my arms around his waist, molding my body to his back.

"My father is...it's complicated. And I never knew my mother. I figure she dumped me on earth after she left my demon sire. I get a memory every now and then, from that time. A flash of a beautiful face, a smile, and her voice—I remember her voice. I waited for her before I found you, but she never came back. Probably didn't want a demon kid."

He tried to pull away, but I held him tighter. I remembered a bit about my dad, too, and like D, I'd waited for him to come back to me, to my family. He left just before I saw my now-missing demon. I wondered if he knew, if he'd seen her before I did. He must have. Why else would he have left? There was only one explanation, or so I'd thought. It was because of me.

Maybe D thought the same thing, but I couldn't see it. The frightened boy who'd come to me all those years ago hadn't exactly been a saint, but he had was a good man. He'd protected my family and provided for us, scrounging for what we needed when we couldn't afford it. True, it could have been a debt of honor. He had lived with us rent-free for over a decade. But he'd given us more than food and working appliances. Every year at Christmas, we'd find a few extra gifts under our scrawny little tree. Megan got new dolls and, when she grew older, dress clothes we couldn't afford on our own. Mom got jewelry and perfume, luxuries she always denied herself in order to make ends meet. I got boots. Beautiful, bedazzled leather cowgirl boots I wore with pride until the soles were falling apart, as least until my little closet elf managed a repair.

He might have given us food, heat, and a working car out of gratitude or self-preservation, but the gifts? Those were pure kindness.

"You aren't bad, either," I said. "You took care of me and my family for years, and you came back here to me. You helped me save Mara, and you feel bad about that summoner's death. I can tell. Whatever you did in the hell realm doesn't matter. You're here, now, doing the right thing."

He didn't pull away, but his back stiffened. Why was he fighting me? Ugh, men and their lack of emotional intelligence—it was a wonder they didn't explode from bottling it all up. I stood with my hand on his back, resisting the urge to squirm. The sunrise was upon us, bathing my room and my demon in the pink, glowing rays of a new day. It would be a day without Hannah, a day no closer to solving my case, but a new day with Dominic. The thought didn't wash away the fear and dread and heartache, but it made the whole thing more bearable. I wouldn't have to go this alone.

"You wouldn't say that if you knew who I really am, but you're right about one thing. I'm here with you now, and I'm going to do the right thing by getting you out of this mess. I won't let anyone take you away from me."

"Oh, yeah?" I said, grinning as he turned in my arms to face me. "What's on your agenda for the day, then? Finding Hannah?"

He nodded. "I'm going to check out the warehouse where you and Lacey found Keith to see if I can find more traces of the magic that killed him and identify it."

Wait, what did that have to do with Hannah, unless... "You think Hannah killed Keith?"

"No other entity could have killed a human in that manner—except, perhaps, an angel."

That was something I hadn't considered, mostly because I didn't think angels did that sort of thing. Honestly, I knew very little about the celestial realm aside from mythology and religious texts. Those had proved less than accurate when it came to demons. But why would an angel kill a human demon summoner?

"Wait, Trinity said that Belial led the Sons of Darkness in a war against the Sons of Light—angels. Celestials. And that text mentioned three realms in relation to the war, so presumably the celestials will be a part of it. Do you think celestials are trying to stop Belial from starting another war?"

"Maybe." D looked thoughtful. "That's not necessarily a favor, though. The enemy of your enemy isn't always your friend when it comes to creatures from the hell or celestial realms. They may have their own agenda."

"Seems you know more about celestials than I do. Have you ever met one?" Demons were my thing, but I'd often wondered about the "other side." Most reported angel sightings in human media were false, like demon sightings. But some demon encounters in the news were legit. No angels had crossed my path, and I'd seen all kinds of non-human entities. I thought they were rare or just didn't bother much with humanity, at least not the segment of humanity I dealt with as a demon hunter. But what if angels were hidden among us, too?

D shrugged. "Not really. I know only what our lore and legends say."

"Which is?" I was growing impatient. I needed answers, damn it, and all I got was the run around—from my boss, from Hannah, and now from D?

He must've read my expression, since he sighed and ran a hand through his hair, a nervous gesture that made me terribly jealous of that hand. "They're haughty, meddlesome, patronizing, and think they should be the supreme rulers of all dimensions. Some of your earth legends about them are true. They spent a good deal of time trying to cast my kind from the earth realm, blackening our names as villains so they could be the saviors of humanity."

He practically spat the word "saviors." Guess all those religious texts got something right. Seemed there was no love lost between demons and angels.

"Okay. There was an ongoing war between the hell realm and celestial realm and earth was caught in the middle, and the angels did a smear campaign on the demons throughout and kept the propaganda machine running. Got it. Why did it end? What happened to celestials? Demons are still roaming the earth, so what about angels?"

He furrowed his brows. "According to legend, celestials and demons reached a truce and agreed earth was neutral ground. Neither side could win, and humans had become collateral damage."

"Really?" I was skeptical, but maybe that came from years of living with Roice and Boice. Those guys thought every myth, legend, and bit of religious lore in the earth realm was a crock of shit, probably because of the whole smear campaign against their species.

D arched a brow. "Ever heard of The Dark Ages? The Black Plague? The crusades?"

"Um, yeah. Collapse of the Roman Empire, flea-ridden epidemics, and religious wars as a pretext for conquest. I did go to school, you know." I ticked each explanation off on my fingers. Take that, Mr. Demon know-it-all.

He grinned. "When you weren't skipping to hang out with me. Anyway, yes, those factors played a role, but who do you think was behind all of that?"

I opened my mouth to answer, but he cut me off. "Before you say demons, remember what I told you about angels and their savior complex? Let me tell you, no one loves war more than angels. People turn to them in times of great distress. Demons may feed on sin, but angels feed on misery."

Damn, my head was spinning. Then again, this was more information than I'd gotten from the boss or Barbatos. I should probably pay attention. I bet Trinity didn't even have this kind of insider information. I'd have to brag later—and have her fact-check.

Surprisingly, D kept talking. After all the secrecy, I dug it. He was like a sexy professor, stimulating my mind as well as my girly parts. "Angels and demons still visited, of course, but they had to abide by the treaty and avoid direct conflict, and both sides agreed to lower their profiles. Aside from demon hunters, most of humanity has no clue that my kind walk among them."

Fascinated, I prodded him for more information. "Angels are still here, too? More than a few? I've never seen one. Could they have something to do with this new rebellion?"

He gave me a lopsided grin. "They're here. You've been so focused on hunting demons that you never noticed them. They aren't your targets. As for the rebellion, I don't know if they have anything to do with it."

"But is there a way to find out? If they're targeting anyone on earth who's helping Belial, maybe they can help us cut off his access to portals and keep him out. Do they use portals, too?"

"Probably. I don't know as much about their mode of travel. You aren't the only victim of cryptic mentors."

His expression changed as soon as the words left his mouth. Maybe he'd had an epiphany. Instead of sharing, he turned away from me and started digging around my room for his clothes. I gasped when he pulled off his pajama bottoms and gave me a killer view of his gorgeous bare ass. The man was amazing, perfect, as if he'd been sculpted by one of those ancient Greek sculptors from long ago, the ones who captured the ferocity and otherworldly beauty of a god. Of course, D was much more impressive in a few areas than your average Greek statue in terms of length and girth. I'd only had a small taste of him, but I wanted more. I wondered if we had time for a quickie.

Oh, and he could share whatever insight had just flashed through his mind while we were at it. Brainstorming and booty—that was my kind of multitasking.

He turned, grinning at me as he zipped his jeans and deprived me of my view. Still, he was shirtless. Those abs had my mouth watering.

"Jane," he said, his gaze raking over me. "I swear to you by all the stars in the sky that I'll have you tonight, and you'll have me. But right now, I have to find the demon, angel, or who knows what other creature it was who killed that summoner."

All work and no play. Le sigh.

He was right, of course, but it didn't stop me from pouting. I consoled myself by digging out a fresh pair of camo pants and tank top from my closet. Time was wasting. I needed to get cracking on the case, too. Couldn't leave all the heavy lifting to D and my teammates. As temporary leader of our little operation, I had to take on the greatest responsibility.

"What are you doing?" D asked.

"What does it look like? I'm getting dressed." Seriously, ask a stupid question... "I mean, as much as I love my pajamas and fuzzy slippers, they aren't really designed for fieldwork."

He reached me in two long strides and pinned me against my bedroom wall.

"D, what the hell?"

My playful lover was gone. In his place stood a demon, a warrior, the creature of nightmare and legend. The hard lines of his sculpted face shocked me. He was angry. Why was he angry?

"You aren't working today."

Oh, hell no. He did *not* just give me an order in my own home, in the sanctity of my own bedroom and in the presence of my favorite sofa. I was going to have to cancel the order I'd put in for his matching kilt if he didn't shape up.

He had me pinned by the shoulders, but I quickly twisted to the side, bringing my right arm up and around in an arcing motion to capture both his arms underneath mine. It wouldn't hold him for any length of time, but it was all I needed to distract him long enough to reverse the motion of my arm and stick my elbow in his face. I didn't want to hit him—yet—so I opted for escape.

I stepped back with my left foot, turning my body ninety degrees to the left while swinging my right arm straight up between our bodies and then down until my right hand met my left hip. The move twisted his arms up and pinned them under my right arm while also putting him slightly off-balance. I'd managed to move my left arm away from him, but I wasn't in an ideal position to use it. My right arm, however, was perfectly set to bend and shoot my right elbow directly into his face. I put it there to let him know I meant business, though I was sorely tempted to bloody his nose or give him a black eye.

Fortunately, he took the hint and let the tension flow out of his body. I let go and spun around to face him. I had no doubt he could regain his hold and give me serious competition in hand-to-hand combat, not to mention whatever magic he could pull out of his ass, but he must have noticed my oh-no-the-hell-you-didn't expression. He held his palms up and said, "Jane, be reasonable."

I got up in his face—had to stand on my toes to do it, but I managed—and said, "Don't you dare tell me to be reasonable after manhandling me and handing me a line of macho bullshit. I'm not sitting at home. It's my neck on the line in case you hadn't noticed."

"Which is precisely why you need to stay put," he said. We were nose to nose, practically snarling at one another. "You're vulnerable without Hannah."

He had a point, but still. "I was apparently without her yesterday and managed to investigate at a murder scene. I've been out tracking and investigating without having to call on my demon before. I'm more than just a host, you know."

"Of course you're more than a host." He spoke through gritted teeth, muscles tense and straining in spite of his obvious effort at self-control. Didn't matter. If he was trying to play nice and conciliatory, he was doing a piss-poor job. "You've got a lot of brain cells lurking in that thick skull. I would suggest you put them to use looking for paper trails and reviewing video surveillance to find out who else is helping Belial in this realm."

"Desk work? Surveillance?" I asked, incredulous. "You know I have demons for that. Boice and Roice are on it, and they're much better at it than I am. I do fieldwork. That's my job. My training and instincts are for hunting. I'll make much more progress sniffing out demons and summoners."

"Don't make me put a binding spell on you," he said, his voice icy.

"Do that and you won't have me tonight or any other night," I said, calling his bluff. He had to be bluffing. Or if he wasn't, he'd think twice about hexing me. D wanted me as much as I wanted him. The evidence was written all over his handsome face, not to mention trying to claw its way out of his jeans.

He threw his hands in the air and turned away from me. Then he slammed his fists against my wall hard enough to leave a crack.

"Hey, when you're done throwing a tantrum and breaking my stuff, how about you make yourself useful and go look for my demon? You know, since you're worried about me being vulnerable and all." I tossed his shirt at him. It didn't have quite the same impact as fists on a wall, but I managed to give him a face full of thick cotton. Nothing wrong with my aim.

I was as angry as he was. Did he honestly think I was going to sit back and act like some damsel in distress? I hadn't been kidding about the desk work thing. My roomies had it covered. I needed to be out in the field, following up on leads, and I knew just where to start.

Losing my demon might have left me vulnerable, but it had provided me with a rare opportunity to get up close and personal with portals and those who guarded them. And I needed a nice walk in the woods to clear my head. But first, I thought I'd pay a visit to the late Mr. Pendergrass's next of kin. D could go off and sulk on his own. I had work to do.

He yanked on his shirt and glared at me, his handsome face twisted with unchecked rage that made him look the part of a full-blooded demon. No matter their forms, demons were formidable creatures. They could be seductive and cruel by turns, using persuasion, trickery, and brute force to get what they wanted.

"If and when you catch up with Hannah," I said to D, "ask her where she was when Keith was murdered."

With that, I grabbed my enchanted knife—which glowed a brilliant red in the presence of my would-be demon lover—spun on the heel of my boots and left him to ponder that while he adjusted his attitude.

CHAPTER TWENTY-TWO

In spite of D's low opinion of my intelligence and ability to be "reasonable," I wasn't stupid. I had no plans to go looking for any murdering demons or demon lords with kidnapping on the brain. I had a degree in criminal justice and a boatload of experience with investigations—in the field, not behind a computer screen. Boice and Roice could handle that much better than I could. That wasn't a cop-out on my part. It was a fact.

Since the twins hadn't managed to hack into Keith's computer yet, I decided to pay a visit to the Pendergrass family and see what I could dig up on the summoner's known associates. He'd been splitting his time between his mother's house and his sister's place. They lived within a few blocks of each other in Antioch. I started at his mom's place, a modest yet tidy ranch home with a decent lawn and nice landscaping out front. Mrs. Pendergrass answered the door in her robe, red eyes rimmed with tears. She was a middle-aged woman with a pretty, round face and gorgeous blond hair. If not for the lines of sorrow etched on her face, she'd have been a knockout.

My heart went out to her. No matter what else he'd been, Keith had clearly been a beloved son.

"Hello, my name is Jane McGee. Are you Mrs. Amanda Pendergrass?" I asked, pulling out the PI license I carried for just such occasions.

"Yes," she said, her voice a soft, hoarse whisper. She barely glanced at my credentials, her tearful gaze glassy and unfocused. My heart ached for her, more so since her son's activities in my world led to his death. Sure, Keith was a lowlife who broke the rules and got in over his head, but the guy's mom had loved him and mourned his loss. I couldn't give her peace or closure. Hell, I couldn't even tell her what really happened to her son.

But I could make the demon or demons who'd brutally murdered him pay.

"I'm sorry for your loss and apologize for disturbing you, but I'd like to ask you a few questions about your son."

She appeared momentarily confused, shaking out of her stupor to glance over her shoulder. I surreptitiously gripped my knife and took a peek at the metal. It glowed a brilliant blue.

She wasn't alone. And the being inside was a celestial.

Damn it, why hadn't I brought backup? Oh, right, I'd been pissed off at my demon boy and had stormed out on my own like I had something to prove. Amateur move, but I had my pride, too. I couldn't even blame it on a tempter. No, this sticky situation was all on my own ego rather than corporeal demons of pride, aptly named egos. Then again, I had the anger of a mace and a healthy dose of stubbornness. I hadn't met any demons that embodied that vice, if single-minded determination bordering on pigheadedness qualified as a sin.

No matter. I'd have to rely on determination, cunning, and more than a bit of luck now. I couldn't let Mrs. Pendergrass fall victim to the monsters who'd taken her son, be they demons, angels, or some unlikely alliance of the two. Whoever killed Keith was tying up loose ends, and his family could be targets.

Clearing my throat, I regained Mrs. Pendergrass's attention. "May I come in?"

She gave me a faint smile and nodded. "Of course. I apologize, I...it's still such a shock."

Stepping aside, she held the door for me as I took a deep breath and crossed the threshold. The space was warm, if dark, filled with wood paneling and pastels muted by the drawn curtains. Vases of flowers and stands with funeral sprays crowded the living room into which Mrs. Pendergrass led me. Wiping her eyes with delicate fingers, she asked me to sit and then, as an afterthought, offered me something to drink.

"No, thank you," I replied, scanning the room for demon signs. We appeared to be alone, but since some incorporeal tempters were sneaky, I figured celestials were, too. I peered into Mrs. Pendergrass's eyes and looked her over for the looking for telltale mark of a demon. What if she'd been possessed by Mephisto, or a demon like him? If a celestial was here, was it to capture the demon at the expense of Mrs. Pendergrass?

My knife was still on the fritz. I couldn't trust its reading.

There were other ways to detect a demon, though I didn't smell the pungent, sulfuric aroma of brimstone, nor did I sense a demonic presence. I had no idea what celestial signs were.

But something not of this earth lurked nearby. Something powerful. I gripped the hilt of my knife, preparing for battle. And since I didn't have Hannah to help me, I had to get Mrs. Pendergrass out of there.

"You said you had some questions about Keith." Her voice broke as she spoke his name. Then, the most extraordinary aura of peace, calm, and tranquility filled the room along with the scents of dark roast coffee and warm apple pie. Mrs. Pendergrass's face changed from its rictus of pain and grief to the same glassy-eyed, slack-jawed expression she'd worn when she'd answered the door.

Alarm bells rang somewhere in the depths of my addled brain before that strange sense of peace curled around me like a blanket. I fought against it, realizing that the feeling was the product of some form of glamour, but not like any tempter demon I'd ever encountered. I surreptitiously slipped the knife out of its sheath and pressed it against the flesh of my thigh, not piercing the skin, but enough to distract me from whatever spell I was in danger of falling under.

Keeping up the pretense of normalcy, I nodded to Mrs. Pendergrass. "I do have some questions about your son. Specifically, I'd like to know more about his online associates."

She smiled as if reminiscing, toying with a stray lock of hair. "Of course. Keith loved role-playing games. He spent hours playing them. Research, really, since he was designing his own."

"How proud you must be."

My snarky comment didn't appear to register to Mrs. Pendergrass. "He was so like his father. Carl spent hours poring over old books. He was a historian, you know. The myths and legends of ancient cultures from around the world fascinated him, especially the darker ones..."

Trailing off, she inhaled deeply and closed her eyes. "I think the brownies will be ready soon. Would you and your colleague like milk with yours?"

Colleague?

A tall, thin figure materialized across the room. I leapt from the sofa and stood in front of Mrs. Pendergrass, shielding her from the intruder with my knife at the ready. It shone with blinding brightness, casting the entity in an ethereal blue glow. The figure smiled at me and spread her arms, palms open in the universal gesture of "I mean you no harm."

I didn't trust it for an instant.

She smiled wider, her weathered teeth gleaming with a preternatural glow, wrinkled skin shining almost as much as the silver-and-white strands of hair that cascaded around her shoulders. Clad in a simple white tunic, all she needed was wings to complete the look.

I tightened my grip on the knife's handle and widened my stance. "Celestial being, I presume?"

The creature laughed, filling the air with soft, soothing notes of some ancient, angelic melody played upon a lyre. "Pleased to make your acquaintance, Jane McGee. I do wish you'd put down that knife. You'll undo my good work with this grieving mortal soul."

"Good work?" I balked. Sure, plenty of humans believed in benevolent angels, but according to my demon associates, that was largely on account of better public relations. The fact remained that visitors from the celestial realm were as powerful, maybe more powerful, than those from the hell realm. Then again, my sources were a tad biased.

But I wasn't stupid enough to take this entity at face value.

"Of course, my dear." New Age Grandma's brows furrowed as she peered over my head, nodding at Mrs. Pendergrass. Feeling foolish—I'd hate to fall for such a lame fake-out this late in my career—I took a cautious step back to get a sidelong glance at the grieving mother.

Grandma wasn't kidding. Mrs. Pendergrass's serenity had apparently fled, replaced by confusion and terror as she stared at my glowing knife. I must've looked like some deranged miniature serial killer. Ethereal energy flooded the room again, and Mrs. Pendergrass slowly returned to her stupor.

"I understand your wariness, Jane. I assure you we have the same goal of protecting this human. If you will allow me to settle her, I will be quite happy to explain."

The scent of baked goods and autumn flooded my senses along with crisp air that sent a pleasant shiver down my spine as multicolored leaves danced in my vision. Good grief, I was surprised the angel didn't throw in pumpkin spice for good measure. I was such a basic bitch.

"You can drop the mojo, Grandma. I'm not falling for it."

"You may call me Cassie," she said with a deep sigh. "My mojo, as you call it, is meant for Amanda Pendergrass. She's sorely in need of comfort."

I couldn't fault the angel's observation. I grudgingly sheathed my knife. Cassie beamed at me before turning her attention to Mrs. Pendergrass. She led the woman down a hallway and into a room, closing the door behind her. I fought the urge to follow and concentrated on clearing my mind of angel Zen mojo so I could keep my wits.

I managed to shake off everything except the smell of brownies. Maybe I was just hungry.

Cassie floated back into the room—literally floated. Her feet didn't touch the ground. Show off. Or maybe it was an angel thing. I was unfamiliar with the ways of celestial beings. Maybe I should keep my biases in check. I opened my mouth, but she held a finger up. "Give me just a minute, dear. I need to turn off the oven. She really was baking brownies."

My stomach rumbled, and the angel laughed. "Don't worry, I'll share."

Damn it. If she was trying to worm her way into my circle of trust, she was doing an excellent job. I was a sucker for brownies.

I sat down on a well-worn floral sofa. The decor was a tad dated, but at least Mrs. Pendergrass's home had hardwood floors and a modern entertainment system. No shag carpet to go with the 70s sofa, thank goodness. I scanned a few of the photos lining the walls, and my heart broke a little when my gaze landed on a family portrait. The younger Mrs. Pendergrass stood beside a handsome devil I assumed was Mr. Pendergrass, their two sons smiling awkwardly at the camera. The younger boy had to be Keith. I recognized the eyes and shape of his face, which held the makings of the dead man I'd seen a few days earlier in spite of the boyish roundness and missing front teeth captured in the old photo.

Poor Mrs. Pendergrass. Her husband was her presumably also deceased, based on how she'd spoken about him. What about her other son? Did she have no one from whom to seek comfort and share grief?

Cassie the helpful angel emerged from the kitchen with a tray filled with brownies and two mugs. She placed the platter on the coffee table and gestured to me to help myself. I hesitated, in spite of the intoxicating aromas of chocolate and coffee wafting from the tray.

Cassie sighed, grabbed a brownie, and took a large bite. After she chewed and swallowed, she said, "See. Not poisoned. Please, have a brownie, dear."

She didn't have to tell me twice.

"Smo, why af you here?"

"Please, dear, don't talk with your mouth full."

The whole *dear* thing would have bothered me had the angel not looked like a sweet little old grandma, not to mention the brownies. She could call me Sugar Pie Honey Muffin if she kept the chocolate coming. It also made the mind-your-manners thing easier to swallow, too.

"Sorry. Why are you here?"

Her brows rose in surprise. "I'm an angel. I'm here to comfort this poor mortal in her time of grief."

"Oh, right, 'cause that's what angels do."

My skepticism must have shown, since she leaned in and whispered, "You've been working with demons too long."

That statement hit a raw nerve. Anger welled from deep within my soul. It had been simmering since Hannah appeared in the mirror all those years ago, but the angel's words turned up the heat and sent the pot of rage boiling over. Speaking of bubbles, that strange sensation that first surfaced back in the alley with Murkowski and later with the boss merged with my rage, coalescing into a storm I couldn't hope to contain.

My voice remained calm in spite of the growing storm of fury. "I've been working with demons too long? Gee, I wonder why? Maybe it has something to do with the fact I've been demon possessed since I was a little kid. Funny how that worked out. Not like I had a guardian angel looking after me."

She smiled at me, a benevolent, patient, and completely patronizing smile that kicked the heat up a notch on my boiling pot of anger. "Oh, child, you have no idea, do you? Your guardian angel has always been with you."

Okay, New Age Grandma had hit a sore spot. No angel had ever come to me in my hours of need, not when I was a scared five-year-old girl newly possessed by a demon, and not now when my life and my family's lives were on the line. Anger surged through me. I stood up, unsheathed my knife, and threw myself in her direction. She disappeared before I landed face first on the love seat where she'd been sitting just a moment before. The old, lumpy chair did little to cushion my fall. Damn, I should've stocked up on D's magic demon healing potion when I had the chance. I couldn't exactly call him now. I had my pride.

He was right, though. I was vulnerable, as my failed attempt to attack the celestial being proved. I extricated myself from the sofa. It was a miracle I hadn't stabbed myself with the enchanted knife. The blade glowed a brilliant blue, its light more intense than the shade it had been when I first entered the Pendergrass home.

Wait a minute...

Demons made the knife glow red—the brighter the glow, the more powerful the demon. Demon power was derived from rank and strength gathered upon feeding. The knife glowed brighter than it had when I first arrived.

And found myself in the presence of a celestial being—a celestial being who'd been "comforting" a grieving mother.

Holy. Shit.

Demons may feed on sin, but angels feed on misery.

D might have been on my bad list, but I owed him for this little epiphany.

I looked around the room, playing a riveting game of where's the angel. "Neat trick with the materializing thing. Can you pull that off any old day, or only after feeding off a grieving soul?"

"Do not be so quick to judge things you don't understand, child."

"I understand when someone's trying to bullshit me." I kept my knife in front of me as I slowly made a circuit of the living room, gaze scanning the area for any sign of my celestial companion. I even checked the row of family photos, halting on the next to last picture in a worn frame. Something familiar about it niggled at my addled brain. Damn my short attention span.

"There is much you do not understand about yourself. How could you possibly recognize when someone's on your side? You cannot distinguish friend from foe, but you will. You're close to the answers that have always been there."

I was about to make some snarky comment when recognition dawned. Not recognition of whatever cryptic pearls of wisdom the angel was tossing my way, but one that sent a shiver of fear down my spine and stabbed a knife of anxiety through my gut. One of the photos showed a teenaged Keith Pendergrass posing in front of a muscle car with another man, his brother. While I'd been focused on his ass the last time I saw the other man, I recognized the startling blue eyes and handsome face. It was Cooper.

Holy guacamole. Apparently summoning was a family business.

A business that had cost Keith Pendergrass his life when he summoned the wrong demon, using his brother's portal, and might cost Keith's brother his life.

"Where are you going, child?" The angel's voice sounded alarmed, but I didn't have time to worry about it.

I only hoped I could get to Cooper before Mephisto or another one of Belial's demon henchmen could.

Or before D got to him.

CHAPTER TWENTY-THREE

My hike to Cooper's portal was a lot easier the second time around. Or it would have been if I hadn't been worried about the health and well-being of my favorite whack job summoner. The trail Lacey and I had blazed the other day remained open. Even better, Lacey wasn't walking in front of me and sending stray branches back to smack me in the head.

Nature was more fun without assault.

I wondered if I could sneak up on Cooper without the assistance of my AWOL demon. Stealth seemed the best approach, considering the guy was likely under attack or in danger of imminent attack. Where on earth—or possibly another realm—had my demon partner gone? It would suck big time if I had to go a few rounds with a powerful demon messenger or demon lord without her. Then again, I did have the skills I'd earned through blood, sweat, tears, and more blood—part of the brutal basic training for demon trackers. Tracking ordinary humans was generally easy. Tracking a powerful demon or Cooper the outdoorsman and wild animal whisperer, however, would no doubt be a real challenge.

Still, if I could pull it off without Hannah, I could tell D to suck it.

I cursed my stupid conscience since it chose that moment to remind me this mission was, in fact, not really about me. It wasn't about my foolish pride, either. Cooper's life might be on the line. Then again, considering D might possibly want to interrogate and possibly murder Cooper since it was his—and Keith's—father who'd summoned him for Belial, I couldn't turn to him for help even if I'd wanted to.

But I couldn't let my impulse-control issues get the best of me either. Not this time.

Considering what we'd learned from the grimoire, I didn't think I could trust the boss, aka The Arbiter, either. That meant HQ and dispatch were out. I dialed my roomies, but the calls went straight to voice mail. Damn it, this was no time to be out of touch. I finally caved and sent a text to Lacey and Alexi requesting backup before I got too deep into the woods and lost cell service.

I hoped they were close. If not, I'd have to rely on my skills, my wits, and that strange power surge that had sprung up within my being again and hope I could control it.

I was so screwed.

I crouched low, choosing my path with care. My footfalls would crack no twig, crinkle no leaf, and disturb nothing in my path. I was the forest, and the forest was me. We were one. My—

Arh-ack-arh-arh-arh-ack-ack

Ricky, my favorite little vixen, came barreling down the path in front of me, doing that weird yip-bark thing all the way.

"Ricky, shh," I hissed. "I'm trying to be sneaky."

She leapt from the path in a streak of red fury and landed on my back. She used it as a springboard to bound on the path behind me—making one hell of a ruckus in the process—and then doubled back to assault me with a slew of licks, rubs, and nips. Her fluffy red tail wagged to its black tip as she scampered around on slim black paws. This was totally going to screw with my efforts at stealth mode, but I could hardly resist the adorable bundle of fur.

"Who's a naughty girl?" I whispered, scratching her behind the ears and down her sleek body as she licked my nose. "Who's the noisiest fox in the park who's going to get me busted by a crazy wild man and a badass demon? That's right, it's Ricky."

She whined as she rubbed her furry little body against me and sniffed. And sniffed. And...sniffed some more. What? I'd showered today. And I didn't have any bacon on me.

"What it is, girl?" I asked.

She cocked her head and regarded me. If I didn't know better, I'd swear she was sizing me up, putting me under a degree of scrutiny beyond that of an animal—albeit a remarkably clever animal.

I snorted. "Are you judging me? I thought only cats did that." Were foxes part cat?

She raised her head and gave a couple of quick fox barks before running off. I stood, hoping she'd spotted some woodland creature to hunt so I could salvage my sneak-up-on-Cooper-and-save-his-ass mission, but she came back. After circling me twice, chirping, and dashing off while looking over her shoulder, I got the message. I was to follow. Hopefully she'd lead me to Cooper.

After chasing a crazy, and possibly rabid, fox through the woods, I wished I had Lacey with me. At least she'd cleared the trail in front of me. Short as I was, Ricky was decidedly closer to the ground and moved with greater agility and speed than I would ever achieve without demonic assistance. At least I didn't hit any spider webs this time, but I did stumble on some tree roots, jacking up my knee and sacrificing dignity in the process.

After about a mile, we approached the clearing that housed the world's ugliest tree and portal to the hell realm. I expected to find Cooper. Actually, I expected Cooper to body-slam me straight back into the forest if I got too close to the protective threshold surrounding the portal. It was his job to keep any demonic entity from seeking passage through his portal without authorization or a legal summons.

Of course, I was no longer a demonic entity. Without Hannah, I was an ordinary human being. Perhaps that was the key to avoiding detection, then. A human could breach the threshold and enter the protected space surrounding a portal and open it, assuming the human could get past the summoner charged with guarding it.

But how would a demon compel or convince a human to do such a thing without possession or some other sort of demon mojo that would leave a trace? Lust, greed, anger, and any of the other seven deadly sins required no magic to be sown in the hearts and minds of people. They were always there. A bribe, a carnal liaison, or a promise to take out a mortal enemy might entice a human to enter the space around a portal.

Murkowski had remembered being in the vicinity of this portal, though his memory was spotty. Did Mephisto leave Murkowski's body temporarily and compel him to cross the threshold? And who was the woman who'd been with them?

When the clearing came into view and I was surprised, not to mention relieved, to find a familiar face there.

Boy, Lacey had gotten here fast. Faster than I had.

Too fast. There was no sign of Cooper or Archimedes, which put me on high alert. My instincts screamed caution. *My* instincts, the ones I'd honed through training and experience as an investigator, as a human, and not as a demon-possessed mortal, were still working. While the bubbly power still surged beneath the surface, it hadn't taken over. This was all me.

I hoped it would be enough.

I bent to scratch Ricky's perky little ears, and so I could whisper some instructions into them. "Hey, girl. I need you to find that cadejo. If he's down for the count, be on the lookout for a wolfman. Maybe some of the other woodland critters you and Coop hang out with. Can I count on you?"

She leaned into the scratch, then faced me and cocked her head to one side. I wasn't sure, but I thought she winked at me before disappearing into the forest. It wasn't the best plan, but it was all I could come up with on such short notice.

"Lacey," I called out as I took a small, tentative step into the protected circle surrounding the portal. "Boy, am I ever glad to see you. Where's Cooper?"

A low moan came from a clump of bushes to the right of the portal tree, just outside the protective boundary. I spotted a pair of large boots sticking out from the mass of low branches, bound at the ankles, and then noticed the circle of stones that surrounded the area. That pattern looked suspiciously like a pentagram.

My gaze darted back to Lacey, who was busy drawing sigils in the air around the portal. Glowing sigils. Enchanted sigils.

Magic sigils.

Crap on a cracker.

I pulled out my knife and took a cautious step toward Lacey. It glowed purple, but the intensity faded as I extended my arm toward Lacey. Simon hovered behind the tree, outside of the boundary, his black shadow quivering. Was he angry, anxious, or scared? I had no idea, but at least I knew for certain Lacey wasn't possessed.

I also knew she'd been the liaison between Mephisto and Murkowski.

"Lacey, you need to stop."

She kept drawing sigils, but she turned her head, leveling her vacant gaze on me. Her voice was flat and devoid of emotion. "I must open the gates."

This was *so* not what I needed.

I'd had a mile-long list of suspects and counting, but I never in a million years would've put Lacey Green on it, assuming Lacey was actually in there and hadn't gone bye-bye thanks to whatever spell she was obviously under. Of course, that begged the question of who or what had bespelled her.

"Lacey, did Hannah put you up to this?"

She frowned. "The Intercessor is undecided, but we can no longer wait. The eve of war is upon us. We must open the gates to the realm of darkness and unleash the seven."

I took another step, wondering if I could disable her. Without our demons, we were evenly matched in terms of strength and skill in hand-to-hand combat. True, I was shorter, but I was also scrappier and not afraid to fight dirty. I didn't see her demon blade. She might have hidden it, or maybe the demon who'd put a spell on her had disarmed her first or compelled her to disarm herself. The demon couldn't very well touch the knife.

Was that demon close by? Was it Belial himself, come to oversee the beginning of his rebellion?

I'd have to ask Lacey and hope she would—or could—answer. "Seven? The Seven Sins, you mean? Seven tempter demon harbingers of war?"

A familiar voice spoke from behind me. "The earth realm is full of tempters. What we need to get this party started are some truly deadly sins."

I whirled around to find Mr. Barbatos smiling at me. "I told you. Shit's about to get real."

CHAPTER TWENTY-FOUR

I stood frozen, uncertain what to do. Barbatos remained outside the protective boundary, presumably held back by his status as a demon. Mr. Traitor Pants was definitely living up to the title I'd just given him. Speaking of pants, who wore a three-piece designer suit on a hike in the woods?

"It was you. You're the one who set me up."

Barbatos laughed. "Yes, pet."

"And you used Lacey to pull off this inside job. She was the go-between for Mephisto and Murkowski, and she...killed Keith?"

The pieces fell into place. Lacey had allegedly been stuck in traffic the night Mephisto tried and failed to extract Hannah and capture us both. She hadn't been there as backup, leaving me to walk into Mephisto's trap alone so he could get to me.

And Hannah.

She must have poisoned Cooper's cadejo as a distraction to gain access to the portal, and when Ricky the fox recognized her scent, Lacey had the perfect cover. I'd sent her to scout portals in west Nashville the night before. As for Keith...

I gulped. D had called it right. The demon in charge—Barbatos—was tying up loose ends. Barbatos had gotten to Keith before D and I could get him back, and he'd used Lacey to do it.

Had she been a willing participant? Had Simon?

Barbatos shrugged. "It wasn't personal. I didn't expect you to get this far, let alone have Dominic show up. Your boyfriend's rather...creative when it comes to interrogation, and the summoner's loyalties were tenuous at best. I couldn't risk him tipping you off."

I shot a glance at Lacey. Her fingers were still working on the sigils, but they'd slowed. She was clearly under the influence of demon magic, but she was also listening. I hoped she could fight the spell. Maybe if I kept Barbatos talking, I could stall long enough for Alexi to arrive.

Damn it, I really needed more backup.

Why hadn't I called D? Oh, right, I was mad at him for doubting my abilities. Stupid. Pride might very well come before my fall.

I turned my attention back to Barbatos. "What's your angle? Did you know what the grimoire predicted, or do you really want to start a rebellion in the hell realm? Doesn't seem like your style."

His gaze widened a fraction, but then he laughed. "You figured it out? I ripped those pages out of the grimoire myself. You *are* full of surprises."

"And you're full of shit."

Barbatos didn't rise to my lame comeback, but at least he kept talking —and the more he talked, the slower Lacey worked. Seemed as though whatever spell he had her under required his attention. I'd have to keep up the distraction, then.

Fortunately, distractions were my specialty. I was good at that.

I wished I was as good at wrapping my mind around whatever conspiracy I'd found myself embroiled in, or maybe the conspiracy in which I found myself embroiled. Crap, that stupid prophecy had apparently affected my grammar.

"I've been stuck in this realm for far too many centuries, pet, and I can't leave without an unsecured portal. I was Mephisto's ticket onto this plane, and he's my ticket off it. Rebellions and prophecies and disposable little demon hunters are not my concern."

Wow. I knew he was an asshole, but I hadn't realized just how ginormous until now.

"So you don't care if your realm becomes a war-torn hell...hole or if you wind up in another epic battle with celestials as long as you get to go home? I had no idea there was a token demon of selfishness."

Barbatos rolled his eyes. "That would be Narcissus. Yes, he's one of ours. Surprised? The Greeks invented drunk history." He began pacing around the protective circle, casually cleaning his immaculate nails with a nasty-looking blade that had appeared out of nowhere. "As for me, I'm a Duke with legions that specialize in weapons production and distribution, which technically makes me a war profiteer. Doesn't matter who's fighting, really. I'll arm the highest bidder. But I'll need to get back home first. Lacey, dear," he said, snapping his fingers. "Focus, please."

Lacey shook her head and lifted her hands once more. She'd almost completed the circle of sigils around the portal. We were almost out of time. Where was Alexi?

"You won't get far without a summoner to let you pass through the boundary. By the way, does the boss know about your plan? Is he in on it?" I took a step toward Lacey. I didn't want to hurt her, but I couldn't let her open that portal. Then again, if she could act as a summoner, I'd have to at least disable her.

Barbatos completed his circuit and stood beside the clump of bushes hiding an unconscious Cooper. He examined his knife and then leveled his gaze on me, clearly enjoying my confusion and distress along with the execution of his diabolical plans. Execution being the operative word since he intended to sacrifice Cooper. I couldn't let that happen either, and not just because the guy had a great ass.

I only hoped he wasn't the summoner who'd sent D back to his dad. Otherwise I might be saving him for nothing.

"The Arbiter is too busy chasing your demon to worry about anything else. After all, she's supposed to unlock the gates to the hell realm according to the grimoire." Barbatos made a moue of disgust. "Seems this so-called Intercessor is about as reliable as you. At least she's kept The Arbiter distracted. Where is she, by the way? I'm surprised you survived separation with your fragile, human constitution."

How did he—

Oh, right. I wouldn't have been able to cross the boundary and get this close to the portal without Hannah. Of course, he also had Lacey the unwilling spy. I was apparently living up to Barbatos's insults. Either I needed to get a grip, or the executive assistant from hell needed some new material.

Probably both.

The bubbly power surge still coursed through me, only this time it seemed to be waiting. Waiting for what, I had no idea. If ever there was a time for extra mojo, this was it. My skin tingled, and my knife flashed with a brilliant purple. If I couldn't count on my demon, I'd have to rely on my wits, my training, and whatever strange power had suddenly and recently grown within me. It had allowed me to stop Mephisto from taking Hannah and helped me take on the boss and walk away unscathed.

Only one problem—I'd also have to control it.

Barbatos raised his hands, and the stone pentagram lifted from the ground. The rocks glowed as if molten and began to swirl with Barbatos's magic. "The blood of this summoner should do nicely. It will give me enough protection to reach the portal."

Damn it. I could disable Barbatos, at least temporarily, or I could tackle Lacey to stop her from opening the portal, but I couldn't do both at the same time. Why couldn't I do cool stuff like astral projection?

I caught a movement out of the corner of my eye, a flash of red. Ricky!

And she wasn't alone. A low growl preceded the appearance of a hulking, frightening shape at the edge of the clearing. I adored Alexi and was glad he'd arrived to help out. But seeing him in full demon-cursed wolfman mode always gave me the creeps. The man was a gentle giant, but the monster within sometimes got a little carried away on missions, making Alexi better suited to brute force than finesse.

Barbatos paused and arched a brow at the large, hairy apparition. Alexi bared his fangs and rose to his full height, muscle-bound body tense as his eyes flashed red. He had Barbatos's attention, which made the pentagram surrounding Cooper flicker. Lacey's hands froze in mid sigil. We'd managed to distract Barbatos, thereby weakening his spell, but appeared to be at a standoff. I took a step toward Lacey, but Barbatos tsked at me and waved his hands over Cooper, making the poor man writhe and scream.

"Stop."

"I can make this quick and easy, or I can take my time. I have missed the delectable flavor of suffering, the sounds of agony and torment. Step away from Ms. Green, if you please." Barbatos raised Cooper's body, making sure to hit every branch and twig on the way up, the bastard, and suspended it in the center of the pentagram. He slashed his knife through the air, opening a gash on Cooper's flank. Crimson bloomed, staining the summoner's camo shirt and dripping down his body into the cup Barbatos had conveniently magicked to catch it. After a few long, agonizing moments, Barbatos lifted the cup and drank deeply.

Ewwwwww.

I stood, knife raised and poised for battle, as the demon took a tentative step past the protective boundary. Crap. His spell worked. He'd managed to breach security around the portal. Now all he had to do was walk through it. Alexi roared and leapt to Cooper, slashing the burning pentagram with his claws. He caught Cooper's limp body and lowered it gently to the ground, sniffing and nudging him with his oversize snout as he whined.

Ricky jumped into the circle and onto Barbatos, clawing, biting, and ripping the fine fabric of his suit, bless her. Apparently unprepared for ordinary threats, Barbatos yelped and swatted at the little vixen. The fox was good. She was a scrappy, pint-sized warrior who wasn't afraid to fight dirty.

Kind of like me. No wonder I liked her.

I took advantage of the situation to go after Lacey. Following the fox's lead, I tackled Lacey from behind and knocked her to the ground. She landed with a nasty thud and gasped. I hoped I'd rendered her temporarily unconscious.

No such luck. My colleague rose, her blank gaze landing on me as she raised her knife. Her instincts seemed unaffected by Barbatos's spell since she dropped into a defensive position rather than going straight for the jugular. We'd received the same training in hand-to-hand combat and learned the hard way about the consequences of rash actions.

I crouched, too, and we moved in a slow circle, gazes locked, gauging one another's intentions as we planned our attack and counterattack strategies. Lacey made the first move, bringing her blade down in an attempt to hit my carotid. I raised my arm to deflect, making an effort to point the blade anywhere away from my body. She tried to redirect my arm down so she could punch into my neck or go around while hooking my weapon arm. Using our height differences to my advantage, I ducked and rolled, which threw her off-balance and allowed me to hit her in the back of her noggin with my knife's hilt.

Lacey recovered and swiped me with her leg, knocking me on my ass, but I managed to scoot away before she could stab me in the leg. She gave me a good slash, though. It stung like a bitch, but I couldn't afford to dwell on the pain. I scrambled to my feet, and she lunged at me again, grabbing my knife arm.

I punched her hard in the crook of the elbow and hooked my arm around the back of her neck, using the leverage to get her on the ground. I hopped on top of her and pinned her arms to the ground. "Lacey, snap out of it!"

She growled and raised her hips, doing her damnedest to throw me off. We must have looked like a pair of armed mud wrestlers. I was glad Boice and Roice weren't around to see it. They'd turn it into a viral video.

I mean, it was kind of hot. Deadly, but hot.

I struggled against the bucking, raging demon hunter beneath me. I had no idea if Barbatos had dislodged my friend the fox, but she'd probably need some reinforcement soon. With a deep breath and a whispered apology, I slammed my head into Lacey's nose. Hard. It made a nasty crunching sound. Crap. I'd totally have to cover the cost of her rhinoplasty, but at least I'd managed to disable her without lethal force.

"Alexi," I yelled at the werewolf as spots danced before my eye. "Catch."

I yanked Lacey up off the ground and half threw her out of the protective circle and into Alexi's massive arms. She shrieked, bleeding like a stuck pig all over his fur and struggling to get out of his hold. He clamped his teeth on the back of her neck, not enough to pierce the skin, but hard enough to let her know he meant business. She took the hint and went limp in his arms.

Simon flew to his mistress and hovered over her, flitting back and forth, clearly agitated. Then the demon froze, at least as much as an immaterial mass of black smoke could freeze, and let out a blood-curdling scream. What the—

The force of the arm around my neck jerked me back and left me gasping. Simon had been trying to warn me. Barbatos twisted my knife arm behind my back and started dragging me toward the portal.

"We don't have much time, pet," he said, his voice punctuated by grunts of effort. I wasn't making it easy for him. I let my feet drag the ground, forcing him to bear all my weight while I struggled to loosen his grip on my neck with my free hand. I managed to dip my chin beneath his arm so I could bite him.

He hissed and twisted my arm tighter. I squirmed in pain since I didn't have enough breath to scream. "Mephisto will pay handsomely for you, demon hunter, and once you're in Belial's army, your demon will soon follow."

"Barbatos." A familiar voice sounded behind us.

Barbatos swung around, and we both stared at the dark mass in front of the portal. It swirled and coalesced into the shape of a red-cloaked man decked out in what looked to be some version of Elizabethan garb, complete with a red leather jerkin covering a puffy-sleeved shirt, tights, soft boots, and a codpiece.

He removed his feathered cap and made a low bow. "Greetings, Your Grace. I'm pleased to see you."

"And I you, Mephisto," Barbatos replied. "I've brought you a gift."

"So I see." Mephisto's red gaze flickered with amusement and apparent delight. "She's quite a handful, is she not?"

Barbatos laughed. "Not to worry. I'm certain your master will find her useful. She needs training, of course." He tightened his grip around my neck. "Send her to obedience school and she'll serve you well. Shall we?"

I'd stopped Lacey, but not before she'd opened the portal. I did *not* want to go to the hell realm. I planted my feet firmly on the ground and then used all the force I could muster to stomp on Barbatos's right foot. The demon howled and lifted me off the ground. I kicked him hard, hoping I could give him a good one in the kneecaps and or the balls.

I must have gotten lucky since he lost his grip on my knife arm. Gritting my teeth through the pain—I wouldn't be surprised if he'd half ripped my arm out of its socket—I spun around in his grip and slashed his cheek with my knife.

He howled in agony as my demon blade cut into his flesh. I used his temporary weakness to my advantage and plunged the knife into his side. Before I could go in for the kill at his neck, he backhanded me hard enough to slam my back into the ugly tree and make my head bounce.

Mephisto laughed. I really hated that guy and swore then and there, someway, somehow, I was going to take his ass out.

My head had just stopped swimming when I caught a whiff of something odd. Something intoxicating and sensual, like sandalwood and sin. What the hell? Had D come? I whirled around, scanning the area for my guy, and immediately regretted the action. A wave of dizziness knocked me on my ass. The scent grew stronger, though, and I realized it was coming from within the protective circle.

Holy guacamole.

Mephisto, or rather a succubus disguised as Mephisto, threw a punch that hit Barbatos square in his angular jaw. The facade of demon messenger disappeared, and I stared in wide-eyed wonder as Mara jumped on Barbatos's back and began pummeling him with her dainty fists. How had she gotten here? How had she disguised herself as Mephisto?

And how the hell had she managed to get past the antidemon protection spell?

"Jinx! Help me get him out of the circle."

Right. Action first, questions later. I staggered to my feet and stumbled over to the grappling demons. I didn't think I had the speed or motor skills to stab Barbatos at the moment, not without risking a fatal blow to Mara. I took a few steps back and then lunged, throwing my weight into the pair of demons and knocking them to the ground. They kept on wrestling on the leaf-littered forest floor, half in and half out of the circle.

Alexi pounced and locked on to Barbatos's arm with his massive jaws, pulling the three of us out of the circle. I struggled to get my footing and grabbed my knife. I was still addled and not at my best, and now I had three demons to fight.

"Alexi, Mara, let go!" My throat was on fire, and the command came out as little more than a whisper, but they heard. I called on the force within me, begging it to give me the last bit of strength I needed to finish the job.

Then, I fell to my knees and plunged my blade straight into Barbatos's heart.

CHAPTER TWENTY-FIVE

"Wow. That's a lot of blood."

My eyelids fluttered as consciousness came back and hit me like a Mack truck. I opened one eye and glared up at Roice. "Thanks, Captain Obvious."

"We thought you were dead for sure," Boice added helpfully. "You look like a zombie."

I coughed and struggled to sit up. The twins helped me, and once I was able to see straight, I took a look around at the situation. Alexi had shifted back into his human form. Someone had brought him pants, but at least I got a nice eyeful of muscle-bound man chest. He was soothing Lacey, who glared at me from two black eyes as she held an icepack to her nose. Mara, the hero of the day, sat cradling a shirtless Cooper in her arms. Someone had cleaned and bandaged the wound in his side, and I was glad to see him alive, if not entirely well.

No worries. The succubus would take his mind off his troubles, at least for a while.

I was about to ask my roomies how they'd pulled off the ruse of the century, but a wave of nausea distracted me. I gently pulled out of their grasps and turned aside to lose my lunch—literally. One of them held my hair for me. They were such sweeties.

After taking a swig of water offered by the other twin, I rinsed my mouth, spat, and worked hard to speak through my aching throat. All I managed was, "How?"

Boice, who'd worn his "That's a HORRIBLE idea...What time?" T-shirt, grinned. "I check my voice mails. So does Roice."

"Mara came up with the idea for the switcheroo," said Roice, brandishing a T-shirt that read, "I may be late all the time but at least I'm fashionable about it." How apropos. "Thanks for the setup, by the way. We weren't sure how we'd manage a distraction."

"No problem," I croaked. "How did you get her across the boundary?"

Boice shrugged. "Blood. Cooper had it to spare. We took a bit before patching the guy up. Barbatos set you up. Didn't see that one coming."

Neither had I, obviously. This was not going to help my trust issues. Speaking of trust...

"Is D around?" My voice was too broken by a near-choking experience to sound pitiful, thank goodness. I probably owed him an apology, but mostly I just wanted to fall into his arms and never leave. Shock was beginning to wear off, and sorrow, grief, anger, and a whole lot of what-ifs started creeping in.

I blinked hard a few times.

Roice grinned wider and put a thumb over his shoulder. "Who do you think gave us a ride?"

I lifted my gaze and lost it. D rushed over and pulled me into his arms, cradling me against his broad chest and enveloping me in his warm, solid presence. I sobbed and clung to him like a life raft as he stroked my back and kissed my hair, whispering words of comfort.

After a while, my sobs slowed to an occasional hiccup, and I lifted my gaze to meet D's. I sniffed and shook my head. "I'm sorry."

His full lips curled into a wry smile. "I'm sorry, too."

"Where were you?" I had no right to ask, of course. I'd stormed off and basically told him to stay out of my way.

He smiled. "I was securing the perimeter. Couldn't risk letting any demons get loose. I put wards up around the park and evacuated the humans in the area with more than a little help from my colleagues."

I craned my neck to get a better look at D's "colleagues," not that there was much to see. The pair of immaterial demons hovered by the tree line. Those must have been the demons D mentioned when he was hunting Keith, the ones who specialized in tracking and concealment magic. Not only had D come for me, but he'd also brought reinforcements.

I choked back another wave of sobs. While I'd been busy getting in over my head, Dominic had been protecting the earth realm and humans in case I failed. Instead of charging in like a raging alpha—because apparently that was my job—he'd kept a cool head and done the sensible thing, the right thing, and had my back.

"I shouldn't have gone off on my own like that. I should've trusted you and brought you along."

"I shouldn't have underestimated you. You had things under control...mostly."

I laughed. "I'm an idiot, and a lucky one. If I hadn't called Alexi and the twins, this could have ended badly. We could've lost Cooper, and Barbatos could have unleashed hell on earth, and—and—"

I was such a blubbering mess.

D held me tighter and shushed me. "You're not an idiot. I told you, you're one of the bravest souls I know. Reckless, pigheaded, and infuriating at times, but brave."

I laughed again through a fresh wave of tears. "Thanks. And thank you for being here, for bringing reinforcements. You guys saved my ass."

He leaned down and planted a soft kiss on my lips. "No, you saved your own ass. You solved this case, secured the portal, and rooted out the traitor in the summoning community in less than five days, not to mention the mole inside our own operation." He spared a look of disgust at the Barbatos's body. "The Arbiter won't be claiming your soul or the souls of your family."

"*We* solved the case," I said, looking around at my bruised, battered, and absolutely amazing team. "I wish Trinity was here, too. She deserves the credit for putting me on the trail of celestials. They're around, you know, and they're a part of the battle that's brewing. We can stop it if we—"

D shut me up with another kiss, this one deeper and full of promise. Eventually he came up for air and spoke. "Trinity sent a report to the rest of the team, and we told her about Hannah's disappearance. She said she had to do some more research, but she thinks she's got a lead on the warrior with the power of three realms."

"Oh, that's easy," I said. "You're the warrior. You have to be."

D arched a brow and cocked his head. "What makes you think so?"

Duh. He was clearly made for battle, with his physique, confidence, cunning, and warrior's bearing. "The warrior is supposed to be imbued with the power of three realms. You're from the hell realm, but you've lived on earth, too. And you know a lot about celestials."

He shook his head. "I'm not from the celestial realm. Never been there."

Well, crap. So much for that theory.

I'd have to let Trinity and Sam work that one out. And we still had a few loose ends of our own, though I wasn't sure which one I dreaded more. "We need to find Hannah, since she's supposed to open the gates to hell."

"She is?"

"Barbatos seemed to think so. It kind of makes sense. According to the grimoire, one who has long slumbered shall awaken, and she's the one who has the power to open the gates to the Realm of Darkness. I mean, she did sort of wake up when Mephisto found us in the alley. That's when she started answering to 'Intercessor' and talking to the boss like they were old pals."

I still wasn't sure what the host of seven was or how one fell from it. My head hurt. And trying to wrap my mind around the conspiracy I'd just unraveled, not to mention what we'd read in the grimoire, had turned my brain into a puddle of mush. The aches and pains masked by adrenaline and the heat of battle had caught up with me, and I was fading fast.

Still, there was one more thing I had to tell D before I went home to lick my wounds and sleep it off.

"D, the summoner who sent you back to the hell realm...I might know who he is," I began with caution. "Or at least, I think I know something about him."

D stiffened, and I swallowed hard. I didn't dare let my gaze wander to Cooper. I shouldn't have said anything, should've investigated first. I didn't know for certain that Cooper had been involved in D's summons. The burly outdoorsman was handsome and appeared young, possibly too young to have been active ten years ago, when someone had sent D back to his father.

Father.

What was it Mrs. Pendergrass had said about Keith? Oh, right. The late rogue summoner had apparently been like his father, a so-called "historian" who spent hours poring over dark myths and legends. If both boys were summoners, it stood to reason that someone close had introduced them to the art, like their dear old dad.

"Ouch. Hey, D, could you lighten up on the death grip?"

"Oh, sorry," he said, loosening his hold on my aching body. His gaze remained hard and steady, anger held on a tight leash, at least for the moment. "What do you know about the summoner who ripped me away from you?"

My chest went tight with the oddest combination of affection, sympathy, and outrage. I'd never thought of it that way, but D was right—the summoner had ripped D away from me, and I'd spent the greater part of the past ten years missing a piece of my heart.

"It was Keith's father," I said through gritted teeth. "It had to be. He taught his sons the art of summoning. Both of them. Keith and Cooper."

D's gaze went wide before he turned to stare at the unconscious summoner, red sparks of anger and murderous intent blazing in it.

I reached out and placed a trembling hand on his cheek. "Cooper wasn't involved. I'm sure of it. He's a good guy."

My demon growled. He actually growled. It would've been sexy in different circumstances, but as it was, it made me worry about Cooper's continued health and safety. "Don't you hurt him—"

A coughing fit interrupted my admonition. I hated it when that happened. It totally ruined the whole stern effect. After clearing my throat, I tried again. "I mean it, D. No intimidation, brutal interrogations, bodily or metaphysical harm. Promise me."

D's lips thinned and that vein bulged from his temple, but he furrowed his brows and appeared to consider my words. I raised my other hand and took his face between them. "We'll find him, D. Cooper will help us find him. And when we do, we'll make him sorry."

He visibly struggled to control the rage coursing through his body and soul, the urge to lash out, to battle, to take his revenge on the blood kin of his enemy. At long last, he nodded and gave me a lopsided grin. "I love it when you talk dirty. And"—he paused to kiss me again before saying—"I think we should date."

I laughed but then sat bolt upright. "What day is it?"

"You need to take it easy." He pulled me back into his arms and forced me to lean against him. "And it's Sunday. Why?"

Crap on a cracker. This day just kept getting better and better. The sun was still out, but not for much longer. I needed a nap, a shower, and possibly stitches, but I'd settle for a shower.

"We have a date tonight, and I think I'm going to need a little more of that magic demon healing potion before I take you to meet my mother."

CHAPTER TWENTY-SIX

By the time we made it to my mom's house, aka my childhood abode—and D's—I was only limping a little. Lacey's knife slash had gone deep, but it was healing. That hell realm potion was super handy. Hopefully my health insurance covered it. I should be back on my feet and in the field by tomorrow night. Good thing, since we still needed to find Hannah. That was priority numero uno. I'd voted to ditch the family meal and return immediately to the hunt, but D insisted we keep the dinner date. Damned overprotective demon.

Then again, maybe he'd missed my family.

Of course, he also knew I was totally trying to weasel my way out of seeing my family and facing my ongoing issues with said family. He called me out on my argument about Hannah and imminent Armageddon, offering the counterargument that she hadn't made any attempts to open any local portals in the past five days and the fact that security had been quadrupled on those portals well before we'd captured Barbatos. To which I counter-counterargued that Cooper's portal hadn't been properly secured because of Barbatos's inside job, which meant there could be other traitors in our midst.

D had then physically carried me to the shower, stripped me down, and unceremoniously dumped me under a rather pleasant stream of steaming water, effectively ending the argument.

He was such a sore loser.

I braced for battle as soon as my feet hit the froufrou doormat that bid visitors welcome to my childhood home. I was pleased to see the freshly painted front porch, shutters, and new red cedarwood siding. Mom had apparently been putting the extra funds I sneaked into her bank account to good use. Maybe someday she'd go for a nice spa day or, even better, a vacation. I swear the woman hadn't gone away for more than a weekend trip to visit family since I'd moved out.

Mom answered the door and took a long look at me, gaze narrowed and nostrils slightly flared. What? I'd showered and put on deodorant. Maybe she was surprised I'd shown up. Or possibly it was the fact that I'd dressed to impress with my neon magenta camo pants and a matching tank top that read, "I'm going to hell on a full scholarship." It was a toss-up.

She took an even longer look at D—not that I blamed her—shook her head as if stunned and turned her attention back on me. "Jane. It's good to see you. Please, come in."

Neither of us went in for a hug. In fact, her crossed arms and stiff posture mirrored my own. Our dynamic had changed little since my childhood, especially since I was still too short to meet her at eye level, damn it. She never did that with Megan. Of course, Megan hadn't made a wrong move since she was eight.

Megan always got hugs. She was the good girl, after all.

Mom's tone was pleasant, perfectly cordial and polite, but distant as ever. She opened her mouth to say something and then, seeming to think better of it, closed her mouth and gave me a slight nod.

Oh, for crying out loud, what had I done this time? Instead of taking the bait, I settled for introductions. "Mom, this is Dominic Bellatore, aka my good friend and colleague from work. Dominic, this is Charlene McGee, aka Mom."

"It's a pleasure to meet you, Mrs. McGee." Dominic, who wore black jeans so tight they shouldn't be legal and a tighter black T-shirt, took her hand in his and leaned down to kiss her softly on the cheek.

Oh, yeah, he was trying to get in good, and it was working. The unflappable woman who'd given birth to me blushed—actually blushed—and did the whole hair twirl thing. With her flawless skin, perfectly coiffed hair, and long, elegant fingers, it worked for her. She was super pretty, with Celtic features courtesy of Grandpa and Grandma's Scottish roots. Always had been, and Megan had inherited those looks. My tan, envy-inspiring olive skin was my gift from my father. Megan also got Mom's height and other features that made men drool and women jealous. Without the burden of working multiple jobs while worrying about raising two daughters solo, Mom had blossomed into a stately and self-possessed mature woman.

I hoped I aged that well, though I would not make the mistake of mentioning that again.

"I'm pleased to meet you, too, Mr. Bellatore," she said, her voice a little husky.

Wow, this was getting awkward. My mom was totally flirting with my almost boyfriend. I needed to get her a date, or possibly a male escort.

I shoved the bouquet of flowers into her hands, grabbed D, and dragged him to the living room. Megan hadn't arrived yet, but her hubby, Brad, was there, decked out in his standard white shirt, boring tie, and slacks that screamed fiscal responsibility.

Brad didn't bother looking up from his phone when I said hello, but he did a double take when he noticed D. He stood and took D's proffered hand in a firm, no-nonsense grip that served as a civilized dick-measuring contest, at least from my point of view. D must've gripped Brad's hand hard enough to pass whatever stupid alpha male test this ritual embodied, since Brad relaxed and offered to grab a beer for him.

Enticing aromas wafted from the kitchen, making my mouth water as a very unladylike rumble from my stomach echoed through the living room. D gave me a sidelong smirk while my mother shot a look of disapproval in my direction.

"Jane, have you been skipping lunch again?"

I cringed. That voice, that maternal glare, the judgment...it was like being five years old all over again, which was why I normally avoided visits. And it wasn't that I'd skipped lunches growing up. I'd *split* lunches with D—on weekends, in the summers, on days off from school. Mom had been okay with nighttime snacks, but being on a tight budget, she'd drawn the line at the extra helpings during lunch and dinner. As soon as D was old enough to begin wandering the streets of Nashville, more food had mysteriously appeared in our pantry.

Before that, however, Mom just assumed I was too lazy or inept to feed myself when Megan and I were on our own. Not a big deal in the grander scheme of reasons I disappointed my mother, but given my raw nerves and general anxiety about being in Mom's cross hairs, I wasn't sure I could take it. Before I exploded with anger, D chimed in.

"We had a busy day at work," D said apologetically. "Jane solved one of our biggest cases today."

After I picked my jaw up off the floor, I risked a glance at my mother. She was clearly surprised by D's testimonial about my general competence. My chest went warm and tight, and my cheeks heated. I couldn't help it. My demon had bragged on me. He winked and gave me one of those lopsided, dimpling grins that melted my heart and made my lady parts tingle.

Mom kept staring in apparent disbelief. Wonderful. She'd never taken my work seriously. Okay, she didn't know what I really did for a living, but that wasn't the point. She still thought of me as incompetent or as the troublemaker in the family, the jinx.

As if sensing my distress, D put a hand on my shoulder and gave it a light squeeze.

"Yeah, tough day, but I promise I'll start brown-bagging it. Can't go wrong with PB and J. So what's for dinner?" I asked a little too brightly. We needed to get the ball rolling on this awkward dinner thing. I wasn't sure how much of Momzilla I could take.

"I made honey lemon chicken with pasta."

I gasped. It was my favorite. She did that. She always did that. She'd take a meat cleaver to my heart and then turn around and do something sweet and thoughtful to completely eviscerate me. Now I felt guilty for skipping family dinners for the past six months. I stared down at my well-worn cowgirl boots, at a loss for what to say.

Mom's uncharacteristic, not to mention unladylike, snort brought me back to attention. I almost got whiplash from jerking my head up, which sucked since my neck still ached from Barbatos's choke hold. I almost jerked again when my gaze landed on my mother's face.

"What?" I asked, genuinely confused.

"Don't act so surprised, Jane. Give me a little credit. I know it's your favorite."

Before I could come up with a funny or snarky comeback, Mom floored me again. "Given how much money you've been sneaking into my bank account, I should've made you lobster thermidor."

I froze. How had she found out? I'd had the twins make it look like some kind of compensation from the insurance company over a car crash we'd had when I was little. Had Megan ratted me out?

D's steady hand on my shoulder was the only thing that kept me from bolting out the door. Crap. I didn't know how I was going to lie my way out of this one. Brad, as usual, picked exactly the wrong time to saunter into the living room with two beers and bated breath. He loved our family drama, probably because it never involved him or Megan. Plus, I had a sneaking suspicion he was jealous of my cash stash. Not that he wasn't doing very well himself, but ever since I'd said no thanks to his investment advice, stock tips, and offers to manage my portfolio, he'd been perplexed and a little angry that I was doing fairly well financially.

The last time I'd attended a famdamily dinner, he'd all but accused me of illegal activity. He leaned against the wall, smirk plastered across his frat-boy handsome face as he looked on. Jackass.

I considered lying. It was my standard MO when it came to Mom, but it was as much for her protection as mine. I couldn't tell her what I did, what I was—or rather, what I had been. Technically, I wasn't demon possessed anymore, but I was in too deep with their kind to get out now, especially with D.

Might as well try the truth, or at least some semblance of it. I held my hands up in the universal gesture of surrender. "Fine, you got me. I've been putting money in your account. You complained about how much I ate growing up. I figured I owed you."

I'd been giving the extra food to D, but she didn't know that.

Mom's nostrils flared, and she opened her mouth but apparently thought better of rising to the challenge I'd issued with that last statement. But it was true. Yeah, we'd been poor, and yeah, she had no idea we had another mouth to feed, but she'd taken it out on me. The glares whenever she checked the pantry, the sighs, the silent tears when she thought Megan and I were sleeping.

She blamed me.

I blamed me, too. But the extra guilt trip had been a heavy burden for the kid I'd been.

Mom heaved a sigh. "Jane, you don't owe me for feeding you. I'm your mother. It was my job."

I should've dropped it, but again, being home brought out my inner five-year-old. And I was tired, and tense, and though I'd never admit it out loud, I was hurt. I'd never had a good relationship with my mom. I craved it, especially in the absence of my dad.

"Yeah, a job you resented every moment of every day."

Mom flinched as if I'd slapped her across the face. Then she took a deep breath, visibly suppressing anger and outrage. She stood to her full height, accentuating my lack thereof, and narrowed her gaze. "Jane Aurelia McGee, that was uncalled for, unfair, and untrue."

I tensed as if for battle, which was weird. I wasn't in the field fighting demons for the lives and souls of unwitting humans. Still, this battle had been a long time coming.

"Jane." D's deep voice was gentle and held a note that sounded an awful lot like pity.

That did it. I jerked out of his hold and glared at my mother. "Uncalled for? Really? You made it crystal clear I was a burden. Megan was fine, but I know I was the bad kid you never wanted. You can stop pretending."

Brad dropped his beer, D swore under his breath, and I clapped a hand over my mouth. Shit. Why had said that? This wasn't like me. I wasn't a petty, vengeful bitch.

Okay, I was, but only when it came to work and only when I couldn't deflect with humor, sarcasm, or interpretive dance. Or when I couldn't use my favorite strategy—avoidance. I never said stuff like that to my mom. It was *way* too confrontational. Crap.

"Forget it," I said through gritted teeth and a forced smile that probably looked psychotic. "Bygones, right? Where's Megan?"

"Here."

I whirled around to face the bearer of the hoarse, broken voice. Megan's eyes were wide and bright with unshed tears. She must've heard my tirade. She hated confrontation more than I did. I should've kept my big fat mouth shut. No need to make everyone miserable with my issues.

At least I'd kept them safe from my boss. They'd never know, but it didn't matter. They were alive, their souls intact, and blissfully unaware of the dangers that came with being related to me. I should keep my distance and protect them from afar. It was better that way.

"You know, this was probably a bad idea. Long days at work make me crazy." I used my best chipper tone. Maybe if I pretended none of that just happened, we could go back to the way things had always been.

I grabbed D's hand and tried to tug him so we could execute a fast getaway. "Let's try this again in a few weeks, okay? I'll even wear some nice slacks and that sweater you bought me last Christmas."

Mom was apparently less than impressed with my gesture. In fact, she looked...hurt. Damn my big mouth. She shook her head and said, "You're just like your father, Jane. Always running away. Even when you were small, you never wanted me too close."

Those words cut me to the core. I needed to get out of there before I said something else I'd regret later. "Come on, D. Let's go."

"No."

We all turned to my sister. She stood in front of the door, hands on her hips, legs apart and braced as if ready to physically prevent me from leaving. Color me impressed. I'd never seen Megan this fierce, this determined, this—

Megan's next words cut off my train of thought. "You don't understand, Mom. She couldn't help it. She's been protecting us for years."

Brad snorted. "From what? Drug dealers? Mercenaries?"

Megan glared at her hubby, which, to his credit, made him shrink back and mutter what sounded like an apology. Then, turning to our mother, she said, "Demons."

CHAPTER TWENTY-SEVEN

I froze. Oh God, this was my worst nightmare come to life. It was worse than my other recurring nightmare involving high school, no pants, and copious amounts of peanut butter.

Brad had dropped the other beer by now, and Mom looked back and forth between Megan and me as if we'd lost our minds. That was new. Not staring at me like that. I'd always been the crazy one, but not Megan.

"Oh, Meg," I said, laughing a little too loud and yanking harder on D's hand. He didn't budge, apparently as shocked at my sister's revelation as I was. Was I the only one with a clear head, master improvisational skills, and the ability to lie out of my ass as easily as breathing?

"She's such a kidder." By now, I was snort laughing, looking around at my family and hoping they would join in. "Earlier this week, I really had her going. I mean, seriously, she thought I might actually be a superhero. Can you believe it?"

I'd let go of D's hand and had stumbled over to Megan in a fit of giggles. I slung an arm over her shoulder as tears streamed down my face. Damn, if Hannah had permanently vacated my premises, I could totally make it in Hollywood. I had mad acting skills.

Megan slipped out of my grasp and took me by the shoulders. "No,

Jane. No more hiding. I know what you are and what you do, what you've always done."

"Oh my God. You know, it was only one time, I swear. Okay, maybe three. They were cute, I'd had a few shots of tequila, and honestly, what else was I supposed to do with that much Nutella?"

I met her gaze and winked, my face contorted into what I hoped resembled a plea for mercy. How the hell had she found out about the demon thing? And how much did she really know? This was not happening. Not now. Not when I was close to freedom and, for the first time, normal.

"Stop."

We all turned to face Mom. Her face had gone pale, and a fine tremor ran through her body. Dread pierced my gut like a thousand shards of broken glass. I'd seen my mother angry, of course, and frustrated, disappointed, sad, and scared, but I had never, ever seen her in the grip of sheer terror.

And that terror seemed to be directed at yours truly.

"What did he do to you?" Mom whispered. Then she looked away as she muttered, "I'll *kill* that bastard."

Wait, what? Someone did something to me? And my mom wanted to kill him? I was totally confused. Holy cow, I needed CliffsNotes.

Everyone started talking at once as I struggled to work out how my sister knew about the demon thing, understand my mom's bizarre reaction, and figure out the quickest escape route. I was debating between sneaking out of the bathroom window versus heading for the back door when D's booming voice commanded silence. Everyone stared at him in wonder, or maybe that was just me. He was so hot when he went all commanding.

Turning his dark gaze on my sister, he said, "How did you know?"

Oh, no, he did not just let the cat out of the bag. "D!"

As usual, they ignored me. Being the youngest really sucked sometimes. Megan jerked her head and said, "That guy who looks like the Terminator told me." Then she turned to glare at me. "You know, the one you sent to follow us?"

I spotted Alexi in the background. For such a big man, he was doing a decent job hiding in the shadows. "Alexi, how could you?"

Alexi's low growl rumbled. "I'm sorry, Jinx. They need to know. You are all still in danger."

"I can't believe you outed me to my sister. Dude, seriously—wait, what do you mean we're still in danger?"

Alexi finally stepped into the light, and I gasped. He wasn't fully wolfed out, but he didn't look fully human. He was more like an oversize backup dancer for *Cats* gone horribly wrong. Wow, no wonder Megan believed him.

I shook my head and shifted back into fight mode. Family secrets and reckonings would have to wait. I apparently had more important things to deal with, and they probably centered on demons bent on rebellion and conquest. Why hadn't dispatch called, and where was my boss?

Alexi bared his fangs. "The boss has your demon cornered, and the rest of the team is on their way. We have to go now."

Megan had gone pale at the sight of Alexi, but she gave a quick nod when I glanced in her direction. I looked over at Brad, or rather, where Brad had been standing, but the poor man now lay in a crumpled heap on the ground. I felt sorry for him for about a nanosecond before turning my attention to D. His eyes glowed with red sparks, and his body had gone tense as a panther's ready to leap on its prey.

Finally, I looked at my mother. She was surprisingly calm and collected, which was weird. The woman had just seen a half-shifted werewolf demon and my full-fledged demon boyfriend, who looked the part, and she'd been informed that her daughter was a demon hunter. Instead of being passed out on the floor with her son-in-law, however, she didn't seem shocked or fear-stricken. If I had to guess, I'd say she was...resigned.

She walked toward me slowly and then surprised the hell out of me by taking both my hands in hers. I must have flinched since she sighed and tightened her grip. "Janie," she said. She hadn't called me that since I was little. "Janie, go. I'll save you a plate. We'll talk later, about your father, about...everything."

My father? What the hell did any of this have to do with my absentee parent?

"Jane." This time, D spoke my name, his voice a low, rumbling growl. "Let's go get your demon."

Mom pulled me in for a quick and completely unexpected hug before giving me a gentle push toward D and the door. "Go."

Still reeling from the evening's revelations, not to mention the bazillion and one questions I had for and about my mother and father, I hopped into D's muscle car. We violated at least twenty different traffic laws as he drove to HQ.

I practically leapt out of the car before D slammed it into park and took off running. I'd just made it inside and was debating elevator versus stairs when a pair of strong hands grabbed me around the waist. One moment I was in front of the elevator and the next I was staring at Barbatos's empty desk outside the boss's office.

"Holy shit!" I staggered out of D's arms and spun around to face him. He'd teleported us. "I knew it. You've totally been holding out on me."

D gave me a lopsided grin. "You've been holding out on me, too." He pointed at my demon knife, which I'd unsheathed. It glowed blue—a brilliant, shining neon blue. Again with the blue, not to mention the purple, when I was supposed to be getting demon red—

I froze, realization dawning.

I pointed the knife toward the boss's door and nearly went blind with the brilliant blue light. "D, it's the celestials. They're in there. What will they do with Hannah and the boss?"

Footsteps echoed in the stairwell like an elephant stomping. Alexi. He'd been right behind us and had managed to keep up on foot even after stopping to pee on a fire hydrant. Hey, a little rebellion was good for the guy. He burst through the door in full wolf demon form, followed by Mara and my roomies.

And my sister.

"Megan, what the hell? You shouldn't be here." I turned to Alexi and put my hands on my hips—being careful with the knife so I didn't stab myself in the side like I'd done when the boss had first bestowed it upon me. "Bad boy."

I learned then that even ginormous, hairy, scary-as-hell wolfmen could do sad puppy dog eyes.

"Oh, no, that's not going to work on me, mister. Get her out of here."

"I'm staying," she said, mirroring my hands-on-hips stance and towering over me. Freakin' tall people.

I flipped the blade and pointed it at her, stabbing the air to make sure she knew I meant business. I wasn't really planning to use it on her. I preferred hand-to-hand combat when it came to my big sis. Ever since I first managed to get her in a headlock when we were kids, it had been my go-to. I had to get her back for all the times she sat on me and tickled my ribs until I nearly peed. Sometimes I had peed.

Screw it. She was going down.

I stepped closer and then froze when the blade glowed blue. What the hell? I pulled back, and the blue glow faded. It returned to its original intensity when I lunged at Megan, who yelped and took a step back. I spun around and pointed it at D. Red—super intense, bright red. Wow. Either he'd been juicing, or he'd somehow leveled up on the demon power mojo. A million questions careened through my addled brain, but I shook my head and focused on the here and now. Red equaled demon, blue equaled celestial. D glowed red, which was no surprise aside from his power signature. Megan glowed blue.

"Oh, holy wow, Meg, you're an angel?"

"What? No, I'm just me. Will you stop swinging that thing around before your hurt someone?"

Now that was just offensive. "I'll have you know I've been through extensive training with this 'thing,' and I even defeated one of our top demon hunters and a rogue demon who set me up. And the knife doesn't lie. You're a celestial."

"So are you."

I spun around again, feeling like a pinball bouncing between two worldviews. Trinity stood with the boss's book in one hand, her other gripping Sam, her demon who could somehow shift from material to immaterial. Dematerializing demons, demons that could be both corporeal and incorporeal, celestials—including my freaking sister?

Wait a minute...

"What did you say?"

Trinity rolled her eyes, let go of Sam to unsheathe her own knife, and pointed it at me. It wavered between red and blue before settling on blue. "I said you're one, too. A celestial."

"That's impossible." I looked around at my colleagues, sister, and almost boyfriend, exasperated no one else seemed to realize how ridiculous the notion was. "Guys, I've been demon possessed since I was five. D-E-M-O-N. Demons and angels don't mix."

"As far as we know," Trinity said. "As far as we were told by the boss, but he didn't tell us everything. We were told demons are either material or corporeal, but they couldn't be both." She held up a finger and nodded at Sam, who vanished in a puff of black smoke.

No, wait, the smoke lingered. Sam was still there. He'd gone immaterial.

A cacophony of voices broke out in shouts of shock, alarm, and accusation. By then, Boice, Roice, and Mara had joined the party, along with Lacey. They must have given her some kind of demon healing potion since she was up and running, but a large bandage covered her nose, and she glared at me out of red, bloodshot eyes that sported twin shiners. Guess she was still pissed off about the headbutt thing. I'd have to tell her how much my head still hurt to make her feel better.

Nah.

Since I was still technically in charge of this ragtag band, it was time to exert my authority. We needed a plan for when we stormed the boss's office. We had to be ready to fight whatever demon, celestial, or other entities were in there including the boss and my former demon. Could I still trust Hannah considering what I now knew about her? Could I fight her? One thing was certain: I couldn't do it alone.

"Okay, listen up. Mission time, people. We've got to get in that office and stop whatever's happening. If it's what the grimoire predicted, then we'll likely have an open portal to the hell realm and some unsavory demons coming through it. Lacey." I turned to my partner in crime, who was still glaring. "We need Simon to take a peek inside to see what we're up against."

Lacey nodded and pulled out her phone. Simon slowly emerged in his smoky form and appeared to hesitate. Lacey reached out and ran a gentle hand through his essence. "It's okay. You can go. I'll be all right, I promise."

Simon swirled and wrapped himself around Lacey in some sort of immaterial demon embrace. It was sweet. Poor little mammon must've been worried about his mistress. Why hadn't he told us about Lacey? Oh, right, Barbatos would have put some sort of binding or silence curse on him, too. Lacey seemed to be holding up well, aside from the nose, but being in thrall to Barbatos the traitor demon had surely affected her. She let her guard down long enough to melt a little in the comfort of her demon, and a gut-wrenching ache for Hannah filled my heart and soul. I turned away to bark more orders while blinking hard.

I spotted Simon slipping through the office door in my peripheral vision, the undulating margins of his incorporeal form blurred by my stupid unshed tears.

"D, did you bring any cool demon magic or weapons to the party?"

He grinned and snapped his fingers. His two incorporeal demon pals materialized beside him, and a couple of long knives appeared in his hands, their blades glowing red with a hint of blue at the tips, which were closest to me. It reminded me of the other elephant in the room.

I turned to Trinity. "Am I really a celestial?"

She unsheathed her own knife and held it up to me, blade pointed skyward. It glowed blue. Then she pointed it at Megan. "Demon steel doesn't lie, and since you both share a bloodline, I think we can be certain you have quite a bit of celestial in your lineage."

My mind reeled as I tried to reconcile everything I thought I knew about myself, my relationship with my demon—not to mention my family. Mom had a *lot* of explaining to do. And Megan? Wow. If I was shocked, she must be questioning her sanity. I'd had a lifetime to accept the existence of demons. Poor Meg. *"Hey, guess what? Demons exist, and your sister was inhabited by one. Oh, and by the way, little sister is actually a celestial being and so are you. Don't be afraid of the werewolf guy who's been following you, though. He's one of the good guys."*

"Megan, you okay?"

Her face was paler than usual, and a slight tremor ran through her body, but she stood on her own two feet and squared her shoulders. She gave me a nod. "I'll manage. You?"

I blinked hard again. Damn it, I would not fall apart. I was owed a nervous breakdown, but it would have to wait. "I'll do. Want a knife?"

D flipped one of his blades, the show-off, and handed it to Megan. She gripped the hilt and examined the blade. "Why knives? They're so... primitive. No guns, tanks, or nuclear warheads?"

"Look at you," I said, rocking back on my heels, totally impressed by my big sis. "And here I thought you were a pacifist."

Megan let out a nervous laugh. "Well, I'm a humanitarian. Crooked politicians and third world dictators are one thing, but demons seem like a bigger threat."

"Not all demons," Roice said.

Oh, crap on a cracker. I sheathed my own knife, walked over to him, took his face in my hands, and made him look at me. "I know. We *all* know. And I don't care what that knife says—I'll always be your demon girl. You and your brother think you can put this place on lockdown? Don't want any humans getting in or bad demons getting out."

Roice jerked out of my hold and muttered something under his breath. Then he looked at D and said, "Can I borrow your buddies? Roice and I will take care of electronic security, but we'll need backup for the supernatural stuff."

The two demons followed my roomies upstairs. Trinity had pulled my sister aside to take her through the basics of knife fighting while Sam conjured sigils over the book, presumably working to translate anything that might help us. Mara comforted Lacey while we waited for Simon's intel. It was quiet on the other side of the office door. I didn't know if that was good or bad, but my hunting instincts and a surge of adrenaline had me itching to fight. That strange, bubbly sensation pulsed through me as well, and I welcomed it. Whatever it was—leftover demon mojo, angel power, or an acute case of overconfidence and overcompensation—I welcomed it. It had helped me stop Mephisto and Barbatos.

I hoped it could help me stop Hannah—without hurting her.

I pulled out my knife, marveling at the intense blue glow. Wow. Maybe I'd gotten a few upgrades, too. Trinity shot me a smug look. "Told you not to underestimate yourself."

"You called it," I said. I hoped I wouldn't prove her wrong.

Simon emerged from the wall and flew straight into Lacey, sending a jolt through her body. Mara took a few steps back. After shaking and contorting her limbs in a manner that would impress a Cirque du Soleil performer, Lacey opened her eyes, irises sparkling red as she merged with her personal demon. It was pretty badass. Scrappy little Simon was a credit and an asset to his mistress.

"What have we got?"

"Simon spotted two celestials. No sign of the boss or Hannah, but they could be incapacitated or using concealment magic. Way too much magical energy in the room to distinguish any particular spell." Lacey paused, probably listening to the voice of Simon in her head. "They seem to be arguing over some sort of large amulet."

"Open portals?" D asked.

"Not yet," Lacey said. "But there are a couple of pentagrams that could be portals in the making."

Crap. Did Barbatos and Mephisto have a backup plan in case they couldn't make it through Cooper's portal? It made sense, but why would celestials be involved. "Does Simon think the celestials are friends or foes?"

"No idea. Good news is they don't seem to be on high alert, so they don't know we're here yet. Probably too distracted by infighting. Not sure for how long."

"It might be a trap." D took a step closer, careful not to crowd or loom over me. He was learning. Of course, his shoulders were tense, and his jaw had gone tighter than a vise grip. He was clearly battling his inner alpha. "Jane, we need to be careful. Especially you. Belial still wants you, and if those portals open, he can get you."

"Then I'll need you to have my back. Can you do that cool teleportation materialization thing with a group of us?"

"Yeah. Who do you want?"

"Lacey and Simon on my left flank, you on my right, and Trinity and Sam guarding the rear and the book." I turned to Alexi. "I need you and Mara and Megan out here in case any demons make it out of the portals. Do not let them get out of this building."

Alexi growled and crouched down on his haunches, ready to pounce. Mara and Megan, both with knives, flanked him. I hoped they could handle whatever came through that door, but I had my doubts. Not about Alexi—he was a seasoned hunter and demon neutralizer. Mara had made a good showing back at the clearing, but she was a trickster, not a fighter, and Meg was a tad undertrained. Still, I knew if the shit hit the fan, Alexi would keep them both safe.

We'd just have to do our best to stop the demons from getting out.

With a deep breath and a leap of faith I wasn't sure I had, I gave a nod to D. He took my hand, Lacey, Trinity, and Sam grabbed D's shoulders, and together we went headlong into battle against the unknown.

CHAPTER TWENTY-EIGHT

We materialized just inside the office door. I'd expected to land in full on chaos, but the space was as quiet as a tomb. No boss, no arguing celestials, and no sound from the television screens and computer monitors. The place appeared deserted.

It made me nervous as all get-out.

I dropped to a defensive stance, back to the wall and knife at the ready. Lacey was right there with me, mirroring my stance. We'd done this dance hundreds of times as partners and operated with a combination of muscle memory, reflex, and trust. I was grateful she still trusted me in spite of a broken nose.

Trinity and Sam took up their own positions with practiced ease, except Sam didn't have a knife. No, Marquess Samagina of the hell realm wielded a long, elegant staff that looked like a cross between a light saber and a two-bladed samurai sword. I was only slightly jealous.

He said some kind of demonic incantation, and the tips of the blades glowed with sparks.

Scratch that. I was hella jealous. If we lived through this, I was totally getting my hands on one of those.

Even though D's knife was similar to mine, he still managed to impress me with his warrior's stance, taut muscles, and the ferocity of his war face. Back against a column and using it as a pivot, D held the knife straight in front of him and made a slow arc with his body and weapon as he scanned the room with meticulous and deadly precision. I did the same on the other side of the room. We spotted the two portals in progress as soon as we materialized, the elevated pentagrams with their enchanted sigils glowing. The last time I'd seen one of those demon-made portals, poor Mara had been in the center, helplessly awaiting her sentence.

These had a few extra features, though. I couldn't see the whole of either diagram from my position, but they were different. Apparently Trinity noticed, too, since she had Sam give her a boost—as in a levitation incantation that lifted her from the ground and allowed her to hover in the air above them. Lacey covered the pair while D and I kept an eye on the perimeter.

"What do you see?" I asked.

"Pentagram with an outer circle and three heptagons. There's an inner circle, too, and lots of writing. Some of it's demon, some of it's a language I don't recognize."

What the hell was a heptagon?

I wasn't about to embarrass myself by asking, so I turned to D. "What do you make of it?"

He frowned. "Not sure. It's not a typical portal. It's more powerful."

That was an understatement. The power emanating from the portal on the right pulled at me like a magnet. The weird, bubbly thing inside me surged in response. D stepped closer to the portal on the left, as did Sam. Lacey seemed drawn to that one as well.

A theory formed in my mind, one that I could test with the one human in the room not under the direct influence of a demon. "Trinity, which portal you feeling?"

I got *the look*—I swear she could scare a demon lord into submission with one of those looks—then, when she realized I was, in fact, being serious, she appeared to consider. "I'm not getting anything. Sam?"

"The one on the left leads to the hell realm. I'd bet my legions on it."

D looked at me, one brow arched in inquiry. I said, "I'm getting a lot of mojo from the one on the right. I'm thinking it must lead to the celestial realm." The oddest mixture of terror and curiosity filled me at the thought. Sure, the knife thing was evidence, but I hadn't been ready to accept I had angel in my lineage. I still wasn't on board with the idea.

But I couldn't ignore the portal and the way it called to me. Denial was one of my usual MOs, but to deny this could prove fatal, and not just for me.

"Wait a minute." Trinity leaned down to take a closer look at the portals. "I think I recognize this. At least the shape and some of the characters. Sam, you need to take a look."

Sam levitated and joined Trinity, placing a gentle hand on her shoulder. Yeah, he was smitten for sure. Then, suddenly, his demeanor shifted. His gaze went wide with astonishment, which matched Trinity's.

"Don't keep us in suspense." Lacey had apparently recovered enough to locate her inner sarcastic pain in the ass. It was a good sign. I hated to ruin it by giggling at her, but she sounded like a goose with a sinus infection.

Trinity's voice jarred me out of that horrible train of thought. "This one"—she pointed to the portal on the right—"It's a Sigillum Dei."

"What's that?" I asked as the bubbly sensation surged through me in a wave of power.

"According to ancient lore, it's a magical diagram, like a pentagram, but more powerful. In amulet form, it's said to give the one who wears it power over all creatures except Archangels. It can also give the wearer visions from God and the angels."

And those celestials Simon spotted earlier had been arguing over an amulet.

"What does it do in portal form?"

Trinity and Sam turned to face me in unison. Their wary expressions dialed my dread level straight to eleven. "The portal summons the Archangels," Trinity said.

"Wait, I thought Hannah was supposed to open a portal to the hell realm and unleash the darkness and the harbingers of doom. What's up with the Archangels?"

"There was more," Trinity said. "A battle between Seven Sins and Seven Virtues, and a warrior imbued with the power of three realms."

Wow, I envied her brains. I was bad at remembering things like poetry, my sister's birthday, and the location of my car. But this was important. Assuming we lived through this, I'd memorize that ancient text and everything related to it. Hopefully D had some hell realm mojo to help me with that.

"So seven virtues are from the Seven Archangels? Wait." I did remember something. "What about the Fallen of the Host of Seven?"

"I am here."

We assumed our fighting stances, scanning the room for the bearer of the voice. It was a rich, lyrical alto, like honey over smooth, single malt whiskey, and somehow familiar. The voice of an angel, a celestial—it had to be. Unlike Cassie, the angel of comfort from the Pendergrass's, this voice had the power of ages behind it. It was Beethoven and Mozart and John Williams all rolled into one cosmic symphony.

She materialized behind the boss's desk, tall and unimaginably beautiful. No wings, which was kind of disappointing. Maybe she only wore them on special occasions. She had the face of an angel. She smelled like home.

I swallowed the lump in my throat and blinked back my tears. "Hannah?"

She graced me with a loving smile. "My name is Haniel, my other, and I slumber no longer."

Holy. Frijoles. My demon wasn't a demon at all. She was an angel. And not just any angel—an Archangel.

I took a step back, struggling to remain upright. "What—how—why have you been living in me instead of ruling in the celestial realm?"

D spoke, his voice low and menacing. "Because she's a fallen. She was banished eons ago, cast out for betraying her kind and joining forces with Belial."

I spun around and stared at him, flabbergasted. "You know her?"

"Yes," he said. "Don't trust her or anything she says. She's a liar and a traitor who'll use you to get what she wants and then toss you aside and crush you under her boot."

Hannah—Haniel—smiled benevolently at us. "Demoriel, you've grown into quite the warrior. I owe you a debt of gratitude for protecting our Jane. Your father will be pleased." She floated closer, and D shoved me behind him.

Shoved me, as in pushed me behind him in a display of alpha macho crap like I couldn't defend myself. Seriously? After I put a knife in Barbatos's heart, not to mention all the demons I'd tagged and bagged over the years, he pulled the alpha thing? What the hell?

Wait a minute...

"You know her." I ducked under D's arm. No, wait, I ducked under *Demoriel's* arm. I was learning so many names today. I wondered if I had another name. "You knew her, and you didn't tell me. And she knows your dad."

Shock and confusion morphed into rage. I'd had enough of secrets and lies. I hit him in the chest and pointed my knife at him. He raised his palms and made to step closer, but I jabbed the blade with enough force to let him know I meant business. He took a step back. "Start talking."

"Jane, there's no time." He gestured to the portals. They'd started spinning and humming with energy. Crap. Every time I was on the verge of getting answers, some apocalyptic nonsense got in the way. The universe was totally info-blocking me.

Melodious laughter brought my attention back to my erstwhile demon-turned-fallen angel. "What's so funny? It's not like you clued me in, either."

"I was imprisoned. Stripped of my identity and my memories and placed in your keeping."

I pointed my knife at her. I wasn't sure if demon steel was a match for an Archangel, but I was pissed. And those minor impulse-control issues hadn't magically disappeared. "I haven't been around for eons. Where were you before? And who put you there?"

She glanced down at my knife and flashed me a feral smile. She was still beautiful, but her features had morphed into something predatory, like a wolf or panther sizing up a tasty morsel of prey. This was totally not helping my trust issues.

"I do not yet know everything. Only that I've been passed from host to host over many generations, humans with celestial lineages, products of unions between angels and earth dwellers. Your power and spirit allowed me to awaken and set me free when Mephisto came. I thank you."

"Don't listen to her, Jane. She's here to destroy earth and the celestial realm."

I didn't trust D at this point any more than I trusted the celestial who'd been inhabiting me, but he had a point. Hannah or Haniel or whoever she was fit the bill when it came to the grimoire's prediction.

One who has long slumbered shall awaken, a Fallen of the Host of Seven, she who has the power to open the gates to the Realm of Darkness.

My teammates all started chattering at once. Sam yelled something about Belial's consort, D pleaded with me to step away from Haniel, Trinity was chanting in a demon language—hopefully conjuring a silence spell—and Lacey yelled at me to do something already. I was inclined to listen to Lacey, but I had no idea what I was supposed to do.

Well, there was one pressing matter. "Okay, Haniel, how about you shut down these portals and then we can talk? You know, angel to angel, so we can get to know each other better?"

She smiled at me, the kind of smile a parent gives to a precocious toddler. It pissed me off. "No. That I will not do. I have a long-overdue reunion and a reckoning with my kindred. They imprisoned me. I shall have justice."

"Okay, you want a little payback. I get it. The earth realm isn't the place, though. Take your quest for revenge to the celestial realm and leave us out of it."

She casually flicked her wrist, and my knife flew out of my hand. D and Sam materialized in front of me, weapons at the ready. Okay, this time I'd take it. Alpha male posturing or guarding, I was clearly out of my league in this fight. Lacey and Trinity flanked me. They hadn't lost their weapons yet. We needed to come up with something brilliant before this powerful and possibly insane—PTSD from prolonged imprisonment, anyone?—Archangel annihilated us.

Sam and D stepped forward, blades at the ready.

Sam made the first move, conjuring a cage of fire around Haniel. "Do close the portals, my dear, before you unleash something you cannot handle. Rumor has it that's what got you into trouble in the first place."

I watched in horror and fascination as the cage began to shrink. Sure, she was powerful and dangerous, but she was still Hannah, my Hannah, and I didn't want to watch her suffer and die. I rushed forward, but strong arms held me back.

"Let me go." I struggled against D's death grip, trying to break free without hurting him. Good grief! Fighting was much easier when it involved capturing and destroying bad demons. "We can't let him kill her."

D pulled me against his body and hissed in my ear. "We have to let her know we mean business."

He had a point, but every instinct I had screamed this was wrong, that I needed to save her. "Why can't Sam just close the portal to the hell realm? He's a demon lord, or marquess, or whatever."

"He didn't create the portal, and he's not a summoner. She has to do it."

"What about the boss? He's the master of all things demon in this realm. Where is he?" I scanned the room, looking for anything that might be out of place. Haniel said she'd been imprisoned for a long time, so it was possible to send her back. And I already knew demons could be imprisoned. The cold metal of the locket that held my black mirror served as a reminder, though it had actually held a celestial disguised as a demon.

A celestial disguised as a demon...or maybe two? If Hannah was an angel in disguise, who or what was my boss? Lacey's demon had observed two celestials arguing before we entered the room, and given that the portals were not open—yet—then the boss had either fled the scene or had been incapacitated and tucked away by the pissed-off celestial who'd once inhabited my consciousness. Fleeing wasn't the boss's style.

That meant the boss was most likely incapacitated and close by. Wow. Sherlock Holmes had nothing on me, baby.

"Jane, get your head in the game." D shook me harder than necessary, but I'd let it slide this time.

"Okay, here's the plan. You and Sam keep Hannah, I mean Haniel, distracted. I doubt that fire cage will hold her for long, but do what you can."

"What are you planning?" D looked skeptical. Seriously, where was the trust?

"I'm going to find the boss and set him free."

"The boss? Free?"

Crap. Life would be easier if my coworkers could just read my mind. True, it would be more awkward, but easier. "Arbiter, Intercessor, and the Warriors imbued with power of the three realms shall tip the balance for good or ill. The grimoire says he's a part of this, so he must be here. I have to find him."

Score one for Jinx's memory. I hoped Trinity noticed.

Before he could question me further, I broke out of his hold, rolled, and scrambled over the floor to retrieve my blade. I held it out, swiping it over every nook, cranny, and knickknack in the office. Trinity, bless her, caught on and started sweeping the other side of the room while Lacey took up a position next to D. I glanced at the fiery cage and spotted some gaps in the flames. Haniel worked fast. And since she probably outranked and outpowered Sam, we didn't have much time.

Okay. Think. If I were an angry Archangel, where would I stash a demon lord?

I didn't know the Archangel, but I knew Hannah. I'd lived all my life with her, and she'd picked up some of my personality traits and habits. If the boss had gotten in my way, I would have stuffed him in something he hated out of spite. What did he hate in this office?

Trash can? Nope, my knife didn't glow when I ran it by the shiny, freakishly clean metal waste receptacle. Desk drawers? Nada. He adored his books, so I'd ruled out the bookcases with a cursory swipe. I glanced at the row of flat-screens lining the walls. All blank, but a tiny orange light glowed in the corner of one screen, like it was in low power mode.

It was the only one.

I ran over and held my knife up, stretching as far as I could to compensate for my lack of height. Bingo. It was faint, but my knife emitted a red glow. I took a few steps back and gauged my target.

With a deep breath and a prayer, I tossed my blade at the screen.

CHAPTER TWENTY-NINE

The screen shattered into a thousand pieces with a sound that set my ears ringing like the bells of Notre Dame. The boss materialized, looked around his office, and then his gaze settled on my blade, which now glowed with a brilliant blue. He picked it up. It shifted to red.

What the hell?

"Are you a demon or an angel or something else? I'm confused."

The boss's gaze landed on me, and I immediately regretted opening my big fat mouth. But come on, it was a legitimate question. And after setting the bastard free, I figured he owed me at least one straight answer.

Apparently guessing my train of thought, he said, "Not one or the other. I'm both, depending upon the circumstance. I am Sameal, the Archangel of Death, also known as the Arbiter, judge of all who dwell within the celestial, hell, and earth realms."

"Okay...now that that's settled, how about we get these portals closed and stop my demon/Archangel from unleashing Armageddon? Oh, and by the way, did you know this whole time?"

He flashed a wicked grin in my direction. "I've been keeping an eye on you since I discovered who and what you were and, more importantly, what you carried within you."

I really wanted to hit him or stab him, but I figured now wasn't the time. Besides, the double-crossing, conniving, sneaky jackass still had my knife. "You know," I said, examining my nails. "This would have been a lot easier if you'd just told me the truth. You're seriously the worst boss ever."

I risked a glance, and if I didn't know better, I'd have sworn I caught the briefest flash of regret. He shrugged. "You aren't the only one with rules to follow."

The sound of clanging metal made me spin around in time to see Haniel wielding a very large and impressive sword against Sam's staff. Knocking Sam off-balance, she spun around and crossed blades with D, thrusting and swinging until she'd forced him into a corner. Lacey charged, but a lightning-fast sweep of Haniel's legs knocked her off her feet. Haniel turned her attention back to D. He was a great fighter and powerful warrior, but a young demon was surely no match for a fallen Archangel.

She raised her hand and lifted D up off the ground, Jedi-style. He managed to toss one knife. It lodged in her shoulder, and crimson bloomed around the glowing blue blade. Haniel used her angel mojo to twist D's arm until he dropped the knife in his other hand. He gasped as he clawed at Haniel's fingers, eyes bulging and face turning red as she choked the life out of him.

No!

"You'll need this."

I turned, and the boss—Sameal, the Archangel of Death, as if I needed another secret identity surprise to keep up with—tossed me my knife. I spun back around, ran, and took a flying leap, grateful for my short, compact body. It came in handy for feats of gymnastics. I landed on Haniel's back and jabbed my knife in her shoulder. She screamed and bucked in pain, dropping D in the process.

Then, she turned her wrath on me.

She slung me off her back, though I kept a grip on the knife, which slid with a slick, sickening ease from her flesh. I hit a wall and then the floor. Everything went from stark clarity to muddled and fuzzy in the space of a heartbeat.

Sounds echoed around me. Shouts from people around me fighting, the low but rising hum of something big—not mechanical, but somehow sinister. What was it? I knew it was something bad and I had to stop it, but how? My thoughts jumbled through the bowl of Jell-O that had once been my brain. I should get up, but I couldn't seem to make my limbs work. There was something important I needed to do. I needed to check on someone. Someone important needed me. My chest went warm and tight, and my heart ached, but I couldn't remember...

I had something in my hand. Moving my head sent unbearable pain ricocheting through my body, so I raised my arm. A knife. It was bloody, and it glowed bright blue. Blood. There was something about blood I had to remember. Think. The humming had become more intense. That wasn't good. But I could stop it somehow with blood.

The image of a bleeding man flashed through my scrambled brain. A creature had taken his blood, used it to go where he was forbidden. The man's blood was connected to that place and could let him go through an open door.

I forced myself to a sitting position as excruciating pain shot through my aching head. I was bleeding, too. Had I cut myself with the knife? No, that didn't make sense. Not by how I'd fallen. How did I know that?

I blinked several times, and my vision focused. The humming sound came from two spinning circles of light—what the hell? The one on the right called to me. I didn't know why, just like I didn't know why the idea of these spinning circles turned my stomach to ice and froze the blood in my veins. Everyone in the room seemed to be engaged in deadly combat, and I got the sense I should try not to attract attention as I crawled along the floor toward the spinning thing.

Portal.

The word floated into my mind and conjured visions of horrible creatures emerging from the depths of some strange and forbidden place. I inched closer and closer, dizzy and light-headed from pain, fatigue, and more than a little blood loss. Head wounds were the worst. Eventually I got close enough to the portal to touch it. Not a good idea, since it burned my fingers. Crap. Now what?

The knife. Use the knife.

Okay. I was reluctant to part with my weapon. Never mind that I was too weak to use it, the idea of plunging it into that spinning circle of mayhem filled me with dread. It would kill me. Then again, I wasn't sure I'd live much longer anyway. I reached behind my head and felt gingerly along my skull. It was sunken in the back. Yuck. I pulled my hand away before revulsion could sink her claws into me. Skull fracture for sure. Swelling, blood loss, memory loss.

Yeah, probably wasn't getting out of this situation. I was in the middle of a raging battle and bleeding out. Some of these fighters were my allies, surely. I could save them. I could shut down at least one portal. My allies would get the other one, and everything would be all right.

Well, I wouldn't be all right, but that seemed minor in the grander scheme of things.

I rose to my knees and then, with monumental effort, got to my feet. I gulped in a breath of air. With the last of my strength, I jabbed my knife into the portal.

I fell back and marveled as the lights of the portal shattered like a million shards of glass. Pretty cool trick for light since it wasn't a solid. At least, I didn't think it was. My head ached worse thinking about the laws of physics, so I just collapsed onto the floor as my limbs grew heavy and my sight grew a bit dimmer.

A beautiful and terrifying woman who seemed to be fighting the other people in the room screamed. She had blood dripping down one arm, but she still managed to fend off the fighters around her. I knew her, I thought. Tears trickled down my cheeks. That was weird. I didn't think I was sad about dying—resigned, yes, but oddly at peace with it. No, I was sad for the woman and for the beautiful, dark man swinging two knives with deadly intent. I didn't want to leave him.

The other portal opened in a brilliant burst of light, and a fearsome man stepped through. He raised his arms, and all movement ceased. The guy wasn't human. I knew that much. And I didn't think he'd come for a friendly visit.

"Lord Belial." A tall, powerful man dressed in black—how original—stepped forward to block his path. "Your presence on the earth realm is unauthorized. Go back to your realm now, and we'll forgive your trespass this one time."

Lord Belial.

My head split as memories came flooding back. Mephisto and Mara, a demon lord bent on rebellion who wanted me and my demon—

No, she wasn't a demon. She was an Archangel trapped as a demon, and she was determined to unleash the hell realm on earth. I'd closed the portal to the celestial realm, not the hell realm. Shit.

My team. The fighters were allies and friends. Belial would kill them all and destroy the earth. I couldn't rely on my broken body to join the fight, so I called to the force within me once more. Whatever power had allowed me to defeat Mephisto and Barbatos could help me with Belial, or at least give us an edge that would help my fellow demon hunters to send him back through the damned portal to hell and close it forever.

Power surged within me, no longer bubbly but with the force of a geyser exploding with enough energy to knock everyone in the room on their collective asses. It lifted my body, and I floated over to Belial, who eyed me with a mixture of fascination and apparent revulsion. That was offensive. Sure, I was no doubt a big, bloody mess, but he was a demon warlord, for crying out loud.

"Thought it would take more than a little blood to make you squeamish," I said. Then again, I was still a bit squeamish myself at the state of my body and brain, which I was pretty sure would fall out of my skull at any moment.

He laughed. "You have spirit. No wonder my son is fond of you." He turned and leveled his red gaze on D, my D.

No, not my D.

Demoriel, son of the demon lord Belial. The resemblance was clear once I bothered to look. Same tall, muscular frame, strong jaw, high cheekbones, and full-lipped sinful mouth, Belial had apparently passed his killer looks on to his offspring.

I was such a fool.

And not just because I'd fallen for D's act—Belial's words threw me off guard, and he used it to his advantage. He grabbed me by the shoulders and pulled me against him. Shock and pain rocketed through my body, and the power within me faltered. He had me, and he was going to drag me with him to hell.

I couldn't see the rest of the team, but I heard shouts from the boss. A gentle hand landed on my back, as cool and soothing as the voice of the fallen Archangel who spoke. "Belial, my love. Let this one go. She's served her purpose, and we're in her debt."

Belial's grip loosened, but he didn't let go. I felt as much as heard his rumbling voice, suddenly soft and filled with something akin to tenderness. No, the demon lord wasn't capable of tenderness, couldn't be. But he could probably fake it. His son had certainly fooled me.

"Haniel." His voice broke. Wow, either he was a good actor, or he was completely smitten.

"Let her go, my love, and I'll come with you. We are free now. They cannot stop us."

"They control the portals," he said.

This time Haniel's laughter cut like a thousand razor blades over my skin. "Not all of them."

I craned my neck, which hurt worse than the sound of Haniel's laugh, and spotted the object in her hand, dangling from a silver chain. An amulet. A Sigillum Dei. Oh, crap. If Trinity was right, and she always was, that thing could allow them to open portals to hell, heaven, and let anyone and anything they wanted through without a summoner.

I bowed my head and gave in to the fine tremors running through my body until I shook in Belial's arms. Shaking turned to sobs as I poured out pent-up grief, fear, and rage and buried my face in Belial's chest in spite of revulsion. Haniel traced patterns over my back with her hand, and she leaned closer, drawn by my misery.

"Give her to me," Haniel whispered.

Belial released me, and I fell into Haniel's arms and let her cradle me to her bosom. She enveloped me in her arms. I accepted the blessed comfort for a precious few moments before I snatched the amulet out of her hand and used the last of my strength to burst free from Haniel's arms. I could have easily stayed with her, lost myself in her warm embrace and angelic power. She would have taken me with her and healed me.

But the price was too high. I wouldn't give up earth and all the people and demons I loved.

Before Haniel could react, I held up the amulet and willed the portal to reverse.

"I'm sorry, Hannah," I whispered. "Good-bye."

Belial and Haniel disappeared through the portal.

"Whoa!"

I turned around to face my bruised and battered teammates, who looked as bad as I felt. But they were alive. They'd recover. Even D, whose gaze I deliberately avoided.

"How the hell did you manage that?" Lacey asked, gracing me with a smirk. Finally! My partner's death glare was getting old.

I shrugged and immediately regretted the action. I wouldn't be able to stand much longer. "Angels feed on misery. I took a gamble on Hannah's instincts, and it paid off."

"Jinx, I need you to—"

I cut Trinity off, which was rude, but I'd had about enough for one week. "Oh, you've got to be fucking kidding me. I'm at death's door, and you want me to do something else?"

"Duck!"

I turned around in time to see a swarm of dark figures racing out of the not-quite-closed portal before the world went black.

CHAPTER THIRTY

I woke up with a jolt and nearly ripped out my IV.

IV?

"If you get blood on our new carpet, Jinx, I swear to Lucifer I'll throw you into the hell realm myself."

I took a moment to get oriented. Spacious room with plenty of windows, a familiar skyline, the sound of rapid keyboard clicks, my ass sinking into well-worn cushions molded to perfection by said ass.

I was home.

"When did we get new carpet?"

Boice didn't bother looking away from whichever computer screen had his attention. "A few days ago when you bled all over the carpet we used to have."

Fair enough. But how did I get home? Why wasn't I dead?

"What happened with the portal?" Ignoring the pain, which was significantly less agonizing than the last time I was conscious, I sat up, disentangled my legs from a mountain of sheets and blankies, and swung my legs over the side of the sofa. When that went well, I pulled myself up, mindful of my IV line and the bandages covering various parts of my anatomy.

"You shouldn't be up." Roice, sporting a T-shirt with a cartoon nurse beneath "You can't fix stupid, but you can sedate it," appeared in front of me and almost gave me a heart attack.

"Roice, what the hell?" I plopped down on the sofa and ran my hand along the back of my head. Big bandage. No surprise there. I assumed they must have shoved my brains back in. Otherwise I'd still be unconscious, possibly paralyzed.

"Did you assholes shave my head?"

Boice spun around in his chair and grinned. He wore a shirt that matched his twin's, only his said, "Welcome to the ER. You're fine. GTFO."

"No. D wouldn't let us. But we did hide your bedpan a few hours ago. Need to pee?"

I did, but I figured it could wait. D...he could wait, too, though I couldn't ignore the anger and hurt cramping my stomach.

D was Belial's son, and he hadn't told me.

Shaking off thoughts of the demon who might have just broken my heart—again—I said, "Well, what's the scoop?"

"You'd better pee first. We'll give you water, and if you keep it down and are a very good girl, we'll brew some coffee and explain everything after the rest of the team gets here.

I waited until I'd locked myself in the bathroom to pull out my IV line, which stung a bit but didn't bleed as much as I thought it might. Why wasn't I dead? Weird. I managed to pee, and after ripping off my bandages and exposing tender and mysteriously tattooed flesh, I took a long shower.

Tattoos? Had the twins inked me in my sleep?

If so, they hadn't achieved the effect they were after. The tats that ran along my arms, torso, and all the way down to my thighs, were elegant and beautiful in shades of black, red, and gold. I'd always wanted some ink, but the swirls and sigils covered more skin than I would have chosen for myself. No, I couldn't blame my roomies' ninja-level prank skills for this—the patterns moved and swirled, and the black ink shimmered with blue-and-red sparkles when the light hit it just right. These weren't ordinary tattoos. They were magic.

At least my ass was all clear. That would have been overkill.

After dressing, I took a deep breath and walked back to my spacious living/working area to face my colleagues and my family. Lacey, who looked much better without the black eyes and crooked nose, was there with Simon and Mara. Trinity and Sam sat next to one another on the sofa, hand in hand. Alexi was rocking his role as bartender, but he wouldn't give me any alcohol. According to him, it would risk my recovery or something. Some friend.

Mom and Megan were there, too, though they'd apparently left Brad at home. Probably for the best. Conspicuously absent was D, aka Demoriel, son of Belial, sent by his father to...what? Catch me and bring me to the hell realm? No, he could have done that any time since his return to earth. Was he supposed to nab Hannah, or Haniel, the fallen Archangel and his dad's long-lost lover?

Maybe he came to protect you?

I shut my inner voice down and walked to my couch that doubled as a sickbed with as much dignity as could muster while still limping. I sat down and took a sip of the coffee I was promised by my roomies, who'd deigned to turn away from their screens, before taking a deep breath and calling our meeting to order.

"Where's the boss?" I wasn't sure if I was still in charge since my time as team leader officially ended with the completion of our mission.

"Out of town," Boice said, a hint of disdain in his voice. "He's working with the Archangels to get us some backup."

I nearly choked on my coffee. Fortunately, I recovered before Mom and Megan dashed over to force me back in bed. "Backup? For what?"

"For the demons who escaped from the portal before it closed. They almost killed you, but it wasn't on purpose," Roice quickly added. "You were kind of in their way, and they were in a hurry. And you were already dinged up pretty bad."

I sat dumbfounded, staring at the faces of my favorite people on planet Earth as the magnitude of my failure settled on my soul, threatening to crush me. A wave of dizziness had spots dancing before my eyes while alarmed voices echoed all around me.

I shook my head and held up my hands to shoo everyone away. "I'm fine. Really, I'm fine. So the boss is AWOL, we've got a fresh pack of demons roaming earth—harbingers of doom by way of seven sins, and there are probably seven so-called virtuous celestial beings out there itching to throw a monkey wrench in the program. Does that pretty much sum it up?"

"She's fine," Megan said, patting my head, which really freakin' hurt. "And I'm sorry for all the times I questioned your life choices. I had no idea."

"That I was such a badass?"

"That you were doing such important work. And speaking of, I've talked it over with your colleagues, and we've agreed it would be a good idea for me to join the team."

I jerked my head back so fast and far that I almost passed out again. Oh, for the love of lollipops, this was totally not happening. "No way. I am *not* working with you. You're way too bossy." There were also the minor issues related to her total lack of training and the danger involved. I crossed my arms and glared at her.

She leaned down, violating my personal space to force a hug on me, and whispered in my ear, "You're not fooling me. I'll be careful. I promise. And I know you'll watch out for me."

I shoved her away and painted a look of shock and indignation on my face. "Oh my God, Megan, I will not set you up with Alexi. You're a married woman."

My werewolf demon buddy turned a deep shade of crimson, and Megan rolled her eyes at me. She put her hands on her hips and arched a brow.

I sighed. "Okay, fine, I guess you can join the team since we're both rocking the celestial DNA by way of Dad, I assume. We'll cover that at the next family dinner, right?" I looked at Mom, who averted her gaze but nodded.

Wow. It was the first time I'd ever seen my mother in such a state.

Hunched shoulders, hands wringing, and not yelling at me or judging me. Not admonishing me to dress like a grownup or eat regular meals or questioning my life choices, like she cared.

But she did care. She'd always cared. The realization hit me like a sucker punch to the gut. I'd kept her at arm's length for such a long time out of necessity and, if I was being honest, out of a desire to protect her.

And I'd justified it by telling myself she didn't want me around anyway, that she never had, but apparently that wasn't the case.

Had she been trying to protect me, too, from my father and his lineage, or maybe from myself? I'd have to think on that. I made a mental note to have Boice check into family counseling providers that served demons and celestials. We had a lot to work out in therapy.

But that would have to wait. First order of business was business, as in what to do about the latest crop of hell realm escapees who were probably wreaking havoc on earth while I sat on my sickbed wallowing. Sure, the grimoire had predicted this could happen, but it was still my fault. I'd failed to close the portal in time. It was my mess, and I'd have to clean it up.

But I couldn't do it alone.

I stood up with some difficulty so I could issue my last executive order. "All right, folks, we've got lots of work to do, but the first order of business relates to leadership. We're going to need someone qualified, knowledgeable, fearless, and smart to run this operation in the absence of the boss, and I think we all know who's in the best position to do that. Trinity"—I turned to face my colleague, who seemed genuinely surprised—"consider yourself promoted."

My team just stared at me in apparent shock. "What? Do I have something in my teeth?"

"No," Trinity said thoughtfully. She eyed me with respect and, if I wasn't mistaken, a hint of calculation. Uh-oh. She was up to something. "I just assumed you'd want more control over your new mission."

"Oh, right," I said, heat creeping into my cheeks. "I'm totally on board to take care of those demons I let out. I just figured it would be more efficient to have you in charge while I'm spending more time in the field since you're, you know, the smart one."

Instead of chastising me—or thanking me, for crying out loud, since I'd just promoted her—she stared at me for a moment, brows furrowed in confusion. Then her gaze went wide before softening. "Jinx, I didn't mean...that is to say...look, it's not your fault. Hannah opened the portal, like she was meant to. The grimoire's prediction came true because that's what prophecies do. And we're all going to be spending more time in the field to fulfill the second half."

I must have looked confused since Trinity took a deep breath and visibly fought the urge to roll her eyes. "You know? The part where the warrior imbued with the power of three realms leads us into battle against the celestials and demons?"

"Oh, right. I knew that." I really did, but I was still confused about the whole warrior thing. D claimed he wasn't the warrior from the grimoire since he didn't have any connection to the celestials. By that logic, none of us qualified. I was human and celestial, like Megan. Alexi had the demon wolf, but as far as we knew, no celestials in the mix. Same for Lacey, though I would be requesting a DNA test for her. You couldn't be that weird without some kind of supernatural mojo. I should know.

Sam and Trinity were out, as were my full demon buddies Boice, Roice, and Mara. Who did that leave?

A truly revolting thought occurred to me.

I planted my hands on my hips and glared at Trinity. She took it well, considering she was my new boss. "If you think I'm going to have some demon's baby and raise it to be an interdimensional warrior, you're out of your freakin' mind."

I was kind of glad D wasn't there. He was the closet I'd ever come to making demon babies.

Trinity rolled her eyes this time, not bothering to suppress the urge. "Seriously? That's where your mind went?"

"Someone should tell her." Boice flashed me a wry smile. "We'll be here all night before she figures it out. She hasn't even asked about the new body art."

Ignoring the insult, I said, "I was getting to that, but since you brought it up, how did I get these?" I held out my arms and turned them over, the swirling patterns undulating through my flesh. "And why is no one else freaked out about them? And..." I took a deep breath and blinked away the tears that threatened to spill down my cheeks. "Where's D?"

"Well," Trinity said, her voice laced with sympathy that made me want to run and hide. "You were mortally wounded in battle, and no amount of demon healing elixir could reverse the damage. Sam offered to patch you up using a demon graft."

I examined my tats with greater appreciation. I had a demon graft, as in demon in me? Wait a minute...

"Who's the donor?" Dread and suspicion settled in my gut as I held my breath, waiting for the answer.

"Donors," Sam said, beaming. "Each of us donated a bit of ourselves since you were quite damaged. Myself, of course, and the young ones." He flicked a hand in the direction of Boice and Roice, who shot daggers with their identical gazes back at him but were smart enough to keep their indignation to themselves for once. "Mara generously contributed, naturally, as did Simon and Demoriel. You are imbued with a bit of all our essences. We're family!"

"D is out looking for the escaped demons," Trinity said. "If and when you're ready to talk, just call him. And Jinx...I know you're mad at him, but he does care about you. Whatever is between him and Belial, he didn't betray you. He almost drained his demon essence dry to save you."

Oh, I was ready to talk to him, all right. He should not have run off without talking to me. No worries. I'd make him pay, and if he really did care, we could both have fun with it if we didn't kill each other first.

"So...I've got demon essences." Dread spread from my gut throughout my body, sending shivers down my spine and straight to my ass. I needed a drink. Or ten. "I'm part human, part celestial, and now I've got demon in me, too, so that makes me..."

"Weirder than the rest of us, that's for sure," Lacey said. "Not that you had far to go."

She grinned. Apparently, I was forgiven for the nose thing. That was the good news. The bad news?

"You're the Warrior," Trinity said. She had the decency to look sympathetic.

#wearesototallyscrewed

**

Thank you for reading! Did you enjoy? Please add your review because nothing helps an author more and encourages readers to take a chance on a book than a review.

Don't miss more of the Jinx McGee series coming soon, and check out the Soul Broker from D. B. Sieders with WAKING THE DEAD

Find all the details about D. B. Sieders including the latest news, giveaways, and more at www.dbsieders.com

You can also sign up for the City Owl Press newsletter to receive notice of all book releases!

SNEAK PEEK OF WAKING THE DEAD

The sound of the crash struck her first.

Her tires screeched after she slammed on the brakes, barely missing the blue Sentra in front of her. It had one of those "Choose Life" stickers plastered on its left bumper, the smiling infant illuminated by the red of taillights.

The image still burned in her brain as she made a sharp left.

Her car fishtailed. She registered more squealing tires and the shriek of metal on metal signaling impact. Her heartbeat hammered above the clamor all around.

Breathe in, breathe out. The car stopped dead. But how?

Am I hit? Did I hit someone? Her airbag hadn't deployed, but the pain in her left shoulder let her know her seatbelt had gotten a workout. *Breathe, focus, look around!* Darkness had already swallowed much of the summer evening twilight's soft glow, but there was still enough light to make out her surroundings. *I'm off the road and half in a ditch, but I think I'm okay. I'm okay. I'm okay. God, what happened?*

There had been an impact. She'd felt it, heard it, but what had she hit? The car in front of her?

With a deep breath, she leaned forward with caution and peered into the ditch. The Sentra had landed in the narrow end of the gorge several feet away from danger. Its driver wrestled with his door, wedged against the side of the trench. When it didn't budge, he gave up, scooted over, and climbed out of the passenger door. Vivian's car teetered over a deeper part of the ditch. She couldn't see them, but knew jagged boulders lurked at the bottom below her front tires. She knew the road well.

It was close to home.

She managed to shift into park with a shaky hand, her right leg cramped from maintaining pressure on the brake. *Get up! Get out!* She turned off the ignition, wincing in pain, and shifted in her seat to remove her seatbelt. Unsure exactly how far her car lurched over the ditch's edge, she moved slow and easy, exiting the vehicle and closing the door. She clicked the automatic door locks and put her keys into her pocket out of habit. Shock and the surreal quality of the unfolding events kept her running on autopilot. The urge to move, to act, forced her to her feet. If she could breathe, she could move. If she could move, she could function. If she could function, she'd be all right.

Judging from the commotion further up the road, someone else involved in the accident was far from all right.

Her feet carried her away from her car and toward the small but growing crowd. The acrid stench of smoke, gas, and burnt rubber assaulted her. The glare of headlights hurt her eyes. She walked forward, ignoring the other spectators who ignored her in turn. Their chatter remained distant—conversations and comfort, tears and terrified mutterings, men and women speaking all around to one another.

No one spoke to Vivian. She spoke to no one.

Sirens wailed in the distance. She walked along the periphery of the crowd, grateful to go unnoticed so she could concentrate and just keep moving. A low rumble of dread gnawed at her gut, warning her to stop, but her legs refused to obey.

Time seemed disjointed, slowing, then skipping like a damaged film reel. She looked back at her car and realized she'd been inches from oblivion. *If I hadn't stopped when I did...if the guy behind me hadn't....* Any sooner, she'd have been rear-ended and launched full into the ditch. A moment later, her car would've been crumpled between the Sentra and the F-350 behind her. But she'd hit the Sentra, hadn't she?

No, no damage to the rear of the vehicle, and her front bumper remained intact, as far as she could tell from the distance. How had she stopped? Shifting her gaze to the F-350, Vivian saw it from the side now, the black truck adorned with a custom flame job painted across the doors and bed. The brawny owner inspected the body for damage. Flecks of dried mud and grime rose from the undercarriage and dulled the flares above. The vehicle's powerful bulk was adapted to rough terrain, like its owner. She and her sleek sedan were not. They'd all been going at least 35, maybe 40 miles an hour. She had to look away. Disaster had come so close.

I should've been knocked into that ditch. How did I miss it?

Shivering, she caught a flash of white in the periphery, but when she turned, it was gone, departing along with the warm breeze that swept in out of nowhere and chased the odd chill that surrounded her away. Infused with energy and a strange sense of urgency, she shook off the remnants of unease and continued.

She had to keep moving.

Another man lumbered across the street toward the crowd. He moved in the long shadows cast by the setting sun, looking from side to side and peering over his shoulder. He seemed as intent on his journey as Vivian was on hers, but unlike the other onlookers, he at least spared her a nod before moving along. Well, she thought he had. The dark green ball cap he wore shielded his eyes, and thus his intent, but he kept walking in the same direction. No one else paid him any mind.

When she turned back to face her destination, she saw what remained at ground zero of the evening's terror. The poor soul in that twisted and crumpled wreckage before her hadn't been so lucky. No one could walk away from this crash.

She took two steps closer. Smoke rose from the damaged engine, along with the occasional spark. Everyone around her stayed back. A man's hand emerged from the driver's side window, along with a soft groan. Another step closer and she heard his ragged breathing.

Vivian took one more step, close enough for her arm to brush the car's cooling frame. She met his stare through the window.

Oh dear God, no.

Her gaze burned a path from his face down to his torso, and then she had to look away from what remained of his body below the waist. The mangled steering column and dashboard covered much of the damage, but not quite enough. *He'll never walk again. He'll be paralyzed. If he took a blow to the head, he'll be a vegetable.*

Vivian's pulse raced. Her hands and fingers went numb.

He'd be better off dead.

Fighting the wave of revulsion, she took one more step toward the car. Every nerve in her body screamed for her to run away, to leave this *thing* that used to be a man and never look back. This was his nightmare, not hers.

She had already lived one of her own.

With palpable effort, Vivian reached for him with one trembling arm and took his hand in hers, gasping when she felt his skin.

Jesus, he's so cold!

The man's grip was iron and it caught her off guard. She hadn't anticipated the strength of it or the effect it would have on her. The bone-deep chill started where their hands joined and spread through her body. She flinched and tried to pull away.

The man squeezed her hand even tighter and tugged, pulling her closer. His brilliant green-eyed gaze was filled with fear, pain, and something she couldn't quite define. Was it anger? He closed his eyes after a moment and a shocking burst of heat traveled through her from their joined hands. His touch chased away the chill, soothing her from ragged fingertips to her battered palm.

When he opened his eyes again, the man's expression mirrored the sudden and inexplicable relief surging within her. No fear, no pain. These weren't her emotions. *They must be his.* But how was she able to experience them as if they were her own? Then a singular emotion reflected in his gaze suddenly pierced her with vivid clarity.

Regret.

Vivian swore she could *see* the gray light of this man's regret emanating from his very pores as it coursed through her.

His expression pleaded, and he spoke to her in a harsh rasp. "I'm...sorry."

"It's going to be okay," she whispered, even though it wasn't.

His chest heaved and his eyes dulled, rolling back as he gasped for air. Two more shallow breaths later, he stilled completely.

"No, please. You have to stay with me. Please, stay with me," she pleaded, shaking his shoulder with one trembling hand even as she felt his grip slipping from her other.

"Oh no, oh dear God, someone help him!"

"Ma'am, I need you to step away from the vehicle," a muffled male voice said from behind her.

"Where the hell did she come from?" asked another man.

"Easy, bro, she must've just wandered in before we put up the barricades."

"No, she didn't. She just popped up out of nowhere!"

Hands gripped her shoulders and tried to pull her away, but she struggled free, refusing to let go of the man in the car. He wasn't blinking. He wasn't moving. His pallor faded to ash even as she begged him to come back.

"Please, ma'am, let us help him."

She yelped when a second set of hands grabbed her around the waist and lifted her off the ground. She wailed in rage and agony when she lost contact with the man's hand. She kicked and clawed at her captor until he dropped her, then she spun around and lifted her hands, ready to fight.

"Jesus, lady, calm down. We're paramedics," one of the uniformed men said. "We're here to help. I'm Ed, and this is Abner." He gestured to taller man beside him. They stood between her and the wreckage. Both began moving forward with outstretched hands as she backed away.

"Why don't you come with us so we can check you for injuries?" Ed spoke in a soft voice, taking slow, measured steps toward her and holding out his hand.

"I'm not injured. I...I can't leave him."

"Were you in the car with him, ma'am?" Abner asked. His sharp tone carried a note of accusation, or perhaps suspicion.

No, not that. He was afraid of her.

"No," she muttered, confused. She shook it off, focusing instead on the overwhelming urge to return to the man in the car.

"What's your name, ma'am?"

"Vivian."

"And his?"

"I have no idea. I don't know him, I just—I saw the crash and I came over. And I need to get back to him. I—I need to help him. Let me go back to him."

"Shh, it's okay. Come on with us now."

Ed lurched forward and grabbed her wrist. She tried to pull away but his scream caught her off guard. He dropped her arm and stumbled back, clutching his hand against his chest and groaning as if in terrible pain. Looking down, she swore she saw a red spark flash out of her fingertips, but by the time she blinked, it was gone.

"Ed? You okay?" Abner stepped away from Vivian and turned his attention to his colleague.

"Jesus Christ, my hand is on *fire*. What the hell did you do to me, lady?" Ed groaned, arm still clutched to his chest and eyes wide with shock and fear.

"Let me have a look." Abner tugged on his buddy's arm. After a quick exam he said, "I don't see anything. Must've been static electricity or something."

"Static electricity, my ass," Ed muttered, wringing his hand and staring at Vivian like she'd sprouted a second head. He and Abner exchanged a few more hushed words before he turned his attention back to the mangled car and the man inside.

Abner spoke louder then, snapping Vivian back to attention. "As for you, you really should go over to the ambulance and let our team have a look at you. The police will want your statement too."

He didn't make any further attempt to touch her. Instead, he pointed to the ambulance parked behind the growing crowd of onlookers while inspecting her with a wary expression. What the hell just happened? Numb with shock and an inexplicable sense of loss, she willed her feet to carry her over to the ambulance, leaving the stranger to his fate.

She paused, glancing back over her shoulder. "Will he be okay?"

"We'll do all we can, ma'am. You just go on now and take care of you."

She made it home two hours later.

Vivian sat on the deck and looked out as far as moonlight allowed. The scent of early summer clover hung heavy in the air and almost masked the fading honeysuckle of spring. Lightning bugs twinkled in the dark while the heat of the day flowed off the land. It wasn't a boon year for cicadas, better known as jar flies in this neck of the woods, but they still sang loud enough to match the volume of the crickets. A few mourning doves cooed in their haunting altos, joined by mockingbirds from time to time.

Her cherished backyard paradise offered little respite from the evening's trauma, or the smaller terrors this night would no doubt offer.

She sighed and drew another long swallow from her glass of wine. Her late arrival back home earned her an earful from the home health-care aide and a fifty-dollar penalty. At least she'd managed to get her car out of the ditch with the help of burly Mr. F-350 and one of the patrolmen on the scene. She could still drive her sedan, but the alignment was out of whack. She'd have to take it in for service tomorrow. What if she had to replace all four tires? Could've been worse. God only knew how she'd managed not to damage her last remnant of the good life. The way things were going, this car would have to last her well beyond its shelf life as a status symbol.

Not that she had any status left, or much of a life.

While still shaken, she wouldn't risk a stronger drink. She had to function. Her sister Mae was likely to have another bad night in spite of the new medications, so neither of them would be getting much sleep. Waiting was the worst. She could only afford about six more weeks off work, maybe eight if she pinched a few more pennies. Having burned through her vacation days and time allotted for family and medical leave, she still couldn't bring herself to return to work.

The irony wasn't lost on her. In the course of her work as a loan officer, she advised countless clients on the merits of financial planning, adequate insurance, and savings. So much for practicing what she preached. But Mae's condition was deteriorating fast according to the doctors, and Vivian couldn't bear to leave her. Besides, insurance only covered twenty hours of home health care per week, hardly conducive to a full-time work schedule.

But more time out of work would be time without pay, forcing her to use more of her scarce savings and dip into her retirement fund. Mae might live even longer. No one would have thought such a wreck of a body could make it thirty-two years.

Her passing would be a mercy for both of them, though the fact didn't offer any comfort, nor did the possibility that Mae might pull through. Guilt enveloped Vivian, wrapping around her like an old worn-out sweater stretched too far. She couldn't throw it out, and she wore it often these days.

Pushing those thoughts aside, she focused on the sights and sounds of her small patch of nature. A light breeze rustled through her favorite maple as its leaves showed their white underbellies. Rain's calling card, as if the heavy slate clouds and palpable humidity weren't announcement enough. A movement in the treeline caught her eye. A deer was always a treat. There weren't many left since the developers got busy in her little corner of the county. As it moved closer, she realized it was something bigger than a deer. No, not *something*, *someone* bigger. She stood and took a step closer to the door.

A man pushed out of the trees and onto the lawn. In the half-light, she saw his hat and heard his footfalls on the soft grass. He paused at the bottom of the stairs, looked up at her, then tipped his hat and raised a hand to wave.

"Evening, ma'am," came his low, gravelly voice. "Didn't mean to startle you." He stopped, perhaps waiting for her response.

"Good evening," she replied, clutching the cell phone in her pocket. "What can I do for you?"

"I just stopped by to see if you was all right after that big ruckus tonight."

She risked a step forward then leaned over the rail to get a better look at him. Yes, she remembered him now. Her visitor was the man who'd given her the nod at the crash site. The outdoor security light let her see him a little better now. He was definitely a local. Clad in well-worn overalls, a weathered John Deere cap, and dusty old boots, the clothes and their owner had more than a few miles on them.

"I'm fine," she said. "You did startle me when you came out of the trees. I didn't recognize you at first."

"You saw me," he said, almost to himself. He seemed to be chewing on some thought or another before he continued. "Oh yes, ma'am, I saw it. Shame too. That boy didn't make it."

"No, he didn't," she said, lowering her eyes. The images were still fresh and buzzed around in her aching head like a nest of angry hornets. Flashes of twisted metal and blood, but not a lot on his face. She'd done all she could for him, holding his hand and whispering words of reassurance. He looked to be about her age, a healthy man with years of life ahead of him.

Until capricious fate cut his life with sudden brutality.

Giving what comfort she could, she'd watched the life drain out of him. The medics had tried to console her that all was not lost. She knew the truth. He was gone. She winced at the thought, closing her eyes at the unexpected pang. Maybe it was just weariness with her own troubles. Death was an old if not welcome acquaintance. Should she try to find out more about him and talk to his family? What would she say? Of course, the police or paramedics would inform them, but the moment she'd shared with the man had been so personal, made her somehow...responsible for him. The voice of her visitor brought her back.

"Hey, now, you all right? I thought you might be pretty shaken up, watching that boy die." When she offered no objection, he took slow, steady steps up the stairs. Something about her visitor dampened the fear running beneath the surface of her civility. Any other night, she'd have run straight inside. It was as if his presence enveloped her in a cocoon of calm and safety.

Maybe she was just lonely.

Once he stood on the deck in front of her, he asked, "Is there someone I can give a holler for you?"

"No, I'll be okay, but it was nice of you to stop by. How'd you know where I live? Are you from the neighborhood?" He didn't look familiar. She'd lived here long enough to know most everyone. The realization should have set off alarm bells, but the warmth in his gaze and down home manner kept her at ease.

"Oh, I'm around here a bit." He smiled. "But I don't like the idea of leaving you all alone after what you been through."

"My sister's in the house, so I'll be fine. She's...she's not feeling well. I really should check on her." Retreating, she asked, "Did you know the man in the accident?"

"Not exactly, but I think we might have something in common," he said with a knowing smile.

His statement and smile poked a big hole in the cocoon of calm, giving Vivian a case of the creeps. Good down-home charm aside, she should never have let him get this close or stay this long. This wasn't like her, especially in light of the evening's stress. Time to end the conversation before the guy went all Jack the Ripper on her.

"Thank you for stopping by. I need to get back inside now. Rain's coming. You should get home before it starts. Good night, Mister...."

"Oh, you can just call me Ezra. It surely was a pleasure to meet you, Miss Vivian," he said, extending his hand.

She hesitated for a moment, but then accepted, tilting her hand slightly to hide the unsightly nails, chewed to the quick. His roughened skin and gnarled knuckles chafed her skin before the warmth of his grasp overwhelmed her.

The shock of it froze her in place, even as warmth suffused her fingertips and beyond—the same heat she'd felt with the wounded man in the car, only more intense and powerful.

When she didn't release his hand, Ezra pulled away gently. He tipped his hat and began his slow descent down the stairs as she stood dazed, still swathed in the pleasant warmth of his presence. Halfway down, he glanced over his shoulder and said, "I'll be seeing you soon. Get on in the house and rest easy now."

"Good night," she said politely, then nipped inside and bolted the door behind her with a sigh of relief and irrational regret.

She tiptoed down the dark hall to check on the shell that held her sister. Entering Mae's room with practiced quiet, Vivian listened. Her sister's breaths were shallow and still plagued by rasps and wheezes. Vivian stood over the narrow bed, regarding her sister with a mixture of love, pity, and resentment.

All of that time they'd borrowed and bought for her, and for what? ˙

God, she was *loathsome* to think such things. What decent person questioned the value of life, especially the life of a loved one? Hell, Mae was the only family she had left since their parents were gone. Good people didn't think of their flesh and blood as burdens, especially someone like Mae. She hadn't asked to be born with her condition, and Vivian had long ago promised to assume responsibility for her should the time ever come.

Still, standing there in the dark, Vivian recalled the horror with which she first contemplated her sister's level of awareness. When she'd prayed as a child, Vivian had hoped God's mercy had spared Mae awareness. She didn't want to think of an intact mind trapped in such a body.

Without thinking, she stroked her sister's cheek and ran her hand over Mae's soft hair. Mae shifted and inhaled deeply. Vivian stiffened, bracing herself for a coughing fit or worse, Mae choking. Instead, Mae's breathing evened out and she drifted further into a peaceful rest. Stranger still, the air around them seemed warmer.

Perplexed, though relieved, Vivian left her sister and forced her own weary legs in the direction of her bathroom. Halfway there, realization dawned. She hadn't actually told Ezra her name.

Had she?

Then again, she'd given her contact information and statement to a half a dozen cops, medics, and even one firefighter at the scene. He'd probably just overheard it. A good chunk of southeast Nashville probably knew how to find her by now.

Still, she could have kicked herself for letting a stranger know she was more or less alone in the house, and for letting him get so close to her. The news and all of those crime dramas on TV tended to blur the line between healthy caution and paranoia. The events of the past few hours weren't helping either.

She didn't notice anything unusual with her hands while completing her nightly routine, other than the slight tremor running through them as she washed her face and brushed her teeth. And the raw skin and mangled nails, of course. Maybe she'd just zapped the paramedic and Ezra with a little static discharge, like the other paramedic had said. But she hadn't been wearing a sweater and it was such a humid night.

Oh God, she'd just touched Mae with that hand. What had she been thinking?

But she'd touched Ezra with it too, and his hot touch almost burned *her*. What the hell? Static electricity didn't travel back and forth like a normal current. Since when had she turned into a battery?

She touched one tentative fingertip to the metal faucet fixture, bracing for a jolt.

Nothing.

Feeling foolish, she touched the brass-plated hoop that held her hand towel, her metal tweezers, and her scissors. Wet or dry, she felt nothing other than cold metal, which should have been a better conductor than flesh.

Vivian shook her head. Maybe things would look a little clearer in the morning.

"Go figure," she muttered, looking at her bottle of sleeping pills. She hadn't even realized she'd pulled them out of the cabinet, though it came as no surprise. Seemed her earlier brush with death had killed the mood.

She put them back with a little hesitation.

After all, they'd still be there tomorrow.

Don't stop now. Keep reading with your copy of WAKING THE DEAD

And visit www.dbsieders.com to keep up with the latest news where you can subscribe to the newsletter for contests, giveaways, new releases, and more.

Don't miss more of the Jinx McGee series coming soon, and check out the Soul Broker from D. B. Sieders with WAKING THE DEAD

The road to hell begins when the reaper darkens her door.

A chance encounter with a dying stranger opens an empathic connection between down-on-her-luck caregiver Vivian Bedford and the world of spirits. Lazarus Darkmore, a grim reaper in a charming and seductive package, seeks to recruit her as a soul broker. Guardian spirit Ezra and his new apprentice Zeke offer protection from the reaper—so long as she works on their side of afterlife management. But these guardians are no angels, and their methods leave Vivian fearing the price of their protection.

Her ability to channel conscious energy from the living, something no guardian or reaper can do, could be a game changer. If she can control it, she can use this power as leverage. And she needs a bargaining chip, especially when she discovers that incapacitated living mortals can supply energy for the spirit realm, making her disabled sister Mae a prime target for guardian and reaper alike.

Can she move from pawn to major player in order to save Mae, and herself, from a horrific fate beyond the simple and fleeting terrors of death?

All reviews are **welcome** and **appreciated**. Please consider leaving one on your favorite social media and book buying sites.

Escape Your World. Get Lost in Ours! City Owl Press at www. cityowlpress.com.

ACKNOWLEDGMENTS

I am so grateful to City Owl Press for helping me make this book baby shine and for bringing it to readers. Tina Moss and Yelena Casale are fantastic publishers! Shout out to my amazing editor, Tee Tate. This book is better for her input, insight, and editorial guidance. To copyeditors and everyone involved with production at City Owl Press, I appreciate your hard work and dedication. My fellow Owls are an incredible group of writers and human beings, and I love being a part of the family. Thanks for the support and love!

Special thanks to Kristin Anders and Jody Wallace for book doctoring early drafts. The pandemic gave me extra time to work on this project, one of the good things that came out of shelter at home. Thank you also to beta readers Eli Jackson and AJ Scudiere. Shout out to Mibl Art for the gorgeous cover art. It captures the world of Jinx beautifully! I'm sending a special thanks to SiederTree Studios for the custom graphic you'll find above each chapter heading. Check out their work on Instagram @siedertreestudios.

And, as always, thank you to my family for giving me the freedom to be a writer, and to my furballs for keeping my lap warm and giving me purrs and love.

ABOUT THE AUTHOR

Award-winning author D.B. Sieders was born and raised in East Tennessee and spent her childhood hiking in the Great Smoky Mountains and chasing salamanders, fish, and frogs. She loved to tell stories while sitting around the campfire.

She is a working scientist by day, but never lost her love of telling stories. Now, she's a purveyor of unconventional fantasy romance featuring strong heroines and the heroes who strive to match them. Her heroes and heroines face a healthy dose of angst as they strive for redemption and a happily ever after, which everyone deserves.

www.dbsieders.com

facebook.com/DBSieders
twitter.com/DBSieders
goodreads.com/dbsieders
amazon.com/D.B.-Sieders/B00D18ZPOY

ABOUT THE PUBLISHER

City Owl Press is a cutting edge indie publishing company, bringing the world of romance and speculative fiction to discerning readers.

Escape Your World. Get Lost in Ours!

www.cityowlpress.com

facebook.com/CityOwlPress

twitter.com/cityowlpress

instagram.com/cityowlbooks

pinterest.com/cityowlpress